Beneath This Man

Beneath This Man

JODI ELLEN MALPAS

FOREVER

NEW YORK   BOSTON

Forever
Hachette Book Group
1290 Avenue of the Americas
New York, NY 10104
www.HachetteBookGroup.com

Printed in the United States of America

RRD-C

Originally published as an ebook
First trade paperback edition: November 2013

11 10

Forever is an imprint of Grand Central Publishing.
The Forever name and logo are trademarks of Hachette Book Group, Inc.

The Hachette Speakers Bureau provides a wide range of authors for speaking events. To find out more, go to www.hachettespeakersbureau.com or call (866) 376-6591.

The publisher is not responsible for websites (or their content) that are not owned by the publisher.

Library of Congress Control Number: 2013947611

ISBN: 978-1-4555-7834-4

For my ladies

Acknowledgments

The This Man roller coaster just gets faster and faster, with more loop-the-loops and twists and turns. I never want to get off. As always, my gratitude to every single person who has joined me along the way is immeasurable.

I continue to bask nicely on Central Jesse Cloud Nine.

Jodi

xxx

Beneath This Man

CHAPTER ONE

I've barely mustered up the strength to make it into work today. It's been five days since I've seen Jesse Ward. Five days of agony, emptiness, and sobbing.

Every time my eyes close he's there, the images flickering from the sure, confident, beautiful man who totally took me, to the hollow, hurtful, drunken creature who destroyed me. Without him I feel empty and incomplete. He made me need him, and now he's gone.

In the darkness I see his face and in the silence I hear his voice. There is no escaping it. I'm unaware of the activity around me, every noise a distant hum, every image a slow blur. I'm in hell. Empty. Incomplete. I'm in absolute agony.

I left Jesse drunk and raging at his penthouse last Sunday. I've not heard from him since that day I walked out, leaving him yelling and stumbling around. There have been no phone calls, no messages, no flowers...nothing.

Sam is still a regular, seminaked presence at Kate's, but he knows better than to talk to me about Jesse. He keeps quiet and well away. I must be painful to be around at the moment. How can a man who I've known a few short weeks make me feel like this? But in those short few weeks I have known him, I've learned that he is intense, hot blooded, and controlling, but he is also gentle, affectionate, and protective. I miss that Jesse so much. But the drunken, hollow man I found at the penthouse was not the Jesse I had fallen in love with. I would gladly take all of his frustrating, challenging ways over the ugliness that was Jesse drunk.

Apparently, Jesse falling off the wagon was my entire fault. He advised me, on a slur, that he'd warned me there would be damage if I left. He had. He just didn't explain what sort of damage or why. I should have pressed for more, but I was too busy being swallowed up by him. I was distracted from everything, blinded by lust and drowning in his intensity. I never anticipated he would turn out to be Lord of the Sex Manor, and I certainly never anticipated he was an alcoholic. I was literally walking around with my eyes wide shut.

I'm lucky that I've managed to avoid any pressing questions from Patrick regarding Mr. Ward's project. When one hundred thousand pounds landed in Rococo Union's bank account, courtesy of Mr. Ward, I was immensely grateful. With so much money paid up front, I could fob Patrick off with an imaginary business trip that's keeping Mr. Ward out of the country and the project on hold. I know I'll have to deal with this eventually, I just don't feel strong enough at the moment, and I'm not sure when I will. Perhaps never.

Poor Kate has tried so hard to pull me out of the black hole that I've put myself in. She's tried to occupy me with yoga classes, drinks at the pub, and cake decorating. But I'm happier festering in my bed. And she meets me without fail every lunchtime. Not that I can eat anything. It's hard enough just to swallow without trying to get food past the permanent lump that's wedged in my throat.

The only thing I look forward to at the moment is my morning walk. I'm not sleeping, so dragging myself out of bed at five o'clock every morning is relatively easy.

In the quiet, fresh, morning air, I make my way to the spot in the Green Park where I collapsed with exhaustion the morning Jesse dragged me around the streets of London on one of his torturous marathons. I sit quietly, picking at the dew-coated blades of grass until my backside is numb and sodden and I'm ready to wander slowly back to prepare myself for another day without Jesse.

How long can I go on like this?

My brother, Dan, is back in London tomorrow after visiting my parents in Cornwall. I should be looking forward to seeing him, it's been six months since I last did, but where am I going to find the energy to put on a front?

My mobile blurts from my desk, dragging me from my daydreams and tapping pen. It's Ruth Quinn. I inwardly groan. Ruth is a new client and proving to be a challenge already. She rang on Tuesday and demanded an appointment for the same day. I explained that I was busy and suggested someone else may be able to make it, but she insisted she wanted me and eventually settled for my first appointment, which happened to be today. She has since called every day to remind me. "Miss Quinn," I greet tiredly.

"Ava, how are you?"

She always asks, which is nice, I suppose. I won't tell her the truth. "I'm good. And you?"

"Yes, yes, fine," she chirps. "I just wanted to check our appointment."

"Four thirty, Miss Quinn." I reiterate, for the third consecutive day. I think I might be pricing myself out of this job.

"Lovely, I look forward to it."

I hang up and blow out a long, calming breath of air. What was I thinking ending my Friday on a new client, and a difficult one at that?

Victoria comes breezing into the office, her long blonde locks fanning over her shoulders. She looks different. She looks orange! "What have you done?" I ask, completely alarmed. I know I'm not seeing particularly clearly at the moment, but there is no denying the tone of her skin.

She rolls her eyes and retrieves her compact mirror from her Mulberry to inspect her face. "Don't!" she warns. "I asked for bronzed." She scrubs at her face with a tissue. "The stupid woman used the wrong bottle. I look like a cheese puff!" She continues to scrub her face while huffing and puffing.

"You need to get yourself some body scrub and head for the shower," I advise, turning back to my computer.

"I can't believe this is happening to me!" she cries. "Drew is taking me out tonight. He'll run a mile when he sees me like this!"

"Where are you going?" I ask.

"Langan's. I'll be mistaken for a Z-lister. I can't go like this!"

This is a complete catastrophe for Victoria. She and Drew have only been seeing each other for a week, another relationship off the back of my cluster fuck of a life. All I need now is for Tom to walk in and declare he's getting married. Selfishly, I'm not happy for anyone.

Sally, our general office dogsbody, comes scuttling out of the kitchen and stops in her tracks when she spies Victoria. "Wow! Victoria, are you okay?" she asks, and I smile to myself as Sally gives me an alarmed look. All of this beautification stuff goes straight over our plain Sal's head.

"Fine!" Victoria snaps.

Sally retreats to the safety of the stationary cupboard, escaping a very riled Victoria and an even more miserable me.

"Where's Tom?" I ask in an attempt to distract Victoria from her fake-tan crisis.

She slams her compact mirror down on her desk and swings around to face me. If I had the energy, I would laugh. She looks terrible. "He's at Mrs. Baines's. It would appear the nightmare continues," she huffs, ruffling her blonde locks around her face.

I leave Victoria and her glowing face, returning to staring numbly at my computer screen. I can't wait for the day to end so I can crawl into my bed where I don't have to see, speak, or interact with anyone.

* * *

I arrive at a stunning town house on Lansdowne Crescent right on time, and Miss Quinn answers the door. I'm completely surprised—her voice doesn't match her appearance in the slightest. I had her down as a middle-aged spinster, piano teacher type, but I couldn't have been further from the mark. She's very attractive, with long blonde hair, big blue eyes, and smooth pale skin, and she is wearing a lovely black dress with killer wedges.

She smiles. "You must be Ava. Please, come in." She directs me through to a horrendous seventies throwback kitchen.

"Miss Quinn, my portfolio." I hand her my file, and she takes it keenly. She has a really warm smile. Maybe I got her all wrong.

"Please, call me Ruth. I've heard a lot about your work, Ava," she says as she flicks through the file. "Lusso, especially."

"Oh, you have?" I sound surprised, but I'm not. Patrick has been delighted by the response Rococo Union has gotten from the publicity of Lusso. I would prefer to forget about all things Lusso, but that doesn't seem likely.

"Yes, of course! Everyone's talking about it. You did an amazing job. Would you like a drink?"

"A coffee would be good, thank you."

She smiles and sets about making drinks. "Please, sit down, Ava."

I take a seat and pull out my client briefing folder. "So, what can I help you with, Ruth?"

She laughs and waves the teaspoon around in the general direction of the room. "Need you ask? It's hideous, isn't it?" she exclaims, returning to coffee-making duties.

Yes, actually, it is, but I'm not about to gasp in horror at the brown and yellow arrangement with faux brick walls.

She continues, "Obviously, I'm looking for some ideas to transform this monstrosity. I was thinking of knocking through and making it a large family room. Here, I'll show you." She hands me a coffee and signals for me to follow her through to the next room. The décor is equally as grim as the kitchen. She seems quite young—midthirties, perhaps—so I'm guessing she's not long moved in. This place doesn't look like it has been touched with a paintbrush in forty years.

* * *

After an hour of discussions, I'm confident that I know what Ruth is trying to achieve. She has good vision.

"I'll draft a few designs in line with your budget and ideas, and get them to you with a schedule of my fees," I tell her as I'm leaving. "Is there anything in particular I should allow for?"

"No, not at all. Obviously, I want all the basic luxuries you would expect to find in a kitchen." She puts her hand out, and I take it politely. "A wine fridge." She laughs.

"Absolutely." I smile tightly, the mention of alcohol making my blood run cold. "I'll be in touch, Miss Quinn."

"Ruth, please!" she shakes her head. "I look forward to it, Ava."

* * *

I drag myself down the street toward Kate's house, hoping she's not home so I can retreat to my room before she resumes mission Perk Ava Up.

"Ava!"

I stop and see Sam hanging out of his car window as he cruises slowly beside me. "Hey, Samuel," I say on a strained smile as I carry on walking.

"Ava, please don't join your evil friend in the Piss Sam Off Club. I might be forced to move out." He parks and gets out of his Porsche, meeting me on the pavement outside Kate's house.

He looks his usual laid-back self, with ridiculously baggy shorts, a Rolling Stones T-shirt, and his mousey brown hair a disheveled mess.

"I'm sorry. Have you moved in permanently now?" I ask on an arched brow. Sam has his own swanky apartment on Hyde Park with much more room, but with Kate's workshop on the ground floor of her house, she insists on him staying at hers.

"No, I haven't. Kate said you would be home by six. I was hoping to catch you." He suddenly looks all nervous, which is making me feel extremely uncomfortable.

"Is everything okay?" I ask.

He offers a little smile, but it doesn't reach his dimple. "Not really. Ava, I need you to come with me," he says quietly.

"Where?" Why is he acting so shifty? This is not like Sam. He's usually so carefree and unapologetic.

"To Jesse's place."

Sam must see the look of horror on my face because he steps toward me with a pleading expression. Just the mention of his name sends me into panic. Why does he want me to go to Jesse's? After our last meeting, you would have to drag me there kicking and screaming. There is no chance in hell I'm returning to that place—not ever.

"Sam, I don't think so." I take a step back, shaking my head. My body has started shaking, too.

He sighs and scuffs his trainers on the pavement. "Ava, I'm getting worried. He's not answering his phone and no one has heard from him. I don't know what else to do. I know you don't want to talk about him, but it's been nearly five days. I've been to Lusso, but the concierge refuses to let us up. He'll let you. Kate said you know him. Can't you just get us up there? I just need to know he's okay."

"No, Sam. I'm sorry, I can't," I croak.

"Ava, I'm worried he's done something stupid. Please."

My throat starts to close up and Sam starts walking toward me with his hands outstretched. I didn't realize I was moving backward. "Sam, please don't. I can't do that. He won't want to see me, and I don't want to see him."

He grabs my hands to halt my retreat, pulling me into his chest and holding me tight against him. "Ava, I wouldn't ask, I really wouldn't, but I need to get up there and check on him."

My shoulders droop, defeated in his embrace, and a quiet sob escapes, just when I thought there were no tears left. "I can't see him, Sam."

"Hey." He pulls back and looks at me. "Just get us past the concierge. That's all I'm asking." He wipes away a stray tear and smiles pleadingly.

"I'm not going in," I affirm, my stomach a knot of panic at the thought of seeing him again. But what if he *has* done something stupid?

"Ava, just get us up to his penthouse."

I nod and wipe away the rolling tears.

"Thank you." He tugs me toward his Porsche. "Get in. Drew and John are meeting us there." He opens the passenger door and directs me into the car.

I climb in and let Sam drive me to Lusso at St. Katherine Docks—a place I swore that I would never return to again.

CHAPTER TWO

As Lusso comes into view, I start hyperventilating. The overwhelming desire to open the door and jump out of Sam's moving car is hard to resist. He glances at me, an obviously anxious look on his cute face, as if he senses my intention to bolt.

Once we're parked outside the gates, Sam comes around to collect me, keeping a firm grip on me as he guides us toward the pedestrian gates where Drew's waiting.

He's dressed in his usual finery, all suited and booted, with perfectly styled black hair, but he doesn't make me feel uncomfortable anymore. I'm more than shocked when he takes over Sam's hold of me, though, pulling me into him and squeezing me hard. This is the first actual contact I've ever had with the man.

"Ava, thank you for coming."

I say nothing because I really don't know what to say. They're truly worried about Jesse, and I feel guilty and even more anxious now. Drew releases me and offers a small, reassuring smile. It does nothing to reassure me.

Sam points up the road. "Here's the big guy."

We turn to see John pull up in his black Range Rover, skidding to an abrupt halt behind Sam's car. He slides his big body out, removes his wraparound sunglasses, and nods in greeting. This is John's usual wordless acknowledgment. Good Lord, he looks pissed. I've only ever got a brief glimpse of his eyes—they are always concealed behind those glasses, even at night or inside, but the sun is shining now, so why he has taken them off is beyond me. Maybe he wants everyone to know how pissed he is. It's working. He looks formidable.

I take a deep breath and punch in the code, pushing the gate open for the guys. I wish this was as far as I had to go. Drew gestures for me to lead the way, ever the gentleman, so I pick my feet up and start my walk across the car park in silence. I see Jesse's car and notice his window is still smashed. My stomach flips as we enter the marble foyer of Lusso quietly, except for the thumping of our footsteps. My insides start churning, my breathing speeding up. So much has happened in this place. Lusso was my first major accomplishment in design. My first sexual encounter with Jesse happened here, as did my final encounter with him. It all started and ended here.

Clive looks up from his big, curved marble desk as we approach, his expression screaming tiresome.

"Clive," I say on a forced smile.

He eyes me, and then the three ominous beings accompanying me, before his eyes settle on me again. "Hello, Ava. How are you?"

"I'm good, Clive," I lie. "You?"

"I'm fine." He's weary, no doubt after having a few heated encounters with the three men escorting me, and judging by his cold reception toward me, they were not pleasant.

"Clive, I'd be grateful if you would let us up to the penthouse to check on Jesse." I load my voice with lashings of confidence, but I feel anything but. My heart is speeding up by the second.

"Ava, I've told your friends here, I could lose my job if I allow that." He flicks a cautious gaze to the boys again.

"I know, Clive, but they're worried," I say, sounding completely detached. "They just want to check he's okay, and then they'll be leaving," I try with graciousness as I know Drew, Sam, and John would have been a lot less than that.

"Ava, I have been up and knocked on Mr. Ward's door and got no response. We've checked some of the CCTV, and I have not seen him leave or return on my watch. Security cannot check five days of continuous footage. I have told your friends this. If I let you up, I could lose my job."

I'm stunned at Clive's sudden turnabout in concierge etiquette. If only he had been this professional and stubborn when I came to see Jesse on Sunday, then we might never have had the altercation we did. But then I would still be blissfully unaware of Jesse's little problem.

I feel Sam press up against my back. "Let us up, for fuck's sake!" he yells over my shoulder.

I flinch slightly, but I can't blame him for being frustrated. I'm feeling pretty frustrated myself. I just want to get them past Clive and go. I can feel the walls closing in on all sides of me, and I can see Jesse carrying me across the marble floor in his arms. All of the images swamping my brain are now all the more clear for being here.

I turn and see John with a face like thunder and his hand on Sam's shoulder, his way of telling Sam to calm down. I didn't want to do this, but tempers are fraying. "Clive, I would hate to resort to blackmail," I say tightly, turning back to face him. He looks at me in confusion, and I can see his brain ticking over, trying to think of what I could possibly blackmail him with. "I would hate for anyone to find out about Mr. Gomez's regular visitors or Mr. Holland's fondness of a Thai girl or two." I watch as Clive's face screws up into a contortion of defeatism.

"Ava, you play nasty, my girl."

"You leave me no other choice, Clive."

He shakes his head and motions us onto the elevator while muttering insults under his breath.

"Brilliant!" Sam chants as they make their way over to the penthouse lift.

I don't have any idea how it happens, but I find my feet lifting and taking small steps behind them, following them to the elevator. "Jesse might have changed the code," I say to their backs.

Sam swings around, looking alarmed.

I shrug. "If he has, then there is no way of getting up there."

All of a sudden, I'm standing in front of the elevator, taking a deep breath and punching in the developer code. There's a chorus of exhales as the doors open and they all get in, and I stand on the outside, looking up at Sam. He smiles, jerking his head mildly, encouraging me to board with them.

I do.

I get in the elevator, Sam and Drew flanking me on one side, John on the other, and I enter the code again. We travel up in an uncomfortable silence, and as the lift doors open, we're faced with the double doors that lead into Jesse's penthouse.

Sam is the first to exit the lift, striding toward the doors and jiggling the handle calmly before he starts hammering on the door like a madman. "Jesse! Open the fucking door!"

Drew and John approach and pull him away, and then John tries the door himself, but it doesn't budge. I can't help but think I might have been the last person to exit the penthouse. I remember making a point of slamming the door as hard as I could.

"Sam, mate, he might not even be here," Drew soothes.

"Where the hell is he then?" Sam yells.

"Oh, he's in there," John rumbles. "And the motherfucker has been drowning in his sorrows for too long now. He's got a business to run."

I'm still standing in the elevator when the doors start to

shut, snapping me out of my dazed state. My natural reflex has my arm flinging up to stop them closing before I step out into the penthouse foyer. I know I said that I would get them up here and leave, I know I should just go, but seeing Sam in such a state has me even more worried, and John's words are prickling me. Drowning in his sorrows or drowning in vodka? If I stay, am I going to be faced with drunken, raging Jesse again?

Drew knocks on the door calmly. It's laughable. If Sam's relentless hammering doesn't get a response, then I doubt Drew's gentlemanly tapping will.

He steps away from the door and drags Sam over to me. "Ava, have you tried calling him?" Drew asks.

"No!" I blurt. Why would I do that? I'm pretty sure he wouldn't want to talk to me.

"Can you try?" Sam asks pleadingly.

I shake my head. "He wouldn't answer, Sam."

"Ava, will you just try?" Drew pushes.

I reluctantly get my phone from my bag and dial Jesse while Sam and Drew watch nervously. I'm not sure what on earth I'm going to say if he answers.

Drew's head snaps toward the door. "I can hear it ringing." He returns to me, obviously waiting for me to speak, but my call goes to voicemail and my heart constricts. He doesn't want to talk to me. I go to reboard the elevator, the hurt enflamed by his rejection of my call, but then an almighty crash sounds out around the foyer.

Sam, Drew, and I all whip our heads around to the double doors leading into Jesse's penthouse and find John on the other side, surrounded by a splintered doorframe. He nods at us, and Sam and Drew fly forward into the penthouse. I find myself following tentatively behind them, remembering the last time I was here.

Turn around! Get in the elevator! Go, NOW.

But I don't. I stand in the doorway and from what I can see, nothing has moved. I step a little bit farther into the open area and hear the guys running around upstairs and down, searching for Jesse. And as the bottom of the stairs comes into view, I notice the empty bottle of vodka is still on the console table. Then I see the terrace doors wide open. I take cautious steps toward them, still hearing the guys running around the penthouse, doors opening and closing, his name being called.

I, however, am pulled toward the terrace. I know why. It's the same magnetism that pulls me toward Jesse every time he is near. Only this time I know it won't be *my* Jesse. Do I want to face him again when he is in such a terrible state, when he is so vicious and hateful? No, of course I don't, but I can't seem to turn away.

As I approach the doors, I try to prepare my eyes for a drunken mess, sprawled across one of the sun loungers, clenching a vodka bottle. But instead, I'm greeted by Jesse's naked, unconscious body face down on the decking.

I choke on my heart, and my pulse starts pounding in my ears. "He's here!" I scream, running toward his lifeless body and throwing my bag down as I collapse by his side.

I grip his big shoulders to try and turn him over. I don't know where I get my strength from, but I manage it, yanking him over so his head is cradled in my lap. I start desperately smoothing my hands over his bearded face, noticing his hand still swollen and bruised, with dried blood all over his knuckles.

"Jesse, wake up. Please, wake up." I plead, giving into hysteria as I look at the man I love, unconscious and unresponsive, lying in my lap. Tears pour down my face and spill onto his cheeks. "Jesse, please." I desperately run my hands over his face, his chest, his hair. He looks hollow, he's lost weight, and his jaw is covered in a week's worth of stubble.

"Motherfucker," John rumbles when he finds me on the terrace with Jesse supported in my lap.

"I don't know if he's breathing," I sob, looking up through glazed eyes to the mountain of a man stalking toward me.

"Here," John gestures, kneeling down and taking Jesse's arm from me.

I look up and see Sam skid to a halt at the door. "What the..."

Tears are invading my eyes uncontrollably and everything has gone into slow motion. Sam makes his way over and lowers himself down next to me. He starts rubbing my arm.

"I'll call an ambulance," Drew says urgently as he finds us all crowded around Jesse's motionless form.

"Hold up," John barks harshly, leaning over Jesse and pulling his dried lips apart, inspecting every part of his limp body. "The stupid motherfucker. He's drunk himself into a fucking coma."

I look at Sam and Drew, but I can't fathom their reaction to John's conclusion. How does he know this? He could be half dead for all John knows. He certainly looks it. "I think we should call an ambulance," I push between sniffles.

John looks at me sympathetically. I've never seen anything but a completely impassive expression on his hard face, so the way he is looking at me now, all sorrowful and like I'm a little naive, is strangely comforting.

"Ava, girl. I've seen him like this, more than once. He needs his bed and some care to get him through this. He doesn't need a doctor. Not that sort, anyway." John shakes his head.

Oh? How many times is more than once? John sounds like he knows the drill. He's not at all concerned by the condition of Jesse lying in my lap, whereas I'm a hysterical wreck. Sam and Drew are not all that good either. Have they seen him like this before?

John clucks my cheek and hoists himself up off the floor. I've never heard him say so much. The big, silent giant turns out to be the big, friendly giant. But I still wouldn't want to cross him.

"What happened to his hand?" Sam asks when he clocks the bloodied, bruised mess.

It really looks terrible and probably needs looking at. "He smashed the window on his car," I sniffle, and they all look at me. "When we rowed at Kate's," I add, almost ashamed.

"Should we get him into his bed?" Drew asks timidly.

"Sofa," John instructs. We're back to a few words.

I watch as Sam gets up and collects an empty vodka bottle from under the sun lounger. He looks at it in complete disgust and dramatically smashes it on the side of a raised planter, making me flinch at the loud noise that echoes around us, but more significantly, it makes Jesse flinch, too.

"Jesse?" I shake him slightly. "Jesse, please, open your eyes."

Sam, Drew, and John all crowd around us, and Jesse's arm starts to rise above his head, flapping around in thin air. I clasp it and place it back by his side, but as soon as I release it, he brings it back up in front of my face, mumbling inaudibly and thrashing his legs about.

"He's looking for you, girl," John says quietly.

I throw a shocked glance at John, and he nods at me. He's looking for me? I reach for his hand again and guide it to my face, spreading his palm against my cheek. He instantly calms. His cold palm on my face offers me little comfort, but it seems to soothe him, so I hold it there and let him feel me, horrified that he has, quite possibly, been out here on the terrace for days, unclothed and unconscious. It might be mild in the daytime, but nightfall brings cooler temperatures. Why did I walk out on him? I should have stayed and calmed him down, not walked away.

"I'll go and get some bedding from upstairs," Drew says, heading back into the penthouse.

"Shall we?" John prompts, nodding at Jesse on the floor.

I reluctantly release Jesse's hand and let Sam and John flank him on either side to coordinate a lift. As he's lifted from my lap, I pull myself up and run ahead to make sure their path is clear and the entire leather corner couch free of a million cushions—all courtesy of me—so it looks more like a bed when I'm done.

As Drew comes down the stairs with his hands full of blankets, Sam and John wait patiently with Jesse's naked weight spread evenly between them. I take a velvet throw from Drew and lay it over the cold leather, and then move back so John and Sam can lower him onto the couch before propping his head up on some pillows and laying another throw over his naked body. I drop to my knees at his side, smoothing my hand down the side of his stubbled face, regret washing over me, tears starting to fall again. I could have stopped this. If I hadn't stormed out, he wouldn't be in this state now. I should have stayed, calmed him down, and sobered him up. I hate myself.

"Ava, are you okay?" I hear Drew's quiet voice over my suppressed sobs, and a hand starts rubbing my back.

I sniffle and wipe my nose with the back of my hand. "I'm fine, sorry."

"Don't apologize," Sam sighs.

I lean over Jesse and rest my lips on his forehead, leaving them to linger for a few seconds, and as I lift myself from the floor, his arm shoots out from under the blanket and grabs me. "Ava?" His voice is cracked and hoarse, and his eyes open slightly, searching around the room. And when they find mine, all I can see are empty pits of nothing; his usual green, addictive eyes are bordering on black.

"Hey." I place my hand over his on my arm.

He starts to lift his head from the pillow, but before I have a chance to push him back down, he gives up trying. "I'm so sorry," he murmurs, his hand starting to pat its way up my arm to find my face again. "I'm sorry, I'm sorry, I'm sorry, I'm sorry, I'm sorry..."

"Stop," I whisper on a quivering voice, helping his hand to reach my face. "Please, just stop." I turn my lips into his hand and kiss his palm, and when I turn to face him again, his eyes are closed. He's gone again.

Taking his hand and placing it under the blanket, I make sure he is tucked in well before pulling myself up and turning to see Sam, Drew, and John, all standing silently watching me tend to him. I had completely forgotten I wasn't alone with Jesse, but I'm not in the least bit embarrassed.

"I'll make some coffee." Sam breaks the silence and heads for the kitchen, John and Drew following.

I take another glance at Jesse, my instinct telling me to crawl onto the sofa and snuggle up to him, stroke him and soothe him. I might just do that, but first I need to talk to the guys. I follow them into the kitchen and find Sam and Drew picking up barstools and John heaving the freezer up from the floor. It wasn't like this when I left on Sunday. Jesse clearly flew into a rage.

"I've got to shoot," Drew says regretfully, placing the last stool upright. "I'm taking Victoria out." He looks a little embarrassed.

"You go, bud." Sam pushes as he hunts for the mugs. "I'll call you later."

"Last cupboard on the right, top shelf," I give Sam the directions to the mugs, and he turns, looking at me quizzically as Drew leaves.

I shrug.

He transports three mugs of black coffee to the island where John and I have taken our seats. "We won't risk the milk, that's if he's even got any. Black okay?" Sam asks.

I nod and help myself, John following suit, putting an incredible four sugars into his coffee. I know there is no milk, but it would be pointless sharing this.

"So," Sam begins, "now we've found him, what are we going to do with him?" he jokes.

Carefree Sam is back and it's quite a relief. Seeing him so fraught had only fueled my own worry, and as it turns out, he had every reason to be anxious. I inwardly shudder at the thought of Jesse alone and suffering for the last five days. How much longer would he have been lying there if I had refused to come? They would have surely phoned the police.

John pipes up. "Everything is running smoothly at The Manor for now. We don't have to worry about that. He'll be back to normal after nursing a weeklong hangover."

"Doesn't he need to go to rehab?" I ask. "Or therapy, I don't know." I have no idea how these things work.

John shakes his head and puts his glasses back on, and I start to wonder about his relationship with Jesse. I thought he was just an employee, but he seems to be the one in the know about all of this.

"No rehab," John states firmly. "He's not obsessed with alcohol, Ava. He drank to lighten his foul mood, to fill a gap. Once he starts, he can't stop." He offers me a small smile. "You helped, girl."

"What did I do?" I don't know why I sound so hurt by John's statement. He has just told me I helped the situation, but I can't help feeling like he's insinuating that I might have helped with the relapse as well.

Sam places his hand over mine on the worktop. "His attention was focused elsewhere."

"But then I left him," I say quietly. I'm just confirming what they are both thinking.

"It's not your fault, Ava," Sam reassures me firmly. "You weren't to know."

"He never told me," I whisper. "If I had known, things would have been different." Really, I'm not sure how things would have been different if Jesse had told me. But I know I never want to see him like he was last Sunday again. If I leave now, will that happen? My head is a jumbled mess. I prop my elbows on the counter and plant my head in my hands. What the hell am I supposed to do?

"Ava?" John's deep rumble pulls my head back up. "He's a good man."

"What made him drink? How bad is it?" I ask. I know he's a good man deep down, but if I know more I might understand better.

"Who knows?" John muses, and then looks at me. "Don't be thinking he was smashed all day every day. He wasn't. How he is right now, that's just because of misery, not because he's an alcoholic."

"And he didn't drink when I turned up?" I can't believe that.

John laughs. "He didn't, although you have brought out some other rather nasty qualities in him, girl."

I frown, but I know exactly what John's talking about, and so does Sam by the look on his cheeky face. I've been told Jesse is usually quite a laid-back type, but I have only ever seen snippets of a laid-back Jesse Ward, and that was mostly when he was getting his own way. Most of the time, all I've seen is an unreasonable control freak. He even admitted himself that he's only like that with me...lucky me.

"I'll stay, but if he comes round and he doesn't want me here, I will be calling one of you two," I warn.

Sam visibly sags. "That won't happen, Ava."

John nods. "I need to get myself back to The Manor and run that motherfucker's business." He gets himself up from the barstool. "Ava, you need my number. Where's your phone?"

I look around for my bag and realize that I've left it on the terrace, so I jump up and leave Sam and John in the kitchen while I go to fetch it.

On my way back to the kitchen, I see Jesse is still out for the count. How long will he be like this, and at what point should I really worry? I have no idea what I'm supposed to do.

I stand silently watching him, his lashes flickering mildly, his chest rising and falling steadily. Even unconscious he looks troubled. Approaching quietly, I pull the blanket up to his chin. I can't help it. I've never looked after him before, but it's instinctive. I kneel and rest my lips on his cold cheek, soaking up the little bit of comfort I get from the contact, before standing and making my way back to the kitchen. John has gone.

"Here," Sam passes me a piece of paper. "John's number."

"Was he in a rush?" I ask. He could have waited for me.

"He never hangs around for longer than necessary. Listen, I've spoken to Kate. She's bringing some clothes over for you."

"Oh, okay." My poor clothes are going to wonder where they live. They have been transported back and forth to this place on numerous occasions.

"Thank you, Ava," Sam says sincerely.

"Don't thank me," I protest, feeling uncomfortable, especially since this is partly my fault.

Sam shuffles nervously. "I know. It's just...well, after last Sunday, The Manor shock."

"Don't, Sam."

"When he drinks, he really drinks." Sam laughs lightly. "He's a proud man, Ava. He'll be mortified that we've seen him like this."

I imagine he will be. The Jesse I know is strong, confident, domineering, and a whole heap of other things. Weak and helpless are not included in the long list of Jesse's attributes. I want to tell Sam that The Manor and its activities have been diluted by this drink issue, but it hasn't. Not really. Now I'm here and

I've laid my eyes on Jesse again, it's all screaming very loudly in my head. Jesse owns a sex club. He also uses the facilities of his own club. Sam confirmed it, even though it was glaringly obvious when I was faced with the husband of one of Jesse's conquests. I knew deep down that he must have slept around, that he was a pleasure-seeking playboy, but I certainly didn't ever imagine how.

*   *   *

We spend the next hour collecting empties and cleaning up the penthouse. I empty the fridge of more vodka, tipping it all down the sink, thinking I won't be drinking it ever again.

Clive rings up to tell me that a young lady is in the foyer by the name of Kate, and after I've advised him of what we've found, we go down to meet her, each dragging a black bin bag full of rubbish and empty bottles. I make a mental note to sort the mangled door out.

When we arrive in the foyer, Kate is waiting under the close observation of Clive. "Hey," she says cautiously as we approach, dragging the clanging bin bags with us. "How is he?"

I release the bag, causing more clanging, and give Clive the eyeball, just to let him know that I'm really pissed off with him. If he had let Sam, Drew, or John up to Jesse's penthouse before now, we may have only found him drunk instead of completely comatose. He has the decency to look apologetic.

"He's asleep," Sam answers her when it becomes obvious that I'm too busy making Clive feel guilty.

When I turn my attention back to Kate, I see Sam slip his free arm around her and give her a hug. She bats him away playfully. "Here." Kate passes me my overnight bag. "I just chucked anything and everything in it."

"Thanks." I take the bag.

"So, you're staying here then?" she asks.

"Yeah," I answer on a shrug. Sam gives me that appreciative stare, and I immediately feel uncomfortable again.

"How long are you staying?" Kate asks.

Good question. How long do these things take? He could wake tonight, or it could be tomorrow or the next day. I have a job to do and an apartment to find. I look at Sam for some clue, but he only shrugs, so I look back at Kate and shrug, too.

I'm suddenly aware that I've left Jesse upstairs alone, and I start to panic. He might wake up and no one will be there. "I should get back up there," I say, looking back toward the elevators.

"Sure, you go." Kate shoos me with her hand and takes the bin bag from the floor. "We'll get rid of these."

We say our good-byes and I promise to call her in the morning before I head back to the elevator, instructing Clive to sort out Jesse's car window and the door to his penthouse on my way. He, of course, gets straight onto it.

When I arrive back on the top floor, I wander into the living room and see Jesse still asleep.

So, what do I do now? I'm still in my taupe dress and heels, so I head upstairs and allocate myself the room at the far end of the landing. Then I change into my ripped jeans and a black T-shirt. I could do with a shower, but I don't want to leave Jesse alone for too long. It'll have to wait.

After making my way back downstairs, I make a black coffee and as I stand sipping it in the kitchen, I figure it would be a good idea to read up on alcoholism. Jesse must have a computer somewhere, so I go in search, finding a laptop in his study. I fire it up, and I'm immensely relieved when it doesn't prompt me for a password. I take it downstairs and settle myself in the big chair opposite Jesse so I can keep an eye on him. Pulling up Google, I type in "alcoholics," and I'm presented with seventeen million

results. At the top of the page, though, is "Alcoholics Anony-
mous." That would be a good place to start, I suppose. John
might have said that Jesse isn't an alcoholic, but I'm doubtful.

*   *   *

After a few hours of browsing the Internet, I feel like my brain
cells have been zapped. There is so much to take in—long-
term effects, psychiatric problems, withdrawal symptoms. I read
a piece about severe childhood trauma leading to alcoholism,
which leaves me wondering if Jesse had something happen to
him when he was a boy, the vicious scar on his abdomen springing to mind immediately. There are also genetic connections, so
then I wonder if one of his parents was an alcoholic. I'm bom-
barded with information, and I don't know what to do with any
of it.

My mind flicks back to last Sunday and the things he said to
me. *You're a fucking prick tease, Ava. I needed you and you left me.*
Then I had left him...again. I shut the laptop in exasperation
and put it on the coffee table. It's only ten o'clock, but I'm totally spent. I don't want to go upstairs to bed in case he wakes
up, so I gather a few cushions, lay them on the floor next to him,
and settle myself, resting my head on the sofa and stroking the
hairs on his toned arms. It relaxes me to have the contact, and
it's not long before my eyes are heavy and I'm drifting off.

CHAPTER THREE

I love you."

I'm vaguely aware of his palm holding the back of my head, his fingers running through my hair, and it feels so comforting...so right. I open my eyes and I'm met by a duller version of the green I know so well.

I jump to my feet and smack my ankle on the coffee table. "Shit!" I curse.

"Watch your mouth!" he scolds me, his voice gritty and broken.

I grasp my ankle, but then I wake up fully and remember where I am. I drop my foot and swing my gaze to the sofa, finding Jesse sat up slightly, looking terrible, but at least he's awake. "You're awake!" I cry.

He winces, clasping his head with his good hand.

Oh, shit!

He must have the hangover from hell, and here I am screeching like a banshee. I walk back the few steps needed to find the chair behind me, and then lower myself onto the seat. I have no idea what to say to him. I'm not about to ask how he's feeling, that is pretty obvious, and I'm not going to hit him with a lecture about personal safety or disregarding his health.

I want to ask him if he remembers our fight.

I want to ask him why he didn't tell me he owns a sex club or that he has an issue with drink.

I want to ask him if he's wondering what I'm doing here and if he wants me to leave.

I want to tell him that I love him.

But I don't. Instead I blurt, "How are you feeling?" and instantly wish I had kept my mouth shut.

He sighs and inspects his damaged hand. "Shit," he states sharply.

He must need some fluids, so I get up and head toward the kitchen.

"Where are you going?" he asks, slightly panicked and bolting upright on the couch.

"I thought you might need some water," I assure him, my heart lifting a little. I've seen that face plenty of times. The domineering control freak usually follows, after he's pinned me down somewhere, but I won't get my hopes up too high. He hasn't got the strength to be chasing, pinning, or dominating me at the moment. I'm disappointed.

He settles at my response, and I carry on to the kitchen, glancing at the clock on the oven as I fetch a glass. Eight o'clock. I've slept for ten hours straight. That hasn't happened since...well, since I was last with Jesse.

I grab a bottle of water from the fridge and fill the glass before returning to find Jesse sitting up on the sofa with his head in his hands, the blanket pooling in his lap.

When I reach him, he lifts his gaze to mine and our eyes lock as I hand him the water. With his good hand, he takes the glass, his fingers resting over mine, and I retract mine quickly, the water splashing out of the glass. I don't know why that happened, and the look on his face makes me feel instantly heartless. He's shaking dreadfully, and I'm wondering if it's withdrawal. I'm sure I read shakiness is a symptom, along with a catalogue of other signs.

He follows my eyes to his hand and shakes his head. This is weird. Things have never been like this between us. Neither of us knows what to say.

"When did you last have a drink?" I ask. This is pink elephant in the room territory, but I've got to say something.

He sips his water and then slumps back on the sofa, his abdominals looking sharper from his slight weight loss. "I don't know. What day is it?"

"Saturday."

"Saturday?" he asks, obviously shocked. "Fuck."

I'm assuming this means he's lost a lot of time, but he can't have been in this penthouse for five days solid, just drinking. Surely he would be dead?

And then the silence falls again and I find myself back on the chair opposite him, twiddling my thumbs and searching my brain for the right thing to say. I hate this. I wouldn't usually think twice about diving on him and throwing my arms around him, letting him smother me completely, but he's so delicate at the moment, which is crazy, considering his tall, if a bit leaner, frame. My strong rogue is reduced to a shaking mess. It's killing me. This man is not the man I fell in love with. Is this the real Jesse?

He sits and fiddles with his glass thoughtfully, and the familiar sight of the cogs turning is comforting, it's a little piece of him that I recognize, but I can't bear this silence. "Jesse, is there anything I can do?"

He sighs. "There are lots of things you can do, Ava. But I can't ask you to do any of them." He doesn't look at me.

"Do you want a shower?" I ask softly.

He leans forward and winces. "Sure."

I watch him struggle to his feet, and I feel like a cold cow for not helping him, but I don't know if he wants me to, and I'm not sure that I can. The atmosphere between us is so awkward.

As he stands, the blankets fall to his feet and he looks down at his naked body. "Shit," he curses, reaching down to retrieve one of the blankets. He wraps it around his waist and turns toward me. "I'm sorry," he says on a shrug.

Sorry?

Like I haven't seen it all before—lots, in fact. In his words, there is not a place on my body that hasn't had him in it, on it, or over it.

My shoulders droop and I sigh as I start walking with him up the stairs to the master suite. It takes a while and we're surrounded by an uncomfortable silence the whole way, but we make it, eventually. "Would a bath be better?" I ask, walking ahead into the bathroom. He looks exhausted after his trek up the stairs, so standing in the shower isn't going to be fun. A good muscle soak in the bath will probably help.

He shrugs again. "I suppose."

I turn the giant mixer tap on and run my hand under it until the temperature is right, while trying my hardest not to think about tub-talk and the fact that Jesse is a self-proclaimed bath man now—but only when I'm in there with him.

I turn and come face to face with the vanity unit. That is where we had our first sexual encounter. This bathroom is where we showered together, bathed together, and had many steamy sex sessions together. It's also where I last saw him.

Stop!

I shake my thoughts away and busy myself finding some bath soak and generally puttering about, while Jesse stands propped up against the wall in silence. The bath takes forever to fill, and I begin to wish I had just shoved him in the shower.

"There," I say once it's full, turning to escape the awkward-ness.

"You're acting like a stranger," he says softly, just as I reach the door, stopping me in my tracks. This is so very painful.

I don't turn around. "I feel like a stranger," I say quietly, swallowing hard and trying to prevent the shakes that are threatening to invade my body.

Silence settles again. I really don't know what to do. I thought the pain couldn't get any worse. I thought I was in the lowest level of hell already. I was wrong. Seeing him like this is crippling me. I need to leave and continue with my battle to get over this man. I feel like I've been knocked back a few steps, now that I've seen him again, but the truth is, I hadn't really made any progression in my recovery.

"Please look at me, Ava."

My heart sprints up to my throat at his words, which are a plea rather than the usual demand. Even his voice sounds different. It's not the familiar deep, husky, sexy rumble I know. Now, it is cracked and broken. He is cracked and broken, which means I am cracked and broken.

I slowly pivot to face the man who is a stranger to me, finding his bottom lip wedged between his teeth as he looks at me through hollow green eyes. "I can't do this." I turn and leave, my heart hammering, but getting slower at the same time. It's going to stop soon.

"Ava!"

I hear him coming after me, but I don't look back. He's not at full strength, so this might be the only time I actually get away from him. What was I thinking coming here? Flashbacks of last Sunday overwhelm my head as I take the stairs fast, my vision blurry, my legs numb.

As I hit the bottom of the staircase, I feel the familiar grip of his hand around my wrist and I panic, flying around to push him away from me. "No!" I scream, frantically trying to release myself from his harsh hold. "Don't touch me!"

"Ava, don't do this," he pleads, grabbing my other wrist and holding me in front of him. "Stop!"

I crumble to the floor, feeling helpless and fragile. I'm already broken, but he can dish the final blow that will finish me off. "Please, don't," I sob. "Please, don't make this harder."

He collapses to the floor with me, pulling me onto his lap and smothering me completely. I sob relentlessly into his chest. I can't control it.

His face pushes into my hair. "I'm sorry," he whispers. "I'm so, so sorry. I don't deserve it, but give me a chance." He squeezes me hard. "I need another chance."

"I don't know what to do." I'm being honest. I feel the need to escape him, but at the same time, I feel the need to stay and let him make things better. But if I stay, will I get dealt that death blow? Or if I leave, will *that* be the death blow...for both of us?

All I know is the strong, firm, assertive Jesse, the Jesse who broods when I defy him, manhandles me when I threaten to leave him, and fucks me until I'm delirious. This is the furthest away from that man.

"Don't run away from me again," he begs, holding me tight. I notice his shakes have subsided.

I pull back, wiping my tearstained face with the back of my hand, my eyes fixed on his stomach, his scar bigger and more obvious than ever before. I can't look at his eyes. They are not familiar to me anymore. They are not dark with anger or sparkling with pleasure—not narrowed fiercely or hooded with lust for me. They are empty pits of nothing, with no comfort to offer me. Despite that, though, I know if I walk out of that door, I'm finished. My only hope is to stay, find the answers that I need, and pray they don't destroy me. He has the power to destroy me.

His cold hand slides under my chin and pulls my face up to

his. "I'm going to make this all right. I'm going to make you remember, Ava."

I stare into his eyes and see determination through the haze of green. Determination is good, but does it eradicate the pain and madness that has come before it? "Can you make me remember the conventional way?" It's not a joke, although he smiles a little.

"I'm making it my mission objective. I'll do anything."

His words, a repeat from the launch night of Lusso, are spoken with as much resolve now as they were back then. He kept his promise to prove that I wanted him. A small flicker of hope lightens my heavy heart, and I sink my face back down into his chest, clinging onto him, hearing a quiet exhale of breath escape his lips as he pulls me closer and holds on like his life depends on it.

It probably does. And mine, too.

*   *   *

"Your bath will get cold," I mumble into his bare chest when we're still crumpled on the floor in a firm hold some time later.

"I'm comfy," he grumbles, and I detect a familiar piece of Jesse in his tone.

"You need to eat as well," I inform him, feeling strange dishing out instructions to him. "And that hand needs seeing to. Does it hurt?"

"Like hell."

I'm not surprised; it looks terrible. "Come on." I pry myself out of his vise grip, prompting him to grumble, but he releases me. Standing up, I put my hand out to him, and he looks up at me with a small smile before taking it and lifting himself from the floor.

We walk quietly up the stairs and back to the master suite.

"In you get," I order quietly, pointing at the bath.

"Are you making demands?" His eyebrows rise.

"Sounds like it." I nod toward the bath.

He starts chewing his lip, making no attempt to get in the bath. "Will you get in with me?" he asks quietly.

I suddenly feel awkward and out of place. "I can't." I shake my head and step back slightly. I want to, desperately, but I know as soon as I surrender to his affection and touch, I'll be sidetracked from my aim to straighten my head, to get answers.

"Ava, you're asking me not to touch you. That goes against all of my instincts."

"Jesse, please. I need time."

"It's not natural, Ava. For me not to touch you, it's not right."

He's right, but I can't allow myself to get swallowed up by him. I need to keep a level head, and as soon as he gets his hands on me, I'm distracted.

I don't say anything. I just look at the bath again before returning my eyes to him. He shakes his head, unwrapping the blanket from around his waist before stepping into the bath and lowering himself gingerly into the water. I collect a cup from the vanity unit and crouch by the side of the bath to wash his hair.

"It's not the same without you in here with me," he grumbles, leaning back and closing his eyes.

I ignore his gripe and start washing his hair and soaping his fine body from head to toe, fighting off the inevitable fizzles streaming through me at the contact.

Lingering around his scar on his abdomen thoughtfully, I quietly hope it will prompt him to explain it. It doesn't. He keeps his eyes closed and his mouth shut. I have a feeling this is going to be a tough ride. He never volunteers information, and he dodges my questions with a stern warning or by distraction tactics. I can't let that happen again. This is going to take all of my strength and willpower. It's just not natural for me to evade him.

I run my hand along his rough jaw. "You need a shave."

He opens his eyes and cups his chin with his good hand, stroking his stubble. "You don't like it?"

"I like you however you come."

Just not drunk!

The fleeting look that passes over his face nearly has me convinced that he's read my mind. "I'm not touching another drop again," he declares confidently, ensuring he maintains our eye contact as he makes his vow.

"You sound confident," I retort quietly.

"I am." He sits himself up in the bath and turns to face me, lifting his battered hand to cup my face and wincing when he realizes he can't. "I mean it, never again. I promise you. I'm not a raving alcoholic, Ava. I admit I get carried away once I do have a drink and I find it hard to stop, but I can take it or leave it. I was in a bad place after you left me. I just wanted to numb the pain."

My heart tightens in my chest, and I feel a sense of relief mixed with a little doubt. Everyone gets a little carried away when they've had a drink, right? I look past him, trying to piece together what I need to say. Millions of words have been trampling my mind for days, but now I can't think of any of them. "Why didn't you tell me sooner? Is this what you meant when you said I would cause more damage if I left?"

His head drops. "That was a shitty thing to say."

"It was."

He returns his eyes to mine. "I just wanted you to stay. I was stunned when you told me that I had a nice hotel." He smiles a little, and I feel stupid. "Things got pretty intense, pretty quickly. I didn't know how to tell you. I didn't want you to run away again. You. Kept. Running. Away."

"I didn't get far, though, did I?"

"I was going to tell you. You weren't supposed to come to The Manor like that. I wasn't prepared, Ava."

That much was obvious. All of the times I had been to the supposed hotel, I'd been chaperoned or confined to Jesse's office. I'm sure people were warned off talking to me, and no one approached Jesse when I was with him. And he's right, things did get pretty intense, pretty quickly, but that had nothing to do with me. God, there is so much to talk about. So many questions. The nasty little creature who Jesse pounded on at The Manor had some pretty interesting things to say. Has Jesse had an affair with his wife?

I sigh. "Come on, you're pruning." I hold up a towel and he mirrors my sigh before pushing himself up on the side of the bath with his good hand. He steps out and I run the towel over his body as he watches me closely.

The corners of his lips lift slightly into the semblance of a smile when I reach his neck. "A few weeks ago, I was nursing *your* hangover."

"I bet your head is banging a lot harder than mine was." I dismiss his reminiscing and secure the towel around his waist. "Food and then the hospital."

"Hospital?" he blurts, his voice startled. "I don't need a hospital, Ava."

"Your hand," I clarify. He probably thinks I want to section him.

I see understanding surface in his eyes as he lifts his hand up to inspect it. The blood has all washed away, but it still looks nasty. "It's fine."

"I don't think it is."

"Ava, I don't need to go to the hospital."

"Don't go then." I turn and walk into the bedroom.

Following me in, he collapses on the end of the bed and watches as I disappear into his huge walk-in wardrobe. I rummage through his clothes, finding him some marl gray sweatpants and a white T-shirt. He needs comfort. I retrieve some boxer shorts from his chest of drawers and walk back over to find him sprawled back on the bed. Just getting him upstairs and bathed has knackered him out. I can't imagine a hangover on this scale.

"Here, put these on." I place the clothes on the bed next to him, and he turns his head to inspect my selection, letting out a heavy, tired breath.

When he makes no attempt to dress himself, I pick up his boxers and kneel down in front of him, holding them at his feet. He's done this to me plenty of times. I tap his ankle and he pushes himself up on the bed, looking down at me, a small twinkle lighting his eyes. It's another familiar trait.

He silently lifts his feet and stands so I can negotiate the boxers up his legs, but then his towel drops when I'm halfway up his body and I come face to face with his huge arousal.

I release his boxers and jump back from him, like it might burn me or something. Not all of him is broken then, I think to myself, trying to ignore the steel rod of flesh within touching distance. I flick a glance up to him and for the first time, his eyes sparkle fully, but it's not what I need right now, although my body is completely disagreeing with my brain. I struggle to control the urge to push him on the bed and straddle him. I'm not risking sidetracking either of us with sex. There's a lot to talk about.

He reaches down to pull his boxers up the rest of the way. "I'll go to the hospital," he says. "If you want me to, then I'll go."

I frown at him. "Agreeing to have your hand looked at won't make me fall to your feet in gratitude," I say curtly.

His eyes narrow slightly at my harshness. "I'll let that slip."

"I need to feed you," I mutter, turning and walking out of the room, leaving Jesse to put his sweatpants and T-shirt on.

CHAPTER FOUR

After showering and changing in the spare room, I head downstairs to find Jesse unconscious on the sofa. I watch the subtle rise and fall of his broad chest for a while, my eyes pleased, despite his evident exhaustion. It takes my mobile to shout and snap me from my daydream, and I quickly track it down, answering without bothering to look at the screen.

"Hello?"

"Ava?"

"Dan!" With all that's happened, I'd forgotten I was supposed to see him today. It's so good to hear his voice. "Where are you?"

"Just pulled into Euston."

"How are Mum and Dad?"

"Worried," he states flatly.

"They needn't be."

"Yeah, well, they are. And me too. Where are you?"

Shit!

"Kate's," I lie. It's not like he'll be talking to her or visiting her to discover the truth. And anyway, Mum knows I'm supposed to be at Kate's, and I'm certain she would have told him.

Silence falls down the phone line at the mention of Kate's name. "I see," he says shortly. "Still?"

Oh, the detachment in his voice. They haven't seen each other for years, but time, it would appear, is not a healer. "It's just temporary, Dan. I'm looking for somewhere as we speak."

"Have you spoken to that twat of an ex?" The spite in his voice is palpable.

"No, but I've heard he's been in touch with Mum and Dad. That's very nice of him."

"Fucking prick. We need to talk about this. Mum filled me in on her little chat with Matt. I know he's a snake, but Mum's worried."

"I called," I defend myself.

"Yeah, and I know you've not given her the whole story. What's with this new man?"

I freeze mid-pace. That's a good question. "Dan, there are some things you can't tell your parents."

"Yes, but you can tell your brother."

"Can I?" I blurt. I highly doubt that. Big brother would probably join my dad in the heart attack ward. This is the reason I didn't go to Newquay: interrogation and nagging. I'll have to face up to it eventually, but not now. I've never been so glad that my parents live so far away.

"Yes, you can. So, when can I see you?" he asks, chirping up a little.

See me or squeeze me for information? "Tomorrow?"

"I thought we were doing today?" He sounds so disappointed.

So am I. I really want to see him, but then in another way I really don't. "I'm sorry. I'm looking at a few places to rent, and then I've got stacks of drawings to finalize." I lie again, but I couldn't possibly muster up the strength to appear reasonably normal in such a short space of time. Maybe by tomorrow I'll have dragged myself out of my hole of depression and uncertainty. I very much doubt it, but at least I have time to try.

"Great, we'll make a day of it." He confirms my fears.

A whole day of evading his questions? "Okay, ring me in the morning," I say, and secretly hope he goes out with all of his mates tonight and suffers a dreadful hangover that delays his call to me. I need time.

"Sure thing. See you tomorrow, kid." He hangs up.

I start thinking of ways to get around this, and after an hour of aimless pacing around the penthouse, I come up with none. I can't avoid him forever.

The intercom phone system chimes and I answer it. "Ava, the maintenance man is on his way up to fix the door. Oh, and Mr. Ward's window has been replaced."

"Thank you, Clive." I hang up and make my way to the door.

I answer to an old boy who is already inspecting the damage. "You have a rhino ram-raid you?" he asks, scratching his head.

"Something like that," I mutter.

"I can secure it for now, but it'll need replacing. I'll get it on order and let you know when it arrives," he says, placing his tool-box on the floor.

"Thanks." I leave him chipping chunks of splintered wood off the door frame and turn to find Jesse half asleep, looking suspiciously at the door.

"What's going on?" he asks.

"John had a fight with your front door when you didn't open it," I inform him dryly.

His eyebrows shoot up, but then he looks worried. "I should call him."

"How are you feeling?" I ask, assessing him and concluding that he looks a bit brighter after an hour power napping.

"Better. You?"

"Fine. Time to get you to the hospital. I'll get my bag." I sidestep him and make my way past.

His hand flies out and grabs my arm. "Ava."

I halt and wait for a follow-up, any words that are going to make this all better, but I get nothing, just his heat seeping into my flesh from his harsh grip on my arm. I look up at him and find him watching me, but he still doesn't open his mouth.

I sigh heavily and pull myself free, but then I remember my car isn't here. How am I going to get him to the hospital? "Shit," I curse quietly.

"Watch your mouth, Ava. What's up?"

"My car's at Kate's."

"We'll take mine."

"You can't drive one-handed." His driving scares the shit out of me at the best of times. No way do I want to go along for a one-handed ride.

"I know. You can drive." He tosses his keys at me, and I panic slightly. He trusts me to drive a car worth more than one hundred and sixty thousand pounds?

* * *

"Ava, you're driving like Miss Daisy. Will you put your foot down?" Jesse moans.

I throw him a scowl, which he chooses to ignore. The accelerator is so sensitive, and I feel so small behind the wheel. I'm scared to death I'm going to scratch it. "Shut up," I snap, before doing as I'm told and roaring off down the road. It's his tough shit if I do bump someone.

"That's better." He looks at me and smiles. "It's easier to handle if you're not pussyfooting around on the power."

I want to smile, but I don't. I could pin that statement on him.

* * *

After three hours in Minor Injuries and an X-ray, the doctor has confirmed that Jesse's hand isn't broken, but he has some muscle damage.

"Have you been resting it?" the nurse asks. "If it's been a few days since you incurred the injury, I would expect the swelling to have subsided by now."

Jesse looks at me guiltily as the nurse wraps his hand in a bandage. "No," he says quietly.

"You should have been," she reprimands him, "and it should be elevated."

I raise my eyebrows at him, and he rolls his eyes while the nurse puts his arm in a sling before sending us on our way. As we get to the entrance, he removes the sling and chucks it in the litter bin.

"What are you doing?" I gasp, watching him walk out of the hospital doors.

"I'm not wearing that thing."

"You bloody are!" I yell, fishing it out of the bin. I'm shocked. This man has no regard for the well-being of his body. He's assaulted his internal organs with gallons of vodka, and now refuses to cooperate so his hand heals properly.

I stalk after him, but he doesn't stop until he gets to the car. I'm holding the keys, but I don't trigger the door release. We glare at each other over the top of the DBS.

"Are you going to open the car?" he asks.

"No, not until you put this back on." I hold the sling above my head.

"I told you, Ava, I'm not wearing it."

"Why?" I ask shortly. The stubborn Jesse is back, but this trait I'm not so pleased to see.

"I don't need it."

"Yes, you do."

"No, I don't," he mocks.

"Put the fucking sling on, Jesse!" I shout over the car.

"Watch your fucking mouth!"

"Fuck!" I hiss back petulantly.

He scowls real hard at me. What must we look like in the middle of the hospital car park, shouting "fuck" at each other over the roof of an Aston Martin? I don't care. He is such a caveman sometimes.

"*Mouth!*" he roars, and then winces at the sound level of his yell, his bad hand shooting up to clasp his head. "*Fuck!*"

I burst into laughter as I watch him dance around in circles, shaking his hand and swearing his head off. That will teach the obstinate fool.

"Open the fucking car, Ava," he shouts.

Oh, he's mad. I squeeze my lips together to suppress my laugh. "How's your hand?" I ask on a giggle that breaks out into a full belly laugh. I can't hold it in. It feels so good to laugh.

When I recover and straighten up, he's looking at me fiercely over the car. "Open," he demands.

"Sling," I snap, throwing it over the roof.

He grabs the material and throws it on the tarmac before returning his furious eyes to me. "Open!"

"You're a child sometimes, Jesse Ward. I am not opening the car until you put that sling on."

I watch as his eyes narrow on me and the edges of his mouth lift into a concealed grin. "Three," he says, loud and clear.

My jaw hits ground. "You are not giving me the countdown!" I screech disbelievingly.

"Two." His tone is cool and casual, while I'm stunned. He leans his elbows on the roof. "One."

"You can get stuffed!" I scoff, standing firm. I only want him to put the damn sling on for his own sake. It makes no odds to me, but this is principle.

"Zero," he mouths, and starts stalking around the front of the car toward me, while I instinctively head around the back. He stops and raises his eyebrows. "What are you doing?" he asks, circling the other way.

I know that face; that's his you're *really* copping it face. I know he won't think twice about pinning me to the ground and torturing me until I submit to whatever he demands.

"Nothing," I say, making sure I keep to the other side of the car. We could be here all day.

"Come here." His voice is that low, husky familiar tone that I love, and another piece of him that's returned. But I'm being distracted.

I shake my head. "No."

Before I can anticipate his next move, he breaks into a full sprint around the car, and I dash off in the opposite direction on a squeal. People are staring as I weave myself through the other parked cars like a deranged madwoman, before I skid to a stop at the back of a high top, four-wheel drive. I peek around the corner to see where he is.

My heart falls out of my mouth, straight onto the tarmac. He's doubled over, his hands braced on his knees.

Shit!

What the hell am I doing encouraging such stupid behavior when he should be recuperating? I run toward him as a few passersby clock him and start to approach. "Jesse!" I shout as I near.

"Is he all right, love?" a man asks me as I make it to him.

"I don't—*what*!" I'm hoisted off my feet with one arm and thrown over Jesse's shoulder.

"Don't mess with me, Ava," he says smugly. "You should know by now, I always win." He reaches up my skirt and rests his hand on the inside of my thigh as he strides toward the car with me draped over him.

I smile sweetly at everyone we pass, but I don't bother to fight him. I'm just happy he has the strength to lift me. "My knick-ers are flashing," I complain as I reach around to smooth my full dress over my bum.

"No, they're not." He lowers me down his body slowly until my face is level with his, my feet off the ground, his chest firm and warm against me. His eyes have won back a bit of sparkle and they are searching mine. He's going to kiss me. I have to stop this.

I wriggle in his arms. "We need to go to the supermarket," I say, focusing my sight on his chest as I squirm my way free.

He sighs heavily, dropping me to my feet. "How can I fix things if you keep dodging my attempts?"

I brush my dress down and return my eyes to his. "That's your problem, Jesse. You want to fix things by distracting me with your touch instead of talking to me and giving me some answers. I can't let that happen again." I trigger the door release and climb into the car, leaving Jesse with his head hanging, chewing his lip.

*   *   *

We pull into the supermarket and I drive up and down looking for a parking space. I've learned something new about Jesse today—he's a crap passenger. I've been bullied into overtaking, cutting people up, and jumping lanes, all in an attempt to gain a few yards. This man is a hothead when it comes to driving. Ac-tually, this man is a hothead full stop.

"There's a space." He thrusts his arm across my line of sight, and I bat it out of my way.

"That's a parent and child space," I dismiss, passing it.

"So?"

"So...I don't see any child in this lovely car of yours. Do you?"

He drops his gaze to my stomach, and I suddenly feel extremely uncomfortable. "Did you find your pills?" he asks, maintaining his stare on my stomach.

"No," I answer, swinging into a parking space. I want to blame him for distracting me from my normal personal schedule, but the truth is, my personal organization skills have always been rubbish. I was forced to pay another mortifying trip to Dr. Monroe to replace the second batch of contraceptive pills that I lost in a week, and I made myself have tests to ensure I hadn't contracted any sexual diseases after constant unprotected sex with Jesse. The suggestion of Jesse's active sex life left me little choice.

"Did you miss any?" he asks, his lips pressing into a straight line.

He's worried I could be pregnant? "My period came last Sunday evening," I say. Like an omen or something, I want to add, but I don't. I switch off the ignition.

He remains silent as I get out of the car and wait for him to eject himself.

"Could you have parked any farther away?" he grumbles, joining me on my side of the car.

"At least I'm parked legally." I walk to the rack of trollies lined up at the shelter and slip a pound in the top to release one. "Have you ever been to a supermarket?" I ask as we make our way up the canopied walkway. Jesse and a supermarket are not things that fit together naturally.

He shrugs. "Cathy does it. I usually eat at The Manor."

The mention of Jesse's super-plush sex club has me bristling and losing all enthusiasm for trying to make conversation. I feel his eyes on me, but I ignore it and focus ahead of me.

* * *

By the time we get back to Lusso, it's six o'clock and we find the door has been repaired. Jesse goes to lie on the sofa, exhausted from a few hours out, and I stand in the kitchen after unpacking the shopping, wondering what to do. It's Saturday evening, and I really feel like settling down with a glass of wine. There is no wine and I can't settle, so instead, I ring Kate.

"What are you up to?" I ask as I plant myself on a barstool with a coffee—not wine, but coffee.

"We're on our way out," she says cheerfully.

"Where are you going?" I can't help feeling slightly envious at her night out.

"Sam's taking me to The Manor."

"The Manor?" I blurt incredulously, all envy disintegrating. Is she winding me up?

"Yes, don't get the wrong idea. I asked him to. I'm curious."

Holy fucking shit! Kate's coolness knows no bounds. While I fled the scene when I discovered exactly what The Manor was, she wants to go and socialize there? Bloody hell. "And Sam's happy to take you?" I ask as casually as I can, but there's no hiding the shock in my voice. I can't believe he's agreed to this.

"Yeah, he's told me what goes down, and I want to see." She sounds so matter-of-fact, while I'm in meltdown just thinking about the place. What must it be like to be so open-minded? And what exactly does go down at The Manor, anyway? "How's Jesse?" she asks, pulling me from my thoughts.

I can detect the edginess in her tone. "He's fine. His hand has some slight muscle damage and he insists he's not an alcoholic."

"I'm glad." Her sincerity is sweet, and I'm relieved she isn't hurling explicit language down the phone and demanding I walk away.

"Listen," I snap my attention back to Kate, "I would say have fun tonight, but I'm more inclined to say...keep an open mind."

"Ava, you don't get more open-minded than me. I can't wait! Speak to you tomorrow."

"Bye." I hang up and run through my times at The Manor, when I thought it was an innocent hotel. I shake my head at myself. How could I have missed it all when everything seems so obvious now? I should cut myself some slack because I was completely diverted by a tall, lean-framed man with dirty blond hair and hypnotizing green eyes. He was perfect. He still is, if a few pounds lighter and a few issues heavier.

I make my way upstairs to change out of my dress, throwing on a pair of cotton shorts and a tank top before removing all of the clips from my hair.

When I get downstairs, Jesse is still asleep on the sofa. I mess around with the TV cabinet for a while, but I can't get the damn thing to open and reveal a television, so I slump into the chair and watch Jesse sleeping, his mangled hand draped over his solid chest and rising and falling with his steady breaths. As my thoughts wander naturally to chocolate éclairs, calla lilies, and "Angels," I drift off to sleep.

CHAPTER FIVE

I love you."

I come awake in a daze of darkness and rub my eyes as I sit up in the chair. It takes me a few moments to figure out where I am, but when I begin to focus, I find a handsome, dark blond man crouched in front of me.

"Hey," he says softly as he brushes my hair from my face.

"What time is it?" I ask sleepily.

He leans in and kisses my forehead. "Just gone midnight."

Midnight? I'm sleeping for England, and I could drift straight back off again, but I'm properly woken up when the shrill sound of a phone ringtone stabs at the silent air.

"For fuck's sake," Jesse complains.

I watch as he yanks his phone from the coffee table and looks at the screen. Who would be ringing at this time?

"John," he greets calmly. "Why?" He glances at me. "No, it's fine...yeah...give me a half hour." He hangs up.

"What's the matter?" I ask, fully awake now.

He shoves his Converse on and stalks for the door, clearly unhappy. "Problem at The Manor. I won't be long."

And just like that, he's gone.

So, I'm wide awake, it's past midnight, and Jesse has just disappeared. I sit in the chair like a loose part and contemplate what is going on at The Manor of such urgency.

Oh no, Kate is there.

I run into the kitchen and find my phone to call her, but she doesn't answer. I try repeatedly, and with each unanswered call, I get more worried. I should just call Jesse, but he seemed pretty pissed off. I pace up and down, make myself a coffee, and sit at the island repeatedly dialing Kate. If my car was here, I would be on my way to The Manor, too. Or would I? It's easy for me to say yes, especially when there is no way I can.

After pacing the penthouse for an hour and calling Kate endlessly, I give in and go to bed, crawling into the plush, soft sheets of the spare room bed and curling up.

* * *

"I love you."

I open my eyes and find Jesse looming over the bed. I'm somewhere between sleep and consciousness, and my mouth won't work. What time is it and how long has he been gone? I don't get a chance to ask, though. I'm gathered into his arms and transported to his room.

"You sleep here," he whispers, lowering me into his bed. I feel him crawl in behind me, and I'm tugged back against his chest.

If I weren't so contented, I would be asking questions, but I am, so I won't. My head hits the pillow, and with Jesse's warmth surrounding me, I'm gone again.

* * *

"Morning."

My eyes open and I'm pinned to the mattress under a heady scent of fresh water and mint. My morning brain is desperately trying to convince me to struggle free, but my body is blocking all of the sensible instructions trying to filter through.

He sits back on his heels. "I need to do this," he whispers, clasping my hand and pulling me into a sitting position.

He takes the hem of my top and slowly pulls it up over my head before leaning into me and kissing the middle of my chest, running his tongue in a light, flicking circle up to my throat.

I'm tense.

He pulls back. "Lace," he says softly as he removes my bra.

I battle between my body's desperate need for him and my mind's strong need to talk. I want to clear the air before I'm dragged back onto Central Jesse Cloud Nine, where I lose all cognitive reasoning. "Jesse, we need to talk," I say quietly as he kisses my throat and works his way to my ear. Every nerve is buzzing, pleading with me to shut up and accept him.

"I need you," he whispers, finding my mouth and claiming it softly.

"Jesse, please." My voice is a breathy whisper as I manage to break away.

"Baby, I do my talking this way." He grips the nape of my neck and pulls me farther into him. "Let me show you."

My body wins.

I surrender to him like the slave that I am. He wraps his arm around my lower back and eases me back down to the bed, sealing our mouths on the way, my entire being jumping to life as his hot, wet tongue slips gently between my lips and glides slowly around my mouth. We're in gentle Jesse mode, and it's as if he knows that this is the best place to take me right now.

His slow, steady breaths tell me he is in complete control as he rests on his forearm and uses his good hand to run his fingertip from my hip bone all the way up to my breast, a steady wave of tingles traveling up my body in time with his touch, leaving my breath shallow and erratic. He finishes by tracing the edges of my nipple wistfully to match the gentle motions of our tongues.

I hold on to his shoulders, feeling all of the misplaced emotions flooding back into me under his gentle touch, his attentive mouth, and his hard body flanking me. My fear was completely justified; I'm lost in him again.

I whimper as he pulls his lips away from mine and sits back on his heels before he uses his good hand to drag my shorts down my legs, taking my underwear with them. "You need reminding."

"This is not the conventional way."

"It's how I do things, Ava." He throws my shorts and knickers to the side and pulls me up, sealing our mouths. "We need to make friends."

I can't fight him anymore. I hook my fingers in the waistband of his boxers and press my lips farther to his as I push his boxers down his thighs. He lets out a long moan, easing me back down onto the bed, causing me to lose my grip on his shorts, so I place my foot into the band and extend my leg to take them the rest of the way. He's leaning half on me, half off, his hard, lean body spreading the length of me as he claims my mouth, pushing his body farther into mine.

Weaving my fingers through his hair, I relish the friction of his long stubble against my face. It's too long to be sharp or coarse, so it feels more like a soft brush is being glided across my face.

He separates our mouths and buries his face in my hair as he cups me between my thighs and draws his palm up the center of my body, slowly over my stomach, and then gradually up between my breasts, finishing against my throat.

"I've missed you, baby," he murmurs against my neck. "I've missed you so much."

"I've missed you, too." I hold his head to me, feeling completely cocooned in strength, but he's not strong at the moment. I feel protected and safe, but I'm aware that it's me who's playing the carer at the moment. I'm overwhelmed, too—completely overwhelmed with intense feelings for this troubled man.

He moves himself so he's cradled between my thighs, and I soon feel the wet, slippery head of his morning erection pushing against me. My mind is a jumble of mixed thoughts, but then he rests on his elbows and gazes down at me, like I'm the only thing that exists in his world. Our eyes say more than words ever could. I move my hands from the back of his head so my palms are on either side of his handsome face.

"Thank you for coming back to me," he says softly as I stare up at him, drowning in his glorious greens, emotion flooding my entire being.

I smooth my thumb across his moist lips and slide it into his mouth, withdrawing slowly and resting the tip on his bottom lip. He plants a light kiss on the end and smiles down at me as he lifts his hips while maintaining our eye contact, my pelvis shifting to meet him.

I sigh in pure, unapologetic pleasure as he slowly, unhurriedly, and reverently slides deep inside of me. My eyes close and my hands slip to the back of his head as he fills me completely and holds still, beating and kicking inside me. His change in breathing to quick bursts of breath is a familiar trait. He's struggling to maintain control.

"Look at me," he demands between pants, and I force my eyes open and gasp a little when I feel him jerk inside me. "I love you," he whispers, his voice cracking.

I inhale sharply at the words I've desperately needed to hear for so long. Does he know? Is that why he's saying it now? Does he think that's all it takes? "Don't, Jesse." I close my eyes, my hands falling away from his head.

"Ava, look at me," he demands harshly. I drag my swimming

eyes open and meet a straight, expressionless face. "I've been telling you how I feel the whole time."

"No, you haven't. You were hijacking my phone and trying to control me."

He circles his hips into me, drawing a collective moan from both of us. "Ava, I've never felt like this before." He withdraws and pushes deep and high. I try to rein in my scattered thoughts, but a moan escapes. "I've been surrounded by naked women with no respect for themselves all of my life." He places his hands over mine, pinning my wrists on either side of my head.

Thrust.

"Jesse!"

"You're not like them, Ava."

Thrust.

"Oh God!" He pulls back and rams back in.

"Jesus!" He stills on a few deep breaths. "You're mine, and mine alone, baby. Just for my eyes, just for my touch, and just for my pleasure. Just mine. Do you understand me?" He withdraws and slowly plunges back in.

"What about you? Are you just mine?" I ask, shifting my hips up to capture the delightful penetration.

"Just yours, Ava. Tell me you love me."

"What?" I cry, when he hits me with a hard drive.

"You heard me," he says softly. "Don't make me fuck it out of you, baby."

I'm stunned. I'm melting beneath him, crippled by pleasure, and now he's demanding I tell him that I love him? I do, but should I confess under duress? It's completely as I expected, though. He's been trying to make me the opposite of everything he knows, keeping me covered, preventing me from drinking, insisting on me wearing delicate lace instead of harsh leather. But what about the sex?

"Ava, answer me." He pushes high and grinds firmly, a sweat breaking out across his brow. "Don't hold out on me."

His words hit me like a lightning bolt. Hold out? He's tried to fuck a love confession out of me before—in the en suite bathroom last Saturday when he rammed into me repeatedly, demanding I say it. I thought he was looking for reassurance that I wasn't leaving. I was wrong. How did he know?

There's another perfect grind, and my internal muscles start to spasm, tremors inching their way into the epicenter of my nerve endings. My legs stiffen. "How did you know?" I cry, throwing my head back in despair, both mentally and physically.

"Damn it, Ava, look at me." He hits me with a full, hard strike of his hips, and I drag my eyes open on an angry yell. "I love you," he shouts, reinforcing his words with yet another slow withdraw and hard, fast attack of his hips.

"I love you, too!" I scream the words that are literally thrust out of me.

He stops his movements completely, our breaths rushed and frantic as he holds my hands in place and looks down at me. "I love you so fucking much. I didn't think it was possible." His words penetrate me deeply, the intensity of our joining making my heart kick into a higher gear as he looks down at me, tears pricking the backs of his eyes. He smiles faintly and slowly withdraws himself. "Now, we make love," he says quietly, rocking gently back into me and capturing my lips in a slow, sensual kiss, full of meaning. He releases his hold of me, and my hands fly to his back, slipping across his damp skin.

His tactic has changed completely. Slowly and leisurely, he drives in and out of me, pushing me up toward complete rapture as I clasp at his damp back, holding as tight as I can. Sex with Jesse has always been beyond compare, but this moment holds a significant power that I never thought possible. He loves me.

I struggle to keep my emotions in check when he pulls back

and holds his face to mine, nose to nose, eyes full of sentiment. I'm coming apart. The consistency of his controlled, deep thrusts has me shuddering and tensing around him as my core convulses and grips his shaft on each and every plunge. The sheen of sweat across his brow and his frown line deep with concentration tell me he's tipping the edge, too. Tilting my hips up on a thrust, I moan as he fills me to my absolute limit. The feel of his rhythmic, meticulous tempo has me wanting to squeeze my eyes shut, but I can't drag them away from his.

"Together," he says, his hot breath spreading across my face.

"Yes," I gasp, feeling him expand and throb in preparation for his release.

"Christ, Ava." A rush of air escapes his lips, and his body goes rigid, but he doesn't remove his eyes from mine. My back arches on reflex when the spiraling rush of pleasure reaches its climax and sends me tumbling into a hurricane of uncontrollable feelings. I cry out in complete despairing pleasure, my body trembling in his hold, my eyes closing to blink back the tears that have developed as my orgasm begins to recede slowly and lazily with his continued, even strokes.

"Eyes," he commands softly, and I obey, opening my eyes again.

He moans deeply, and I tighten all of my muscles at my core to grip him and extract his release. I can see the battle he's having with his instincts to hammer into me and throw his head back, but he's keeping a rein on his control. And then you can almost hear the snap of his release as his cheeks puff out and he pushes himself into me, long and hard, holding himself there, my muscles obliging his throbbing erection and continuing with their slow, easy constrictions as he pours into me.

"I love you," I say quietly as he looks down at me, his chest heaving. There. I've put it out there. My cards are well and truly on the table, and he didn't technically fuck that one out of me.

He rests his lips on mine. "I know you do, baby."

"How did you know?" I ask. I know I've never told him. I've screamed it in my head a thousand times, but I have never actually voiced it.

"You told me when you were drunk," he smiles, "after I showed you how to dance."

I do a quick run-through of the night when I got ridiculously drunk and relented to his persistent pursuing again. I remember admitting it to myself, but I certainly don't remember blurting it out to him. Mind you, I don't remember much after Jesse escorted me from the bar. I was in a state. That's his fault, too.

"I don't remember," I admit, feeling bloody stupid.

"I know you don't." He grinds his hips, and I sigh. "It was so fucking frustrating." It all comes flooding back. He really was trying to fuck a love confession out of me. He watches me as I figure it out, and his mouth forms an O on a small smile.

"You knew all along?" *Drunken confessions.*

I had beaten myself up about it for days and days, and he knew all along? Why didn't he say something? Why didn't he just talk to me instead of trying to fuck it out of me? So much could have been so very different.

His smile disappears and is replaced with a stoic expression. "You were drunk. I wanted to hear the words when you were of sound mind. Women get drunk all the time and confess their undying love to me."

"Do they?" I blurt.

He almost laughs. "Yes, they do." He drops his eyes, "I wasn't sure if you still did after . . ." His teeth start a vicious workout on his bottom lip, "Well, after I had my little meltdown."

I inwardly laugh. Little meltdown? Bloody hell, what would be a big meltdown? Women tell him they love him? What women and how many are there? I screw my face up in my own private disgust. I'm extremely uncomfortable with how resentful

I'm feeling about any other woman having him or loving him. I need to put these thoughts right out of my mind and fast. No good could come of me knowing.

"I love you." I reinforce my words, almost grinding them out, like I'm telling all of those women who claim to love him, too. I feel his whole body relax over me before he continues slowly circling deep inside me.

Pulling him down, I wrap my entire body around him. I feel like a weight has been lifted from my shoulders, but then it occurs to me that I'm in love with a man and I have no clue how old he is.

"How old are you, Jesse?"

He pulls his face up and I can see the cogs of his mind start revolving. I know he's thinking whether or not he should just tell me his real age and stop with his silly diversion. "I can't remember."

Oh, I might be able to play this to my advantage. "We were at thirty-three," I prompt.

He smirks at me. "We should start again."

"No!" I pull his face down and rub my nose across his rough cheek. "We got to thirty-three."

"You're a rubbish liar, baby." He laughs, nuzzling into my face. "I like this game. I think we should start again. I'm eighteen."

"Eighteen!"

"Don't play games with me, Ava."

"Why won't you just tell me how old you are?" I ask, exasperated. It really doesn't matter to me. He's forty, maximum.

"I'm thirty-one."

I sag beneath him dramatically. He does remember. "How old are you?"

"I just told you, I'm thirty-one."

I narrow displeased eyes on him, and one side of his mouth

lifts into a semblance of a smirk. "It's just a number," I moan. "If you ask me anything in the future, I won't answer—not truthfully, anyway."

His semblance of a smirk falls away immediately. "I already know everything I need to know about you. I know how I feel, and nothing you could tell me will make me feel any different. I wish you felt the same."

Oh, that's below the belt! It wouldn't make a jot of difference to the way I feel about him. I'm just curious, that's all. "You said before that I might run a mile if I know," I remind him. "I'm not going anywhere."

He laughs. "No, you're not. Ava, you've found out the worst about me and not run a mile. Well, you did, but you came back." He kisses my forehead. "Do you honestly think I'm bothered about my age?"

"Then why won't you tell me?" I ask, exasperated.

"Because I like this game." He resumes nuzzling into my neck.

I heave a sigh and increase my squeeze around his warm, sweat-dampened shoulders, locking my thighs tightly around his hips. "I don't," I grumble, burrowing my face into his neck and breathing him into me. I exhale in contentment and trace my fingers across his firm back.

We lie silently for the longest time, but when I feel his body shaking, it diverts my thoughts to what lies ahead for us. "Are you okay?" I ask nervously.

He squeezes me tightly. "Yeah, what time is it?"

That's a point. What time is it? I hope I've not missed Dan's call. I wriggle under Jesse and he moans into my neck. "I'll go check the time."

"No, I'm comfy," he complains. "It isn't that late."

"I'll be two seconds."

He grumbles and lifts himself slightly to slip out of me and then heaves his body off of mine, rolling onto his back. I jump up to go and find my phone, discovering it's nine o'clock and Dan hasn't called. That's a relief, but I do have twelve missed calls from Jesse.

I walk back into the bedroom and find him leaning against the headboard, brazenly naked and unashamed. I look down at myself. Oh, so am I.

"I've got twelve missed calls from you," I say in confusion, holding my phone up to him.

A disapproving look jumps onto his face. "I couldn't find you. I thought you had left. I had a hundred heart attacks in ten minutes, Ava. Why were you in the other bedroom?" He fires the words accusingly at me.

"I didn't know how things stood." I may as well be honest.

"What does that mean?"

He sounds offended.

"Jesse, the last time I saw you, you were a stranger who told me that I was a prick tease and had caused you untold damage. Forgive me for being a bit apprehensive."

His affronted look falls away instantly and is replaced with one of regret. "I'm sorry. I didn't mean any of it."

"Right." I sigh.

"Come here." He pats the mattress and I walk over to slide in beside him. We lie on our sides facing each other, our heads resting on our bent forearms. "You'll never see that man again."

I hope I don't, but I'm doubtful. "Will you never drink again?" I ask nervously. Now is as good a time as any to get the information I need.

"No." He places his fingertip on my hip bone and circles lightly.

I shiver. "Never?"

He pauses midcircle. "Never, Ava. All I need is you and for you to need me. Nothing else."

I frown. "You already made me need you. Then you destroyed me," I say quietly. I don't mean to make him feel guilty, but it's the truth.

He inches closer to me so our noses are nearly touching and his hot, minty breath is spreading all over my face. "I'll never hurt you."

"You said that before."

"Ava, the thought of you in pain, emotionally or physically, is appalling to me. Completely unspeakable. I feel crazy just thinking about it. What I've done to you makes me want to plunge a knife straight through my own heart."

"That's a bit over-the-top, isn't it?" I blurt.

He scowls at me. "It's the truth, just like I feel violent when I imagine another man lusting after you." He shakes his head, as if shaking away images that are cropping up in his mind.

"You can't control everything," I say on a furrowed brow.

"Where you're concerned, I'll try my best, Ava. I already told you, I've waited too long for you. You're my little piece of heaven. Nothing will rob you from me. Nothing." He presses his lips to mine to seal his declaration. "As long as I have you, I have purpose and reason. That is why I won't be drinking and that is why I will do everything in my power to keep you safe. Understand?"

Actually, I don't think I do, but I nod anyway. His determination and grit are commendable but ridiculously ambitious. What does he think will happen to me? I can't be stitched to his hip permanently. Crazy man.

I reach forward to brush my thumb over the jagged line of his scar. "How did you get this?" I try my luck. I know he won't answer me, and I know it's a sore subject, but I'm compelled to extract as much information as I can. I now know the worst of him, so what harm can it do?

He looks down at my hand on his scar and sighs. "Inquisitive this morning, aren't you?"

"Yes," I confirm. I am.

"I already told you, I don't like talking about it."

"You're holding back on me," I accuse, and he rolls onto his back on a heavy sigh and rests his forearm across his face. Oh no, he's not evading this. I straddle his hips and pull his arm away. "Why won't you tell me about your scar?"

"Because, Ava, it's in my past, where I want it to stay. I don't want anything affecting my future."

"It won't. It doesn't matter what you tell me. I'll still love you." Does he not understand that?

I frown when he smirks. "I know," he says too confidently. He's pretty cocksure of himself this morning. "You already told me that when you were legless," he adds.

Hmm, I told him a lot when I was drunk. "So why won't you tell me?"

He places his hands on the juncture of my thighs. "If it won't change how you feel about me, then there is little point in tarnishing your pretty little head with it"—he raises his eyebrows—"is there?"

"I'm not going to tell you anything if you ask me," I sulk.

"You already said that." He sits up and seals our lips, my arms mechanically wrapping around him, but then I think of something else.

"Did you ever find out how the gates came to be open? And the front door?" I try my hardest to sound casual.

"What?" He pulls away from me, looking perplexed.

"When I came to The Manor on Sunday, the gates opened without me pressing the intercom and the front door was ajar." I know it was her.

"Oh. The gates malfunctioned, apparently. Sarah had it sorted out." He pushes his lips to mine again.

"That's very convenient. Did the manual front door malfunction, too?" I ask, my sarcasm potent. I can't believe he bought that feeble explanation. I know what happened. The tramp intercepted my message, relishing the thought of me turning up unannounced and discovering The Manor's offerings.

"Sarcasm doesn't suit you, lady." He gives me a very scornful look, but I don't care. That woman is a deceitful tramp. Oh, I feel full of determination all of a sudden, but slightly sympathetic for Jesse. He actually thinks she's a friend? Should I share my verdict? "What would you like to do today?" he asks.

Oh shit! I've got to see Dan today and I can't take Jesse with me. What would that look like? I can hardly introduce Jesse to Dan. That's a disaster waiting to happen, what with Dan's older brother protectiveness and Jesse's trampling tendencies. How am I going to play this?

"Well, there's just one thing I have—" Jesse's phone starts ringing, halting my announcement.

"For fuck's sake," he curses, lifting me from his lap and placing me on the bed. He gets up and answers his phone before walking out of the bedroom. "John?" He sounds a little impatient.

I lie on the bed, running through all of the ways I can break it to him that I really must go and meet Dan. He'll understand.

"I've got to go to The Manor," he says sharply, stalking back into the room and heading for the bathroom.

Again? I haven't even asked him what dragged him there last night, and I notice Kate hasn't called me back. "Is everything okay?" I ask. He looks pissed.

"It will be, get ready."

What?

Oh no! I am not going to that place! I've still got to wrap my head around it all. I hear the shower turn on and I jump up to go and explain, finding him in the shower already. He smiles know-

ingly and gestures for me to join him, so I walk in and grab the
sponge and shower gel, but he takes them from me and loads
up the sponge himself before turning me around and beginning
to wash me down. I stand quietly, searching my brain for a way
to approach this, as he works the sponge slowly across my body.
Surely he won't have a hissy fit over my unwillingness.

"Jesse?"

He kisses my shoulder blade. "Ava?"

"I really don't want to come," I blurt, and then scold myself
for not being a little more tactful.

He pauses with his swirling circles for a few moments before
he continues, "Can I ask why?"

He can't be so thick-skinned he has to ask that question. "Can
you just give me some time to get used to it?" I ask apprehen-
sively, while mentally begging for him to understand and be
reasonable.

He sighs and wraps his forearm around the tops of my shoulders, pulling me back to him. "I understand," he kisses my
temple. "You're not going to avoid it forever, are you? I still
want my new bedroom designs."

I'm in shock at his reasonableness. No questions, no trampling or sense fuck—just an okay? Have we turned a corner?
This is good, and as for the new extension? I hadn't given it a
thought, but he's right. I can't avoid the place forever. "No. Anyway, I'll have to come to oversee the work once we finalize the
designs."

"Good."

"What's going on at The Manor?"

He releases my shoulders and starts washing my hair with his
men's shampoo. "The police turned up last night," he says, totally detached.

I tense all over. "Why?"

"It's just some idiot playing games. The police rang John this morning to arrange a few interviews. I can't get out of it." He turns me around and places me under the spray to rinse my hair. "I'm sorry."

"It's fine," I assure him. I won't tell him why it's fine. I can meet Dan without worrying about a Jesse-style trample. "Kate was at The Manor last night." The concern in my voice is obvious.

"I know." His eyebrows rise. "It was quite a surprise."

"Was she okay?"

"Yes, she was fine." He kisses my nose and slaps my bum. "Out you get."

Once we've dried and Jesse has adorned me in lace underwear before leaving, I waste no time. I grab my phone immediately to call Dan and we arrange to meet at Almundo's, a little coffeehouse in Covent Garden. I run across the landing and dress in record time, calling down to Clive to order me a cab between drying my hair and pinning it up. I'm super excited.

CHAPTER SIX

I scan the masses of people having brunch and spot Dan in the corner with his face in the Sunday paper. He looks so well, all tanned and dazzling. I fly across the café and all but dive on him.

"Whoa!" He laughs. "Pleased to see me, kid?" He wraps his arms around me, and I fall apart all over him. I'm so happy to see him, and all of the built-up stress and emotion of the last few weeks just spills out of me...again.

He takes my hand in his. "Get rid of those tears, right now." He smiles. "This will be the best thing that ever happened to you. You're well shot."

Oh, he thinks I'm in a state over Matt? Should I let him carry on thinking that? The alternative is explaining a whole lot of other shit, and I can't do that. I would be here for months. I wipe my eyes. "I know. It's been a shitty few weeks. I'm fine, really."

"Forget about him and get on with your life." He rubs my arm affectionately. "What about this other bloke who Matt's been whining on about?"

"His name's Jesse. It's nothing. He's just a friend," I shrug.

"Just a friend?" He eyes me suspiciously as my hand reaches up to find a stray tendril from my updo.

"Just a friend and a few stretched truths." I need to change the subject. "How are Mum and Dad?"

He gives me a warning look. "Threatening to pay a visit to London and sort you out. Mum mentioned a strange man answering your phone last week. I suspect he might be the stretched truth?"

My attempts at diversion have failed miserably. "Yeah, okay. Can we change the subject please?"

Dan holds his hands up in defense. "Okay, okay. I'm just saying, be careful, Ava."

I sag, considering exactly what my parents will make of Jesse, and none of it is good.

We order and chat about Dan's job, Australia, and his future prospects. His friend is expanding the surf school business and wants Dan to partner with him. I'm pleased for him, but quietly disappointed for my own selfish reasons. He won't be coming home anytime soon.

"How's Kate?" he asks, while picking at the corners of his pastry, blatantly feigning disinterest.

I should refrain from mentioning Sam. I can't imagine Dan would appreciate such information. I abruptly remember that I've not taken my pill and start rummaging through my bag. "She's still Kate," I say casually. I locate my pill packet and pop one out before taking it with some water, watching over my glass as Dan drops into deep thought. I need to snap him out of that immediately. "What about you? Any female interests?" I ask on an arched brow, swapping my water for coffee.

"No." He smirks. "Nothing permanent, anyway."

I'm about to lecture him on being a player when my mobile starts dancing around the table and the Temper Trap's "Sweet Disposition" blares from the ringer. I smile. His telephone manners haven't improved.

It's just gone one o'clock. I thought he would be longer than this, but maybe he's still at The Manor and just checking in on me.

"Hey, I love that track!" Dan exclaims. "Let it ring." He starts singing along to it.

I laugh. "I just need to take this." I leave the table with my phone and Dan with a furrowed brow. I know he's going to be suspicious that I'm removing myself from his presence to take this call. I'll say it was Kate.

I walk out into the sunshine. "Hey," I say cheerfully.

"Where the fuck are you?" he bellows down the phone.

I pull it away to save my eardrums. "I'm with my brother, calm down."

"Calm down?" he yells. "I get home and you've run out!"

"Fucking hell," I whisper to myself, but not quietly enough.

"Watch your fucking mouth!"

I look up to the sky in despair. "I've not run out. I've come to meet my brother. He's back from Australia," I state calmly. "I was supposed to see him yesterday, but I got a little caught up elsewhere." I didn't aim for sarcasm, but it comes naturally.

"I apologize for inconveniencing you," he hisses.

"Excuse me?" I'm stunned by his hostility.

"How long will you be?" His tone hasn't changed; he still sounds like a pig.

"I said I would spend the day with him."

"Day!" he shouts. "Why didn't you tell me?"

Because I knew he would trample it! "Your phone interrupted me and you were sidetracked with problems at The Manor," I spit.

It goes quiet down the phone, but I can still hear his labored breathing.

"Where are you?" His voice has softened slightly.

"I'm at a café."

"Where?"

There's not a chance in hell I'm telling him that. He'll turn up, I know it, and then I will be left explaining to Dan who he is and where he came from. "It doesn't matter where. I'll be back at yours later."

It goes quiet, and I wait, finally hearing him sigh. "Come back to me, Ava." It's definitely a demand.

"I will."

The silence spreads between us again, and I'm very abruptly reminded of the small part of Jesse that sends me crazy. Did I really wish this back?

"Ava?"

"I'm here."

"I love you," he says softly, but it's strained. I know he wants to rant and probably haul me back to Lusso, but he can't do that if he can't locate me.

"I know you do, Jesse." I hang up and exhale an exhausted breath. I'm beginning to wish I didn't know about Jesse's alcohol issue because now I'm worrying myself stupid that I will push him to have another gorging session. I've always been an advocate of *knowledge is power*, but at the moment I'm favoring *ignorance is bliss*. Then I could hang up and think that he's an unreasonable control freak and be content to let him stew. But now I know, I've hung up, and I'm worried I've just dangled the proverbial bottle of vodka under his nose.

"Is everything okay?"

I turn and see Dan approaching with my bag over his shoulder. I give a small smile. "Fine."

"I settled the bill. Here." He hands me my bag.

"Thanks."

"Are you all right?" He frowns.

No, I'm bloody not. The stretched truth is stretching my patience. "Yeah, fine." I plaster on a cheery face. "So, what do you want to do?"

"Tussauds?" he asks with a big smile. I return it.

"Absolutely, let's go."

He holds his arm up for me to link and off we go. I've lost count of the number of times we've roamed the halls of Madame Tussauds. It's tradition. There's not one waxwork that we haven't got a photo with. We've snuck around the place, entered restricted zones, and done whatever it took to get the photographs we needed to keep our scrapbook up to date. Childish, but it's our thing.

* * *

We have an amazing day. I've laughed so much my cheeks ache. As it turns out, the only new waxworks in Tussauds are royalty. I had a photo with William and Kate, and Dan was captured squeezing the Queen's boobs. We had dinner at our favorite Chinese in Chinatown and a few cheeky wines in a bar.

I hug Dan tightly as we say our good-byes at the tube. "When are you going back?"

"Not for a few weeks. I'm going up to Manchester tomorrow to catch up with some university friends, but I'm back in London next Sunday so I'll see you again before I leave, okay?"

I release him from my squeeze. "Okay. Call me as soon as you're back in London."

"I will, take care, kid." He kisses me on the cheek. "I'm on my mobile if you need me."

"Okay." I smile.

He strides off and leaves me wishing he could stay forever. I've never needed him so much.

* * *

As I enter the foyer of Lusso, Clive is on the telephone. I walk straight past his desk on my way to the lift. I really don't feel like chatting.

"Thank you, good-bye. Ava!" he shouts after me, and I stop and roll my eyes before turning to face him.

"Yes?"

He shoves the phone into its cradle and hurries toward me. "A lady stopped by. I tried calling up to Mr. Ward, but he didn't answer. I'm afraid I couldn't let her up."

"A lady?" He's got my attention now.

"Yes. Mature woman. Nice, with blonde, wavy hair. She said it was urgent, but of course, you know the rules."

Oh yes, I know the rules, and for once I'm relieved he's stuck to them. Blonde, wavy hair? Not Sarah, surely. "How mature?"

He shrugs. "Midforties."

I don't like Sarah, but she definitely doesn't look like she's in her forties. "What time was this, Clive?"

He looks at his watch. "Only a half hour ago."

"Did she give her name?"

He frowns. "No, she didn't. I met her at the gate. She was expecting to go straight up to the penthouse, but when I wouldn't let her through and said I would have to call Mr. Ward, she started getting a bit vague with me."

"No worries, Clive. Thanks." I board the lift and punch in the code. A vague lady who thought she could march up to the penthouse unannounced?

I exit the elevator to find Jesse's front door open. Does this man have no regard for home security? I shut the door behind me and instantly feel on my guard. The sound system is playing. It's not as ear piercing as last time, but it's the track playing that has me on edge.

"Angel."

I run through the penthouse, leaving the music on. Finding Jesse is more important than turning off the tormenting song that reminds me of the awful day I found him drunk. I head straight for the terrace, but he's not there. I dump my bag and take the stairs two at a time and bolt into the bedroom. Nothing.

Panic starts to flood me, but then I hear the shower running, and I fly into the bathroom, coming to an abrupt stop when I see Jesse sitting on the floor of the shower, his running shorts soaking wet and clinging to his thighs. His shirtless back is against the cold tiled wall, his knees pulled up and his arms resting on top of them. His head in slumped as the water crashes down around him.

Lifting his head to meet my gaze, he smiles, but he can't hide the torture in his eyes. How long has he been like this? I exhale a long breath of relief, mixed with a little exasperation, before walking straight into the shower fully clothed and settling myself in his lap.

He buries his head in my neck. "I love you."

"I know. How many laps did you do?"

"Three."

"That's too much," I scold him. We're talking twenty miles here. That's not a quick jog around the park to alleviate some stress. His body is not strong enough for this at the moment.

"I freaked out when you weren't here."

"I kind of got that," I say with only a light dash of sarcasm. He shifts his hands to my hips and tweaks my hip bone. I jerk.

"You should have told me," he says sternly.

"I was always coming back," I assure him. "I can't be joined at your hip." And he can't be running a marathon every time we're apart.

He snuggles deeper into the crook of my neck. "I wish you bloody could be," he grumbles. "You've had a drink."

I suddenly feel awkward, uneasy. "Have you eaten?" I ask, not knowing what else to say. He's probably burned off a million calories running like Forrest Gump.

"I'm not hungry."

"You need to eat, Jesse." I moan. "I'll make you something."

He tightens his grip on me. "Soon, I'm comfy."

So, I let him be comfy for a while. I sit on his lap, my dress clinging to my body, my hair sopping wet, and just let him hold me. It can't be like this every time we're apart. I'll never settle. We most certainly haven't turned a corner, and I'm sorely disappointed.

"I hate this song," I say quietly, after we've sat in a tight clinch for an age.

"I love it. Reminds me of you."

"It reminds me of a man I don't like."

"I'm sorry." He nips at my neck, drawing his tongue up the length to my jawbone. "My arse is dead," he mumbles.

"I'm comfy," I mock. He moves his hand and grasps my hip bone, causing me to flinch and yelp. "Stop!" I cry. "I need to feed you!"

"Yes, you do. And I want my Ava, stripped naked and lying on our bed so I can binge on her." He stands himself up with me wrapped around his body, and with little effort, considering his injured hand and depleted body.

My Ava? That's fine. Our bed? I will file that away for now.

"I'm all for that, but I need to feed my man. Food now, loving later."

"Loving now, food later," he challenges as he walks us out of the shower and positions me on the vanity unit.

"Where's your bandage?"

He picks a bath sheet up from the pile on the shelf and starts rubbing the wetness from my hair with his good hand. "It was getting in my way." He drapes the towel around my back and uses the corners to pull me into him, kissing me hard on the lips. I catch him wince.

"Please, let me feed you."

He pulls back on a little pout. "Okay, food now, loving

later." He smirks and nuzzles our noses, then kisses my forehead. "Come on, you need some dry clothes." He goes to lift me off the unit, but I brush him away. "Hey!" He scowls at me.

"Your hand. It's never going to heal if you're hoofing me all over the place." I jump down, kick off my sodden ballet pumps, and undo the side zip of my dress before pulling it over my head. I'm then thrown up over his shoulder and carried out of the bathroom.

"I like hoofing you about," he declares, chucking me onto the middle of the bed. "Where's your stuff?"

"In the spare room." He makes a point of demonstrating his disgust with an audible grumble before he stalks out of the room and returns moments later with all of my things spread between his good hand, under his arms, and in his mouth. He dumps it all on the bed. "There."

I reach into my bag and retrieve some clean knickers and my oversized black sweatshirt, but my comfortable cotton knickers are soon snatched out of my hand. I frown as I watch him riffle through my bag and pull out a pair of lace replacements.

He hands them to me. "Always in lace." He nods in approval of his own demand, and I comply without hesitation or complaint, putting the lace knickers on, and then my oversized jumper. I watch as Jesse ditches his wet shorts and swaps them for a blue jersey pair, seeing new definition in his back and arms as his muscles roll and flex when he pulls them up. I sit and admire from my position on the bed before he picks me up again and carries me down to the kitchen.

First, I turn the music off on a little shudder, then I stand in front of the fridge scanning the shelves. "What do you want?"

"I don't mind, I'll have what you're having." He comes up from behind and reaches past me to grab a jar of peanut butter, dropping his lips to my neck.

"Put that back!" I make a grab for the jar, but he evades me and beats a hasty retreat to the barstool, shoves the jar under his arm to unscrew the cap before dipping his finger in to scoop a big dollop out. He smirks at me as he slides his finger into his mouth and forms an O with his lips as he pulls it out.

"You're a child." I settle on chicken fillets, grabbing them from the fridge.

"I'm a child because I like peanut butter?" he asks over his finger.

"No, you're a child because of the *way* you eat peanut butter. No one over the age of ten should finger-dip jars, and as I'm being kept in the dark over your age, I assume that you're over ten." I fire a disgusted look at him as I find the tinfoil and wrap up the fillets with some Parma ham, then put them in an oven dish.

"Don't knock it until you've tried it. Here." He thrusts his peanut butter-covered finger over the island and into my line of vision. I screw my face up. I detest peanut butter.

"Pass," I say, putting the chicken in the oven. He shrugs and then licks it off himself.

I get some sugar snap peas and new potatoes from the fridge and load them into the built-in vegetable steamer, then fiddle with a few knobs before it kicks into action.

Lifting myself up onto the worktop, I watch him on a small smile. "Enjoying that?"

He pauses midscoop and looks up at me. "I can eat the stuff until I feel sick." Another finger goes in.

"Do you feel sick?"

"No, not yet."

"Do you want to stop now before you do and save some room for the well-balanced meal I'm making you?" I fight to prevent a grin.

He doesn't. He smirks and slowly screws the lid back on. "Why, baby, are you nagging me?"

"No," I correct him. I don't ever want to be a nag. "I'm asking you a question."

He's watching me carefully, his eyes dancing. I shiver from top to toe. I know that look. "I like your sweatshirt," he says quietly, running his eyes down my front to my bare legs. It's oversized and it covers my bum. It's hardly sexy. "I like black on you."

"You do?"

"I do," he asserts quietly. He's trying to distract me again.

"It's Monday tomorrow," I say positively. I don't know why I choose that tone.

"And?" He folds his arms over his chest.

I drum my fingers on the worktop next to me. "And nothing, I was just wondering what you might have planned?"

A fleeting look of panic sweeps over his stubbled face. "What have *you* got planned?"

"Work," I answer, watching as he starts chewing his bottom lip and those bloody cogs start turning again. "Don't even think about it. I've important meetings to keep," I warn, before he has a chance to spit out what I know he is thinking.

"Just one day?" He pouts at me playfully, but I know he's deadly serious. I'm bracing myself for a countdown or a sense fuck.

"No, you must have lots to catch up on at The Manor," I affirm assertively. He has a business to run and he's been unconscious for a whole working week. John can't be expected to run things forever.

"I suppose so," he grumbles.

I mentally cheer. No countdown? No sense fuck? We really are moving forward.

"Oh, Clive said there was a woman here earlier."

"He did?" He looks surprised.

"He said that she was trying to get up to the penthouse. She wouldn't give her name and you didn't answer your phone when Clive tried to call you. Blonde woman. Mature. Wavy hair." I watch for his reaction, but he just frowns.

"I'll have a word with him. Is my well-balanced meal ready yet?"

That's it? He'll have a word with Clive? "Who was it?" I ask as I get down from the worktop to check the steamer.

"No idea." He jumps up himself and gets some cutlery from the drawer.

"You really don't have any idea?" I ask doubtfully, while removing the chicken from the oven and putting it in the pan to finish it off.

"Ava. I really have no idea, but I assure you, I will speak to Clive and see if I can establish who she was. Now, feed your man." He sits back down and holds his knife and fork in his hands, upright from the counter.

I go about serving up and present him with the first meal I've ever made for him. I hate cooking.

He tucks straight in. "Yum," he mumbles around a mouthful of chicken. "How was your day with your brother?"

"Fine," I answer, sitting next to him.

"Just fine? This is really good."

It's good to see him eat something other than peanut butter. He's like a different man again—so confident and self-assured, but in the next breath he's falling to pieces. Do I really have that much of an impact on him?

"We had a great day. We did Madame Tussauds and went to dinner at our favorite Chinese."

"Tussauds?"

"Yeah, it's our thing." I shrug.

"It's nice to have a thing." He sounds sincere. "You've eaten already?" He looks at my plate and I blush. "Are you eating for two?" he asks, looking up at me. I nearly choke on a potato.

"No!" I splutter around my food. "Stop worrying," I grumble, returning to my dinner.

He continues eating while making appreciative sounds around his fork every now and again. I would think he might be taking the piss, but I've tasted it—it's good.

Once we're done, I load the dishwasher and my thoughts start drifting. Him brushing off the mystery visitor is eating away at me. He's being vague and it's bothering me.

I turn to challenge him and crash straight into his hard, naked chest. "Oh!"

He towers over me, breathing hard, and my eyes weld to his huge erection tenting the front of his jersey shorts. "Lose the sweatshirt," he demands, his voice low and husky.

I look up into his green eyes and wisely note that he's not in a fucking-about mood.

I grasp the hem of my sweatshirt and slowly draw it up over my head, then drop it to the ground.

He runs his eyes appreciatively down my body, over my exposed breasts, and settles his gaze on the juncture of my thighs. "You're impossibly beautiful and all mine." He links his fingers into the top of my knickers and slowly drags them down my legs, falling to his knees as he does.

He taps to lift my foot and then repeats on the other before wrapping his big hands around my ankles. His eyes find mine. "I think I'll let you come first." His voice is gravelly. "Then I'm going to rip you clean in half."

I gasp at his fierce promise as he runs his palms the full length of my legs, from my ankles to the back of my thighs, and then yanks me onto his waiting mouth. His invasion of me reduces me to a moaning mess in his grasp as he works his tongue over every part of me—expertly, meaningfully. My hands find his hair and my hips roll onto his mouth, with no encouragement from my brain.

My head falls back. "Oh shit," I groan, the thrum at my sex accelerating into a constant vibration.

"Mouth," he mumbles against my flesh, which only serves to propel me that little bit closer to utter ecstasy.

I feel one of his hands move from the back of my leg and slide up the inside of my thigh. His finger slips inside me, and on a desperate cry, I release his head to lean back on the worktop for support, his circling finger stretching me and brushing my front wall on each rotation. I'm buzzing, my muscles grabbing onto his finger greedily.

"Tell me when, Ava." He replaces one finger with two and pushes deeper into me.

That, and the vibration of his lips on my clitoris, finishes me off. "That's it!" I cry, pushing my hips forward onto his mouth in an attempt to take the edge off the peak.

I'm wiped out from the onslaught of his mouth, and I sag against the worktop on a violent round of shakes, my heart clattering in my chest as he reins in his rhythm and laps gently, letting me drift down on a long, satisfied sigh.

"You're too good." I drop my head down to find his eyes.

He looks up, but keeps his mouth on me, circling gently and thrusting his fingers lazily in and out. "I know," he gloats. "Aren't you lucky?"

I shake my head at his self-assuredness as I watch him slowly crawl up my body, trailing his tongue as he goes.

When he reaches my nipple, he bites it lightly, and then clasps his arm under my bum, lifting me so I'm eye level with him. "Are you ready to be fucked good and proper, baby?"

"Knock yourself out," I challenge, draping my arms over his shoulders.

He smashes his lips against mine possessively and attacks my mouth. When he's like this, I forget about his weak moments—the moments when I'm comforting him, holding him, and reassuring him. Not at the moment, though. Right now, he is brutally sexy and domineering. I love it, and I've really, really missed it.

He keeps our mouths fused as he carries me out of the kitchen, toward the gym, and kicks the door open, setting me on my feet as he leans down to maintain our kiss and accommodate our height difference. He bites my bottom lip gently and starts walking forward, prompting me to step back in time with his advance, and after a few steps, he stops and kisses up to my ear, his hot breath igniting all of my senses. I'm mentally begging for him.

"Fancy a workout?" he whispers.

"What did you have in mind?" I nuzzle my cheek into him as he laps at my ear, causing the heartbeat at my core to kick in again, subtle and slow. He steps back from me, and the absence of his warm body in front of mine leaves me chilly, wanting to pull him back to me.

He's watching me with promising, lust-filled eyes, as he reaches for his shorts and pushes them down his legs, his arousal springing free.

I gasp. I don't know why, I've seen it enough times, but it still makes my breath hitch. I glide my eyes up, past his scar and to his perfect pecs. I will never tire of staring at the fine physique of the man standing in front of me—not ever. He's a work of art, carefully sculptured and polished to complete perfection.

He nods behind me and I slowly pivot, but all I see is the rowing machine and his punch bag, so I turn back and face him. His face is completely impassive, and he slowly nods again, indicating that what he has in mind is, indeed, behind me.

It dawns on me. He said he was going to rip me in half.

Oh good Lord!

"Oh," I whisper.

He starts walking slowly toward me, and the potential of his intention has me fidgeting on the spot. Taking my hand, he leads me to the rowing machine and then lowers his big, naked body so he's sitting on the seat. His erection stands up vertically from his body, and the prospect of this scenario suddenly has me panting with anticipation.

I'm tugged forward to stand in front of him, and he reaches forward with his injured hand to guide my leg over the runner so I'm straddling his legs. I look down at him, my heart kicking into its maximum speed limit as I wait for his next instruction.

He reaches up and cups my breasts with his big palms and softly, slowly massages them until they ache with heaviness. I don't miss the small wince on his face, but he doesn't stop, and I'm not about to try and stop him myself.

"Hmmm..." My head rolls back and my lips part, letting out short, rapid rushes of air.

"Ava, you fucking kill me," he says quietly. I pull my head down so our eyes meet. "I love you," he whispers, sliding his hands down to rest on my hips. I jerk and the corner of his mouth twitches. "I love how you flinch when I touch you here." He circles his index fingers in the sensitive hollows. I struggle to keep my legs steady. "I love how wet you are for me here." He slides his finger into me and I moan. "I love how you taste." He slips his finger into his mouth and pulls it out slowly while he watches me, then taking my hand again, he tugs me toward him and guides me down onto his waiting arousal.

I cry out when he impales me, the thick hardness of him completely spearing me.

He rests his forehead against mine. "I love how it feels to be inside you." He locks his hands around my lower back. "Wrap your legs around me."

I hook my legs around his waist and loop my ankles, pulling myself in closer to him. His breath falters as I reach forward and place my hands on the front of his shoulders.

"I. Love. You," he states firmly as he begins to slide us slowly forward on the seat, the abrupt halt at the end of the runner causing me to jerk slightly on a small cry.

His eyes clench shut.

Yes, now I am beginning to see the benefits of this. His penetration is deep, but it won't take many of these slides and hits to have me begging to let go.

When he opens his eyes, I lower my mouth to his and he accommodates my demand for mouth contact. I love his mouth. I love what he can do with his mouth. I love the words and the tones that come out of his mouth. I love the way he chews his bottom lip when deliberating something important to him.

"I love you," I say against his lips.

He pulls back, his handsome face looking content. "I can't tell you how happy that makes me." He slowly slides us back up the runner. "Do you need me?"

I brace myself for the jolt that I know will come, and when it does, we both moan together. "I need you."

"That makes me happy, too. Again?" He's already on his way back down the runner.

"Please." We jolt again at the end of the line, and the ache in my stomach transforms into a slow climb to climax.

We're traveling back up the runner, a bit faster this time.

Jolt!

"Oh!"

"I know," he whispers. "More?"

"Yes!" I plunge my tongue into his mouth desperately.

He slides us down slowly, but doesn't let it hit the end this time. Instead, he pushes off with his feet and sends us gliding up the runner. We hit the end with such force, our bodies collide hard and I have to release his lips and bury my face in his shoulder on a choked scream.

"Oh shit!" He strains, and repeats the same delicious move.

Slide and hit!

This is intense. I've never felt him so deep. I rest my mouth on his shoulder, resisting the urge to clamp onto him with my teeth, my hands moving onto the back of his head to hold myself steady as he slides us back down the runner, ready for another crash to the top. My insides are furling, and I can feel him twitching and kicking inside me. He catapults us back up the runner, and when we hit the top, my teeth sink into his shoulder and I cry out in pure, exquisite pleasure.

"Fuck, Ava!"

I release my teeth and kiss my bite mark as we descend again.

"Get your teeth back into my shoulder!"

I do as I'm bid and moan against him as I bite his shoulder on a crash.

"Shit, I'm going to come," he yells, letting us roll back down the runner. "You ready?"

"Yes!" I wrap my mouth around his shoulder and clamp my teeth lightly, ready for his assault.

He lets loose.

There are no more controlled movements. He slides and crashes us relentlessly as I clamp onto him with my teeth and fingernails. The intensity of his muscled length pounding me deeply has me screaming his name against his shoulder. I start to feel fireworks fizzing as he continues with the slides and hits, pushing me toward ultimate detonation. The relentless throbbing and beating of his erection deep inside me has me sprinting to the finish and I'm gone, pushed into ecstasy on a loud crash and a cry from both of us. I sink my teeth in once more, sending Jesse into a bucking fit as his hips fly up and he shouts loudly.

Oh my God!

I'm still pulsing and riding out my orgasm when I'm vaguely aware of being gently rocked back and forth, the slight motion draining everything he has to give me.

I pull my face away from his shoulder and plant a kiss on the bite mark.

"You're a savage, lady." He twists his head to take a look at himself, and then his eyes flick to mine.

Taking possession of my mouth, he kisses me deeply and I squeeze him in my arms, joining him in his blissful oblivion. I could stay like this forever, completely encased in Jesse.

"I'm going to take you to bed and sleep all night buried deep inside you." He slowly begins to lift, keeping us connected. "Kiss me, now," he commands as he starts striding out of the gym with me wrapped around his waist. I run my hands through his hair and gently yank it before slowly lowering my lips to his.

"Savage," he says against my lips.

I smirk and open my eyes as he takes the stairs, finding him staring at me as our tongues dance leisurely between our mouths. I hold his eyes with mine the entire way to the bedroom, where he lowers me to the bed under him. I can feel him hardening inside me again. This man is relentless.

Hooking his arm under my lower back, he shifts me up the bed until my head finds a pillow, our mouths and bodies remaining locked for the whole journey.

"Stay with me," he says, pulling back and brushing my hair away from my face. He studies me intently, his eyes sparkling with satisfaction at having me in his arms.

"I'm here."

"Move in with me." He drops his face and circles my nose with his.

Does this man know the meaning of the word gradual? He's being a bit hasty, and we still haven't discussed any of the more important stuff—like The Manor and work and his challenging ways.

"I want you here when I go to sleep." He licks my bottom lip.

"And I want you here when I wake up. Starting and ending my day with you is all I need."

I'm fully aware that if I don't give the answer he wants, I'm facing an attack of the sulks or a sense fuck, and I don't want to spoil this moment. I need this moment. "Don't you think this is all a bit soon?" I ask.

He pulls his face up, his expression not quite sulky, but well on its way. "You obviously do."

"It's been two days," I try to reason with him.

He frowns. "Two days since what?" He lifts his torso up and slips out from me a little, planting his forearms into the mattress on either side of my head. He plunges forward and my breath catches in my throat. "I want this every morning and every night." He smirks, knowing damn well what he's doing to me. He's going to hit me with a sense fuck. "And maybe a bit in between." He lazily pulls back and slowly pushes forward again. I clench my eyes closed. I'm not fooled that he is about to make love to me. Maybe, if I agree, I'll get gentle Jesse, but I'm really not sure about living with him.

"You only want me for my body." I feign shock on a rushed breath.

He gasps and drives long and controlled into me. "You don't want this?"

I throw my head back and moan. "You don't play fair, Mr. Ward."

He withdraws slowly. "Say yes!" he shouts as he pounds forward, knocking the wind right out of me, forcing my arms to fly back to brace myself on the headboard. "Have I got to fuck some sense into you, Ava?"

Oh, here it comes. He's going to fuck some sense into me that makes no sense at all. Moving in with him? It's way too soon.

My muscles tighten and my blood heats, sailing through my veins at a ridiculous speed. I hate that he does this to me. All sensibility is well and truly derailed. "No!" I snap, and he thunders into me again, grunting as he does. He reaches forward with his bad hand and slides his palm under the back of my head, pulling me up to face him. I'm not sure if the scowl on his face is because he's mad or because his hand is hurting.

"Say it," he orders, and then charges forward again.

I'm not going to give in on this. It really is too soon. He won't stop this; he's too far gone himself. "No," I state firmly and precisely on a pant.

He growls and hammers forward, pounding mercifully into me. I grip onto him with the muscles of my womb as he forces me farther up the bed. "Fucking hell, say it, Ava!" he roars. A bead of sweat trails down his temple and his frown line jumps into position.

"No!"

"Ava!" His shout echoes around the bedroom before he smashes our mouths together viciously. I buck and writhe under his forceful body and greedy mouth as my pending release simmers low in my groin. "You like that?" he gasps against my mouth as he persists with his relentless pounds.

"Yes!"

"You want this every day?"

"Yes!"

He yanks my hair tighter and grinds his hips harder. "Say it then." I feel the wound-up coils snapping inside me as I fly into a bottomless pit of pure pleasure beneath him. All reason is lost as he takes ownership of my body, soul, and mind.

"Yes! Yes! Yes! Fucking hell. Yes!" I scream.

"Watch your fucking mouth!" His booming voice is piercing as he joins me in my pleasure and releases my hair before punching his fist into the mattress. That had to hurt! He pushes himself into me as deep as he can and holds himself there, his head rolling back.

He groans.

I feel his hot release pumping deep into me, and I bring my hands down from the headboard to rest on his chest. His head drops, his eyes find mine, and he slowly circles his hips against me, easing us both down.

"That wasn't so hard, was it?" His voice is hoarse and dry.

I smooth his solid chest under my palms. "I was under the influence," I say, and then mentally slap myself for my poor choice of words.

He can't hold me to this, surely. But then I realize...this is Jesse, my unreasonable control freak. He can, and he will.

He smiles a glorious, full smile and kisses me tenderly, then rolls us over so I'm sprawled across this chest. His finger traces the column of my spine and he smoothes my hair. I snuggle happily into him.

"I can't be with you every second of the day," I say, though how I feel right now, it's tempting. Why wouldn't I want this day and night, and a little bit in between as well?

He exhales, long and wearily. "I know you can't. I wish you could."

"I have a job, a life."

"I want to be your life."

"You are," I argue softly. He can be so vulnerable and delicate, and I know I'm the answer to that. It's miles away from the domineering brute who just fucked some sense into me. Is it sense, though? Or just pure craziness?

CHAPTER SEVEN

I'm freezing cold, and I wince at the invasion of light that's attacking my eyes as I open them and bolt upright in bed.

Where is he?

I brush my hair out of my face, jump out of bed, and rush into the bathroom. He's not there. In a blind panic, I hotfoot it downstairs and skid to a stop at the kitchen entrance.

"Morning." He puts his coffee down and gets up from the island, walking casually toward me. It's like I'm looking at a different man. Have I dreamt the last couple of days?

He is clad in a charcoal-gray suit, crisp white shirt, and a soft pink tie. He's clean shaven, his messy blond hair has been manipulated to the side, and his green eyes are twinkling in delight. He looks stunning.

"Urh...morning," I stutter.

He reaches for me and wraps an arm around my waist, then hoists me off my feet and up to his lips. "Sleep well?" He brushes his mouth against mine.

"Hmmm," I hum. I'm staggered. I was sure that I would be set for battle this morning with Mr. Challenging.

"You see, this is exactly why I want you here morning, noon, and night," he muses.

"Why?" So he can do this every morning? Maybe moving in with him wouldn't be such a bad idea after all.

He lets me slide down his front, then stands back to look me up and down, clasping his newly shaved chin with his bad hand and arching a brow on a mild grin.

Oh fucking hell! I'm naked!

"Shit!" I turn and make a hasty retreat to the stairs, but I don't get very far. He catches me halfway up, wrapping his arm around my waist and lifting me from my feet. "Watch your mouth!" He takes me back to the kitchen, sitting me on the breakfast bar.

"Oh!" I yelp, as the coldness of the marble spreads across my bare backside.

He laughs and separates my thighs before settling himself between them. "I want you to come down for breakfast every morning just like this." He trails his finger from my knee to the apex of my thighs. I'm more than awake now. I'm tense, too.

"You're confident I'm going to be here every morning," I say as casually as any woman can when a godlike creature is lightly brushing his forefinger across her pubic hair. He can't hold me to things when I've agreed to them midorgasm.

He's fighting a grin. "I *am* confident, because you said yes. Or was it..." He looks up to the ceiling in deep thought and then back at me. "Oh, I remember. It was...'Yes, yes, yes, fucking hell, yes!'" The corner of his mouth lifts cheekily as he slips his finger inside me.

"I was caught at a weak moment." I can't hide the lust in my voice. He's got me.

He circles his thumb over my clitoris and my leg muscles start aching. I shift on the worktop slightly to give him better access. I'm so bloody easy.

"Do I need to remind you why it was a good decision?" he asks, and then takes my lips, trading one finger for two and plunging straight into me, whipping me into a desperate, wanton state.

No, he doesn't. It's nonsensical, but I'll take the reminder. I grab his suit jacket, clench my fists, and moan into his mouth. I feel him grin against my lips before he releases them and pushes me down on the worktop. The coldness of the marble radiates through me, but I'm beyond caring. I need him...again.

With his eyes burning into mine, he undoes his belt and trousers urgently, then yanks his boxers down, freeing his morning erection. In a coordinated set of moves, he clasps me under my thighs and pulls me forward onto his waiting cock.

"This is another reason," he growls, pulling back and then hurling forward.

"Oh God! Jesse!" I drop my head back onto the worktop and arch my back into him. Oh good Lord, he has the moves. He starts a punishing rhythm of drives that have me clamping my hands on the edge of the worktop to stop myself riding up the marble. His breathing is hard and loud, and he lets a gruff bawl escape his lips on each advance.

"Fuck! You feel perfect, baby." He rams forward again, hitting me hard, a despairing yelp bursting from my mouth.

I don't know what to do with myself; he's relentless with his momentum as he charges forward over and over and over. I'm dizzy. He places his hand on my breast and massages hard, all in time with his solid thrusts.

"Remember yet?" he barks, but I can't answer. Speech has totally evaded me. With each powerful drive, he's edging me closer and closer. I inhale and hold my breath as I reach the summit. "Answer the question, Ava," he demands. "Now!"

"Yes!"

"You're staying with me?" His grip of my breast tightens, his hips powering forward relentlessly.

"Oh God! Oh God! Jesse!"

"Answer the fucking question, Ava!" His unremitting blows are sending me wild, my head spinning, my core trembling violently.

"Yes!" I scream on a rushed release of air as I'm rocketed skyward in a deliriously wonderful sensation of satisfaction, buzzing from top to toe, my back arching, my body in fits of spasms.

"Oh yes!" He collapses on top of me, pinning me to the worktop.

I flop my arms above my head on an exhausted sigh and let my muscles naturally contract around him as we lie panting and sweating on the island. I'm completely and utterly shattered. I could go back to bed, but I've got to go to work and, not that I would admit it to Jesse, I really don't want to. I would rather he carry me upstairs and love me all day long—maybe longer.

He lifts his head up to look at me. "God, I fucking love you."

"I know you do. You shaved." I breathe. I really could go back to bed. I feel like I've been on one of his torturous runs.

"You want me to grow it back?"

I reach up and run my palm down his newly smoothed face. "No, I like seeing all of you."

He turns his face into my palm and kisses it, then pushes himself up and plants a kiss on my stomach before withdrawing from me to sort his trousers out.

He stares down at me as he refastens his belt then wipes his moist, lush lips with the back of his hand. "I've got to go. Get out of my sight before I take you again." He clasps my hand and pulls me off the counter before dropping a long, sensual kiss on my lips. "Now."

I debate remaining exactly where I am—I want more, but he seems content with getting on with his day without me, and that has to be a good thing. I don't want to derail him, so I saunter off butt naked and well aware that he's watching me. I stop at the archway and turn to face him, finding him standing with his hands in his pockets, his eyes twinkling. He's studying me very carefully.

"Have a nice day." I smile, reaching down and running my finger over my moist cleft, and then up to my mouth. Oh, I really am a little temptress.

"Fuck off, Ava," he warns.

I grin and pivot, taking myself upstairs. I am such a slut! But I don't care. I'm pleasantly surprised by his happy persona this morning. I had been bracing myself for a challenge, trying to get myself out of the penthouse Jesse-free. This is progress. I'm pleased.

It's Monday and I have a lot of work to sort out. I feel power-ful and I need to power dress to enhance my confident attitude. Thank God Kate took the initiative to pack some work clothes and...my black, sleeveless pencil dress.

I shower and make the best job I can with my hair before slipping my dress on and grabbing my red heels on the way downstairs, but I come to an abrupt halt at the door.

Shit!

I haven't got my car and some of the files I need are in there. I exit the penthouse hastily and race downstairs to find Clive taking a delivery outside the foyer. I run out into the sunshine toward him while putting my shades on. "Clive, I need a cab!"

"Ava, how are you this morning?" He beams at me. "Your transport is here."

"My transport?"

He points toward a black Range Rover, and I see John leaning against the hood on his phone. He has his customary shades on and his black suit, and he nods at me, as per his usual greeting.

I start walking toward him, but remember something and swing back to face Clive. "Did Jesse speak to you about the visi-tor he had yesterday?"

"No, Ava." Clive makes his way back to his desk.

Hmmm. I thought not. I carry on my way and as I approach John, I catch the tail end of his conversation.

"She's here, Jesse, I'll be there soon." His rumbling voice always makes him sound like he's in a bad mood. He hangs up and nods at the car, his indication that he wants me to get in, so I take myself around the front and climb in. If I weren't in such a rush, I would probably complain.

"Why are you here?" I ask as I settle in the passenger seat.

"Jesse asked me to take you to work." He doesn't sound impressed.

"I need to get my car. Do you mind? It's at Kate's, she lives in Notting Hill."

He nods his acceptance, lets his window down, and leans his arm on the frame. He looks like one mean motherfucker.

"Did you get the gates sorted?" I ask.

His face turns slowly toward me and I see his forehead slightly wrinkled, an indication that he's frowning. I hold his stare, but he still doesn't answer.

"The gates of The Manor," I prompt. "They malfunctioned last Sunday."

He starts nodding and turns his face back to the road. "All sorted, girl."

I bet they are. The niggling need to push this is irritating, but if there is one thing I know about John, it's that he isn't a big talker.

We travel in silence, except for John's humming, and he drops me at Kate's. "Thanks, John," I call, jumping out of his car.

"S'all good," he rumbles, and he's gone.

It's eight. I have time, so I run up the path to Kate's house.

I head straight through to find her beating a gigantic bowl of sugar and butter. "Hey." I dunk my finger in her bowl.

She swats it with her spoon. "Out! I've got so much to do! I got absolutely nothing done yesterday." She's really flustered, which is a million miles away from her usual calm and collected façade.

"Oh yeah?" I smirk.

"Fun!" she snaps, tipping flour onto the measuring scales. I make the sensible decision to leave it right there. "How's your brother?" she asks.

"He's good." I won't go into too many details.

"Jesse?" she asks, her tongue hanging out as she bends down to gauge the scales.

"Yeah." I flop down into one of the tub chairs.

She straightens up and looks at me questioningly. I haven't got time at the moment to go into too many details, there is far too much to get her opinion on.

"Ava?"

I sigh. "He wants me to move in. I said yes, but that's only because he fucked some so-called sense into me after I said no. He followed it up with a reminder fuck this morning." Kate gapes at me.

"Wow!

I laugh. "Yes."

"Isn't it a bit soon?"

The question shocks me, but I'm glad she's of the same mind-set as me. "I think so. He wants me day and night and a little bit in between. He's bad enough already, with his demands, control, and worrying."

"Have you told him that?" She tosses the flour into the bowl and starts mixing again.

"No. Hey, what went down at The Manor on Saturday night and why didn't you answer any of my calls?"

She shoots her bright blues to mine. "Nothing!' she barks defensively. "I forgot to call you back."

"I was referring to the police turning up," I say with a raised brow.

"Oh!" She returns to mixing her cake a little too frantically. "I don't know. Jesse turned up and the police left shortly after."

"Hey, chick!"

Sam's cheerful voice comes from the doorway and we both look up in unison. He's completely naked, except for one of Kate's minuscule Cath Kidston aprons, and as he walks past me, my eyes drift and I get a right eyeful of his tight, naked butt.

I cough, looking anywhere and everywhere, except at Sam. "Hi." I wave a flappy hand in his direction, feeling my face burning up as I glance at Kate in desperation, silently begging her to do something about the cheeky sod.

"Samuel, put some clothes on." Kate scorns him on a small smile.

"I've come to help," he whines.

"You've already put me way behind." Kate moans, slapping his naked rump with a spatula full of cake mixture.

"I hope you're going to dispose of that now!" I laugh. She shrugs and starts licking the spatula on a smile.

Sam turns to face me with the biggest grin on his cheeky face, clearly enjoying my embarrassment, too. And then he bends slightly, shoving his arse in Kate's face. "Now you're going to have to lick it all off."

I jump out of the tub chair in a complete fluster. "I'd better be going," I blurt, my voice high and squeaky. I don't want to witness the impending clean-up operation of Sam's naked buttocks.

"See ya!" Kate laughs as I make my escape, not daring to look back for fear of what I might see. Kate's curt response to my enquiry about The Manor is making my head spin. I don't even want to *think* what I'm thinking.

* * *

I arrive at the office on time to a huge bunch of calla lilies lying across my desk. I sigh. How does he arrange for flowers so quickly?

I find the card.

> *You're a savage and a tease.*
> *You drive me crazy,*
> *I love you.*
> *Jx*

I drive him crazy? The man is delusional. I fire a quick text to him:

> I know u do. Flowers r beautiful. Thank u for the ride . . . 2 work.
> Ax

I settle at my desk and bring up my e-mail and list of things to do, but I'm quickly distracted from my work when I remember that I've not taken my pill. I grab my bag from the floor and rummage through, but after a good few minutes of searching, I have my bag turned upside down on the desk and everything sprawled all over the place.

"Shit shit shit! Please, not again."

"Morning, flower," Patrick strolls into the office.

"Morning." I don't look up from my futile searching. I deserve a medal for being so bloody careless.

"Nice flowers." I don't miss his questioning tone.

"Oh yes. My brother," I blurt out quickly.

"How lovely." He smiles, making his way to his office.

My phone starts dancing across my desk, alerting me of a text.

> YOU are beautiful and I know you know. Cheeky! I miss you.
> Jx

I melt all over my desk. I miss him, too, but I'm now dreading having to go back to Dr. Monroe for the third time. This is ridiculous.

With my phone in my hand, I decide I may as well get the one call I really don't want to make out of the way. I dial Matt, and it rings twice before he answers.

"Ava?" He sounds pleased to hear from me.

"I could do with picking those bits up," I get straight to the point. If I didn't need my things, I wouldn't call him at all. Talking to him has me physically itching. I was with him for four years. How did this happen?

"Of course."

"Can I swing by after work on Thursday? Say, six-ish?"

"Sure, I look forward to it," he replies cheerfully.

I want to hiss down the phone, *Why did you ring my parents, you worm?*, but I know he is probably expecting some sort of backlash from me. I'm not going to indulge him.

"Great, see you then." Why did I say that for? It's not great at all.

"Yeah, see you later." He sounds almost smug.

I shudder and hang up. If I could, I would send Kate around to get my things, but I know that will just end in tears and possible police intervention. I'll be in and out in ten minutes. I can resist the urge to pound on him for that long.

"You want a coffee, Ava?"

I look up and see Sally fiddling with her ponytail. There's something different about her. "Please. Did you have a good weekend, Sal?" She shuffles on the spot and blushes ten shades of crimson, and then I notice that her high-necked blouses have been replaced with a scoop-neck top. Wow! Sal has great tits! Who would have thought?

"I did. Thank you for asking, Ava." She scuttles off to the kitchen.

I grin to myself. Our dull, dreary Sal may have had some male action at the weekend. I put my phone down and start working through my files, ready for my appointment with Mr. Van Der Haus on Wednesday.

As ten thirty approaches, I gather my things to go on a few site visits. "Sal, tell Patrick I've gone to check on a few sites. I'll be back about four thirty."

"Will do," she sings enthusiastically, while filing some invoices. Yep, she's definitely had some male interest. Do men really have that impact on us women?

I pass Victoria and Tom at the door.

"Darling, how was your weekend?" Tom croons.

"Great," I say, accepting his air kiss. "I've got to dash. I'll be back about four thirty."

"Excuse me," Victoria barges past me.

"What's up with her?" I ask Tom.

Tom rolls his eyes. "Oh, bugger me if I know. She rang on Saturday declaring she was in love, then I meet her this morning and she has a face like a slapped arse!"

"Drew?"

Tom shrugs. "She doesn't want to talk about it. Not a good sign. I'll see if I can pump any info out of her. Speak to you later."

I make my way to the tube and stop off at the chemist to replace my depleted gloss. I'm drawn to the vitamins, remembering reading about deficiency when I was doing my research on the Internet about alcoholics. I read what feels like a million labels, then decide to speak to the pharmacist.

After a vague chat, he recommends a few things, but strongly advises seeking medical help if I'm worried. Am I worried? Jesse insists he's not an alcoholic and he certainly doesn't scramble for the hard stuff when he sees it. I buy the vitamins anyway. They can't hurt.

When I'm walking up Kensington High Street, I hear Bill Withers singing "Ain't No Sunshine" from my bag. I smile and don't think twice about answering. I don't need him flying into panic over a few missed calls and bombarding me during my client visits. I need to keep him stable, and if that means a quick telephone conversation, then so be it.

"Hey," I greet.

"God, I miss you." He sounds so forlorn. It's only been four hours since he had me spread on the kitchen worktop.

"Where are you?" I ask.

"At The Manor. Everything is under control. I'm not needed here. Do you need me?"

I can't see him, but I know he's pouting. "Always." I know that's what he wants to hear.

"Now?" he asks hopefully.

"Jesse, I'm at work." I try not to sound tired, but I have a ridiculously busy day ahead of me.

"I know," he grumbles dejectedly. "What are you doing at this precise moment?"

"I'm on my way to a client and I've just got here, so I'll have to sign off." He might not be needed at work, but I have a diary to keep.

"Oh, okay." He sounds so miserable, and I feel guilty for brushing him off.

I stop outside my destination and look up to the heavens. "I'll stay at yours tonight," I say, hoping this will placate him.

"I would hope so, you live there!"

I roll my eyes. Of course I do. "I'll see you later."

"You will. What time?" he presses.

"Six-ish."

"Ish," he whispers. "I love you, lady."

"I know you do." I hang up and make my way up the steps to the front door of Mr. and Mrs. Kent's new home.

*   *   *

"Nice flowers."

I look up and see Victoria standing at my desk. She is less orange, but no less miserable than she was this morning. "Are you okay?" I ask, wondering if Tom managed to extract any information.

"Not really."

"Do you want to elaborate?" I prompt.

She shrugs. "Not really."

I try not to look bored, but it's bloody hard. I haven't the energy to tease information out of her. I get up and head for the kitchen to get some biscuits. I need a sugar hit.

I find Sally washing up.

"Hi, Ava," she says happily.

Now, I really *am* prepared to push Sally for information. I'm dying to know what's put a huge smile on her face and provoked the introduction of scoop-neck tops. "What did you get up to at the weekend, Sal?" I ask casually as I dip into the biscuit tin. I catch her blushing again. I'm definitely onto something here. If she says she's done a cross-stitch and cleaned the windows, I'll hang myself.

"Oh, you know...I went for a drink." She's trying to sound casual and failing miserably.

I knew it! "Nice. Who with?" I feign disinterest. It's hard. I'm desperate to discover that our Sal—dull as dishwater, plaid-skirt-wearing, high-necked bloused, office dogsbody—is a dominatrix or something.

"I had a date," she says, maintaining her failing casual tone.

"Really!" I blurt. That came out so wrong. I didn't mean to sound shocked, but I am.

"Yes, Ava. I met him on the Internet."

Internet dating? I've heard nothing but bad things about it.

They look like underwear models on their profile pictures, but when they turn up they are more akin to serial killers. Sal seems quite happy, though. "Did it go well?"

"Yes!" she screams. I nearly choke on my biscuit. I've never seen her so animated. "He's perfect, Ava. He's taking me out again tomorrow."

"Ah, Sal, I'm really happy for you."

"So am I!" she sings. "I'm off now. Do you need anything before I go?"

"No, you get going. I'll see you tomorrow." She dances out of the kitchen and I remain against the counter as I work my way through another three chocolate biscuits.

* * *

When I pull up outside Lusso, the gates open immediately. Jesse's car isn't here.

I enter the foyer, weighed down with flowers and bags, and see Clive clicking various buttons on his high-tech surveillance system. "Hi, Clive."

He looks up and smiles. "Ava, how are you?"

Rubbish! I've had a ridiculously busy day, I want to shower, get into my sweats, and have a glass of wine. I can do none of those things, and I'm pissed off that Jesse's made a big fuss about me being here and he's not even here himself. "Tired," I mumble, heading for a big sumptuous sofa. I might fall asleep.

"Here, Mr. Ward left this for you."

I look up and see Clive holding up a pink key. He left me a key? So he knew he wouldn't be here and he didn't even ring to tell me.

I walk over to Clive and take the key. "When did he go?"

Clive continues clicking and switching while studying the monitors. "He dropped by at around five to leave it."

"Did he say when he would be back?" Am I just expected to hang around and wait?

"Not a word, Ava." Clive doesn't bother looking up at me.

"Did he ask you about the woman who stopped by?"

"No, Ava." He almost sounds bored.

He didn't ask because he bloody knows. And he's going to tell me.

I leave Clive playing with his equipment and make my way up to the penthouse, letting myself in with my pink key and heading straight to the kitchen. I go to the fridge and yank the door open and am immediately confronted with rows and rows of bottled water. I shut the fridge door with more force than it deserves—it's not the fridge's fault there's no wine in it.

I sit myself on a barstool and gaze around the immense kitchen that I designed. I love it and never in a million years did I imagine that I would have the opportunity to live here. Now I have, though, I'm really not sure about it. I love him, but I fear living with him will just encourage his controlling behavior and challenging ways. Or would he be better? More reasonable?

My stomach does a little flip and a growl, reminding me that I should really get something to eat. I've only picked on a few biscuits today. It's no wonder I feel exhausted.

I'm just about to convince myself to lift my tired arse from the stool when I hear the front door open, and a few moments later, Jesse walks into the kitchen looking as wiped out as I feel. He doesn't say anything for the longest time. He just stands there and looks at me, and I notice his hands shaking slightly, his brow looking damp. My craving for a glass of wine diminishes instantly.

"Are you okay?"

He slowly walks over and stands me up. Reaching down, he clasps the hem of my dress and pulls it up to my waist and then grabs me under my bum and lifts me up to straddle his waist.

He buries his face in my hair and walks us out of the kitchen. I can feel his heartbeat clattering against my chest as I hold on to him while he takes the stairs silently with me in his arms. I want to ask him what's wrong, I've got lots of things to ask him, but he seems so despondent.

He walks us to the bed and crawls on with me beneath him, settling on top of me with his weight spread all over my body. It's soothing. Locking my arms around him, I breathe into his neck and soak up his fresh-water smell. I sigh contentedly. He might be a significant contributing factor to my stress and tiredness, but he makes it disappear just as quickly as he triggers it.

"Tell me how old you are." I break the comfortable silence after I've held him until his hammering heart has returned to its usual, steady speed.

"Thirty-two," he says into my neck.

"Tell me."

"Does it matter?" he asks tiredly.

It doesn't matter, but I want to know. He might like this game, but I don't and it's not going to make any difference to how I feel. I just think I should know. It is mandatory information, like his favorite color, food, or track—all of which I don't know. I know so little about him. I correct myself in an instant. Black, peanut butter, and "Angel."

"No, but I would like it if you told me."

He nuzzles in my neck. "All you need to know is that I love you."

I sigh and start to think about my introduction of a truth fuck into our relationship. Something has got to wheedle this small, insignificant piece of information out of him. I know my persistently asking him is having no satisfactory results.

"How was your day?" he asks, his voice muffled in my hair.

"Stupidly busy, but very constructive." I'm quite pleased with what I managed to get done, considering I thought my day would be a bombardment of calls and texts. "And you need to stop sending flowers to my office."

His head lifts and I'm greeted with a disgusted look. "No. Have a bath with me."

I roll my eyes at his stubbornness, but I could think of nothing better than having a bath with him at the moment. "I'd love to."

He pulls himself up so I have to release his neck, and he drops his lips to mine. "You stay here, I'll sort the bath." He jumps up and takes his jacket off as he goes to the bathroom.

I hear the water start running and I turn onto my side, feeling content and tranquil. He makes me feel like this, and it's these times when I know why I'm here. It's how attentive, loving, and tender he is. Perhaps living with him wouldn't be so bad after all. But then I give myself a quick reminder that I'm currently on Central Jesse Cloud Nine. I won't be thinking like this once I've not conformed to one of his demands. It will come, and it might even be about all of this moving-in business.

He strolls back into the bedroom, and I lie back and admire his incredible gait as he pulls his tie loose and throws it on the nearby chaise longue, then starts working his shirt buttons. He lets his shirt hang loose and leans down to take his shoes and socks off. He's barefoot with his trousers resting on those glorious, narrow hips, his shirt open, revealing the sharp lines of his chest. I could sink my teeth into him. He would probably enjoy that.

"Enjoying the view?"

I look up and find green pools studying me. That look alone renders me a soaking-wet mess. "Always," I answer, my voice all throaty.

"Always," he confirms. "Come here."

I slide off the bed and slip out of my heels.

"Leave the dress," he demands softly.

I pad over to him, keeping hold of his hypnotizing eyes. My heart is ricocheting off my rib cage, and I part my lips to let subtle streams of air escape, watching him as he slowly runs his tongue over his bottom lip.

"Turn around."

I obey and slowly pivot away from him. I feel his palms rest on my shoulders and the contact, even through my dress, zaps my nerve endings to life.

He leans down and rests his mouth near my ear. "I really like this dress." Both of his hands travel inward until they arrive at my nape. He gathers my hair and places it over my shoulder, and then slowly draws the zip of my dress all the way down.

I flex my neck muscles in an attempt to control my overwhelming need to shake off the shudders that he's instigating, but I give up when I feel his lips rest against my upper back and his tongue glide up to the nape of my neck. Every fine hair stands on end, and I arch my back in response to his long, hot stroke.

"I love your back." His lips vibrate against my skin, generating even more shudders. He moves his mouth back to my ear. "You have the softest skin."

My head rolls onto his shoulder, and my face turns into his neck. He adjusts his head so his lips find mine as he hooks his hands into the front of my dress and pushes it down my body.

"Lace?" he asks.

I nod and his eyes sparkle with lust as he kisses me gently, like I'm glass. Our tongues slip and slide over each other with little effort from either of us, and I lean back onto him for support. I'm relishing his gentleness and soft touch.

His hands find my breasts and he pinches my nipples through the lace of my bra, teasing them to firm peaks.

"See what you do to me?" He grinds his hips into my lower

back, demonstrating exactly what I do to him, before dropping a chaste kiss on my lips. "I'll die loving you, Ava."

I know how he feels. I don't see a future without him in it, and I'm excited and apprehensive about it all at once. It's the unknown. He is still unknown. I need more than his body, his attention . . . his challenging ways.

He yanks the cups of my bra down, exposing my breasts, and skims the flats of his palms over the tips of my nipples. "You and me," he breathes in my ear, sliding one of his hands down my front and straight to the apex of my thighs.

My knees wobble when his hand cups me over my underwear, a deluge of liquid fire descending on me, my hips rolling forward against his hand to get more friction.

"Do I turn you on, Ava?"

"You know you do." I pant and then moan as he thrusts his hips forward.

"Wrap your arms around my neck," he says quietly. I reach back and link my hands behind his neck. "Are you wet for me?"

"Yes."

He hooks his thumbs in each side of my knickers. "Only for me," he whispers, dragging his tongue lightly down the edge of my ear.

"Only for you," I agree quietly. I need nothing else except for him.

I feel a sharp tug and a tear, and I look to see my knickers hanging from his index finger in front of me. He lets them slide off the end of his finger and takes his other hand to my hip.

I jerk slightly, and he laughs in my ear. His fingers shift as his big hand wraps around my hip, spreading from my front to my back, his other hand hovering in front of me.

"What shall I do with this, Ava?" He flexes his good hand in front of me. "Show me."

My hammering heart does nothing to regulate my short, sharp breaths. I want that hand on me. I remove my arm from around his neck and reach forward to take his hand, slowly guiding it down to the inside of my thigh and flattening his palm against my flesh.

I start applying pressure on his hand and drawing up until his flat palm glides over my sex, the moisture ensuring it travels with ease. I gasp, my hips whipping back and colliding with his groin, provoking a moan to escape his lips and my head to fall back. I need him to kiss me.

I turn my face into him, and he takes my hint, brushing his lips across mine. My teeth clamp down lightly on his bottom lip, and I pull back to let it slowly drag through my grip, his eyes locked on mine as I continue to work his hand up and down in a slow, steady caress.

"Don't come." His voice is rough.

I immediately withdraw his hand and bring it up to his mouth and he watches me as he runs his tongue straight down the center and onto his fingers. Oh Lord, I'm desperate for him, but I can't disobey him—not during these moments.

My bra is unclasped and I'm turned to face him before he brushes my hair back with his hand. "Promise me you'll never leave me."

I look up into his troubled eyes. I can't get used to this unsure part of him. I don't like it, but at least he's asking, not demanding. "I'll never leave you."

"Promise me."

"I promise." I take his wrists one at a time and undo the cuffs of his shirt, then push it from his shoulders. He lets his arms hang by his side, his head dropped to watch me as I undo the button and zipper of his trousers. My palms slide around his hips and under his boxers to drag his trousers and underwear over the tight, smooth flesh of his arse and down his thighs, his thick, pulsing length jutting straight out from his hips invitingly. It triggers all sorts of desperate wants in me, not helped by his abdominals rippling under my touch as I skate my hands up his torso, marveling at his beauty.

"I can't wait anymore. I need to be inside you." He steps free of his trousers and lifts me to him, my legs wrapping around him. I flinch when his cock brushes against my slickness as he carries me toward the wall, where I'm pushed up against the cold paint, feeling the hot, slippery crown of his erection pushing at my opening, breaching my entrance only a little. He breathes heavily and lets his head fall into my neck, as if preparing himself for his invasion of me. I can't wait. I swivel my hips and bore down on him, taking him all the way.

"Oh, you fucking kill me," he moans as he stills inside me.

I want to tilt my hips and instigate movement, but I know from the jolting and twitching of him inside me that he's holding back, so I keep still and sweep my hands through his dark blond hair while he gathers himself, his heart pounding so hard I can almost hear it.

"Are you holding on to me?" He brings his face up to mine.

"Yes." I weave my fingers together around his neck and tighten my thighs.

He growls with approval and releases his hands from my back, planting them onto the wall on either side of me. Then he slowly eases back on a steady breath before plunging forward on a sharp exhale.

I moan, the sensation of his hot, throbbing assault of me has me shifting my hands and clawing at his back. Resting his forehead against mine, he slowly begins rocking in and out of me.

I sigh on every plunge as he works me up steadily. Oh fucking hell, he feels so good. My grip begins to slip on his sweat-dampened skin, our breath mingling together in the close space between our mouths.

"Kiss me," he gasps, and I push my lips to his mouth, tackling his tongue.

I feel a scream bubbling in my throat as he rears back and pushes forward, sending me sliding up the wall. I clench my thighs to lift myself farther and then bore down on him.

"Good God, woman! What the hell do you do to me?" He thrusts forward again and again, pushing me up the wall, swallowing my small cries as he kisses the life out of me. "I've waited all day for this." He hits me with another thrust. "It's been the longest fucking day of my life."

"Hmmm, you feel so good." I'm reveling in his attention.

"I feel good? Fuck, Ava, you do serious things to me." He bucks forward.

"Jesse!" I'm a despairing wreck. The calm, smooth motions are fading fast, being replaced with firmer, more aggressive strikes.

"Ava, wherever I'm going from now on, I'm taking you with me, baby."

Thrust!

Holy shit, I'm struggling here. My nails dig harshly into his flesh.

"Shit, Ava!" He fires into me, beads of his sweat dripping onto me. "You're going to come."

"Hard!"

He mumbles in my mouth. I can't hold back anymore. He strikes with ferocious power and I snap, the coils of pleasure peaking and firing off, my nails sinking into his flesh, my teeth gripping his lip harshly. I drop my forehead to his damp, salty skin where his neck meets his shoulder and rock my head from side to side as I jerk uncontrollably against his big body.

"Ava!" he shouts, as he pulls back and then smashes forward, slowly withdrawing before hammering into me again, finding his own release as wave after wave of contractions sweep through me.

He moans, then sinks us to the floor and falls onto his back, heaving and sweating. I drag myself up and sit astride of him, planting my hands on his slick chest and gently grinding myself on his hips. His arms fall back over his head as he looks up and watches me work us both down. We are both wet, out of breath, and thoroughly satisfied. I'm exactly where I should be.

"What are you thinking about?" he puffs, looking up at me.

"About how much I love you," I tell him the truth.

His lips curve at the corners and a look of pure satisfaction spreads across his handsome face "Do I still qualify as your god?"

"Always. Am I still your temptress?" I grin and circle my hands on his chest.

"That, baby, you most certainly are. God, I love your grin." He gives me his own roguish one.

I reach down and pinch his nipples. "Bath, god?"

He jolts upright, nearly headbutting me in the process. "Shit! It's still running!" He jumps up with me still in his arms and still buried inside me, hissing as he grips me too hard with his bad hand.

"Put me down!" I try to peel my body away from his, but he just increases his grip.

"Never." He takes us into the bathroom, where we find the huge bath is not even three-quarters of the way full. He reaches over to the waterfall tap and flips it off.

"You could leave that bath running for a week and it wouldn't be full," I say as he steps in and lowers us down.

"I know. The designer of all this Italian shit obviously has no regard for the environment or my carbon footprint."

"Says he with twelve superbikes," I quip, and then sigh happily as I'm sunk into the lovely relaxing water, still astride his lap, still full to the hilt with his semierect cock. "I could look at you all day." I run my fingertip over every square inch of his hard, lightly tanned chest, swirling and flicking as I go. The silence is comfortable as he watches my delicate touch skate all over his body, my fingers working their way up to his neck, his chin, his lips, and they part, his eyes twinkling as I lower myself to rest on his chest, my mouth meeting his.

"I love your mouth." I drop kisses all the way around the edges of his lips until I'm back to where I started. "I love your body." My hands drift down his arms, my tongue slipping into his mouth. "I love your crazy mind, too." I coax his tongue from his mouth and lap gently as I trail my hands back up his arms until my palms wrap around his neck and my body arches into him.

He moans. "*You* make me crazy, Ava. Just you."

I feel his big palms slide up my back until he's cupping the back of my head and pushing me into him, our mouths continuing to work each other slowly, our bodies slipping against each other slightly. I know I make him crazy, but he makes me crazy, too.

I pull back and look at my crazy man. "Crazy."

"-ish." He smiles and lifts me from his lap, turning me until I'm seated between his parted thighs. "Let me wash you." He grabs the sponge and starts squeezing the hot water all over me, resting his cheek against the side of my head. "I need to talk to you about something," he says quietly. There is no mistaking his apprehension.

I tense all over. "What?"

"The Manor."

He has ceased squeezing warm water over me, and I can almost hear those fucking cogs clanking around in his handsome head. I do not like the direction of tub-talk today. I want to get out and have a shower.

"The anniversary party." The worry is clear in his tone and it bloody should be.

"What about it?" I'm not going to get myself worked up be-cause I really, really am not ever, not in a million years, going. Never—no way. Is Kate still going? I cringe. Undoubtedly.

"I still want you to come."

"You can't ask me to do that. You asked me to go before I knew."

"Are you going to avoid my workplace forever?" he asks sar-castically.

I don't appreciate his tone of voice—not in the slightest. "I might do."

"Don't be stupid, Ava." He recommences soaking me in water and presses a kiss to my temple. "Will you please just think about it?"

I sigh tiredly. "I'm making no promises, and if you even think about trying to fuck some sense into me on this, I'm leaving," I threaten. I'm being completely dramatic, but I want him to know how much I don't want to go.

He nuzzles my ear and wraps his legs around the outside of mine. "I want the woman who keeps my heart beating with me."

Oh God! That's emotional blackmail if ever there was any. Damn you, Jesse Ward, of an age I *still* don't bloody know. I let him continue to wash me while I think about using this to my advantage. Maybe I could negotiate his age from him in return for my presence at The Manor's anniversary party. I need to think hard about how much I want to know his age compared to how much I *don't* want to go to the party? That's a tricky one.

"Did you speak to Clive?" I know he hasn't. I'm being sneaky.

"About what?"

"The mystery woman."

"No, Ava, I didn't have time. I promise you I will ask, though. I'm just as curious as you are. Now, are you hungry?" He circles his tongue around my ear. It could send me to sleep. At least he hasn't lied about talking to Clive.

"I'm not going to sleep until you tell me who that woman was."

"How can I tell you if I don't know?"

"You do know."

"I don't fucking know!"

I jump at his harshness, and then feel his arms lock tighter around me. "I'm so sorry, baby."

"Okay," I say quietly. But it's not. *I'll* speak to Clive in the morning.

"My lovely lady is exhausted," he whispers. "Takeaway?" He bites at my earlobe, smoothing the soles of his feet down my shins.

"You have a fridge full of food. It's a waste."

"Well, can you be bothered to cook?"

No, I can't, but I notice he doesn't offer himself. Then again, he openly admits that cooking is one of the only things he's not amazing at. He was serious as well, the arrogant arse. "Takeaway," I agree.

"I'll go and order while you wash your hair." He lifts himself out of the bath and leaves me in the massive tub, and I watch his wet nakedness stroll out of the bathroom, returning a few moments later with shampoo and conditioner. I'm eternally grateful. My poor hair has been mistreated way too much lately. He gives me a grin and leans down to kiss my forehead. "Wear lace."

CHAPTER EIGHT

I stretch myself out and I'm immediately aware of Jesse's absence in the bed. Propping myself up on my elbows, I spy him sitting on the chaise longue, bending down.

Oh no!

I lie back down as quietly as I possibly can and shut my eyes. He might not have noticed I woke—if I'm lucky. After a few silent moments, I feel the bed dip, but I keep my eyes firmly shut, silently begging him to leave me alone.

An age of me pretending to be asleep passes by, and he still hasn't nudged me, so I cautiously open my eyes and find green pools of delight staring down at me. I groan, very loudly, as I watch the semblance of a small smile tickle his lips. I flip myself over onto my front and cover my head with a pillow, then hear him laugh as the pillow is whipped from my head and I'm turned over onto my back.

"Good morning," he chirps, and I screw my face up in disgust at his cheery, break of dawn happiness.

"Please don't make me," I plead, pulling my most solemn face.

"Up you get." He grabs my hand with his good one and pulls me into a sitting position. I make a big display of moaning in repulsion at his idea of starting the day, and then nearly start crying when he presents me with my freshly laundered running kit that he, so generously, bought me.

"I want sleepy sex," I complain. "Please."

He hoofs me off the bed and draws my lace knickers down my legs before tapping my ankles to lift. "It will do you good."

I lift as instructed. "This is torture," I grumble. It's all right for him, running stupid distances on a daily basis.

"I like having you with me."

I remain grumpy but silent as I let him dress me and lead me down to the foyer of Lusso. We emerge into the dawn sunlight to birds chirping and the hum of delivery vehicles. I start to stretch before any instruction from Jesse, and he smiles as he watches me, at the same time carrying out his own muscle sweep. I want to be a grump, but he is just too delicious in his black shorts and tight white tank, his hair a disheveled mess and his morning stubble at just the right length.

"Ready?" I chirp, as I bounce off toward the pedestrian gates. I punch in the exit code and start jogging toward the Thames. I feel better already.

"Just think," he muses, as he joins my side and we start running steadily together. "We can do this together every morning."

I cough on a sharp inhale of air. Fourteen miles every morning? I don't think so, the mad bastard.

We jog at a steady pace, and I'm reminded of the relaxing advantages of running at this time of day. It really is very peaceful and mind cleansing.

After we conquer the Green Park, we make our way onto Piccadilly, passing the point at which I collapsed the last time. I glance across to the spot where I sat every morning, picking at the grass and soaking up the dew through my trousers. I can see myself there—a pasty, empty waif—a half-complete woman.

"Hey."

I snap from my daydream and look up at Jesse, finding a concerned face. "I'm fine," I puff, shaking my head and giving him a reassuring smile.

I shake off my sad thoughts and mentally applaud myself. I'm going to do this! I feel Jesse's elbow nudge me, and I look up to see a look of recognition on his face at my achievement. But then I do a quick calculation in my head and figure that we're probably only two-thirds done, and at the thought of at least another four and a half miles, I hit the proverbial runner's wall...again. My lungs seem to drain of all air and my body starts burning up along with them.

I'm not going to do this.

I battle on for a few hundred yards, and then enter the park at the next entrance, dramatically collapsing on the damp grass...again. I heave valuable air into my scorching lungs and pant like a dog in heat.

I watch through my slightly blurred vision as Jesse approaches me and stands over me. "I did better than last time," I splutter between dragging in long, wheezy breaths.

He smiles. "You did, baby." He drops to his knees beside me and lifts my leg, rubbing firm, slow circles into my calf muscle. It has me groaning and him laughing. "I'm proud of you. Give it a few days and you'll fly through it."

What? My eyes bulge under my closed lids. If I had spare breath, I'd cough in disgust, but I don't so I lie on the grass as he works his magic hands on every burning muscle, but all too soon, he pulls me up into a sitting position and waves a twenty under my nose.

"I came prepared. Coffee?" He nods past me, and I look to see a Starbucks over the road.

I could kiss him. I throw my arms around him in gratitude for his forward thinking. I've been rubbed back to life and now

I get a Starbucks. The run was worth it. He laughs and stands with me still wrapped around his neck.

"Come on." He pries me from his body and takes my hand, and we stroll over to Starbucks, getting served super quick due to the early hour.

"Do you want something to eat?" Jesse asks.

"No," I answer quickly, dragging my eyes away from the mouthwatering temptations in the glass cabinet.

He smiles and wraps his palm around the back of my neck, pulling me into him and resting his lips on my forehead before turning his attention back to the swooning sales clerk. "A cappuccino, extra shot, no chocolate, a strong black coffee, and two blueberry muffins, please." He smiles brightly at the young girl, who giggles nervously. He returns his eyes to me. "Go and get a seat."

I find a window seat and flop down in the leather couch. What a perfect way to start the day, ten-mile run aside. I would still take sleepy sex over this, though. I would take sleepy sex over anything.

It's not long before my mind starts drifting to Jesse's plea for me to go to The Manor's party. What sort of party would it be, anyway? Visions of seminaked people milling around, hazy, dim lighting, and erotic music all invade my worried mind. And hooks, hoists...whips.

Fucking hell!

It would be like a giant gangbang with kinky toys! Oh Jesus, good Lord above. Not only do I *not* want to go myself, I'm not that crazy about the thought of Jesse being there either. An assault of jealousy spikes at me repeatedly as I imagine women drooling all over him, trying to entice him with promises of wicked sex. There's no doubt he's up for a bit of rough, and he's bloody good at it, too. He's used to all of that shit. I'm having a mental breakdown in Starbucks, and again I'm reminded that Jesse has had lots of practice... with sex... and toys and...

Stop!

I saw the look on those women's faces when I was at The Manor. I *was* an interloper, and I can imagine the reception I would get if I *did* go to the party. It certainly wouldn't be any warmer than my previous visits. I would be, in effect, gate-crashing their gangbang. This is horrible.

"Dreaming?"

I pull my eyes from the lush greenness of the park across the road, to the lush greenness of my Lord of the Sex Manor. I feel depressed and slightly inadequate all of a sudden. And really, really bitter—resentful and consumed with jealousy.

I smile a really unconvincing smile, and he eyes me suspiciously while arranging the coffees and muffins on the table. I start picking at the top of my muffin as I stir my coffee. "I'm not coming to the party," I say to my cappuccino. "I love you, but I can't do that." I add the last part in an attempt to soften the blow. My Lord doesn't take *no* well. I know he's watching me, but I can't muster up the strength to appear fine. I'm not, and after a few silent moments pass, I glance up to establish what expression his handsome face is displaying. There's no rage or scowl, but his frown line has jumped into position and he is chewing his bottom lip.

"It's not going to be how you think it will be, Ava," he says quietly.

"How do you mean?"

He takes a sip of his coffee and sets it down on the table before shifting forward in his chair and resting his elbows on his knees. "Has The Manor ever given you the impression of a seedy sex club?"

"No," I admit.

"Ava, there won't be people wandering around naked and

propositioning you. You won't be manhandled up the stairs to the communal room. There are rules."

"Rules?"

He smiles. "The only places people are permitted to remove their clothes is in the communal room or one of the private suites. The ground floor, spa, and sports facilities are run like any other exclusive resort. I don't run a brothel, Ava. My members pay a lot of money to enjoy everything The Manor provides, not just the privilege to pursue their sexual preference with like-minded people."

"What's your sexual preference?" I ask quietly. I know I'm blushing, and I could kick myself. Of all the things I could ask, I ask this? What the hell is wrong with me?

He grins that roguish grin and pops a piece of muffin in his mouth, chewing purposely slowly and watching me as I writhe under his potent gaze. "You."

"Just me?"

"Just you, Ava." His tone is husky and determined, and I can't help the small smile tickling the corners of my mouth. He's just cranked up his sexual magnetism tenfold.

"Good." I take my first real mouthful of my muffin, immensely satisfied by his response. Just me. I like that answer. Do I even care about what goes on at The Manor, as long as Jesse isn't involved? I just have to disregard the fact that he has been. To what extent has he been involved, though? And is it compulsory for me to know?

We watch each other for a short while, him running his index finger across his bottom lip, me marveling at how damn sexy he looks doing just that.

"You'll come?" he asks, instead of demands. He's being really rather reasonable for Jesse. "Please," he adds, hopefully, on a pout.

Oh, I just can't refuse this man. "Only because I love you."

His pout transforms into a killer smile, and I pool on the couch. "Say it again."

"What? That I'll come?"

"Oh, you'll come all right. No, tell me you love me again."

"I do." I shrug. "I love you."

He grins. "I know you do. I love hearing you say it." He raises his glorious body slowly and puts his hand out to me. I take it, falling into his chest when he tugs a little. "If you had kept running, we would be at home by now and I would be lost inside you."

He drops a long, lingering kiss on my lips and then proceeds to toss me onto his shoulder and stride out to the street.

I catch a glimpse of the young girl who served Jesse looking longingly at me being carted out over the shoulder of my Adonis. I smile to myself. This is what every woman wants, and I have it. No one is taking him away from me, so if I have to go to the stupid anniversary party just to fight off the pack of lions waiting to sink their claws into him, then I will. I'll trample.

I'm tossed in a taxi and subjected to a torturous journey home. I can see the obvious, solid-iron length under Jesse's shorts, and I'm fidgeting to try and dispel the buzzing hijacking me between my thighs.

* * *

"Morning, Clive," Jesse says urgently as he drags me through the foyer. It's a good job I have my trainers on; I may as well be sprinting. He bundles me into the elevator, smashes his code into the keypad, and pins me against the mirrored wall, attacking my mouth hungrily.

"I might have to fuck you *before* my run in future," he growls into my mouth. His primal tone has me falling to pieces under his hard body. My hands are fisted in his hair and pressing his mouth closer to mine, our tongues urgently battling in our mouths. This is going to be a shock-and-awe moment. We are way past sleepy sex territory and if those elevator doors don't open soon, that moment might happen here.

The doors slide open and I'm walked into the penthouse foyer backward, our mouths remaining fused and our tongues relentlessly dueling. I don't know how he manages it, but he gets the door open without breaking our contact, and I'm having my sweaty running kit ripped from my body before the door is closed. He wants in quick, which is absolutely fine by me. I kick my trainers off as he yanks my shorts down my legs, and I start pulling his shirt up over his head. I'm released from his mouth for the few seconds it takes me to get his shirt past his face before his mouth is crashing back to mine again and he's walking forward, directing my backward steps toward the wall by the front door.

He turns me around. "On your knees, put your hands on the wall," he spits urgently, and I waste no time following through on his command while he rids himself of his trainers and shorts.

I drop to my knees and spread my palms on the cool paint, panting and impatient. He grabs my hips tightly, and I jerk under his hold, but he doesn't ease up. He pulls my hips back slightly, knees my legs apart, and positions himself behind me.

"Don't come until I say. Understand?"

I nod and clench my eyes shut to try and ready myself for the onslaught of power that I'm about to welcome into my body. I should know by now that when he is like this, no amount of mental psyching up can prepare me for him.

I feel the head of his cock pushing at my entrance, and as soon as he's leveled it up, he pounds forward on a garbled yell. He gives me no breathing space to adjust or accept him. He immediately yanks me back onto himself and begins to piston in and out of me ruthlessly. He's a man possessed.

Holy fucking shit!

My eyes fly open in shock and I shift my hands on the wall, desperately trying to steady myself as he continues to wildly buck into me. "Jesus, Jesse!" I scream around the delightful invasion of my body.

"You knew this would be hard, Ava," he barks, smashing on. "Don't you dare fucking come."

I try and focus on anything but the immense, fast accumulation of pressure that's building up in my groin, but his relentless and barbaric strikes are not helping my desperate situation. I won't be able to hold out for long at this riotous rate.

"Fuck!" he roars frenziedly. "You. Fucking. Drive. Me. Crazy!" He punctuates each word with a hard, sharp thrust. I'm sweating more now than I did on my ten-mile run.

His hands slide up my back from my hips to grip onto my shoulders, and my head rolls back under his warm, firm hold. I'm delirious with pleasure. The telltale signs of him tensing travels through his arms, straight to my shoulders. I'm relieved. I'm past the point of return, but I can't fully let go until I get the okay. What the hell would he do if I defied him and gave in to my demanding release, anyway?

He continues to buck and slap against me, and on an ear-piercing roar, he slams into me with such force, tears stab at my eyes. He stills and leans against my back, pushing me forward onto the wall, circling his hips deeply. I'm buzzing, my body teetering on the edge. He reaches up and grabs my ponytail, pulling my head back to rest on his shoulder, moving his damaged hand around my front to the inside of my thigh.

He pulls my hair so my face turns into his, my hazy vision met with dark green. "Come," he demands, softly sliding his finger down the center of my core and sweeping his tongue through my mouth.

His words and his touch trigger a shift of pressure in my

groin that seizes me from every angle, and I explode on a stretched-out, blissful moan into his mouth.

I sag in his hold and let him softly massage me through my climax. "You *are* a god," I mumble against his mouth, moving my hands from the wall to link around the back of his neck.

I feel his grin against my lips. "You're so lucky."

"You're an arrogant god."

He slips out of me and turns me around in his arms. I maneuver with him, draping my arms back around his neck. "Your arrogant god loves you so fucking much." He showers my sweaty face with kisses. "Your arrogant god wants to spend the rest of his life smothering you with his love and his body." He stands us up, dragging me with him.

I'm delighted, but I'm also ignoring the small part of my brain that is trying to remind me that with Jesse's love and body also comes Mr. Challenging Control Freak.

"What's the time?" I ask around his morning-stubbled face.

"I don't know." He carries on with his smothering, and I start walking backward toward the kitchen so I can get a look at the clock. He follows, still wrapped around me and still dropping kisses all over me.

I catch a glimpse of the cooker clock. "Shit!"

"Hey! Watch your fucking mouth!"

I wriggle free of his hold and start running toward the stairs. "It's quarter to eight!" I yell, as I take the stairs two at a time. Where has the time gone? My arrogant god is too much of a distraction. I'm going to be super late.

Throwing myself in the shower, I make quick work of ridding my body of sweat and cum. I'm frantically rinsing my hair when I feel Jesse's hands slide over my wet stomach, and I wipe my eyes to find him towering over me with his dirty, roguish grin spread across his beautiful face.

"Don't," I warn. I'm not being distracted by him anymore. He pouts and works his hands up to my shoulders, yanking me forward onto his mouth. "I'm going to be late," I argue feebly, trying to fight off the budding craving as he teases my lips with his.

"I want to make an appointment," he says, licking my bottom lip, pushing his groin into my stomach.

"To fuck me? No appointment necessary," I quip, trying to pull away from him.

He growls and yanks me back. "Mouth! I already told you, I don't need to make an appointment to fuck you. I do that whenever and wherever I please." He rubs his groin back into me, and it's now I know that I have to escape before I'm swallowed up again.

"I've got to go." I duck out of his hold and hastily leave him in the shower, sulking like a schoolboy. He just had me, although I could go again, too.

I brush my teeth and make my way into the bedroom, sitting myself in front of the floor-length mirror with my makeup bag and hair dryer. I commence a fast blast dry, quickly pin it up, and start applying my makeup.

Jesse walks out of the bathroom, gloriously naked and unashamed. I scowl at his naked back, dragging my eyes away to continue with my makeup. I'm being distracted.

Leaning forward, I sweep my mascara wand over my lashes and pull back to find Jesse standing to the side of me, leaning into the mirror. I look up and come face to face with the broad head of his semierect manhood. My eyes are fixed, absolutely delighted, and then my greedy stare travels up his naked body and finds him looking in the mirror, coaxing his hair to the side with some wax. He knows what he's doing.

I take a calming breath and return to my makeup, but then he makes a point of brushing against me, his firm leg sweeping lightly over my bare arm. I shudder and glance up to find a twitching lip as he tries to feign ignorance. The swine.

He looks down at me in the reflection of the mirror, his eyes swimming with all sorts of promises, and then he lowers himself behind me until he's sitting cradling my body. Shifting forward, he pushes his front into my back, wrapping his arms around my waist and resting his chin on my shoulder. I hold his gaze in the mirror.

"You're beautiful," he says softly.

"You are, too," I reply, tensing slightly when I feel his hardness pushing into me.

He fights a smile, knowing damn well what he's doing. "Don't go to work."

I knew this was coming. "Please, don't."

He pouts. "Don't you want to fall into bed and let me pay special attention to you all day?"

I could think of nothing better, but if I relent on this, I'm fully aware that I'm setting a rod for my own back. He can't keep me to himself all of the time, although I know he doesn't think that his ambition is unreasonable. "I have to work," I say, clenching my eyes shut when he turns his lips into my ear.

"I *have* to have *you*." He circles his tongue lightly in my ear.

Oh God, I need to escape now! "Jesse, please." I wriggle in his embrace.

He scowls at me in the mirror. "Are you denying me?"

"No, I'm delaying you," I reason, wriggling harder and turning myself around in his arms. I push him down to his back and lie on his front, pushing my lips onto his, his arms falling above his head as he moans around my kiss. "I need to work, god."

"Work me. I'll be a very grateful client."

I pull back and smile. "You mean to say that instead of busting a gut keeping clients happy with drawings, plans, and schedules, I should just jump into bed with them?"

His eyes turn black. "Don't say things like that, Ava."

"It was a joke." I laugh.

I'm flipped over and pinned under his body. "Do you see me laughing? Don't say things that will make me crazy mad."

"I'm sorry," I blurt quickly. I need to cop onto his zero-tolerance approach to lighthearted jokes that suggest me with another man.

He shakes his head and lifts himself from my body, strolling off to the wardrobe. Taking the loss of distraction as an opportunity, I finish my makeup. I've really upset him.

An unexpected and very unwelcome image of Jesse with another woman jumps into my head, making me do my own little head shake. It's like my subconscious is giving me a taste of my own medicine. I screw my face up in disgust and throw my eyeliner into my makeup bag. It worked. I feel my flesh prickling with possessiveness.

After smothering myself in cocoa butter, I slip on my lace underwear and my red shift dress.

"I like your dress."

I swing around and my eyes are assaulted by a devastatingly handsome, navy-suited beast. I sigh in appreciation. He is just too bloody perfect and he's not shaved. I swoon on the spot. He looks like he's got over his little strop.

"I like your suit," I counter.

He grins and finishes straightening his gray tie before pulling the collar of his white shirt down. If I were any other woman and I found out about The Manor and the god who owned it, I would join, too.

I throw my bag on the bed, retrieve my phone, sweep some gloss across my lips, and grab my shoes, all under his watchful eye. I have another futile rummage through my bag for my pills, but I know I'm searching in vain.

"Lost something?" He splashes some aftershave on.

"My pills," I grumble with my head practically inside my

oversized leather shoulder bag. I run my fingers around the stitching of the lining to check for rips.

"Again?"

I look up at him and smile apologetically. I feel stupid, and I'm not relishing the thought of visiting Dr. Monroe again. I need to sort that today before I miss any more.

"I'll see you later." He lands me with a chaste kiss on my cheek and leaves me to carry on searching for rips in the lining of my bag. Maybe I should just get the jab and save myself all of this embarrassment.

I freeze on the spot, my brow furrowing, my mind jumping the gun . . . I think.

No, he wouldn't. Why ever would he?

CHAPTER NINE

As I walk into the foyer, I find Clive rubbing the cuff of his jacket on the marble desk, buffing it to a shine.

"Morning, Clive."

"Good morning, Ava," he says happily.

I return his cheeriness with an over-the-top smile. "Clive, I don't suppose you could show me the CCTV footage from Sunday, could you?"

"No!" he blurts quickly, suddenly becoming busy and frantically typing on his keyboard.

I eye him suspiciously, but he won't look at me. "Has Jesse spoken to you?"

"No." He shakes his head and keeps his eyes down.

"Of course." I sigh, turning and walking out of the foyer. The Lord is cute, and I'm suspicious.

"Oh, Ava!" I hear Clive coming after me. "Maintenance rang. The door is on order, but it's coming from Italy so it may be a while." He walks beside me.

"You should call Jesse and let him know." I carry on walking, and he carries on flanking me.

"I did, Ava. Mr. Ward advised me that I should consult with you on anything regarding the penthouse."

I skid to a halt. "I'm sorry?" I sound confused.

Clive looks nervous. "Mr. Ward, he said you live here now and anything concerning the penthouse should be run past you, especially as you designed it."

"Oh, he did, did he?" I grind, feeling only a little guilty for sounding so menacing. "Clive, do me a favor. Ring Mr. Ward and tell him I *don't* live here."

Clive looks like I've just told him that he has two heads. "Of course, Ava. I'll…urhhhh…do it now."

"Good," I snap, and carry on outside the building. I'm fuming. He moves me in under the persuasion of a sense fuck followed by a reminder fuck, and then expects me to become Molly Mop? No amount of sense or reminder fucking will work in his favor this time.

I stand and rummage through my bag for my sunglasses and car keys, completely riled, and as I slip on my glasses, Massive Attack's "Angel" creeps into my ears.

"Oh no!" I screech. I'm even madder now. He knows how I feel about that track. I grab my phone and connect the call. "Stop messing about with my phone!"

"No! Reminds me of you," he yells. "What do you mean, you don't fucking live there?"

"I'm not your fucking maid!" I shout back.

"Watch your fucking mouth!"

"Fuck off!"

"Mouth!"

The cheek! If he thinks I'm going to be playing the dutiful domestic lady, he's got another thing coming. Looking up, I spot John leaning against his Range Rover. His signature wraparound glasses are on, but I can see his arched brow above them. He's enjoying this.

"What's John doing here?" I snap.

"Have you calmed down yet?"

"Answer me!"

"Who the hell do you think you're talking to?"

"You! Are you listening? Why is John here?"

"He's going to take you to work."

"I don't need a chauffeur, Jesse." I've calmed my voice slightly. How undignified of me, shouting and swearing like a drunken football hooligan, and in front of the newest, most prestigious residential complex in London. John's grinning. It's new to me. I've never seen him display any humor.

"He was in the area. I thought it would be easier than you trying to park." Jesse has calmed his tone, too.

"Well, at least tell me what's happening if it involves me," I spit down the phone and hang up.

Controlling pig!

I make my way over to John and my phone starts singing again en route. I'll be changing that ringtone. I flash my screen at John as I pass him, and he grins again. "Yes, dear?" I quip, rather bravely, fully aware that I'm digging myself a hole here. But he's out of touching distance so there's no risk of any kind of Jesse-style fucking to put me in my place.

"Don't be sarcastic, Ava. It doesn't suit you."

I climb into the Range Rover and put my seat belt on. "You'll be pleased to know that I'm on my way to work with John." I glance over at John, and he nods. "Would you like confirmation?" I thrust the phone under John's nose. "John, make yourself known."

"S'all good, Jesse." He smiles and I notice a gold tooth.

I put the phone back to my ear. "Happy?"

"Very!" he snaps. "Ever heard of a retribution fuck?"

The very words send shivers down my spine. I glance at John. He's still grinning. "No, are you going to demonstrate?"

"If you're lucky; I'll see you at home." He hangs up.

I put my phone in my bag, feeling coils of anticipation

springing into my groin. Then I look at the beast of a man sitting next to me. "Were you really in the area?"

John stops with his signature hum. "What do you think?"

As I thought. "How old is Jesse?" I ask casually. I don't know why I choose that tone. It's ridiculous that I don't know his age.

"Thirty-two," John replies, completely deadpan.

Thirty-two? That's how old Jesse said he was last night. I look at John, who has started humming again. "He's not thirty-two, is he?"

He smiles again, flashing his gold tooth. "He said you would ask."

I shake my head, at a total loss on the subject, but as John seems to be in a talkative mood, I'll take another angle. "Is he always so challenging?"

"Only with you, girl. He's actually quite laid-back."

"I obviously bring out the worst in him," I grumble.

"Ah, girl. Go easy on him."

"Do you want to live with him and his challenging ways?" I ask, exasperated.

"So, you've moved in then?" His eyebrows appear over his shades as he turns his face to me. I hope John isn't jumping to the same conclusion as Sarah did—that I'm after his money.

I suddenly have the urgent need to defend myself. "He asked me and pretty much bullied a yes out of me, but I'm not so sure. It's a bit soon. That's what that little spat was about. He doesn't like being told no." I wave my phone at John.

The corners of John's lips turn down, and he starts nodding his head thoughtfully. "He certainly has a way with you."

I scoff and do my own little thoughtful head shake. He certainly *does* have a way with me. It's frightening. "How long have you known him?" I may as well get my fill. He might shut up and not start talking again.

"Too long." He laughs, and it's a deep, rumbling belly sound that has him developing a few more chins as his neck retracts.

"I bet you see some sights at The Manor." Now that I know what the place is, John's role is all the more clear.

"It's all in my job description," he says casually.

Ah, which reminds me... "Why were the police there?"

John turns an almost threatening face to me, and I wither slightly. "Just some idiot playing games. No need for you to worry, girl." His attention is turned back to the road, leaving me put firmly in my place. Information. I need some damn information.

I'm dropped off at my office, and John nods his farewell.

* * *

"Morning, Ava!" Sally says cheerfully.

She has on the same top as yesterday but in a different color. Today's is red. "Hi, Sal. Are you okay?"

"Yes, thank you for asking, I'm very good. Can I get you a coffee?"

"Please."

"Coming up!" She flashes me a lovely smile and skips to the kitchen. I notice she has nail color on, and it's not nude or clear. It's firecracker red! This must be in preparation for her date. I like sparkling Sally. I hope she doesn't get crapped all over.

I load my computer up, crack on with some estimates, and prepare a heap of invoice requests for Sally. My in-box is flooded with new e-mails, mostly junk, so I start to plow through them.

At ten thirty, I hear the office door open, and when I look up, I see a fan of calla lilies spread across the arm of Lusso girl. I knew he wouldn't take any notice of my request. She rolls her eyes, and I give her an apologetic shrug. After exchanging flowers and signatures, I retrieve the card.

Looking forward to your retribution fuck?
Your god.
X

I smile and send him a text.

Yes I am and yes u are. Your Ax

I'm well and truly on Central Jesse Cloud Nine. After a morning of knuckling down, I decide to give Kate a call while I'm taking a few minutes out for lunch.

"Well, hello!" she sings down the phone in greeting.

"Hey, you okay?"

"It's all good in the hood! How's my favorite boyfriend to a friend?" She laughs.

"He's fine," I answer dryly. She only loves him so much because he bought her Margo Junior.

"Listen, I'm on my way to Brighton to drop off a cake in Margo Junior. Do you want to do lunch on Thursday? I'm a bit hectic tomorrow. I've got stacks to catch up on."

"Being distracted, are we?"

"Fun!" she snaps. "Do you want to do lunch or not?"

"All right!" I blurt. Her oversensitivity is making me super suspicious. "Thursday, one o'clock at Baroque."

"Perfect!" She hangs up.

Blimey, I think I just hit a nerve. Fun my arse! She's skirting around this and brushing it off far too hastily. I hear the door of the office open and look up to see Tom arriving. "Tom, we need to have a word about your attire!"

He looks down at his emerald-green dress shirt with bright pink tie. Color clash in Tom's world is highly offensive. "Fabulous, isn't it?" He strokes his tie.

No, it's not. In fact, it's a crime. If I were looking for an interior designer and Tom turned up on my doorstep, I'd shut the door in his face. "Where's Victoria?" I ask.

"Appointment in Kensington." He throws his man-bag on his desk and takes his glasses off to clean them on the tail of his shirt.

"Did you find out what happened?'

"No!" He slumps into his chair. "She moped and sulked all day." He leans forward and scans the office. "Hey, what do you make of our Sal?"

He's noticed, too. It's hard not to. "She had a date," I whisper loudly.

"No!" he gasps.

He puts his glasses back on in a dramatic gesture that suggests he needs to see my face, given the news. It's ridiculous. They're a fashion statement and Tom's attempt to appear professional.

"Yes! And a second date tonight." I nod.

His eyes bulge again. "Can you imagine how boring he is?"

I recoil, suddenly feeling extremely guilty for engaging him in such a conversation. "Don't be a bitch, Tom," I scorn.

Sally walks through the office, stopping our gossip dead in its tracks. Tom raises his eyebrows and grins as he follows her path to the photocopier. If I were close enough, I would kick him.

He turns back to me, catching my disapproving expression and holds his hands up. "What?" he mouths.

I shake my head and return to my computer, but my peace is short-lived.

"So," Tom calls from his desk. "Victoria tells me you've moved in with Mr. Ward."

I look up from my screen in shock and see him casually flicking through a catalogue. How does she know? Of course...Drew. "I've not moved in with him, and I need you to be quiet, Tom." I carry on deleting junk e-mails.

"Fancy that, living in the ten-million-quid penthouse that you designed," he muses thoughtfully, still flicking pages.

"Shut up, Tom." I glare at him when he lifts his eyes from the catalogue that he's not even reading. He takes the hint this time, shutting up and carrying on about his business.

I don't know how I'm going to get around this with Patrick. It doesn't look very good, me dating a client, and all I need is Tom blabbering off in the office for all to hear.

*   *   *

As five o'clock hits, I sit tapping my pen on my desk, deep in thought, and I have a bloody fantastic idea.

I jump up from my desk and quickly clear it of drawings and files, then grab my bag and flowers and head for the office door. "I'm done, see you tomorrow, guys," I call, as I all but sprint out of the office. I have half an hour. I can make it.

I head for the tube and to my intended destination.

*   *   *

After my last-minute shopping trip, I run from the tube to Lusso. I need to be showered and ready before Jesse gets home. I bypass any conversation with Clive and jump into the elevator, puffing and panting from my exertion. My poor body has really taken a hammering today. Flying into the bedroom and throwing my flowers and bag on the chest, I start unpacking all of my purchases, shoving them in the wooden trunk and quickly jumping in the shower, eager to ready myself for the evening ahead. I'm careful not to wet my hair as I frantically wash the day away and not so frantically shave.

Stepping out to grab a towel, I slam straight into a familiar, solid, and very naked chest.

"Oh!" I yelp, shocked.

"Surprised to see me?" His voice is low and threatening.

I slowly lift my gaze to his and find hooded, dark green eyes and a deadly serious expression. Dominant Jesse has arrived, and he's completely screwed my plan up.

"A little," I admit.

"Thought so. We have a small issue to resolve and we're going to do it now."

I stand frozen in place, dripping wet and clutching the towel, with his menacing, lean frame towering over me. That and his heavy breathing tell me I'm in no position to protest...but I just can't help myself. "What if I say no?"

"You won't." His self-assured tone pumps the blood faster through my veins as he pushes himself into me, the warm, slippery head of his erection probing at my lower stomach, prompting a small gasp of air to escape my mouth. His eyes burn with dark promise as I wait for him to make his move, anticipation having the muscles at my core convulsing.

"Let's not play games, Ava. We both know you'll never say no to me." His fingertip trails the length of my wet arm, across my shoulder and up my neck until it reaches the hollow under my ear.

I close my eyes. He's got me again.

"Do you believe in fate, Ava?" His voice is silky smooth, but sure and serious.

I open my eyes on a frown. "No," I answer honestly.

"I do." He reaches down and cups me, his hot touch making me tense further. "I believe that you're supposed to be here with me, so you advising the concierge that you don't live here just fucks...me...off." He accentuates the last three words clearly and sharply.

He reaches up with his other hand, grasping my nipple between his thumb and forefinger, and starts rolling, elongating my already stiff peak. I close my eyes as I'm sliced in two by waves of pleasure. He slowly inserts two fingers inside me.

"Oh God." I moan, my head falling back, the towel dropped in favor of Jesse's shoulders.

He takes advantage of the access to my neck and bends, pressing his lips to the center of my throat, licking a firm, wet stroke all of the way up to my chin, his fingers sweeping big punishing circles inside me, stretching me. He's preparing me for him.

"I'm going to fuck you until you scream, Ava." His husky voice is playing havoc with my desperation for him. I have every faith he will.

He yanks my face down to meet his eyes. He's in control, but so frenzied, too. I don't know what to make of it. The only thing I seem to be able to concentrate on is the wildfire spreading throughout my body and slamming straight between my thighs on a powerful, determined thud.

"Go and kneel on the end of the bed. Face the headboard," he throws his order at me, and I follow through immediately, taking myself to the bed, kneeling, and resting my backside on my heels.

What has he got planned?

I feel his chest press up against my back and he reaches in front of me, clasping my hands and flattening my palms. Then he guides them to my breasts and circles my palms over my nipples so they lightly skim the tips, the burning friction having me pushing my breasts forward to get better contact. But he just tsks me and pulls my hands farther away. I protest with a disjointed cry.

He pushes his mouth to my ear. "Do you trust me?" he asks.

"With my life," I confirm, a little confused.

I hear him growl in approval. "Have you ever been handcuffed, Ava?"

What?

Before I have a chance to register what is happening, my arms are yanked behind my back and a pair of handcuffs are snapped over my wrists. *Where the fuck did they come from?* I jiggle my wrists, hearing the metal clank.

"Keep your arms still, Ava," he chastises me, letting my hands rest at the top of my bum.

Oh Jesus fucking Christ!

I've never mentally sworn so much. This is so unexpected and has just blown my truth fuck right out of the fucking water! He's never used playthings before. I do and I don't want to stop this, but I can't seem to utter the words.

I still myself and try my hardest to relax my arms while I consider whether he's done this before. I inwardly laugh. Of course he has, you stupid woman. Why didn't I see this coming?

He leans into me. "Good girl." He pulls the pins out of my hair and runs his hands through my long waves, spreading them across my bare back.

I shiver and try to steady my erratic breathing. It's no good. My heart is sprinting in my chest and nothing is going to slow it down. This is unknown territory to me. I have never, not for a minute, allowed myself to consider the prospect of being trussed up, defenseless, and at a man's mercy. It's ironic, really; I'm at Jesse's mercy with or without handcuffs.

He drags his fingertip slowly down the column of my spine to my arse, down the center crease of my bum, and then I feel his arm wrap around my lower stomach, his other hand pressing into my back. "Down you go," he says softly as he eases me down to the mattress. I'm face-planted on the mattress at the end of the bed with Jesse standing behind me. I'm completely exposed and vulnerable.

"Do you realize how fucking amazing you look like this?" His tone is full of approval, but I'll take his word for it. This isn't me at all. "I'm not going to take your arse." He drops a kiss at the small of my back and then I feel his solid cock skim my raw, damp flesh. A surge of relief flies through me. I don't think I could have handled that on top of the handcuffs.

And then he's pushing at my opening.

He grips my hips harshly, making me jerk. "Don't move," he grits through a clenched jaw, and I force myself to still. I feel him enter me, and I instinctively tense around his lush invasion.

"You want it all the way?" His voice is low and dark. I don't recognize it, but I'm desperate for full penetration.

"Yes," I splutter. *Oh God, help me.*

He withdraws his half-submerged arousal, and I moan at the loss of fullness. I need all of him. I push myself back impulsively and then feel the sharp thrash of his hand across my backside.

"Fuck!" I scream. The sting radiates across my cheek, and my shoulders tense against the bed.

He pushes into me but only halfway again. "Mouth," he spits. "Don't move!"

I start gasping as the sting mingles with the delicious semi-invasion. "Jesse!" I plead.

"I know." He skates his palm across my cheek as he withdraws again, and I clench my eyes shut, willing my body to relent to my brain's instructions to relax.

"I can't do this," I whimper into the mattress as I pull at the handcuffs. It's too much and it's come out of the blue. Or has it? I know his business, I know he can be animalistic during sex and I love that, but he can also be romantic, gentle, and loving. Is this the next level?

"You can do it, Ava. Remember who you're with." He powers forward, slamming into me and knocking every ounce of breath from my lungs.

I scream, my throat instantly hoarse.

He pulls out slowly and with control. "What did I say you

would do, Ava?" he asks on a grunt, slamming back into me again.

There is no air in my lungs, and he is striking so deeply, my brain is being blown apart. No cognitive thought is possible, let alone speech.

He repeats the mind-blowing move. "Answer me!" he roars and slaps my arse again.

"Scream! You said I would scream!" I choke on the words as he smashes forward again.

"Are you screaming?"

"Yes!"

He groans and then bangs forward again and again and again, driving me into orbit. "Is that good, baby?"

Oh God, it is! The sting of his slaps and the pounding of his cock have taken me to a whole new level of pleasure.

"Where do you live, Ava?" he shouts on another ferocious blow.

I want to cry. Cry with shock, cry with pain, cry with de-light...cry with absolute mind-numbing pleasure. My brain is in meltdown and my body is wondering what the hell is going on. I can't think or see straight. This is wild, intense, and fuck-ing amazing, but other more unwelcome thoughts are fighting to the front, worming their way into my scrambled brain. How many women has he done this to? How many women have had the pleasure of a retribution fuck? I feel sick.

"Ava! Where the fuck do you live?" He punches out each word. I'm numb. Numb with absolute, intense, mind-blowing bliss. "Don't make me ask again!"

"Here!" I shout. "I live here!"

"Damn fucking right you do." His palm collides with my cheek again, reinforcing his words, before he's clenching my hips again and pulling me back on each and every hard, punishing blow against my body.

Sparks start launching, the pressure at my core set to detonate loudly. I scream in delighted despair. This is way past severe. I really won't be able to walk tomorrow. Is this part of his plan to keep me at home? Because if so, it's going to work.

I feel his palm collide with my arse again, and that last stinging slap rockets me into the most powerful, splintering climax I've ever experienced. I scream... very loudly—an echo around the room, sore throat, despairing, thrilling, satisfied scream.

"Fuck!" Jesse roars. I feel him tense and then the grinding circles of his hips against my backside.

He moans.

I moan.

I'm shaking all over. Proper, uncontrollable, tingling, rippling shakes.

One of my wrists is released from the cuffs, and I pull my arm above my head as he collapses on top of me, flattening me beneath him. He holds himself inside me, jerking and kicking as he grinds around and around, extracting every modicum of pleasure from me.

I'm surprised at myself and my revelation. I'm a filthy, kinky minx! The heady combination of pleasure and soreness has totally knocked me out, and despite my reservations, I'm glad I saw it through. That has just proved, beyond a doubt, I could never deny him.

He lays his arms over mine and dots light kisses at the nape of my neck while moaning and lazily gyrating his hips into me. "Friends?" he whispers softly in my ear, nibbling my lobe. His soft velvet voice is a million miles away from the brutal sex lord I've just encountered.

"Where did that come from?" I ask. I'm still in shock. I've met many levels of his sexual capabilities, but this one has dazed me completely.

He drags my lobe between his teeth. "Tell me we're friends."

"We're friends." I sigh. "Tell me where that came from."

He reaches up and releases my other wrist from the cuffs, the absence of the heavy burden a relief. He slips out of me and flips me over, holding my wrists at either side of my head. I look up at him, waiting for an answer, but it doesn't seem forthcoming. Should I keep my mouth shut?

He eventually speaks. "I like hearing you scream." He grins. "And I like knowing that I'm the one making you scream."

Mission accomplished. "I have a sore throat." I pout.

He drops a kiss on my lips. "Are you hungry?"

"No." I'm really not, and I'm not getting out of this bed either. It's not even eight o'clock.

"I'll go and get you some water and then we can snuggle, deal?" he asks, circling his nose with mine.

"Deal."

He gives me a light kiss before peeling himself away from me, and I crawl up the bed, settling on my front and reveling in his scent all over the sheets. I'm absolutely bushed and my arse stings a little. If I weren't so satisfied and sated, I would be enormously pissed off that he has just gotten the upper hand. He doesn't know it, but he has just derailed my evening plans. I'm way too tired to pursue my truth fuck now.

I roll over onto my back, stare up at the ceiling, and battle away the unwanted thoughts that are raiding my exhausted mind. How many women? I've maintained that I really don't want to know, but unreasonable curiosity is making its unwanted presence in my mind hard to ignore. If I weren't so shattered, I might give that direction of thought more attention, but I am, so I close my eyes and quietly thank Jesse for draining me of any energy to pursue it.

"Baby, have I fucked you unconscious?" The bed dips and I feel his warm, hard body flank me. I drag myself onto my side.

"Strawberry?" He brushes the cool, plump fruit across my bottom lip, and I open to take a bite. "Good?"

"Very," I say around my mouthful of delicious, ripe strawberry. I'm definitely hungry for these.

He starts grazing on his lip, his eyes darting around the room. Oh no. What's he thinking? "You didn't mean it, did you? When you said you didn't live here?"

I pause midchew and look at the worried face in front of me. His frown line is slowly creeping across his brow. "You want me to live with you, but you won't even tell me how old you are." I raise my eyebrows. He has got to see the weirdness in this. There's a whole lot of other stuff as well, stuff that I'm trying my hardest to ignore—and failing—but I'll stick to this minor detail for now.

"What difference does my age make?" he asks as he pops a strawberry into his own mouth.

I shake my head, watching him chew. "Okay," I swallow. "What do I tell my parents when they ask about your profession?"

The cogs commence and he shrugs, slipping another strawberry past my lips. "Tell them I own a hotel."

I accept his offering but keep talking. I'm not going down easily here. "What if they would like to see this hotel?" I mumble around my munching.

"Then they can see it." He smiles. "*You* thought it was a hotel.'

I scowl at him. "You had me escorted around the premises by staff and locked me up in your office so no one could talk to me. Are you going to do the same with my mum and dad?"

"I'll show them around on a quiet day," he answers swiftly.

Has he thought about this already? I can't believe I'm talking about the possibility of him meeting my parents. "What if they want to stay at this hotel?" I fire back. "They live in Newquay, so they'll be staying in a hotel if they come to visit."

He starts laughing. "Should I put them in the communal room?"

I jab him in the stomach, which only serves to increase his amusement. "I'm glad you find my turmoil so funny." I grab a strawberry and shove it in my mouth.

He recovers from his laughing fit and turns serious eyes onto mine. "Ava, it would seem you're looking for any excuse to get out of this." He reaches over and drags his finger across my bottom lip. "If your parents ask how old I am, then make an age up, however old you want me to be, I'll be that. If they come to visit, then they will stay here. There are many spare bedrooms, all with bathrooms. Stop fighting it. Now, is that all?" He arches an expectant brow at me.

"Are you going to trample my parents?"

"If they get in my way," he says seriously.

I have a mental meltdown on the spot. I need to avoid the meeting-my-parents scenario for as long as possible—maybe even forever.

"Why were the police at The Manor?" I shoot at him.

He rolls his eyes. "I told you, some idiot is playing silly games."

"What sort of silly games?"

"Ava, it's nothing for you to worry about. End of." He presents me with another strawberry, and I reluctantly take it. He's trying to stop me from asking irritating questions by keeping my mouth full.

"What about this mystery woman?"

"She's still a mystery," he answers swiftly and shortly.

"So you asked Clive?"

"No, Ava, I haven't had time." He's very annoyed. He bloody has asked Clive, and he's also asked him to keep his mouth shut. I need to be cute here, too. I scowl at him, but he continues. "When can I take you shopping?"

What?

He must catch my alarmed face because his irritated expression softens immediately. "I owe you a dress, and with the anniversary party coming up, I thought we could kill two birds with one stone."

"I have plenty of dresses," I grumble. A shopping trip with Jesse is at the top of my *avoid-to-do* list. I'll walk out of the store looking like an Eskimo.

"Are you going to defy me at every turn today, lady?" He narrows his greens on me, and I give him my own little scowl in return, but I'm too exhausted to quarrel. Instead, I move myself into his chest and snuggle up to him. He might be an arrogant, challenging arse, but I'm completely in love with him and there is nothing I can do about it.

CHAPTER TEN

I peel my eyes open and find myself tucked closely into Jesse's chest. It's not quite daylight, which means it's very early, and Jesse isn't awake, so it's definitely before five. My brain snaps awake immediately, and I begin the meticulous task of freeing myself from his body without disturbing him. It's hard. He seems to hold on to me as tight in his sleep as he does when he's awake.

I tentatively edge myself away from him, pausing and tensing every time he shifts or sighs in his sleep. My body is rigid as I creep my way to the edge of the bed, and once I'm free, I release the breath that I've been holding and look down at my handsome man with two days' worth of stubble. I want to jump straight back into bed with him, but I resist. What I have planned spurs me to leave him sleeping peacefully while I rootle quietly through my bag for my phone.

It's five o'clock. Shit! Okay, I've got to be quick or he'll be waking soon to drag me around the streets of London on one of his torturous marathons. I creep about the bedroom like a naked burglar, retrieving my stash from the wooden trunk and easing out the contents. The bag crumples, and I grit my teeth, freezing in place as he rolls onto his back on a moan.

I remain like a statue until I'm sure that he's settled, then make my way over to the bed, padding quietly across the thick carpet.

I gently grasp his wrist and tug it up over his head to the wooden headboard. I struggle; his arm is heavy, but I manage to get him in position and slip the handcuff over his wrist, then attach it to one of the wooden bars of the headboard. I stand back and admire my handiwork, feeling rather pleased with myself. Even if he does wake up now, he's not going anywhere.

I collect the other set of cuffs and make my way around the other side of the bed. I have to kneel on the bed to reach for his arm, but I'm not so worried about waking him now that I have at least one arm secured, although this will work better if he can't lay any hands on me.

I maneuver his arm cautiously above his head and fasten the other handcuff around the wrist of his damaged hand. It's looking much better, but I'm mindful that this could hurt if he fights against them.

I'm smug. That was way easier than I thought, and he's still dead to the world. I practically dance my way back over to the bag and finish my preparations before slipping into some stunning black lace underwear that I picked up on my last-minute shopping exhibition.

Oh God, he's going to go spare. I make my way back over to my sprawled, restrained, naked god and climb up to straddle his hips. He stirs, and I smile when I feel him begin to harden under me. I sit patiently and wait.

It's not long before his beautiful lashes start flickering and his lids start to twitch. His eyes open and find mine immediately, his morning erection now in full firmness beneath me.

"Hey, baby." His throat is husky as he squints and gains focus. I run my eyes down his torso, his muscles bunched and taut from the position of his arms. "Hey." I smile brightly and watch closely as he gains full consciousness and then moves his arms, clanging the metal on the wooden headboard. The abrupt yank on his wrists has his eyes snapping wide open, and I hold my breath, watching his sleepy face as he frowns and looks up over his head.

He jiggles his arms again. "What the fuck?" His voice is still hoarse. He swings his eyes to mine. They are all wide and stunned. "Ava, why the fuck am I handcuffed to the bed?"

I fight the grin from my face. "I'm introducing a new kind of fuck to our relationship, Jesse," I state calmly.

"Mouth!" He rattles his wrists again and takes another look at his restrained hands. I see realization dawn on his handsome face as he turns his eyes back to me. "These are not my handcuffs," he says warily.

"No, and there are two pairs. I'm sure you've noticed." I can't believe how calm I'm being. I'm crapping it. "So, like I was saying, I've invented a new fuck, and guess what?" I ask with a little excitement in my voice.

He doesn't scorn me this time. Instead, he arches a nervous brow. "What?"

Oh, I could cuddle him. "I thought of it just for you." I grind myself onto him teasingly and his chest expands, his jaw tensing. "I love you."

"Oh, fucking hell," he groans.

I place my hands on his chest and lower myself down to his face. He watches me as I descend, his eyes shimmering in anticipation and short pants of breath escaping his parted lips. "How old are you?" I murmur, brushing my lips lightly over his.

He lifts his head to try and make better contact, but I pull back. He scowls, dropping his head back down. "Thirty-three," he pants, and then moans in despair as I grind down again.

I drop my mouth to his neck and nibble my way up to his ear, licking and lapping as I go. "Tell me the truth," I whisper, and then bite his lobe gently.

His cheeks puff out. "Holy shit! Ava, I am not telling you how old I am."

I sit up on his chest and shake my head at him. "Why?"

His lips form a straight, annoyed line. "Undo the cuffs, I want to touch you."

Ah!

"No," I toss back at him, grinding down again, rubbing him in just the right spot. I'm not unaffected myself, but I have to keep my control here.

"Fuck!" He yanks his hands and jerks his legs slightly, causing me to jolt forward. "Remove the fucking cuffs, Ava!"

I steady myself. "No!"

"For fuck's sake!" he roars. "Don't play games with me, lady!"

Oh, he's angry. "I don't think you're in a position to tell me what to do," I remind him coolly. He stills, but he's heaving long, heavy, and very frustrated breaths. "Are you going to stop being unreasonable and tell me?"

His eyes narrow good and proper. "No!"

Oh, he really is a stubborn arse. "Fine," I say calmly. I fall down onto his chest and clasp his face in my palms, and he gazes up at me, waiting for what I'm going to do. I plant my mouth on his and moan as he parts his lips, his tongue darting out, seeking mine.

I pull back.

He growls in frustration.

Shifting off of his lap, I wickedly give his erection a long, slow lick straight up his shaft.

"Ohhhh, fucking hell," he moans despairingly. "Ava!"

I smile, sitting on my heels between his legs before collecting my weapon of mass destruction and holding it up in front of him. His head lifts, his eyes nearly falling out when he registers what I'm clasping.

"Oh, no! Ava, I swear to God!" He throws his head back on the bed. "You can't do this to me. *Fuck!*"

I smile and flick the on switch of the diamanté embellished vibrator that Jesse took an immediate dislike to on our shopping trip in Camden. He really doesn't want to share me with anyone or anything. The vibrating kicks in and he moans, thrashing his head to the side.

This is going to kill him. "Wow!" I blurt, getting the full force of the vibrator in my hand. "This is one powerful machine," I muse to myself.

His eyes are clenched shut, the muscles of his jaw ticking. "Ava, remove the fucking cuffs!" He grates the words through his clenched teeth.

I couldn't have hoped for a better response. I will get his age out of him, even if I have to keep him here all morning. In fact, I hope he holds out for a little while. I think I might enjoy this.

I turn the vibrator off, placing it down on the bed, and he slowly opens his eyes. I wait for them to fall on mine. "Are you going to tell me how old you are?" I ask, completely composed.

"No, I'm not."

"Why are you being such a stubborn arse?"

"Am I not your stubborn god?" he asks on a small smirk.

He won't be smirking in a minute. I lift myself to my knees and hold his eyes while I tuck my thumbs into the top of my lace knickers. "This morning you're an arse." I slowly draw my knickers down my thighs to my knees, and he follows their path with lust-filled eyes. I can see the pulse in his erection beating regularly. "Wouldn't you like to help me out here?" My voice is seductive and soft as I slowly lick my fingers and slide them down my front to my thighs.

His cheeks puff out again as he watches my hand slip between my legs. "Ava, undo these cuffs now so I can fuck you until you're seeing stars." His voice is calm, but I know he is anything but.

I slip my fingers over my clitoris and brush gently on a little gasp of air. It's not Jesse, but it still feels good. "Tell me."

"No." He rests his head back. "Remove the cuffs."

I shake my head at my stubborn man and drop my hands to either side of his hips.

Stars? Oh, he'll be the one seeing stars. I rest my lips on his lower stomach next to his scar and circle my tongue in a few slow, sweeping laps before crawling up his body and kicking off my knickers on my way. I look down at him, but he refuses to open his eyes, so I kiss the corner of his mouth. It works. His head turns instinctively and his lips part as he takes my mouth. I press down on his groin, my wetness causing me to slide up and down with ease.

"Oh Jesus, Ava, please."

"Tell me." I bite his bottom lip and drag it through my teeth, but he just shakes his head lightly, so I break our fused mouths. "Fine, have it your way." I rise and reposition myself back between his thighs and collect my weapon of mass destruction from the bed.

"Put it down." His tone is full of warning, but I ignore him. I flick it on again, saying nothing. "Ava, I swear to God!" The anger is returning. I hold his eyes as I slowly take the vibrator down to the apex of my thighs. "Don't!" He throws his head back in total misery.

I can't believe he's putting himself through this. He can stop it in a heartbeat. Damn it, I want him to look at me. I swiftly change my destination and hold the vibrator out, slowly skimming it over his beautiful, beating cock. He jerks erratically. The bed shakes.

"Fuck! Ava, fucking fuck, fuck, fuck!" he yells, but his eyes are still firmly closed. I can't make him look at me, but I'll make damn sure he hears me. I return the vibrator to myself and rest the drumming head at the top of my clitoris.

Holy fucking shit!

I gasp, my knees shaking, as I jerk at the full force of its power stabbing me straight at my core. "Ohhhhhhh Goddddd!" I moan, and then increase the pressure slightly. That feels really nice.

His eyes snap open, his breathing all over the place, and a heavy shimmer of sweat has formed a river in the crease on his forehead. His face is pure torture. I almost feel guilty.

"Ava, all of your pleasure comes from me."

"Not today," I muse, closing my eyes on a sigh.

"Ava!" he barks, clanging the cuffs against the headboard. "Fuck! Ava, you're pushing it!"

I keep my eyes closed. "Hmmm," I hum, jerking slightly as the consistent vibrations tickle the tip of my clit.

"I'm thirty-seven! For fuck's sake, woman, I'm thirty-fucking-seven!"

My eyes fly open, and my mouth drops open in shock, the vibrator falling to the bed. He told me? It bloody worked! I want to do a little jig on the bed and scream to the heavens in glory. Why didn't I think of this before? I'm not going to try and kid myself that I will get away with this again—he'll probably sleep with one eye open for the rest of his life, so perhaps I should take advantage of his vulnerable state and pump him for some more answers, like where that scar came from, how many women there have been, and what the hell the police are doing at The Manor. Oh, and the mystery woman and Sarah...

He glares at me, and I'm suddenly yanked straight out of my mental celebration dance and right into panic.

"Take...the...fucking...cuffs...off." He emphasizes each word slowly on a hiss.

Oh bloody hell. In all of my meticulous planning and execution of the truth fuck, I hadn't given a second thought to the aftermath. He's seething mad, and now I've got to release him. What is he going to do? I sprint through my options, but it doesn't take long because there are only two: release him and take my punishment or leave him handcuffed to the bed forever.

I watch him with wide, cautious eyes as he watches me with dark, furious ones. What am I going to do? I place my hands on his strong thighs and inch myself up his body until my face is hovering above his. I need to lighten his mood.

Smoothing my hands through his hair, I drop my lips onto his. "I still love you," I mumble around my kiss. Maybe it's the reassurance he needs. Eleven years is nothing, really. What's the problem? He's still my handsome, roguish god.

He moans as I give his mouth some extra special treatment. "Good, now take the cuffs off."

I kiss my way to his neck and nuzzle. "Are you mad at me?"

"Fucking crazy mad, Ava!"

I sit up and look at him. He really is crazy mad, and now I'm shitting myself. I give him my best cheeky grin. "Can't you be crazy in love?"

"I'm that, too. Remove the cuffs." He looks at me expectantly.

I shift to ease myself up and shudder when his arousal falls to my opening, the throbbing, wet head slipping over my entrance.

He bucks. "Damn it, Ava! Take the fucking cuffs off!" He's completely deranged and now I know…I'm not taking the cuffs off. I get off the bed and stand at the side, looking at him rage.

"What are you going to do?" I ask nervously.

"Take them off." He looks almost murderous.

"Not until you tell me what you're going to do."

His breathing is heavy, his chest expanding. "I'm going to fuck you until you beg me to stop, and then you're going to run fourteen miles." He raises his head and stabs me with ferocious greens. "And we won't be stopping for a muscle rub or a coffee break!"

What? I'll take the fuck, but I'm not running anywhere, except out of his penthouse. He already made me do ten miles yesterday. That will be his way of regaining control, making me do something that I really don't want to do, and I definitely don't want to run fourteen miles.

"I don't want to go for a run," I state as calmly as I can. "You can't make me."

His eyebrows jump up. "Ava, you need to remember who holds the power in this relationship."

I back away in disgust and then flick my eyes to his restrained wrists before returning them to him. "I'm sorry, who has the power?" My sarcasm only serves to notch his fury level up a little more—if that was possible.

"Ava, I'm warning you!"

"I can't believe you're being so cranky over this. It was okay for you to handcuff me!"

"I was in control!"

That's stupid! "You're a power freak!" I shout back, and he wriggles a little more. "I'm going to get a shower." I stomp off.

"I'm only a power freak with you!" he yells at my back. "Ava!"

I slam the bathroom door and remove my bra. The arrogant, power obsessed, controlling arse! My delight in the fact that my truth fuck worked has been well and truly trampled. I throw myself in the shower and listen to my name being yelled repeatedly. If I weren't so affronted, I would laugh. He really doesn't like not being able to touch me, and he really, really doesn't like relinquishing power.

I shower and brush my teeth at a leisurely rate. It's still super early. I have plenty of time.

When I walk back into the bedroom, I find Jesse has calmed

down slightly, but there is definitely still a hint of anger in his expression as he looks up at me.

"Baby, come and free me, please."

His sudden turn in mood has me suspicious and on my guard. I know his game, and I'm not falling for it. As soon as I free him, he'll be on me like a lion before manhandling me into my running kit and dragging me around the streets of London. I'm not denying that I would love to have him all over me right this minute, but I'm not hanging about to be tortured by fourteen miles. Unfortunately, they come as a package deal.

I sit myself in front of the floor-length mirror to start drying my hair, glancing at the reflection every now and again, seeing him watching me. But he just scowls and throws his head back like a brooding schoolboy whenever I catch him.

I apply my makeup and smother myself in cocoa butter, and when I put on the cream lace underwear set that Jesse bought me, I hear him whimper. I smile smugly to myself. I may as well. I don't know how long I'm going to be holding this power. I slip my white ruffle blouse on with my black, slim-fit trousers and black heels.

I'm ready. Walking over to my handcuffed man, I lean down to drop a long, lingering kiss onto his parted lips. I don't know why I'm doing this. My bravado is commendable.

He sighs and brings his knees up so the soles of his feet are flat on the bed as I reach down and wrap my hand around his still-erect cock. I'm seriously in for it when he catches me.

He jerks. "Ava. I love you so fucking much, but if you don't undo these cuffs, I'm going to fucking strangle you!" His voice is a mixture of pleasure and pain.

I smile around his mouth and give him a chaste kiss on the lips before leaning down and kissing my way from his chest to his solid cock, and then all the way to the tip, finishing off with a little swirl before taking him deep into my mouth.

"Ava, please!" he moans.

I release him and retrieve the key to the handcuffs from the chest of drawers. As I walk back over, he lets out a relieved breath. I don't know why; I'm not freeing him completely. I undo his damaged hand and it falls limply to the bed. A pang of guilt assaults me as he gingerly flexes his fist to try and get some life back into it. Making my way over to the chest, I place the key back on top.

"What are you doing?" he asks on a frown.

"Where is your phone?"

"Why?" The confusion in his face is clear.

"You'll need it. Where is it?"

"It's in my suit jacket. Ava, just give me the key." He's losing his patience again.

I scan the room and spot his jacket on the floor where he obviously dumped it last night before he pounced on me in the bathroom. I find his phone in the inside pocket and place it on the bedside table, just out of reach. I don't want him calling for assistance before I make my escape.

Fetching my bag, I stride out of the bedroom, leaving him a massive mess of unexploded male. I am so going to cop it later, but at least I released one hand. It might be his damaged one, but he'll be able to sort himself out ... if he doesn't grip too hard.

CHAPTER ELEVEN

Hello, flower." Patrick comes out of his office as I take my seat. "You're bright and early this morning." He sits on the edge of my desk and performs his usual snort of disgust as the desk performs its usual creak of protest. "What have you got to tell me?'

"Not much." I turn on my computer. "I have a meeting with Mr. Van Der Haus at lunchtime to go over my designs."

"Oh, good. What about Mr. Ward? Have you heard from him yet?"

I feel my face flood with heat as I turn to my computer. "Urhhh, no, I'm not sure when he's back from his business trip," I reply, mentally praying he leaves it right there.

"It's been nearly two weeks, hasn't it? I wonder what's keeping him," he asks, and I suspect my boss is frowning but I can't look to confirm it.

I cough. "I really don't know."

Patrick rises from my desk on a long creak. "Oh, by the way, our Sally is poorly. She won't be in today," he says as he makes his way back into his office.

Sally is ill? That's not like her. Oh! It was her second date last night. Either it went very well and she's pulling a sicky to cavort in bed all day with Mr. Mystery, or it went very badly and she's pulled a sicky to mope in bed all day with a box of tissues. I guiltily suspect it's the latter. Poor Sal.

I sag in my chair on a long exhale and then jump when I hear "Angel" seeping from my bag. Oh dear Lord. He's obviously freed himself. I'm not answering it. It rings off and immediately rings again, but it's my normal ringtone this time. I scoop my phone from my bag and take Miss Quinn's call.

"Good morning, Miss Quinn," I greet cheerfully.

"Hi, Ava. Please, it's Ruth. I was just checking in. Have you managed to get the ball rolling yet?"

"Yes, I've prepared a schedule of fees for my services, Ruth, and I've drafted a few ideas to send over."

"Brilliant." She's so enthusiastic. "I'll look forward to receiving them. Where do we go from there?"

"Well, if you are happy with my fee structure and draft ideas, then we can start putting together some firm designs."

"Great, I'm so excited!"

I smile. That much is obvious. "Okay, I'll get the fee structure and drafts over to you by the end of play today. Bye, Ruth."

"Thanks, Ava." She hangs up, and I immediately set about scanning the designs into my computer. I love working with people who are as passionate about their home as I am.

* * *

As ten o'clock hits, I've been in the office for three hours and I've got mountains of work done.

I swing around in my chair to go and make a coffee, nearly having a seizure when I'm confronted with my arrogant god, who's looking down at me with raised, cunning eyebrows. His handsome face spreads into his customary roguish grin. I'm instantly on high alert, and he looks bloody glorious in his gray suit and pale blue shirt, open at the collar with no tie. He has two days' worth of stubble. My eyes are delighted, but my mind is racing with uncertainties.

"How lovely to see you, Ava," he says smoothly as he reaches forward and puts his hand out. His jacket sleeve rides up, revealing his gold Rolex.

Shit!

I go stone-cold when I see a collection of red welts around his wrist, his Rolex doing nothing to conceal them. It's his damaged hand, too. I flick my startled eyes up to him and he nods in acknowledgment. I mentally kick my stupid self around the office. I've hurt him. I feel hideous. I don't blame him for being so furious.

I place my hand in his, but I don't grip it. I don't want to hurt him any more. "I'm so sorry," I whisper the words quietly, full of remorse. My unreasonable desire to know his age has marked him. I really am going to be in for it.

"I know you are," he answers coldly.

"Ah! Mr. Ward." Patrick's cheerful voice invades my ears as he approaches my desk from his office. I release my hold of Jesse. "How very good to see you. I was just asking Ava if she had heard from you."

"Mr. Peterson, how are you?" Jesse gives him his full-on, melt-worthy smile, usually reserved for women.

"Very good, how was your business trip?" Patrick asks.

Jesse's eyes swing to mine briefly before returning to Patrick's. "I secured my assets," he replies, completely composed. "Did you receive the deposit I made?"

Patrick's face lights up. "Yes, absolutely. Thank you." I notice he doesn't advise Mr. Ward that it is far too much for an initial upfront payment.

"Good, as I said before, I'm eager to get things moving. My *unexpected* trip has put us a bit behind."

"Of course, I'm sure Ava will sort you out." Patrick places his hand on my shoulder affectionately, and Jesse's eyes fall straight onto it.

"I'm sure she will," he muses quietly, his eyes still firmly fixed on Patrick's hand.

He's sixty years old, silver haired, and about five stone overweight. Surely Jesse can't be threatened by my big, cuddly bear of a boss?

He shoots his eyes back to Patrick. "I was going to ask Ava if she would like to join me for some brunch so we can go over a few things. You don't mind."

That last part was definitely not a question. He's trampling.

"Be my guest," Patrick chirps happily. I notice he doesn't ask me.

"Actually, I have an appointment at lunchtime," I pipe up. I point to the page in my new diary, which is absent of the big, black, permanent marker lines that Jesse put through every day of my last diary. I want to delay this confrontation for as long as possible. I'm not at all comfortable with the wily look all over his handsome face. But then he catches a glimpse of my new diary and he frowns, his jaw ticking wildly.

Yes, I replaced it!

"That's not until noon," Jesse points out, and I cringe. "I won't keep you too long," he adds on a husky, promising voice that also harbors a bit of threat.

"There you go!" Patrick sings as he walks off to his office. "It was nice to see you, Mr. Ward."

I sit tapping my front tooth frantically with my nail while I try to think of a way out of this. There is none, and even if I had a valid reason, I would only be delaying the inevitable. Looking up at the man I love beyond measure, I am literally trembling in my heels.

"Shall we?" Jesse asks, as he puts his hands in his pockets. I collect my phone from my desk and stuff it in my bag, along with my file for the Life Building. I'll need to head straight to the Royal Park for my meeting with Mikael after my *meeting* with Jesse.

He holds the door open for me, and Tom comes barreling through before I have a chance to exit. His eyes go all wide and shocked when he clocks who's holding the door.

"Mr. Ward!" he splutters. It's ridiculous for him to be addressing Jesse so formally. He's been out drinking and dancing with him.

"Tom." Jesse nods, all businesslike.

"I'm just going for a business meeting with Mr. Ward." I tilt my head to the side and flash a telling look. I hear Jesse laugh lightly.

"Oh, I see. A *business* meeting, huh?" Tom chuckles. I could kick him in the shins And when he performs an over-the-top wink, I decide that the next time I see Tom, I *will* kick him in the shins. Exiting hastily onto the street, I'm relieved to be away from the office and the possibility of being ratted out, but nervous that I am now pretty much at Jesse's mercy. I'm not deluded enough to believe that just because we're in public, he won't have me pinned to the nearest wall as soon as he can.

We walk along, side by side, until we hit Piccadilly. I don't know where we're going, but I keep up with him. He makes no attempt to take my hand and he doesn't speak. I'm getting more apprehensive by the second. I glance up at him and find his face is completely straight and he doesn't return my gaze, although I know he knows that I'm looking at him.

"Excuse me, have you got the time?" a mature businesswoman asks Jesse.

He takes his hand from his pocket and looks at his watch. I wince at the sight of the marks on his wrist. His hand is still bruised from the beating he gave his car, and I've added to it.

"It's ten fifteen." He flashes his smile reserved only for women, and she pools on the pavement in front of him.

I'm spiked with immense possessiveness as she gushes a thank-you. She's probably closer to Jesse in age than I am, the brazen hussy. You can't possibly tell me she hasn't got a phone she could check, and why didn't she ask the bald, sweaty, over-weight businessman in front? Rolling my eyes, I wait for Jesse to take the initiative and lead on, and after he's spent a few moments blasting the woman with his knockout smile, ensuring she gets the full-on experience, he carries on his way, me following. As I look back, I see the woman glancing over her shoulder. How desperate and unashamed can someone be? But then I laugh to myself. I'm that desperate when it comes to Jesse, and I'm also completely unashamed.

We cross the road and approach The Ritz, and I'm stunned when the door is opened for us. Jesse signals for me to enter. We're having brunch at The Ritz?

I say nothing as he leads me to the restaurant and we're seated in the most obscenely regal space. This isn't Jesse at all, and it certainly isn't me.

"We'll have the Eggs Benedict twice, both on granary; a cap-puccino, extra shot, no chocolate; and a strong black coffee. Thank you." Jesse hands the menu to the waiter.

"Certainly, sir." He picks up my fancy, fabric napkin and lays it across my lap and repeats the same carefully executed move on Jesse before backing away from the table. I gaze around at the affluent surroundings, full of well-bred, wealthy folk. I feel un-comfortable.

"How is your day going?" he asks casually, with no hint of any emotion in his tone. This just increases my unease further, the question dragging me back to his dark presence across the swanky table. He removes the napkin from his lap and places it on the table, his face expressionless as he regards me.

What the hell should I say? It's not even ten thirty and I'm already having a pretty exclusive day. So far, I've discovered his age, used a vibrator, handcuffed him to the bed and left him there, and now I'm having a late breakfast in The Ritz. They're certainly not your usual daily happenings.

"I'm not sure," I answer honestly, because I have a feeling there are going to be a few more exclusives I can add to that list.

His eyes lower so his super lashes fan his cheekbones. "Shall I tell you how my day is going?"

"If you like," I whisper. My voice is full of nervousness. I'm not even confident that he wouldn't cause a scene in the most posh hotel in London in front of the most posh people in London.

He sits back in his chair and hammers me with his potent green gaze. "Well, my morning run was waylaid by a challenging little temptress, who handcuffed me to our bed and tortured me for information. She then abandoned me, leaving me helpless and in desperate need of her." He starts fiddling with the fork at his place setting, and I wilt under his stare. He takes a deep breath. "I eventually got hold of my phone, which she left just…out…of…reach…" He pinches his thumb and index finger together. "And then waited for a member of my staff to come and free me. I ran fourteen miles in my personal best time to expel some of the pent-up frustrations that she presented me with, and now I'm looking at her beautiful face and wanting to bend her over this wonderfully dressed table and fuck her into next week."

I gasp at his crass words spoken with no concern in the middle of The Ritz. Oh God, what must John think of me? I hope he laughed. He seems to find Jesse's reactions and behavior toward me quite amusing.

The waiter places our coffees down, and we both nod a thank-you before he backs away again.

I pick up my fancy—probably solid—silver spoon and start slowly stirring my coffee. "You have had quite an action-packed morning." I glance up nervously and find him fighting a grin. He wants to laugh, but he wants to be angry with me, too, and it makes me feel so much better.

He eventually sighs. "Ava, don't ever do that to me again."

"You were crazy mad." I breathe on a long, relieved exhale, disintegrating on my yellow throne.

"I was way, way past crazy mad, Ava." He reaches up and starts circling his temples, as if trying to rid himself of the memory.

"Why?"

He pauses midrub. "Because I couldn't get to you." He says it like I'm stupid. He must catch my look of confusion because he moves his fingers to his forehead and rests his elbows on the table. "The thought of not being able to reach you actually made me panic."

"I was in the room!" I blurt a bit too loudly. I take a quick glance around to make sure I've not drawn any attention from the posh clientele.

He scowls at me. "You weren't in the room when you left!"

I lean across the table. "I left because you threatened me." This is most definitely not a conversation for the plushness of The Ritz.

"Well, that's because you made me crazy mad." He widens his eyes at me. "When did you get those handcuffs?" he asks accusingly as his palms hit the table, the bang silencing the other diners surrounding us.

I sit back in my throne and wait for them to continue with their conversation. "When I left work yesterday. You kind of pissed all over my plan with your retribution fuck," I grumble moodily.

"Watch your mouth. I pissed on your plan?" he asks incredulously. "Ava, let me tell you, nowhere in my plan was it written that you would have me restrained and at your mercy. So it is *you* who pissed all over *my* plan."

We both cease all speaking of plans, retribution fucks, and handcuffs when the waiter approaches with our food. He places it in front of me first and then Jesse, swiveling the plates around so the presentation—which looks more like art—is at its best position for us to admire before we attack it with our knife and fork. I smile my thanks.

"Is that all, sir?" the waiter asks Jesse.

"Yes, thank you."

The waiter removes himself from the table and leaves us to resume our inappropriate conversation.

I sink my knife into my dish. It looks too good to eat. "You should know your temptress is extremely pleased with herself," I say thoughtfully as I wrap my lips around the most delicious piece of granary toast, topped with smoked salmon and hollandaise sauce.

"I bet she is." He raises his eyebrows. "Does she know how crazy in love with her I am?"

I melt on a sigh. I'm in The Ritz, eating the most incredible food and looking across the table at the most devastatingly handsome man I've ever laid eyes on—my devastatingly handsome man. All mine. I'm back to basking in the sun on Central Jesse Cloud Nine. "I think she does."

He turns his attention back to his dish. "She had better not just think."

"She knows."

"Good."

"What's the problem, anyway?" I ask. "Thirty-seven is nothing."

His eyes flick to mine. He looks almost embarrassed. "I don't know. You're in your midtwenties and I'm in my late thirties."

"So?" I watch him closely. He really does have a complex about his age. "It bothers you more than it does me."

"Maybe." He fights a smile from his lips. I can see he's relieved at my lack of concern. I shake my head, returning to my dish. My arrogant playboy has an insecurity, but I love him all the more for it.

We eat in a comfortable silence, the waiter checking if everything is to our satisfaction at regular intervals. When we're done, he clears our plates swiftly and Jesse asks for the bill.

"So, when are we going dress shopping then?" he asks before taking a sip of his coffee.

I can't prevent the long exasperated breath of air escaping my mouth. I'd forgotten about that, and I know that if I defy him on this, I'll be promptly ejected from Central Jesse Cloud Nine. I shrug. "Friday lunch?'

His frown line jumps into position. "That's cutting it a bit fine, isn't it?"

"I'll find something." I finish the most scrumptious coffee I've ever had.

"Put me in your diary for Friday afternoon...all afternoon."

"What?" I feel my brow knit.

He takes a wad of notes out of his pocket and puts five twenties in the leather-bound book that the waiter has just left. One hundred pounds for breakfast? That's my new dress!

"Make Mr. Ward a Friday afternoon appointment. Say, one-ish." His greens are dancing with delight. "We'll go dress shopping and there will be no rush to get ready for the party."

"I can't book out my whole afternoon for one appointment!" I splutter in disbelief. Mr. Unreasonable is back.

"You can and you will. I'm paying him enough." He stands and makes his way to my side of the table. "You need to tell Patrick that you're living with me. I'm not pussyfooting around him for much longer."

I stand, taking the hand he has offered, and let him lead me out of the restaurant. No, he won't pussyfoot around. He'll just keep trampling him instead. "It will make things awkward," I try to reason. "He won't be impressed, Jesse. And I don't want him to think that I'm slacking instead of working if I should have any *business* meetings with you."

"I couldn't give a fuck what he thinks. If he doesn't like it, then you'll retire," he says, marching on, dragging me behind him.

Retire? I love my job, and I love Patrick, too. "You're going to trample him, aren't you?" I say warily. My man is like a rhinoceros.

The valet hands him his car keys and Jesse slips him a fifty. A fifty? Just for parking and returning his car? Granted, it is a very nice car, but still.

He turns into me, grazes his palm down my cheek and circles his nose on mine. "Are we friends?" His minty freshness hits me like a bulldozer.

"Yes," I submit, but judging by the last few minutes' conversation, I don't expect we will be for long. "Thank you for breakfast."

He smiles. "Anytime. Where are you going now?"

"The Royal Park."

"Near Lancaster Gate? I'll take you." He presses his lips hard onto mine and pushes his hips gently forward.

I gasp.

He can't thrust me outside The Ritz! I hear him laugh at my shock before he pulls me toward his car. The valet opens the door for me, and I smile sweetly before climbing in. After Jesse has slid in behind the wheel and given my knee a quick squeeze, he roars off into the midmorning London traffic at his usual alarming speed. "What am I going to tell Patrick?" I turn and look at him. Oh, he's so handsome.

"What, about us?" He flicks his eyes to me. His frown line is firmly in place.

"No, about our business breakfast. What have we discussed?"

He shrugs. "Tell him we've agreed fees and that I want you at The Manor on Friday to finalize the designs."

"You make it sound so simple." I sigh, sitting back in my seat and looking across the parks.

He places his hand on my knee and squeezes. "Baby, you make it sound so complicated."

* * *

Jesse screeches up outside the Royal Park and waves a delighted-looking valet away when he approaches to collect the car.

"I'll see you at home." He wraps his palm around the back of my neck and yanks me over to him, taking his time to say his good-bye. I let him, with no concern for the valet standing close by, staring longingly at the DBS.

"Six-ish," I confirm as he kisses the corner of my mouth.

He grins. "Ish."

I know it's not the right time to approach the subject, but it's going to eat away at me for the rest of the day. He can't be serious, surely? "I can't retire at twenty-six."

He sits back in his seat, the stupid, sodding cogs kicking into action. It worries me instantly. He *is* serious. "I told you, I don't like sharing you."

"That's stupid," I blurt, which was obviously wrong, judging by the scowl that has just flashed across his face.

"Don't call me stupid, Ava."

"I wasn't calling you stupid. I was calling your ambitious intention stupid," I argue quietly. "I'm never going to leave you." I reach over and slide my hand across the back of his neck. Does he need reassurance on this?

His lip disappears between his teeth as he stares at the steering wheel of the DBS. "That doesn't stop people from trying to take you. I can't let that happen." He turns tortured eyes onto me. It punches a massive hole in my stomach.

"What people?"

He shakes his head. "No specific people. I don't deserve you, Ava, but by some fucking miracle, I've got you. I'll protect you fiercely—eliminate any threat." His hands slide over the steering wheel, his knuckles turning white from his harsh grip. "Okay, we need to stop talking about this because I'm feeling a bit violent."

I sit and look across at my beautiful, neurotic control freak and wish I could give him the reassurance that he needs. My words won't ever work. I'm beginning to realize that now.

I undo my belt and crawl across the car to straddle his lap. Sod the valet. I pull Jesse's face up to mine, cupping his cheeks and lowering my lips to his. He moans and slides his hands around to clench my bum and pulls me in toward his hips. I want him to take me back to Lusso right now, but I can't brush off Mikael.

Our tongues slowly sweep together, rolling, pulling back, and plunging again, time and time again. I ache with need for this man—painful, constant aching, and I know he feels exactly the same about me.

I pull back and find his eyes clenched shut. I've seen that look before, and the last time I saw it, it was because he had something to tell me. "What's wrong?"

His eyes fly open quickly. "Nothing's wrong." He brushes away a loose tendril of my hair. "Everything is right."

I stiffen in his lap. He's said that before, too, and everything really wasn't right. "You have something you want to tell me."

"You're right, I do." His head drops, and I feel sick—stomach-churning sick, but then his eyes lift again and find mine. "I crazy love you, baby."

I recoil slightly. "That's not what you want to tell me."

He reduces me to a pool of steam on his lap when he blasts me with his smile, reserved only for women. "Yes, it is. And I'll keep telling you until you get fed up of hearing it. It's a novelty to me." He shrugs. "I like saying it."

"I won't get fed up of hearing it, and don't be saying it to anyone else. I don't care how much you like saying it."

He grins, a real boyish, cheeky grin. "Would that make you jealous?"

I scoff. "Mr. Ward, let's not talk about jealousy when you've just vowed to eliminate any threat."

"Okay, let's not." He pulls me in and rolls his hips upward, unearthing a wicked beat at my very center. "Let's get a room instead," he whispers, flicking those damn delectable hips up once more.

I frantically scramble out of his lap, eager to escape that mind-melting touch before I rip his suit off here and now. "I'm going to be late for my meeting." I grab my bag and press my lips briefly on his. "I need you waiting in bed when I get home."

He smiles a satisfied smile. "Are you making demands, Miss O'Shea?"

"Are you going to deny me, Mr. Ward?"

"Never, but you do remember who has the power, don't you?" He makes a grab for me, but I bat his hands away quickly, jumping out of the car before he completely swallows me up.

I pop my head back in. "You do, but I need you. So could you please be naked and waiting?"

"You need me?" he asks, a triumphant look on his face.

"Always. See you at yours." I shut the door, hearing him yell *"ours"* as I walk off. I'm aware of eyes drilling into me, and I turn to find the valet with the biggest grin on his face. I blush profusely and scuttle up the steps into the hotel.

* * *

I'm shown to the same snug where Mikael and I last met, and Mikael is already waiting for me. He has the mood boards laid out on the table and is studying them. He looks more casual today, his suit jacket removed, his tie loose, but his pale blond hair still perfectly styled.

He looks up when I walk in. "Ava, very good to see you again." His lightly accented voice is as smooth as ever.

"And you, Mikael. You received the drafts?" I nod at the boards as I set my bag down on one of the large green leather couches.

"Yes, but the problem is I love them all. You're too good." He puts his hand out, and I take it.

"I'm glad." I smile brightly.

He releases me and turns back toward the table. "I'm veering toward this one, though." He points to the cream-and-white scheme that I'm favoring myself.

"That would be my choice, too. I think it encapsulates your aspiration best."

"It does," he agrees, smiling warmly at me. "Take a seat, Ava. Would you like a drink?"

I perch on a sofa. "Water would be good, thank you."

He signals to the waiter at the doorway before lowering himself onto the sofa next to me. "I apologize for the holdup on our meeting. Things didn't go as swiftly as I planned back home."

That would be his divorce then. I can't imagine things would go smoothly when you are as rich as Mikael. His wife is probably trying to take him for every penny. I don't say anything, though. I suspect Ingrid shouldn't have divulged as much as she did, and I don't want to get her sacked.

"It's not a problem, really." I smile and return my eyes to the mood boards. "So, we're swinging toward this one then?" I place my hand on the cream-and-white scheme.

He shifts forward. "Yes, I like the simplicity and warmness. You are very clever. One would think it would come across insipid and cold, but it doesn't at all."

"Thank you. It's all about the fabrics and tones."

He smiles, his blue eyes shimmering. "Yes, I guess it is."

*　*　*

We spend a few hours discussing the time frames, schedules, and budgets. He is really quite easy to be around, which is a huge relief. After rejecting his dinner invitation, I was worried things would be awkward, but he took my answer on the chin and has said no more.

"It will all be sustainable materials, yes?" He runs his finger across the drawing of a large four-poster bed I've sketched.

"Of course." I indicate the many items of other furniture. "I understand the forestry commission in Scandinavia is serious business."

"It is." He laughs. "We all have to do our bit for the environment. We got a little bad press after Lusso."

My mind's eye is flooded with images of twelve superbikes and a petrol-guzzling DBS. "We do," I agree.

After a bit more discussion I excuse myself to use the ladies'. I'm pleased with how the meeting is progressing, and I'm eager to get back to the office to start working on the master design. Standing in front of the mirror, I ruffle my hair, pinch my cheeks, and then exit the ladies', walking across the lobby of the hotel and back to the snug.

But my positive mood is soon trampled all over when I enter the room and nearly choke on thin air. What the fucking hell is he doing here?

CHAPTER TWELVE

J esse is standing next to Mikael, bold as bloody brass, looking over my designs. Oh, he's gone too far this time. He's going to trample my business meeting. Oh God, he is going to trample Mikael, and he doesn't even know that he's previously asked me to dinner.

I'm at a loss as I stand and watch them chat, all businesslike, while I try to figure out how to handle this. As per my usual reaction to Jesse's wayward ways, I want to scream at him, but with Mikael here, that's out of the question.

As if he has sensed my presence—he always does—Jesse turns to face me. I flash him a you're-pushing-it look and slowly approach them.

"Mikael," I say, muscling my way between them at the table. I feel Jesse tense from head to toe at my informal acknowledgment to my client. He can go and take a leap off the nearest cliff! The man deserves everything he gets. And he wants me to move in? He can forget it, and there will be no sense fucking to change my mind either.

Mikael smiles at me. I don't miss the arched eyebrow. "Ava, let me introduce you. This is Jesse Ward. He bought the penthouse at Lusso. I was showing Mr. Ward your designs. He's as impressed as I am."

"That's nice," I say without even acknowledging Jesse, turning my back on him to face my client instead. "Should we schedule our next meeting now?" I feel ice-cold air emanate from Jesse.

"Yes, that would be good," Mikael says. "Does Friday afternoon suit? We can meet at Life and get a rough idea on quantities. Maybe I could buy you lunch?" His eyebrows rise suggestively, and while I know I shouldn't be encouraging this sort of behavior, I just can't help myself.

"Friday afternoon suits me fine and lunch would be lovely." I smile, but then feel Jesse's warm, minty breath on the back of my neck. He's standing pretty damn close for someone who supposedly doesn't know me.

"I'm sorry to interrupt," Jesse pipes up.

Oh God, he's going to trample Mikael.

He grasps my shoulders, and I watch as Mikael frowns in confusion. He slowly turns me around until my stunned face is looking up at him. "Baby, have you forgotten that I'm taking you shopping?"

Oh fucking hell!

He really doesn't have any regard or shame. Mikael is going to be calling Patrick to complain, then Patrick is going to find out about Jesse, and I'm going to get sacked! I can't even find the strength to fire him a disgusted look as he looks down at my dumbstruck face, his eyes twinkling.

"I didn't realize you knew each other," Mikael says, clearly confused. We've just been introduced and neither one of us informed Mikael that we're already acquainted. We are so much more than acquainted.

Jesse knocks Mikael out with a killer smile. "I was in the area and I knew the love of my life was here." He shrugs. "I thought

I would slip in and get my fix. I'm not going to see her for another four hours." He bends down and brushes his lips over my ear. "I missed you," he whispers.

He turns me around so I'm facing Mikael and pulls my back to his chest, wrapping his arm around the tops of my shoulders and kissing my temple. This is so unprofessional. I want to die on the spot. I look up at Mikael and find him observing Jesse's little trampling session thoughtfully.

"I'm sorry, when you mentioned you were here to meet your girlfriend, I didn't realize you were referring to Ava," Mikael says coolly.

"Yes, isn't she beautiful?" He presses his lips to my temple again and inhales in my hair. "And all mine," he adds quietly, but loud enough for Mikael to hear.

I feel my face getting hotter by the second, my eyes darting everywhere except in Mikael's direction. Is he trying to eliminate Mikael? He's a client, not a threat. Not that Jesse knows of, anyway. God help me if he finds out about my dinner invitation.

My eyes land briefly on Mikael. He's watching me carefully. I feel so uncomfortable.

"Mr. Ward, if I had an Ava, I've no doubt I would do exactly the same." He flashes me a smile, and I feel my face burning up further. "Perhaps Monday would be more suitable?"

I find my voice. "Of course, Monday will be fine." I try to subtly wriggle free of Jesse, but he has a firm hold of me, and I know that even the whole British army would struggle to get me from his arms.

Mikael puts his hand out to me. "I'll call you to arrange a time once I've checked my diary."

I take his offering. I'm ending an important business meeting with a very important client and I'm completely coated in my neurotic, possessive control freak. I'm mortified. "I look forward to it," I say enthusiastically, earning myself a sharp little nudge in my back. Is he winding me up?

Mikael exits the snug, and I notice him glancing over his shoulder as he leaves. I just about capture the thoughtful look on his pale face, and I can't help but think that Jesse has just set a challenge for him. I could collapse with exasperation. "I can't believe you just did that," I say quietly as I stare at nothing in particular. "You've just trampled my most important client."

I'm swung around in his arms to find his face level with mine as he bends to accommodate the height difference between us. "Who is your most important client?" he asks on a heavy furrowed brow.

I roll my eyes. "You're my lover, who happens to be a client."

"I am more than your lover!"

I look at the panicked face close to mine and curse myself for wanting to head straight to the hotel bar and down a large glass of wine. No, actually, make that a bottle.

I exhale in complete despair. "I need to get back to work." I turn away, but feel his hand clamp around my wrist, the usual heat his touch instigates ever present.

Jesse walks around so he's in front of me, keeping hold of my wrist. "You encouraged him on purpose," he shoots accusingly.

Yes, I did! Just like he rocked up to The Royal Park on purpose to hijack my meeting, and for what? I look up at him through the fog of tears glazing my eyes. "Why?" I ask. It's a simple question.

"Because I love you," he says quietly.

"That's not a reason." My tone suggests I'm completely defeated, which is fine because I am.

His head snaps up in shock, and he pins me in place with his appalled glare. "Yes, it is. And anyway, he's a known womanizer."

Okay, now he's just making up excuses to justify his unreasonable behavior. If he loves me, then he should support me in my work, not try to sabotage it.

"You can't hijack every meeting I have with a male client," I say tiredly, with no faith in my attempt to reason with him.

"I won't, just him. And any other man who may be a threat."

I want to throw my head back and scream at the heavens. Jesse sees every man as a threat. "I have to go." I try and regain possession of my body, but he refuses to release me.

"I'll take you," he informs me, reluctantly releasing my wrist. "Collect your things." He walks over to the table and starts scooping up my mood boards. "These are really very good."

I can't join him in his enthusiasm. I feel despondent and flat. I can see my dream career flushing down the pan before my very eyes, and worst of all, there is the little niggling fear that I will push him to get steaming drunk if I don't comply with his unreasonableness. How can I go from being so immensely elated to so incredibly defeated, all in such a short space of time?

*　*　*

Jesse drops me at the corner of Berkeley Square at my request so I'm not spotted by Patrick getting out of Mr. Ward's car nearly four hours after I went for a breakfast meeting with him. I need to think about how I'm going to break this to Patrick, and I pray on all things holy that Mikael doesn't tell him first. This needs to be handled with care.

I give Jesse a chaste kiss on the cheek and leave him watching me, his bottom lip getting a grueling chew as I drag myself from his car. I say nothing, and neither does he.

*　*　*

"You've been a while, flower," Patrick says, as I settle at my desk.

"Mikael and I had a lot to go through. It's looking good," I offer by way of an explanation.

It seems to do the trick. He smiles instantly. "He is happy?"

"Very," I confirm, and that broadens Patrick's smile by a few more inches.

"Wonderful!" he exclaims, retreating to his office looking delighted.

I open my e-mail and hear the office door open. Looking up, I see a massive bunch of calla lilies floating toward me. Really? I left him five minutes ago.

They land on my desk, and the young girl sighs. "I don't know why he doesn't just buy you the shop. Sign here, please." She thrusts the clipboard under my nose, and I scribble my name.

"Thanks." I hand her back the clipboard and find the card.

I'm sorry-ish
Jx

I fall back in my chair. What he means is . . . he's sorry because he knows that he has upset me, but he's not at all sorry for trampling Mikael or my day. Maybe I should stay at Kate's tonight. I could do with some time, a big bottle of wine, my own thoughts, and no distractions.

The office door swings open again, and I look up to see Ruth Quinn beaming at me. Why is she here? I only spoke to her this morning. Her blonde hair is shining and bouncing as she struts to my desk, waving excitedly.

"Ava!" she sings.

"Ruth." I frown, but she doesn't seem to notice my confusion.

"I was just in the area and I thought I'd drop by." She places her neat, slender body on a chair in front of my desk.

"Oh?" I say, looking at her to continue.

"Yes." She smiles, but doesn't elaborate.

I glance at the clock. It's not even three o'clock. I've got another three hours to get her designs over by e-mail. "Was there something that you wanted to add to the specification?" I ask.

"No. Not at all. I'm sure I'll love the designs."

I'm not sure what to say. She's dropped by for nothing? No reason?

"Are you okay, Ava?" Her smile fades a little.

I shake myself up. "Yes, I'm fine." I force a happy face. I'm not fine, but I want to mood over it in peace, not make pointless conversation with a client. "I've prepped everything, Ruth. I'll get it across to you before the day's out." I know I've already told her this on the telephone, but what else can I say? Should I offer her a coffee?

"Lovely." She strokes her hair, and then flicks it over her shoulder. "Are you doing anything nice this weekend?"

Now I really am frowning. She's not a clinger on, is she? "I'm not sure."

"We should have drinks!"

I inwardly groan. She wants to be friends. Never mix business with pleasure—my new rule applies to female clients, too. What should I say? "Sure." The word slips past my lips and stuns me. I don't want to have drinks with Ruth.

"Are you sure you're okay?"

"Yes, fine." I try to smile.

"Man trouble?" Her fair, precisely plucked eyebrow rises.

"No." I shake my head.

"Ava, I know a woman in turmoil when I see one." She laughs. "Been there, done that."

"Honestly, Ruth, there is no man." I need Kate for this line of conversation, not a client. Wine and Kate.

She gives me a knowing smile and stands. "They're not worth the trouble."

I return her smile, but only because I'm pleased that she appears to be leaving. "I'll get your designs over soon, Ruth."

"Can't wait! We'll talk soon...about drinks." She breezes out of the office, leaving me to the turmoil she knows I'm in.

* * *

At the end of the day, I don't go to Kate's. I leave the office and I'm pulled toward St. Katherine Docks by the magnet that is the Lord of the Sex Manor. I said I wouldn't leave him, and I need these mounting questions answered, like this mystery woman.

"Evening, Ava."

"Hello, Clive. Can I speak to security, please?"

"They are all off-site at the moment." He diverts his attention to his computer, his way of halting this conversation from going any further—his way of dodging me.

"Right." I sigh, carrying on to the elevator. When the doors open to the penthouse, I let myself in with my pink key and head straight for the kitchen, kicking my shoes off and looking for wine that I know won't be there before finding a vase to put my flowers in. I remember the bunch upstairs that I hastily dumped on the chest in favor of delivering one truth fuck, so I take the stairs tiredly and enter the master suite to retrieve them.

Oh...dear.

My new diamanté-embellished vibrator is in a million pieces all over the far end of the bedroom floor, and there's a hole in the wall opposite the bed. The bedroom is vast, so he must have lobbed it with some force. I'm suddenly thinking that leaving before he got free was a decision well made.

I look across the room to the bed and see the handcuffs still dangling from the headboard, mental images of Jesse flying into a rage instantly starting to assault my brain. This man has issues—big, unreasonable, bloody issues...with control...with me.

I kneel and collect up all of the pieces, taking them to the bathroom and depositing them in the bin before I start running a bath. Picking up the calla lilies that are in desperate need of some water, I make my way back downstairs.

I get halfway down and hear the front door shut quietly, and I'm halted in my tracks as I watch Jesse come into view. He stops at the bottom of the stairs and looks up at me, his handsome face expressionless and his usually bright eyes a little glazed. He removes his suit jacket and reaches up, undoing his shirt buttons slowly as he watches me. He drops his shirt to the floor to join his jacket, then kicks off his shoes, socks, trousers, and boxers. My eyes are pulled to the red marks around his wrists when he removes his Rolex and throws it on top of his pile of clothes. I'm never handcuffing him again.

"You're not laying a finger on me until you tell me who that woman was." This might take all of my strength, especially if he starts the countdown, but I'm not backing down here.

"I don't know." His face is completely expressionless.

"So you've not asked Clive to stop me from looking at the CCTV?"

He almost smiles. "My beautiful girl is ruthless."

"My god is evasive."

"Ava, if I didn't need you all over me right now, I'd be challenging you."

"But you do, so you'll tell me."

"I slept with her."

I'm not displaying surprise. That much I had already figured out. "So why was she here?"

"Because she heard I was missing."

"That's it. She was worried?"

He shrugs. "Yes. That's it. Now I get you all over me."

"Why didn't you just tell me this before?"

He shrugs. "Because it was no big deal until you made it one."

He starts up the stairs slowly, completely naked and stunningly spectacular, and scoops me up without stopping, prompting me to drop the flowers and wrap myself around his body. "You made it a big deal by evading my questions."

He doesn't reply. I want to rip strips off him for trampling my day. I want to stamp and scream in a temper, but I can't seem to find the strength or the inclination to do it. He talked, and now I just want him all over me, too. My mind is fuzzy, but my body is fizzing...for him.

He places me on my feet and starts slowly undressing me, watching his hands work over my clothes as I stand quietly and let him do his thing. I would have put my money on a retribution fuck after my performance this morning, but instead I'm confronted with gentle, soft Jesse. I don't mind. I need soft and loving right now.

Once we're both naked, he takes me down to the thick, cream carpet and swaths me in his body, burying his face deep in my neck and breathing me into him. I mirror him and take my own hit of minty fresh-water loveliness, wrapping my arms firmly around his back to pull him closer, eradicating any space that may have been between us.

We lie on the floor in the middle of the bedroom and hold each other for the longest time while I stare up at the ceiling and stroke his hair, taking all of my comfort from his strong heartbeat thudding against my chest.

"I've missed you," he mumbles into my neck.

I shudder when I feel his hot tongue running circles around the delicate flesh under my ear. We've been apart for less than five hours. I would say he was unreasonable, but I've missed him, too. "Thank you for the flowers."

"You're welcome." He kisses up to my lips, brushes my hair from my face, and gazes down at me. "I want to drag you to a desert island and have you all to myself forever."

He drops a kiss on my lips and rolls us over so I'm straddling his hips. I can feel the evidence of his mood wedged between our bodies and it triggers all of my usual desperate needs for him. My nipples pucker under his watchful eye, and his grin widens into his signature, melt-worthy smile, reserved only for women. I want it to be reserved only for me. An unreasonable pang of possessiveness assaults me.

"I fucking love you," he sighs.

"I know you do." I circle my palms over his chest and pinch his nipple. "I love you, too."

"Even after today?"

"You mean after you stalked me all day?"

He pouts playfully and shifts his arms under his head. I dribble as his muscles bunch and flex. "I was worried about you."

I raise a mocking eyebrow at him.

"I was," he argues.

He wasn't worried about me at all. He had an unreasonable and unwarranted attack of possessiveness. "You were over-the-top and stupidly possessive. My challenging man needs to relax."

He scoffs. "I'm not challenging."

"You're challenging and in denial."

His brow furrows. "What am I in denial about?"

"Being challenging and unreasonable. Your performance today was way off the scales." I need to know he won't hijack every business meeting I have with a male client. He said it would be only Mikael, but then followed it up with *and all other male threats*. His idea of a threat is a million miles away from my idea of a threat. He's going to trample all of my male clients, I know it. My work diary is going to be padlocked and so is my mouth. I'm not telling him anything.

He looks at me with a little scowl. "Mikael would have made a move on you, and then I'd *really* have to trample him."

I laugh lightly. He doesn't need to know that Mikael has

already made his move. I will be keeping that snippet of information to myself. "Well, I think you made your point pretty
clear. It was embarrassing."

"It was necessary," he mutters, and I roll my eyes, making a
dramatic display of my exasperation.

"You should run more. Oh, the bath!" I jump up and run into
the bathroom.

"No, I need you more," he calls to my back.

"Don't you have me enough?" I flip the tap off, thinking he
could never leave me a whole day without some kind of trampling session or intrusion on my working day. Would I want
him to *not* interfere? I like the flowers and the messages; it's the
tramples I have an issue with. If I refused to let him speak to me
while I was at work, would he be tempted to have a drink to try
and get through the day? Could I risk it? My relaxed brain begins to ache...again.

I make my way back into the bedroom, finding him still
sprawled on the floor. He is just too delicious. I walk over and
settle myself back on his hips.

"Have you enough?" he asks. "No, I don't. I need you every
second of the day, just like you need me. Constant contact."

He reaches up and pinches my nipple, and I jerk on top of
him, catching a full-on rub from his erection. He gives me his
roguish grin.

"What if you couldn't have me all day?" I ask. There will be
times in the future when he might actually be on a real business
trip. Or, perhaps, I will.

His grin disappears instantly and is replaced with a glare
pointed straight at me. "Are you going to try and stop me?"

"No, but there may be situations when you can't have instant
access to me. I might be unobtainable."

A fleeting look of panic flies across his face and his bottom lip
disappears between his teeth.

"Would you make a grab for the vodka?" There. I've said it.

He laughs, and I frown.

"I promised you I will never have another drink. I meant it," he says surely. He sits up and rests his hands on my hips. I jerk, and he smiles. "Bath. I want your wet, slippery skin all over mine."

"Your confidence is commendable," I mumble sarcastically as I ease myself up and put my hand out to him.

He looks at me with narrowed eyes and reaches up to take my hand, yanking me forward and spinning me onto my back. He rests his big body all over me and drops his lips to mine in a long, lingering kiss. "It is all very easy because I have you. Unravel your knickers, lady."

Easy for him to say. I'm dealing with a neurotic madcap. "So, tomorrow I'll be undisturbed all day?"

He pulls his head back to look at me, chewing his lip again. "Lunch?"

"I'm meeting Kate for lunch."

He pouts. "Can't I come?"

"No," I state firmly. I need time with Kate to talk about him and his challenging ways.

"I think you're being unreasonable."

I throw my head back on a laugh, but suddenly jerk and buck as he grabs my hip bone and squeezes. "Stop!" I screech.

"No!"

"Please!" Tears jump into my eyes as I try to fight him off. I can't bear it.

"Lunch," he says calmly, as he continues tickling me.

"Absolutely not!" I cry through my uncontrollable laughter. This isn't fair. I'm not submitting. No way!

"Maybe a sense fuck will do it." He releases my hip and I relax, trying to get my erratic breathing under control.

"Jesse, I can't be with you every second of the day," I try to reason.

"If you give up work you could be." He's deadly serious.

My eyes widen in disgust. Never! I love my job. "Now who's being unreason...Ohhhhh!" I lose my trail as he plunges deep into me. Oh God, here comes the sense fuck, but what is he trying to get me to submit to? Lunch or retiring?

He wastes no time breaking me in. He powers into me like a madman. My legs fall open and he pins my wrists on either side of my head. "Lunch?" he asks as he thrusts hard.

My brain has just turned to mush, but it still registers that this is a lunch sense fuck. I'm relieved. Lunch will be easier to relent to, but I still don't plan on going down easily. Mr. Challenging has a challenge on his hands.

"No!" I shout defiantly.

He growls and surges forward, his firmness stroking me hard and fast as he drives in and out like a wild animal. "You are so receptive to me."

I am! He lays one finger on me and I'm all over the place. "Jesse, please."

He hits me hard with his hips and grinds firmly. "Baby, let me have lunch with you."

I shake my head, holding my breath.

"Do I feel good?"

"Yes!" I shout on a rushed exhale. The crest of a booming orgasm descends on me, and his grip tightens around my wrists.

"Say yes," he insists harshly, and I know he's on his way to explosion, too.

What if I don't say yes? What if I hold out on him? "No!" I'm not giving in. He can't fuck sense into me every time I don't agree to something.

He hammers on, my thighs tensing, my mind knotted. "Ava, give me what I want."

"Jesse!"

"You're going to come."

"Yes!" I cry. All of the pent-up stress of the day is going to come rushing out at any moment.

"Oh, fuck, baby, you do serious things to me." He hits me with another powerful thundering of his hips.

My mind goes blank, and I'm about to detonate when he stops dead in his tracks, subsequently stopping my imminent orgasm dead in its tracks. "What are you doing?" I scream, completely stunned. I tilt my hips to try and get the friction I need to tip me over the edge, but he pulls his own hips back until he is only just inside me. "You bastard!" I spit.

"Watch your fucking mouth! Say yes, Ava," he pants, but his words are controlled. How is he doing this? I know he's ready to come.

"No," I affirm.

He shakes his head and then locks eyes with me as he plunges, oh so slowly, and swivels his hips.

"Ohhh," I groan. "Faster."

"Say the word, Ava." He repeats the teasing move. "Say it, and you'll get what you want."

"You don't play fair," I complain.

"You want me to stop?"

"No!" I shout in frustration. This is torture at its worst.

He flexes his hold on my wrists. "I'll ask you one more time, baby. Lunch?" He flicks his hips forward as he asks, and I lose any determination I had to defy him.

"Fuck me," I cry as he looks down at me, amusement plaguing his expression.

"Watch your mouth." He's grinning. "Was that a yes?"

"*Yes!*" I scream.

"Good girl," he praises, and then powers forward, hammering into me and tossing me straight back into a fast buildup to release. I stiffen from head to toe as sizzling hotness travels through my bloodstream, and my skin heats from the friction of being pushed across the carpet by his manic momentum.

"Jesse!" I'm gripped from every direction by stabbing shots of pleasure flying through my nervous system, exploding at my core.

I scream.

His drives become more urgent and his breathing loud and erratic as he smashes against me on carnal shouts and releases everything he has, my core muscles clenching greedily onto him, my limp, exhausted body completely helpless to his unforgiving blows.

He collapses on top of me in a sweaty heap and rocks gently against me. "My work here is done," he pants in my ear.

I lie under his hard, warm body, trying to gather my senses and breath, and wonder if it will always be like this. He gets the results he wants, so, yes, it probably will be. I've got to learn to deal with this. I've got to train myself to repel him. I laugh at such a pointless exercise. I don't want to repel him.

He pushes himself up on his hands, and it's only now I notice he doesn't wince. "Your hand!" I cry.

He lifts it up and I can still see slight bruising, but the swelling has subsided massively. "It's fine. Sarah had me keep ice on it for most of the afternoon."

"Sarah?" I blurt without thinking about what tone I should use. It comes out accusingly.

He frowns at me, and I hate myself for sounding so shocked. "She was just being a friend," he says coolly, but this only heightens my concern. Another woman looking after him doesn't sit well, and the fact that it's pouty lips really has my jealous streak racing to the surface.

I suddenly feel extremely uncomfortable with my possessiveness. Good God, I ridicule Jesse for this. I'm a bloody hypocrite, and the way he is staring down at me, gauging my mood, isn't helping. He's a very desirable man who assaults women with that fucking smile and has them in puddles at his feet.

I wriggle underneath him to get free and he obliges, letting me up on a frown. I head straight for the bathroom and immerse myself in the hot bath. I'm really not comfortable with these feelings. I've never been jealous in my life, and now I'm going to be fighting women off on a daily basis. That's a full-time job in itself. Maybe I *will* need to retire.

"Has someone got a touch of the green-eyed monster?"

I look up and see him standing in all of his naked glory by the bathroom doorway. "No," I scoff. I couldn't be more obviously jealous if I tried.

He walks over to the bath and steps in behind me, lowering his body until I'm cradled between his legs. He drapes his arms over my shoulders and pulls me back to rest on his chest. "Ava, you are the only woman for me," he says softly in my ear. "And I am all yours." He picks up the natural sponge from the edge of the bath, dips it to soak up some water, and then starts running it across my breasts.

"You need to tell me more about yourself."

I feel his chest lift on a sigh. "What do you want to know?"

"Is The Manor strictly business or have you mixed it with pleasure?" The sponge pauses between my breasts for a few seconds, but then he continues smoothing it over my body.

"Dive straight in, why don't you," he says dryly.

"Tell me," I press.

He sighs so heavily I almost turn around to glare at him, just so he knows I don't appreciate his bored reaction to my question. "I've dabbled."

Dabbled?

I'm not sure I like the sound of dabbling, especially in this area of inquiry. "Are you still dabbling?"

"No!"

"When was the last time you dabbled?"

His sponge strokes pause again. Please don't tell me he has to think about this.

"Way before I met you." He continues caressing me with the sponge.

"How long before you met me?" I need to shut the hell up. I really don't want to know about this part of him. But I can't stop the stupid questions flying out.

"Ava, does it matter?"

"Yes," I retort quickly. No, actually, it doesn't, but his short, huffy answer is prickling my curiosity.

"It wasn't regular." He's doing his best to avoid this.

"That didn't answer my question."

"Is anything I tell you going to change the way you feel about me?"

That question has me prickling further. What has he done? "No," I say, but I'm not so sure now. He clearly thinks it will.

"So, can we drop it? It's in my past with a whole heap of other stuff, and I would rather leave it there." His tone is final. I feel slighted. "There is only you. End of." He kisses the back of my head. "When are we moving the rest of your stuff in?"

I inwardly groan. He fucked that sense into me as well. I notice all of this so-called sense he's fucking into me only makes sense to him. "I'm here," I remind him. "I've got to pick up the rest of my stuff from Matt." Did I really just say that out loud?

"No, you fucking won't!" he shouts in my ear, and I recoil at his booming voice. "I'll send John. I told you, you won't see him again."

Right, I'm dropping this. I'm not going to get anywhere with it; I'm not stupid. I've already arranged my pickup, anyway, and Jesse will never know. Well, he will, when I've got my stuff, but it will be too late for him to stop me by then.

I think of something else. "Tell me where you went when you disappeared on me."

He tenses beneath me. "No," he spits the word out fast.

Okay, now I'm getting mad. I turn myself over to lie on his front so he's forced to look me in the eyes. "The last time you held back on me, I left you."

His eyes widen slightly, but then narrow. He knows I've got him. "I locked myself in my office."

"For four days?" I ask doubtfully.

"Yes, for four days, Ava." He looks past me, refusing to meet my eyes.

"Look at me," I demand harshly.

His eyes fly to mine in obvious shock at my order. "Excuse me?" He almost laughs. It's patronizing, and I don't appreciate it.

"What were you doing in your office?"

"Drinking. That's what I was doing. I was trying to drown out thoughts and images of you with vodka. Are you happy now?" He tries to shift me from his body, but I tense from top to toe in an attempt to make myself a dead weight.

I fight with him, pushing his slippery body back down into the bath. He gives in and lets me. I know he could overpower me if he wanted to, so he doesn't really want to escape. I slide my body up his so our noses meet.

"I'm sorry," he whispers. "I'm so sorry, baby."

"Please, don't be." I push myself into him, tackling his mouth, desperate for him to know that I couldn't care less. I feel responsible...guilty.

"When I saw those bruises on your arms, I realized I was in deep, Ava. Way too deep."

"Shhhh," I hush him, covering his whole face with my mouth, kissing every square inch of him. "Enough, now."

He cups my bum and pulls me up, burying his face between

my breasts. "It won't happen again, I'll kill myself before hurting you again."

He doesn't have to use such strong words. I understand. He's regretful. I am, too. I should never have walked away from him. I should have stayed, thrown him in a cold shower, and sobered him up. "I said enough, Jesse."

"I love you."

"I know you do. I'm sorry, too."

He releases his hold and I slide back down his body until we're eye to eye. "What have you got to be sorry for?"

I shrug. "I wish I hadn't left you."

"Ava, I don't blame you for walking out on me. I deserved that, and if anything, it will only make me more determined not to drink. Knowing I could lose you is enough of a motivation, trust me."

"I'll never walk away from you again. Never," I affirm.

He smiles lightly. "I hope you don't, because I'd be finished."

I mirror his smile and lay my cheek on his chest, letting him surround me in his warmth and comfort.

*　*　*

I open my eyes and it's still dark. I'm vaguely aware of the bed vibrating under me, and I'm wet.

It takes me a few moments, but when awareness finally hits me, it really hits me hard. I scramble over to flick the lamp on and the light slams into my eyes like gravel. I squint to gain focus and find Jesse sitting up in bed, rocking back and forth with his knees clenched to his chest. Holy shit, he's drenched and his pupils are huge black saucers. He looks petrified. "Jesse?" I speak quietly, not wanting to startle him. He doesn't respond. He just continues with the rocking, but then he starts mumbling.

"I need you," he says quietly.

"Jesse?" I place my hand on his arm and shake him gently. He looks so scared. "Jesse?"

"I need you, I need you, I need you." He repeats the mantra over and over. I want to cry.

"Jesse, please," I plead. "Stop, I'm here." I can't bear to see him like this. He's shaking uncontrollably, and sweat is pouring from his brow, his frown line by far the deepest I have ever seen it. I try to position myself in his line of sight, but he doesn't acknowledge me. He just carries on with the rocking and mumbling, staring straight through me. He's asleep. I pull his legs down away from his body and climb onto his lap, wrapping my arms around his sodden back, holding him as tight as I can. I don't know if he is aware, but his arms come up and grip me, and his face buries deep into my neck.

We sit like this forever while I whisper in his ear, hoping he will recognize me and snap out of his night terror. "Ava?" he mumbles in my neck after an age. His voice is cracked and throaty.

He's awake. "Hey, I'm here." I pull back and cup his face with both of my hands. His eyes search mine, looking for something. I'm not sure what.

"I'm so sorry."

"What are you sorry for?" He's worrying me even more now.

"For everything." He falls back, taking me with him so I'm lying across his wet chest. My body is soaking, but I don't care.

My head rests on his chest and I listen as his heart rate slows. "Jesse?" I say nervously, but he doesn't answer, so I lift my head to look at him and see he's fast asleep, looking peaceful. What was that all about?

I lie on him for hours, my mind racing with reasons for him to be sorry. Bloody hell, maybe I *am* reading too much into this.

There's plenty for him to be sorry for. Lying to me, deceiving me, drink, his unreasonableness, his possessive streak, his neurotic behavior, trampling my meeting today, his...

I doze off, running through all of the reasons why Jesse could be sorry.

CHAPTER THIRTEEN

I love you."

I feel familiar lush lips brush over mine as I come awake, my eyes opening to stunning green shining down at me. "Wake up, my beautiful girl."

I raise my arms over my head and stretch. Oh, that feels good. Blinking up at him, I note he's dressed, and my sleepy brain quickly registers that with Jesse dressed already, there is no danger of being dragged around London on one of his punishing runs.

"What time is it?" I croak.

"You're fine, it's only six thirty. I've got a few early supplier meetings at The Manor. I needed to see you before I go." He leans down and kisses me, and I get a taste of his minty breath.

Supplier meetings? What sort of supplies would that be? I snap a lid on those thoughts immediately. It's too early.

"My eyes don't have to be open for *you* to see *me*," I complain, as I reach around his back and pull him down. He smells yummy.

"Come and have breakfast with me." He pulls me up from the bed, and I wrap my naked body around him in my usual chimp-ish fashion. "You're creasing me," he says with zero concern, carrying me out of the bedroom and down to the kitchen.

"Put me down then," I bite back, knowing he won't.

"Never."

I smile smugly as I absorb him in all of his fresh-water loveliness. "I don't need a reminder fuck. You can still come to lunch."

"Mouth." He laughs. "I'm sorry. I really needed to see you before I go."

I stiffen instantly at his words. Well, one word in particular; *sorry*. Shit! I had forgotten about his midnight meltdown. He places me gently on the work surface.

"You woke up in the night."

"I did?" His brow furrows. I don't know whether to be relieved or worried.

"You don't remember?"

"No," he says on a shrug. "What do you want for breakfast?" He leaves me on the counter and goes to the fridge. "Eggs, bagel, fruit?"

"You said you need me." I throw it in the air and hope he catches it.

He doesn't. He lets it drop straight to the floor and tramples all over it. "And? I say that when I'm awake." He doesn't even turn away from the fridge.

"You said you were sorry." I place my hands under my thighs. Now he turns. "I've said that when I'm awake, too."

This is true, he's said it all when he's awake, but he was in such a state.

He smiles. "Ava, I was probably having a bad dream. I don't remember." He turns back to the fridge.

"You were just a bit frantic, I was worried," I say timidly. It wasn't normal.

He shuts the fridge door, harder than is necessary, and I immediately regret bringing this up. I'm not scared of him, but the way he's holding himself is making me wary. I don't want to start a fresh day on a quarrel. It was just sleep talk, after all.

He wanders over to me chewing his bottom lip, and I watch him with caution. When he reaches me, he muscles between my legs and takes my hands out from under my thighs, holding them between us and stroking the tops with his thumbs.

"Stop worrying about what I say in my sleep. Did I say I didn't love you?" he asks softly.

I feel my brow knit. "No."

His green eyes twinkle as one side of his mouth tips upward at the corner. "That's all that matters." He plants a kiss on my forehead.

I pull away from his lips. He's doing it again. He's evading. "That wasn't normal. And I'm getting pissed off hearing that tone." I scowl. "You either talk, or I'm gone." His gaping mouth shuts, but he still doesn't speak. I've shocked him. "What's it to be?" I press.

"You said you'd never leave me," he says quietly.

"Okay. Let me rephrase that. I won't leave you if you start answering me when I ask you something. How about that?"

He's chewing his lip and staring at me, but I don't look away.

"It's not important."

I laugh in disbelief and make to move, but he moves in closer, hampering my attempts to get myself down from the counter.

"I dreamt you were gone." He fires the words out quickly, almost panicky.

I stop with my struggle to free myself. "What?"

"I dreamt I woke up, and you were gone."

"Gone where?"

"I don't fucking know." He releases his grip on me and his hands plunge straight into his hair. "I couldn't find you."

"You dreamt I left you?"

His frown line is fierce. "I don't know where you went. Just gone."

"Oh." I don't know what else to say, and he refuses to look at me. He got himself in that state over me leaving him?

"It wasn't a nice dream, that's all." He won't look at me, and I suddenly feel a little guilty. This is a serious hang-up.

"I'm not leaving you," I try to reassure him, "but we've got to talk. I have to torture information out of you, Jesse. It's exhausting."

"I'm sorry."

I reach forward and pull him back between my thighs. This is one of those moments—the ones where I'm the strong one. They are becoming more frequent as I'm working out this man. "Have you had bad dreams before?"

"No." He accepts my hold and squeezes me tight to him.

"Because you drank."

"No, Ava. I'm not an alcoholic."

"I didn't say you were." I hold him tightly, feeling a little sad for him, but quietly pleased that he's opened up.

"Can I make you a well-balanced breakfast now?" He pulls out from my clinch, clearly keen to take his power back.

"Yes, please."

"What do you want?"

"Toast."

"Toast? It's hardly well-balanced," he mutters, releasing me to put some bread in the toaster.

I lower myself down from the island and take a seat on a stool to admire him as he putters around the kitchen. He looks as handsome as ever this morning. He's not shaved, and I love the one-day stubble on him. He's hasn't got a full suit on, just charcoal-gray trousers and a black shirt. I may change my mind about lunch just so he's forced to give me a reminder fuck.

I watch him gather the butter, knives, and plates and place everything in front of me on the island. Then he finds a jar of peanut butter and settles next to me, dunking and sucking on a hum. "So, what's in your diary today?"

I choke on my toast, and he frowns.

"What's so shocking about wanting to know what you're going to be doing?"

I swallow my toast. "Oh, nothing." I chew a bit more. "If I thought you were genuinely interested and not planning a trampling mission."

"I am genuinely interested." He looks hurt. I'm not falling for it.

"I'll meet you at Baroque at one. I've still got to ring Kate and advise her that you're gate-crashing our ladies' lunch."

"She won't mind. She loves me."

"That's because you bought her Margo Junior."

"No, it is because she told me so."

"When?"

"At The Manor."

My jaw hits the marble counter. I know they were both at The Manor on Saturday. "What was she doing at The Manor?" I try to sound casual, but by the look on his face, I've failed.

"That is none of our business." He smiles as he jumps up from the stool and chucks his empty peanut butter jar in the bin. "I've got to scram."

"Scram?"

"Skedaddle...go...leave." He winks at me, and I pool on the stool in a soppy mess. He's in a good mood this morning, all roguish and playful, and I love it. Easygoing Jesse is becoming a more regular visitor these days.

"I've decided that maybe lunch isn't such a good idea. I don't want Kate to think we're joined at the hip." I turn away from him and carry on eating my toast in the most blasé manner I can muster. It's hard when my man is bristling and snarling behind me.

He grabs me, and I squeal as he flips me around and walks me to the wall, pinning me under his delicious body with my toast still in my hand. His eyes are uncertain, and I almost feel guilty...almost.

I know what's coming.

I fight to conceal the grin that's tickling the corners of my mouth as he bends, leans into me, and rolls his hips up so I get a full-on stroke at my core. I moan in pure, sneaky satisfaction.

"You didn't mean that," he says, sliding his hand over my stomach, down toward the apex of my thighs.

"I did," I challenge, and then jerk as his thumb slips over my sensitive flesh. Oh God, I'll never get enough of him.

"Someone is going to be quick," he muses, as he continues to ride me with his hand. I sigh, savoring his talented touch working me. "Don't play games with me, Ava." He withdraws his hand and steps back from me.

What?

I want to yank him back and shove his hand down below. I look at him, all *what-the-hell*, and he smirks at me.

"I'm already late because I wanted to make sure you ate. If I knew you were going to play games with me, I would have fucked you first and fed you after." He steps in and makes a point of grinding his ever-loving hips against me, moaning in my ear. "One o'clock," he whispers, before he bites into my suspended toast and pulls away. "I love you, lady."

"You don't," I snap. "If you did, you wouldn't abandon me halfway to orgasm."

"Hey!" he yells. He looks pissed. "Don't ever question whether I love you. It'll make me mad."

I try and plaster an apologetic look on my face, but in my unexploded state, I'm struggling to convince my brain to do anything other than yank him back into me and make him sort me out. He's turned on, I can see it. How can he walk away?

"Have a nice day." His eyes soften as he leans down and rests his lips on my cheek. "I'm going to miss you like crazy, baby."

Oh, I know he will. But it's only six hours until our lunch date. He'll live.

*   *   *

Once I'm ready, I make my way downstairs, clinking on my heels through the foyer as I delve through my bag for my sunglasses.

"Morning, Ava," Clive calls.

"Morning." I slip my shades on and emerge into the sunshine, coming to an abrupt halt when I spot John leaning against his Range Rover.

Really?

He lifts his glasses up and shrugs his big shoulders at me.

I walk over. "John, I can drive to work," I say in a tired tone. I need my car today so I can collect my stuff from Matt's after work.

"I don't think you can, girl," he rumbles. What's he talking about? "Your car's being cleaned." He shrugs again and slides behind the wheel. I swing around and see an army of men cleaning my car.

Oh, for God's sake. I drag my keys from my bag and find my car key missing. Later, I will be explaining to Mr. Control Freak that snooping through a woman's handbag—and phone—is bloody rude. This is bad news. I need my car to collect my things from Matt's after work. I'll ask Kate.

I jump in next to John, who's wearing his usual ensemble of black suit and black shirt. How many black suits can one man have?

"Do you think he's unreasonable and challenging?" I ask casually, flipping the visor down to put some lip gloss on.

"Yes, girl," he rumbles. "But, like I said, only with you. He's never cared before you."

I sit back in my seat and listen to John commence humming to match his taps. Jesse can't have *never* cared for anyone. He's thirty-seven.

"How old is he?" I ask on a smile, earning myself another dazzler from John.

"He's thirty-seven. But you know that now, don't you, girl?"

I die a thousand deaths on the spot and turn a thousand shades of red. I'd forgotten Jesse had to be rescued. I bet John got a right eyeful. I start laughing to myself when I think of what John must have walked in on—a bedroom with one naked god handcuffed to the bed, a diamanté embellished vibrator, my black lace, and the aforementioned god then making a hole in the wall with said vibrator. I'm beyond embarrassed, and my sinking body into the passenger seat confirms it.

We make the rest of the journey in silence, except for John's humming. He drops me off at Berkeley Square and I run to my office to escape my discomfort, giving him a quick wave over my shoulder while wondering how the hell I'm ever going to face him again. I wander to my desk and see Sally at the filing cabinet. She looks suicidal. The high-necked polyester blouse is back and the firecracker nail polish has disappeared. It is definitely as I suspected. Men are such wankers. I elect not to mention it, she won't appreciate it.

"Morning, Sally." She lifts a heavy head and offers a small smile before returning to her filing. I feel bad for her. "Where is everyone?"

She shrugs. Oh, this is bad, so I resign myself to shutting up and getting on with things.

* * *

I enter the bar at one and spot Kate at our usual table. I sit down and come face to face with a big glass of wine. "Fuck! Kate, get rid of it!" I shove it to her side of the table.

She gives me daggers. "I thought you might need it."

Yes, I really do, but Jesse will be here soon, and what would it look like if I'm sitting here slurping wine? That would be cruel and extremely thoughtless. I make a grab for Kate's glass, but she throws herself on it.

"Kate, he'll be here soon."

"Hey! Put the wine down!" she demands in a stern voice. "He's not my boyfriend."

She refuses to let go, and I glare at her as I release her glass. She picks it up and takes a long swig while watching me.

"You cow!" I toss at her, and she grins around the rim. I grab my wine and down the lot in one fell swoop. Kate bursts into laughter. Oh God, that was good. It's been almost two weeks since I've had a drink, which is an all-time record for me. I let out a long, satisfied gasp.

"You did need it," Kate confirms the obvious.

"Yes. And probably another." I sulk. Guilt washes over me at my weakness, and I look over my shoulder before running to the bar to deposit my empty. I feel like a delinquent child. "Oh, and don't tell Jesse you love him. It makes his head swell." I moan as I sit back down. "Can you run me to Matt's after work to get my stuff?"

"Sure, just don't ask me to speak to him," she spits. "Shall I pick you up from your office?"

"At six. Is that all right?"

"Sure it is. Have you spoken to him?"

"Yeah, he's expecting me, but Jesse doesn't know I'm going and it has to stay that way," I say warningly. Kate raises her eyebrows but says nothing. "He'll trample." I shrug. I think that wine has gone straight to my head. I feel woozy. "How's Sam?"

"He'll be here soon."

"He will?"

"Yes." Her short, sharp reply leaves no room for further questioning. "He mentioned Jesse joining us, so I thought why not?" I have nothing to say to that, so I change the subject. "Hey, do you know what's happened with Victoria and Drew?" I ask eagerly. Kate must know something.

Her eyes widen. "Oh, you won't believe it!"

"What?" I sit forward, completely rapt with the obvious sign of dirt to dish.

"Drew asked her to go to The Manor. Little prissy was not impressed!" Kate is delighted, but I'm suddenly filled with dread.

If Victoria knows about The Manor, does that mean she knows who owns The Manor? Did Drew tell her everything? Oh good God, I pray not. If she has worked it out, then there would be no doubt that she has told Tom, and the last thing I need is Tom and Victoria on my case and spouting off around the office.

"What do you want to eat?" Kate asks, snapping me from my worrying thoughts.

"I'll have a BLT on granary, please."

"What about Jesse?"

I frown to myself. I have absolutely no idea. I don't even know what any of his favorite foods are. "Ask if they have peanut butter."

"Peanut butter?" She screws her face up in distaste. "Oh, here he is." Kate tips her glass in the direction of the door, and I turn to look, sighing in appreciation, as does Kate when Sam follows in behind him with Drew. Jesse plants a chaste kiss on my cheek, and then pulls over a chair from another table for himself. He sits down next to me, slightly facing me, resting his hand on my knee. The warmth of his palm spreads up my leg, smacking me straight between the thighs. He does me no favors when he slowly strokes and squeezes, strokes and squeezes.

"You took my car keys." I narrow accusing eyes on him.

"Everyone okay?" he asks, ignoring me and starting to circle his thumb on the inside of my thigh. I glance at him, finding he's smiling, knowing damn well what he's doing. I try and pull my leg away but he has none of it. Whenever and wherever.

"I'm good," Kate chirps. "And I'm ordering. What's everyone having?" She gets up.

Everyone throws their order at her and she disappears to the bar, leaving me with the men.

Jesse leans into me. "You've had a drink."

I tense. "It was an accident."

"I don't mind you having a drink if I'm with you, Ava." He turns his attention back to the boys. He doesn't mind?

I sit and watch Jesse be completely normal with Drew and Sam, talking about sports, mostly extreme, and generally carrying on like any normal man would. This is easygoing Jesse. He laughs with them, his eyes twinkling, keeping his hand exactly where it is. I smile to myself. It's a pleasure to see, and then he glances over at me and winks, and I want to straddle his hips and eat him alive.

"So, how is Victoria?" Kate chucks the question at Drew as she takes her seat, and everyone looks at him. She is such a shit stirrer.

"Don't ask." He takes a swig from his bottle of beer. I notice no one else seems to be uneasy about the whole alcohol presence. Am I handling this all wrong? "She's sweet, but God, she's got to lighten up."

I recoil in my chair. Drew's lightening-up comment is a bit harsh, especially if he's hit her with an invitation to The Manor. He can't knock her for being skeptical.

"Why did you ask her to go?" I blurt the question before my brain engages. Isn't it obvious why he asked her? Jesse gives me a sideway glance, and I feel my face burning up.

Drew shrugs. "It's who I am, it's what I like."

"Amen," Sam says, and raises his bottle.

Kate clinks Sam's bottle with her glass and he grins at her. My eyes widen—she's had some action at The Manor!

Holy fucking shit!

Does Jesse know this?

"Anyway," Drew continues, "I've got to make the most of it. Get to thirty-five and it's a slippery slope down to a saggy arse and man boobs. I'll think about a woman who loves me for me and not for my body when I need to."

I feel Jesse tense next to me. He's thirty-seven, but there's most certainly no saggy arse or man boobs on him. I shift my legs and cross one over the other, prompting him to tighten his grip. Out the corner of my eye, I see his lips form a straight line.

"Well, I've only got nine years left, so I'd better get my fill," Kate says sardonically.

My eyes are wide, my mouth gaping. I'm at a table in a normal bar, in normal London, with normal people, and they're all talking about The Manor like it's a perfectly regular setup. No, not normal people. How can they be? These three men have all dabbled, and now Kate has been dragged to the dark side, too. I need more wine.

"It hits us women worse than you lot," Kate continues, waving her wine glass in the general direction of the men. I catch Sam winking at her. I'm not sure this is a good thing, even though Kate insists it's just fun.

"Is that what happened to you, Jesse?" I ask coolly, taking a sip of my water. His hand shifts up my thigh slightly, and I clench my legs shut.

"No." He turns to me. "Do you think I'm lacking in the body department?" He arches an expectant eyebrow at me.

What a stupid question if ever there was one. "You know I don't."

He grins. "So, I'm still your god?"

I flush and scowl at him at the same time. "You're an arrogant god," I mutter.

He leans in and wraps his palm around my neck, dragging me toward him and hitting me with a completely over-the-top kiss. Despite my surroundings, I let him take me. As usual, my mind goes blank and nothing else exists except for Jesse and his power over my entire being. Swallowed, swamped, taken...

When he finally releases me, I look at the others, suddenly hugely embarrassed at his blatant display of affection. There is a chorus of mushy vocals and one vomiting gesture. Jesse pulls me into his arms.

"Seriously, you guys," Kate scorns. "Here's the food, so enough with the sloppy shit."

Sam reaches over and plants a kiss on her cheek. "Feeling left out?"

She bats him away as the waiter places our lunch on the table.

Everyone tucks in, including Jesse, and we chat and laugh between eating. It doesn't escape my notice that Sam and Drew often flick fond looks over to my and Jesse's side of the table.

"I better get back to work," I say regretfully. It's been nice being relatively normal at lunch—as normal as it can be when you're eating with the owner of a super-plush sex haven and two of its members.

"I'm coming." Jesse chucks the remaining half of his BLT down on his plate and gets up from his chair.

"It's a two-minute walk around the corner," I say tiredly, but halt any further objections when he glares at me, and instead make my way around the table and kiss them all good-bye, shoving Kate some money for my and Jesse's lunch.

She trusts it back in my hand. "Jesse already settled the bill."

He did? I look at Jesse, but he is too busy shaking hands with the boys to notice. He collects me and starts leading me out of the bar.

"Hey!" Kate shouts to my back. "Saturday night, girly drinks?"

I stop and spin round to face her, flashing a *what-do-you-think-you're-playing-at* look. She doesn't seem to notice my reaction. No, she is too busy watching for Jesse's reaction to her request. I see Sam and Drew both watching intently, too, waiting for Jesse's response. I can feel him twitching uncomfortably next to me.

"Maybe next week," I say as confidently as I can.

"You can go," Jesse says quietly.

I can go? What does he mean, I *can* go? "No, we have The Manor anniversary tomorrow. I'll be knackered," I affirm. I do want to go, but I know he'll prohibit alcohol, the bloody control freak. I don't get legless all of the time, and the last time I did, it was his fault. I've got so much to dump on Kate as well. Both of us have, by the sounds of things. This little lunch has only clipped the corners.

"Hey, he said it's cool," Kate complains.

"I'll speak to you later," I say dismissively, hoping she will take the bloody hint and shut her gob.

"Oh yes, of course." She winks. "Later."

I want to throw my bag at her, but then I feel Jesse tug me slightly, preventing me from following through on my intention, so instead, I toss another dirty look at her before turning and letting Jesse lead me out of the bar.

We walk out onto Piccadilly into the lunchtime crowd, and I can feel the mild tension between us. He drops my hand and drapes an arm around my shoulder, pulling me into his side.

When we turn into Berkeley Street, I stop and face him. "If I go out, I won't be drinking, will I?"

"No," he says flatly. I roll my eyes and carry on walking. "You can have a drink at the party." He catches up to me and replaces his arm over my shoulder.

Yes, I can have a drink at the party because he'll be there to watch over me. The problem is, I'm not comfortable drinking in front of him.

"Would you get the doormen to spy on me, too?" I grumble.

"I don't ask them to spy on you, Ava. I ask them to watch over you."

"And call you if I don't follow the rules?" I quip, earning myself a little nudge on the hip.

"No, and call me if you are rolling around on the bar floor," he says dryly, "with your nonexistent dress around your waist."

I look up at him and find accusing eyes. Okay, yes, I was on the bar floor, but I wasn't rolling, and I wasn't steaming drunk. Not that time, anyway. Kate was and she took me down with her. As for the dress? Well, that's a trivial issue, and one that's now in a dozen strips after neurotic man here shredded the damn thing. I could go out, have a couple of glasses of wine, wear something acceptable, and not roll around on the floor. Then no red alert would need to be issued by the doorman. Maybe I could stay at Kate's so I'm not rubbing his nose in it. I laugh to myself at my ambitious idea. He will never let me stay at Kate's.

I let him hold me close to his side as we carry on our way to my office. "You've got to let me go now," I say as we near. Patrick might be there and I've not mentioned any sort of *business* lunch with Mr. Ward. This is painfully difficult.

"No," he grumbles.

"What are you going to do for the rest of the day?" This I really want to know. Please let him say that he's got a stack of business to occupy himself with so I can get to Matt's and get my stuff without worrying about fobbing him off. Withheld information isn't the same as lying.

He pouts. "Think about you."

That doesn't make me feel any better. "I'll be back at yours as soon as I finish work," I say, realizing instantly that I've just lied. I use every ounce of energy to stop myself reaching for my hair.

"Ours!" he corrects. "What time?"

"Six-ish." Give or take an hour, I add to myself.

"You like that tag-on, don't you? Ish . . ." He narrows his eyes on me, and I feel scrutinized.

"Ish," I counter, leaning on him for a kiss.

He grabs me and leans me back over his arm in a ridiculous theatrical performance before kissing the life out of me in the middle of Berkeley Square. People sidestep us and tut as they pass, but I couldn't give a toss.

"God, I fucking love, love, love you."

I grin. "I know you do."

He pulls me back up to a vertical position and then buries his face in my neck to chew my ear. "I can't get enough of you. Let me take you home."

I'm tempted to jump work and let him, when my phone starts singing, snapping me from my rebellious thoughts. I fish around in my bag while letting Jesse stick to my neck, and when I lay my hands on it, I hold it above Jesse's head to see who it is. I groan. Of all the times Mikael could call, he calls now?

Jesse pulls back and looks at me with an inquiring eye. "Who is it?"

"Just a client." I shove my phone in my bag. I'll call him back. "I'll see you at your place." I go to walk away, but he grasps my wrist.

"Damn it, Ava. *Ours!* Who was it?" His sudden change of temper catches me off guard.

"It's Mikael," I grate. "Just a client." I yank my wrist free from him and start the short remaining distance to my office.

My phone starts ringing again, and I retrieve it as I enter the office. "Mikael," I greet.

"Ava, I'm calling to confirm our Monday appointment." His soft voice seeps into my ears. It's really quite sexy. "Would midday suit?"

I collapse in my chair and swivel to face my desk, horrified to find Jesse standing over me, prowling like a raging beast, his chest heaving. Tom and Victoria are at their desks watching intently, making no attempt to hide their interest. I glance over my shoulder to find Patrick in his office, but, thank God, he's oblivious, looking completely wrapped up in something on his computer screen.

"Ava?"

"Mikael, I'm sorry." I look up at Jesse questioningly, but he ignores me, continuing with his menacing performance with no regard for our location or spectators. "Yes, fine." I try to sound professional and assertive. I fail miserably.

"Ava, are you okay?"

"Yes, fine, thank you."

"Good. So, you broke your own rule?"

My heart skips a few beats. "Pardon?" I squeeze the word through my sudden nervous breathing.

"Jesse Ward. He's a client, yes?"

I don't know what to say. No, he wasn't a client, not when I was working on Lusso, but I'm not stupid enough to point that out. Mikael must know that I'm supposed to be working for Jesse. *Supposed* to be. I haven't been back to The Manor yet, and Jesse hasn't pushed it.

"How long you have been seeing him?"

My blood runs cold as I search my brain for the right thing to say. "Urhhh, a month-ish," I stammer down the phone. Why is he asking this?

"Hmmm. That's very interesting." My blood runs even

colder. Why would that be very interesting? I'm still staring into the green eyes of the man I would die for, and I've got another man on the end of the phone sounding like he's got something to tell me—something that's going to send me crashing and burning from Central Jesse Cloud Nine, not that I'm on it at this particular point in time.

"Why would it be?" I ask. I sound terribly nervous, which is fine because I am. What does he know?

"We will discuss that when we meet."

"Okay." I hang up. That was unbelievably rude, but I don't know what else to do or say. Jesse is crowding my desk, looking like he might rip my head off, but for what? Bloody hell, in the space of five minutes, we've gone from cavorting on the pavement to a staring standoff.

We burn holes into each other with our stares, until I relent and flick my gaze over to Tom and Victoria, who seem to have settled in for the show. Then I look back at Jesse, but I'm reluctant to make the first move for fear of it all blowing up and Patrick coming to investigate the commotion. I can't sit here all day looking at him, though. "I'm at work," I say quietly and tightly, with no faith in my feigned staunchness. He looks fit to burst with rage.

"You won't see him again." He grinds out the words clearly and slowly.

"Why?" I don't bother pointing out that Mikael is a client. He knows that and judging by the look on his face, he doesn't care.

"You just won't. It's not a request, Ava. You won't defy me on this." He starts chewing that fucking lip, still brooding, still shaking with anger.

I can't do this here—not in the middle of my office. I also can't withdraw from the Life contract. "I'll see you at Lusso," I say quietly.

"Yes, you will." He turns and stalks out.

I flop back in my chair and release a long rush of breath that I hadn't realized I was holding.

"Gosh, that man can do a sexy brood," Tom chirps. "Been to The Manor lately, darling?"

Victoria starts giggling for the first time in two days. So much for wondering if she's figured it all out.

I feel fit to burst with frustration and stress, but luckily for Tom and Victoria, Patrick saves their bacon before I let loose on them.

"Flower," he says as he perches on the corner of my desk. It creaks its customary protest. "Mikael Van Der Haus has been in touch and insisted on a research trip to Sweden."

Oh fuck.

After we were awarded the design contract at Lusso, Mikael's partner had demanded genuine Italian everything, so I was sent to Italy on a research and sourcing trip. Mikael has stressed his desire for sustainable materials on Life, but I didn't anticipate this.

A trip in aid of Mikael's project will probably send Jesse to the grave.

"Is it really necessary?' I ask. *Please say no, please say no.*

"Absolutely, Mikael insisted on it. I'll look at flights." He creaks his way back up from my desk and returns to his office.

I'm in trouble here. There is not a chance in hell that I'll get to Sweden without Jesse trampling someone, and then where will that leave me? Jobless, that's where. I break out in a sweat.

"Coffee, Ava?" Sally appears from the stationary cupboard, looking as miserable as she did earlier. I need wine desperately.

"No thanks, Sally."

I look up and see Tom and Victoria with their heads down. Good. I can spend the rest of the afternoon worrying about my life drama in peace. I suddenly wish I didn't have to pick my stuff up after work. Seeing Matt is the last thing I want to do.

CHAPTER FOURTEEN

Six o'clock approaches and I start clearing my desk. Everyone else has left, so it's down to me to do the office checks and lock up. Kate pulls up in Margo Junior and I jump in.

"What's going on with you and Sam?" I fire at her immediately as I settle and put my belt on. In my huffy state, I begrudgingly marvel at the comfort of Kate's new van.

"Nice to see you, too." She pulls into the traffic.

"Come on. Spill. What's going on with you and Sam?"

She shrugs. "Nothing."

I roll my eyes on a dramatic sigh. "Nothing. Of course."

"What are you wearing to this big bash?" she asks, in an obvious diversion from my inquiries.

I inwardly groan. Am I even going now? "I don't know, Jesse is supposed to take me shopping."

"Oh? He is, is he?" she muses. "Make the most of old money-bags."

"I'm not looking forward to it. I've not been there since last Sunday, and that pouty-faced tramp will be there," I grumble. I sit back in my seat and think of all the other things I would prefer to do tomorrow night, and now that Jesse is quite clearly raging with me, my enthusiasm has not lifted. It's me who should be raging. He's got some explaining to do in light of Mikael's brainteaser. "I do know how old he is now, though."

She grins as she flicks her eyes over to me. "How old, and how did you find out?"

"Thirty-seven. I handcuffed him to the bed and tortured it out of him."

Kate bursts into laughter and I join her. I suppose it is rather funny.

*   *   *

We pull up outside my old flat, and I see Matt's white BMW. My heart sinks, but I knew he would have to be here to let me in.

"Do you want me to come in?" Kate asks.

I mull over the question for a few seconds but decide it's probably best if she waits in Margo Junior. Kate is a feisty bugger when she wants to be, and all I have to do is get in, be polite, and get out.

"No, I'll bring it out to you." I open the van door and get out, feeling sicker by the minute.

I make my way up the steps and press the buzzer for our apartment, looking up at my building and feeling unexpectedly sad that I don't live here anymore.

"Hi," Matt's happy voice comes over the intercom.

"Hi," I say as informally as I can. I don't want to get into friendly conversation with him. I'm still pissed he had the nerve to call my parents.

"I'll buzz you in."

I hear the door mechanism release and I look back at Kate, giving a little wave to indicate I'm going in. She puts her thumb up and flashes her mobile at me. Nodding my understanding, I step into the corridor of the downstairs entrance hall.

Making my way up the stairs, I take calming breaths while giving myself a mental pep talk. I must not mention the call to my parents, and I must not get involved in too much conversation.

When I reach the top, I see the front door open slightly, so shaking myself up, I walk straight in. I don't shut the door; I don't plan on being here long. I look in the kitchen and lounge for Matt, but he is nowhere to be seen, so I head for the bedroom and find my stuff piled in bags and boxes. With Matt nowhere to be found, I start collecting a few bags up in my hands, but when I turn to leave the room, Matt is standing in the doorway with a glass of red wine in his hand. He's wearing his beige suit. I've always hated that suit, not that I've told him. His dark hair is in its usual side parting and combed neatly.

"Hi," he says on an over-the-top smile.

"Hey, I looked for you," I explain as I lift the bags. "Kate's waiting in her van. I'll take these down to her." There's no hiding the hostility that develops at the mention of Kate's name, but I ignore it and walk with purpose to the door, stopping when he makes no attempt to get out of my way.

"Excuse me." My politeness is killing me.

He smiles at me, then takes a cocky swig of his wine before standing back a fraction, giving me just enough room to slip past and make my way down to Kate. When she sees me emerging from the building, she jumps out of her van and runs around to open the back doors.

"That was quick," she says, taking the bags from me.

"He's packed for me," I reply, nodding at the bags on an arched brow.

She smirks. "That's very civilized of him."

I return to the apartment and grab a few more bags, thinking how much quicker this could be over with Kate's help, but adding her to the mix is sure to send the situation into anarchy.

And with no offer of help from Matt, I traipse back and forth, collecting my worldly possessions by myself.

"How many more?" Kate asks as she thrusts my ninth and tenth bags into the van.

"Just one box," I say on an about-turn. He better have packed everything because I don't want to come back.

Making my way back up and grabbing the final box, I turn to make a hasty exit, but I find Matt blocking my escape again.

"Ava, can we talk?" he asks hopefully.

I cringe. "Talk about what?"

"Us." He waves his hand between our bodies.

"Matt, I'm not going to change my mind," I say as surely as I can, but before I know what has happened, he's on me trying to shove his tongue down my throat. I drop the box and use all the strength I possess to push him away from me. "What the hell are you doing?" I screech.

He pants a bit and then scowls at me. "Reminding you of why we're good together."

I actually laugh. It's a proper belly laugh. He's reminding me? Of what? How much of a twat he is? Please! A Jesse-style reminder it is *not*.

"Are you still seeing someone?" he asks.

"That's none of your business."

"No, but your parents were very interested."

I take a long, steady breath to prevent my hand flying out and cracking him one. I'm not even going to justify his actions with a response. "Get out of my way, Matt." I'm immensely proud of myself for keeping my voice even.

"You stupid cow."

My eyes widen. I'm stunned. I knew he had a nasty streak, but is this really necessary? I see red. "Yes, I am still seeing someone, and do you know what, Matt? He's the best I've had."

He laughs a sly, slap-worthy laugh. "He's a raving alcoholic,

Ava. Did you know that? He's probably drunk out of his skull every time he fucks you."

I falter and Matt's cocky grin widens. He thinks I'm shocked because he's just dropped the alcohol bombshell on me. I'm not. I'm shocked because he knows something about who I'm seeing. How?

I want to wipe his smug grin off his face with one swift slap. "Well, even pissed he's a better fuck than you ever were."

"You're pathetic," he snarls.

"No, Matt. I'm making up for four years of shit sex with you."

His face drops a little. He doesn't know what to say. I lean down to get the box from the floor and whip my head up when I hear the thunder of heavy footsteps charging up the stairs.

Oh fuck!

"Ava!" he roars.

Any hope I had of leaving Matt and his bewildered expression kind of commotion free has been well and truly trampled. How does he know I'm here? I'll kill Kate if she's tattled on me.

He comes bulldozing through the door and any notion I previously had that I've seen him at his angriest is thoroughly obliterated. He looks rampant, and I'm actually afraid. Not for myself, for Matt. Jesse looks capable of murder.

He looks straight at me and I wilt under his intense, furious stare. "What the *fuck* are you doing here?"

I physically tremble in my heels, silently wondering how he knows I'm here. But I dare not ask, so instead I stand with my mouth firmly shut.

"Answer me!" he roars.

I flinch. It's pretty obvious what I'm doing here, he doesn't need my confirmation, and he must have seen the bags in the back of Kate's van.

Matt wisely stands back and keeps his mouth shut. He's been on the receiving end of one of Jesse's rages before.

"I fucking told you! Don't ring him, don't come here. I said John would do it!" He waves his arms around like a deranged screwball. "Go and get in the fucking car."

I hear a snigger escape Matt's lips, and I whip my eyes around to him. He looks at me and I see a glint of sick satisfaction in his eyes. It tips me over the edge. I'm not standing here being screamed at, especially in front of my twat of an ex-boyfriend. I grab my box and steam out of my apartment, thanking all things holy that Jesse didn't walk in a few seconds earlier.

"We kissed." I hear Matt's smug voice and then Jesse's unmistakable fist in his face.

I could cry. Does Matt not know when to shut the fuck up? Jesse's thumping footsteps tail behind me as I walk out onto the street and see Kate. Sam is here—oh, and John, too.

The big guy's leaning up against his Range Rover—wraparound sunglasses in place—looking as menacing as ever, but his face is completely impassive. Kate is pacing beside her van with Sam standing to the side looking a bit concerned. Is it really necessary for everyone to be here? I give her a *don't* stare as I approach her.

She takes the box from me. "Holy fucking shit, Ava," she whispers, throwing it in the back of her van.

"Did you tell Sam I was here?" I ask shortly.

"No!' she screeches. I believe her. She wouldn't do that to me.

"John!" Jesse yells as he emerges from my building. "Put her stuff in the Rover." He shakes his recovering hand and a flash of concern twangs inside me. The bloody idiot. Couldn't he have used his left hand? And then his referral to me registers.

Her?

"Leave it, John!" I shout, halting John in his tracks. "I'm not going with him. Kate, come on." I start toward the passenger side of Kate's van and when I get to the door, I look up and see Sam with his hand on Kate's arm. She looks at Sam and he shakes his head faintly, then she looks back to me. I can see she is torn.

"Get the bags, John!" Jesse thunders down the steps.

"Leave them!" I shout.

I see John blow out an exasperated breath of air and look at Jesse for guidance, but he must decide that my wrath is the lesser of two evils because he starts transferring my things into the Range Rover. He can take my things. It doesn't mean I'm going. I get in Kate's van and throw myself back in the seat in total aggravation.

Within two seconds, the door is flung open. "Out!" His voice is shaking with anger. I couldn't give a toss.

I grab the handle to yank it shut, but he moves his body to block me. "Jesse. Just fuck off!"

"Mouth!"

"*Fuck off!*" I scream. My throat is sore, my vocal cords pleading for some calmness. I've never shouted so much. I'm shaking, trembling with fury. How dare he? How dare he behave like this after everything I've been through with him?

"Watch your fucking mouth!" He leans in and grabs me.

I fight him off, but my strength compared to his is pathetic. He manhandles me out of Margo Junior and stands me with my back facing his front, while I persistently struggle to bat him away. Wrapping an arm around my waist, he lifts me clean from the ground, carrying me to his car while I kick and scream like a three-year-old.

"Get off me!"

"Shut your filthy mouth, Ava," he grates, which only assists in encouraging me to fight him some more. I'm mortified, being manhandled in the middle of Notting Hill under the shocked stares of my best friend, her boyfriend, and John. I want to scream at the heavens. I struggle some more, trying to pry his grip from my body.

"Stop making a scene, Ava."

Looking up, I see numerous bystanders halted in their daily business, all watching the dramatic happenings unfolding before their eyes. I give in with my struggle, but mainly because I'm thoroughly exhausted. I let him bundle me into his car, batting my arms at him when he tries to put the seat belt on me.

He grabs my chin and tugs my face to his. "You had better stay fucking put!" His green eyes are brimming with fury as I stare at him defiantly before pulling my face away. I sit in the warm black leather trying to catch my breath as I watch him walk back over to John, Kate, and Sam. They're talking, but I have no idea what about. Jesse's head drops and I see Kate place a hand on his arm. Fucking traitor! Why is he the one getting all of the sympathy and reassurance when I'm the one who's just been abducted by a wild fucking maniac?

John shakes his head and clips the side of Jesse's jaw with his knuckles, but Jesse pulls back from it harshly. I lip-read John's *calm down* and watch as Jesse walks away, throwing his arms in the air before yanking his dark blond disheveled hair in frustration. John shakes his head and this time I know he just said *motherfucker*.

Good! This is an indication that John agrees with me. *Nasty qualities*, I think John said. You don't get much nastier than this. He's completely lost the plot.

I look out of the passenger window when he climbs back in the car, starts it, and roars off down the road, flinging me back in my seat. His normal driving mood is frightening enough. I'm not looking forward to this journey.

"How did you know I was here?" I keep my eyes firmly on the view whizzing past my window.

I hear him wince as he takes a corner, and out of my peripheral vision, I see him shake his hand. "It doesn't fucking matter."

"It does matter." I turn and look at his scowling profile. He's still a handsome beast. "I was fine until you turned up."

He whips his head around to face me. I meet his stare with the same fierceness he's giving me. "I'm fucking infuriated with you. Did you kiss him?"

"No!" I shriek. "He tried and I beat him off. I was just leaving." My forehead muscles are aching from scowling so much.

I jump when he punches the steering wheel. "Don't ever fucking tell me I'm possessive and over-the-top, do you hear me?"

"You are stupidly possessive!"

"Ava, in two days I've caught two men trying to get in your knickers. God knows about the times when I've not been there."

"Don't be stupid," I scoff. "You're imagining things." I'm fully aware that he's not. "How do you know Mikael?"

"What?" he snaps.

"You heard me." I can tell by the disappearance of his bottom lip between his teeth that he's thinking hard about this.

"I bought the penthouse, Ava. How do you think I know him?"

"He thought it was very interesting when I told him that we had been seeing each other for a month-ish. Why would he?"

His head whips around. "Why the fuck are you talking to him about us?"

"I wasn't, he asked the question and I answered! Why would he think it's interesting, Jesse?" I can feel myself losing control. I look away from him, trying to take some calming breaths.

"That man wants you, trust me."

"Why?" I shout, throwing my face in his direction again, but he refuses to look at me.

He punches the steering wheel again. "He wants to take you away from me!"

"But why?"

"He just fucking does!"

I jump back in my seat, shocked and unsatisfied by his vague, furious answer. This conversation will get us nowhere. He needs to calm down and so do I. I'll ask my questions when he's not looking like he may put his fist through the window.

*   *   *

He pulls up outside Lusso and I exit the car before he turns the engine off. I notice John pull into the car park as I enter the foyer, and I completely ignore Clive as he comes out from behind his desk. I head straight for the elevator.

I expect Jesse to stop the doors from shutting so he can get in, but he doesn't. He's obviously concluded that we both need to calm down as well.

I exit the lift and fish my key from the side pocket of my bag to let myself in before I slam the door behind me and chuck my bag on the floor in a temper. "Fucking man!" I curse to myself.

"Hello," a small voice says.

I look up and see a gray-haired middle-aged woman standing in front of me. I suppose I should be concerned by this strange woman in Jesse's penthouse, but I'm too angry. "Who the hell are you?" I blurt nastily. The woman recoils slightly and it's then I clock the can of furniture polish and duster in her hand.

"Cathy," she says. "I work for Jesse."

"What?" I ask impatiently, but then the anger dominating my entire being gives way to allow that little piece of information to sink in—that and the furniture polish in her hand.

Oh shit!

The door opens behind me, and I turn to see Jesse walk in. He looks at me and then at the woman standing in front of us both. "Cathy, you should probably get off now. I'll speak to you tomorrow," he says calmly, but I can still detect the anger in his voice.

"Of course." She places her polish and duster on the side table and then takes her apron off, folding it hastily, but neatly. "I've put dinner in the oven. Give it thirty minutes." She picks up a carpet bag from the floor and stuffs her apron in the top. God bless her, she smiles at me before leaving. It's more than I deserve.

Jesse gives her a peck on the cheek and a reassuring rub of the shoulder as she leaves. I watch her walk out into the foyer, and see John and Clive transporting my bags from the elevator. That's a waste of time because I'm not staying here. I stomp into the kitchen and yank the fridge open, hoping a bottle of wine might have magically found its way in there. I'm sorely disappointed.

Slamming the fridge door, I steam out of the kitchen and up the stairs. I can't even look at him at the moment. As I enter the bedroom and slam yet another door, I stand and wonder...what now? I should just leave—give us both some space to calm down. This is too intense, too quickly. It's poisonous, crippling.

I sigh wearily, putting my head in my hands in desolation, feeling the tears brimming and a lump in my throat forming. I'm head over heels in love with a man who has the most extreme temper and challenging ways. At the other end of the spectrum, though, he's the most loving, sensitive, protective man in the universe. If John's right, and he is only like this with me, should we be together? He'll be dead by the time he's forty from heart failure, and it will be my fault. With Jesse, when times are good, they are incredible, but when they are bad, they are unbearable.

I thought I was beginning to find out what I needed to know but as time goes on, it's becoming obvious that I haven't. And it doesn't look like I'm going to find out anytime soon—unless I ask Mikael...

The door flies open and Jesse comes crashing in, looking like he's been electrocuted. He's visibly shaking and the main artery in his neck is bulging. He holds up something in his hand.

"What the *fuck* is this?" He looks like he could spontaneously combust at any moment. I frown but then realize he's holding up a sheet of flight details. Patrick must have slipped them into my bag.

Oh Jesus, I'm in for it now.

Hang on a minute. "You've been through my bag!" I'm shocked. I don't know why, he invades my privacy all the fucking time. He doesn't look ashamed or apologetic. He just waves the paper in front of my face while his chest puffs in and out erratically.

I push past him and storm downstairs to my bag, hearing him follow me, his heavy breathing almost louder than his charging footsteps. I rip my bag from the floor and take it into the kitchen.

"What the hell are you doing?" he shouts. "It's not in there, it's here." He thrusts the paper under my nose as I dump my bag on the island and start rummaging through it.

I have no idea what I'm looking for.

"You are not fucking going to Sweden or Denmark or any fucking where, for that matter!" His voice is somewhere between anger and fear.

I look at him. Yes, there is definitely fear in there. "Don't go through my bag." I grind the words out through my incensed frustration and look at him accusingly.

He backs away a little and chucks the paper on the island while maintaining his infuriated glare. "Why, what else are you hiding from me?"

"Nothing!"

"Let me tell you something, lady." He stalks forward, getting his face right in mine. "I will die before I let you leave the country with that womanizing prick." A wave of pure dread travels across his face.

"He won't be coming!" I shout, slamming my bag down for effect. I don't know that for sure, and in actual fact, I suspect he probably will. He's got a plan and a motive.

"Yes, he will. He'll follow you there, trust me. He's relentless in his pursuit of women."

I actually laugh. "Just like you?"

"That was different!" he barks. He closes his eyes and lifts his fingertips to his temples to start rubbing away the tension.

"You're impossible," I spit.

"And what are you doing taking vitamins?" He scowls good and proper. "You're pregnant, aren't you?"

I grab the vitamins from my bag and throw them at his head. His eyes widen as he ducks stealthily out of the way and they crash against the wall before falling to the kitchen floor. I need to regain some control. I'm losing it in a big way.

"I bought the vitamins for you," I yell, and he looks at me like I could possibly be a fruit loop. I'm close.

"Why?" He looks at the bottle on the floor.

"You put your body through the mill. Have you forgotten?"

He scoffs. "I don't need pills, Ava. I've told you." He stalks forward and grabs my arms, pulling me close to his face. "I am not a fucking alcoholic. If I drink now, it will be because *you* make me crazy mad!" He shouts the last bit in my face.

"You blame this all on me," I state. I'm not asking it as a question, because he has already shouted it in my face.

He drops me and walks away. "No, I don't." His hands yank on the back of his hair in frustration. "What else are you keeping from me? Business trips with rich Dutchmen." He glares at me. "Cozy visits to the ex-boyfriend?"

"Cozy?" I splutter. He thinks seeing Matt was cozy? "You stupid fucking man!'

"Mouth!"

"Get lost!" I shout. He's on another fucking planet! If he knows me as well as he claims he does, then he wouldn't be throwing such stupid insinuations around.

"I can't be around you right now," he bellows. He clenches his teeth, and I see the muscles of his jaw ticking. "I fucking love you, Ava. So fucking much, but I can't look at you. This is fucked up!" He stalks out of the kitchen.

I hear the front door slam and moments later, an almighty crash. I run out to the penthouse foyer, and Jesse is nowhere to be seen, but the mirrored door of the elevator is shattered into a million pieces. Through my derangement, I instantly think of what further damage he has done to his poor hand. Then I cry. Hopeless, howl-at-the-moon blubbering. I feel completely helpless and out of control. I feel like I'm being tested, like he is trying me to see if I have the strength to get him through this total mess, and on top of that, I'm battling with the incessant niggling thought that it's me who has made him like this. It's not healthy.

I walk back into the big open living area and see all of my bags placed in a neat row at the side of the stairs. What should I do with them? Am I staying?

I leave them, and not knowing what else to do, I go and sit myself on a sun lounger on the decking area and cry to myself—loud, shoulder-shaking, pouring-tears crying, while I try to find some direction and guidance. I'm staring into space and feeling nothing but abandoned. Familiar feelings, all of which I never wanted to feel again, are flooding back into me—the empty feeling, the lost, lonely, and dejected emotions that had me residing in the lowest level of hell while Jesse wasn't in my life. How have I come to need him so much? How has this happened to me? He's walked out, and now I've got a good idea of how he felt when I did the same to him. I feel like a massive part of me is missing.

It is.

I take myself back upstairs and have a shower and stand for an age under the spray, absentmindedly soaping my body. Everywhere I turn I see us—Jesse and me on the vanity unit, against the wall, in the shower. We're everywhere. I hurry out, suddenly desperate to escape the reminder of our intimacies, and dry my hair before flopping on the bed. I'm not sure how long I'm sitting, staring blankly at the ceiling. Minutes. Hours. The dry tears making my skin stingy and tight should tell me. I try not to, but I reflect back, thinking of the times we have been apart when he's had a drink. Will he have a drink now? The thought has my heart starting a painful gallop in my chest, working its way up to my mouth. The idea of Jesse mixed with alcohol is enough to have me dashing to the kitchen to get my phone.

As I enter, I get a waft of something smelling really good. Oh! I run to the oven and turn it off, grab my phone, and dial John.

His low rumble seeps down the phone after the first ring. "He's here, Ava."

"The Manor?" I'm so relieved but at the same time, I wonder what he's doing there.

"Yeah," John sounds regretful. It makes me straighten up.

"Should I come?" I don't know why I'm asking when I'm already on my way upstairs to get dressed.

He hums down the phone, "Probably, girl. He went straight to his office."

I hang up, throw some clothes on, and head for the door. My car keys. Jesse hasn't given me my car keys back. I dive into the boxes of my belongings, praying I'll find the spare set, and eventually lay my hands on them.

I'm in the foyer of Lusso in no time at all, running through, my heels clinking fast over the floor. I notice Clive kneeling down behind his desk but I swiftly pass him without a word. I've no time for him this evening. The poor man will wonder what he has done to upset me.

"Ava!" I hear him yell after me. I wouldn't stop, but it sounds like something is seriously wrong. Maybe the mystery woman has been back.

"What's up, Clive?"

He runs toward me in a panic. "You can't go!"

What's he talking about?

"Mr. Ward," he pants, "he said you mustn't leave Lusso. He was very insistent."

"Clive, I haven't time for this." I carry on my way, but he grasps my arm.

"Please, Ava. I'll have to call him."

I don't believe this. He's got the concierge performing prisoner guard duties now? "Clive, it's not your job to do this," I point out. "Please, let go of my arm."

"Well, I did say as much myself, but Mr. Ward can be very insistent."

"How much, Clive?"

"I don't know what you're talking about," he says quickly, rearranging his hat with his spare hand. He couldn't look guiltier if he tried.

I pull my arm free from Clive's grasp and walk over to the concierge desk. "Where do you keep Mr. Ward's numbers?" I ask, scanning the high-tech display screens in front of me. I notice Clive's mobile sitting on the desk, too.

Clive walks over with a befuddled look on his face. "It's all linked to the phone through the system. Why do you ask?"

"Do you have Mr. Ward's number on your mobile?" I ask.

"No, Ava, it's all preprogrammed into the system. Resident's confidentiality and all."

"Good." I yank out the wires leading from the phone system

to the computer and drop them in a tangled mess to the floor
where they meet Clive's jaw.

I hear the poor old boy's shocked mumbling on my way out
and feel a small pang of guilt. That will be yet another repair
bill falling on the doormat of the penthouse. Jumping in my
car, I immediately notice a small back box on the dashboard and
knowing what it is, I press it and the gates to Lusso begin to
open.

The whole way to The Manor, I pray repeatedly that I'm not
going to find Jesse with a drink in his hand. This will be the first
time I've been back since my discovery of its offered activities,
but my need to see Jesse is overriding any nerves or reluctance I
have.

CHAPTER FIFTEEN

John opens The Manor door before I reach it and offers me a small, reassuring smile. "Has he calmed down?" I ask as we walk past the bar and reach the summer room. There are people scattered around the seating areas, drinking and talking, probably discussing what the evening may have in store, and I'm assaulted by a dozen inquisitive stares. I tense all over.

"Damn, girl, you affect that motherfucker." John laughs, giving me a glimpse of that gold tooth.

I let out a rush of breath in agreement. "My man is challenging."

John looks over at me and smiles. "Challenging? That's a word. I call him a fucking pain in the arse. I've got to admire his determination, though."

"Determination?" I feel my brow knit. "Determination to be challenging?"

John stops as we reach Jesse's office. "I've never seen him so determined to live."

"What do you mean by that?" I can't help the confusion in my tone. I can't see any determination to live. All I see is determination to kill himself off from stress. He's completely self-destructive.

My breath hitches in my throat.

Self-destructive. Jesse has said that before—when he took me on his bike.

"Trust me, it's a good thing." John looks at me affectionately. "Be easy on him."

"How long have you known him, John?"

"Long enough, girl. I'll leave you to it." He takes his mountain of a body and strides off down the corridor.

"Thanks, John," I say to his back.

"S'all good, girl. S'all good."

I stand outside Jesse's office with my hand hovering over the doorknob. John's unexpected information, albeit vague, has piqued my curiosity more. My mind is racing with thoughts of alcohol, dabbling, lack of leathers, and scars. I turn the handle and walk, with caution, into Jesse's office.

And I don't like what I see.

Jesse is in his big office chair facing Sarah, who is perched on the corner of his desk. A thud of possessiveness slaps me in the face, but it's the bottle of vodka on Jesse's desk that has me more fretful. I can fight off unwanted female attention, as long as it's unwanted. The vodka is another matter entirely.

They look up at me in unison, and she flashes me an insincere smile. Then I notice a bag of ice resting on Jesse's hand. I was right to have a touch of the green-eyed monster. They look, in Jesse's words, very cozy. Now there is absolutely no doubt in my mind that these two have had a sexual relationship. It's written all over her face. I feel sick, jealous. and dangerously possessive.

I look at Jesse, and he meets my gaze. He's still in his charcoal trousers, but the sleeves of his black shirt are rolled up. His dirty blond hair is a glorious mess on top of his beautiful head, but despite all of his loveliness, he looks fearful and uneasy. I don't blame him. I've just walked in on him looking cozy with another woman and with a bottle of the evil stuff in front of him. It's my worst nightmares wrapped into one.

He slowly turns his chair with his feet, away from Sarah and toward me.

"Have you had a drink?" My voice is even and strong. I feel anything but.

He shakes his head. "No."

I'm uncertain as to whether the small voice is due to the woman or the vodka. He drops his head slightly, and the silence is awkward, but then Sarah rests a hand on Jesse's arm, and I want to dive on the desk and yank her hair out. Jesse flinches and snaps his eyes to mine.

Who the fuck does she think she is? I'm not naive enough to believe that she is trying to be a supportive friend. I'm suddenly furious with myself for allowing another woman the opportunity to comfort him, especially this woman. That's my job.

"Do you mind?" I look directly at her so there's no mistaking whom I'm talking to.

She looks up at me but makes no attempt to remove her hand from Jesse. "Excuse me?"

"You heard me." I flash her a don't-fuck-with-me glare and she smirks an almost undetectable smirk.

Jesse pulls his arm away and her hand falls to the desk. Then he flicks his eyes nervously between us. God bless him, he's keeping his mouth firmly shut, but then the bitch only leans down and kisses him on the cheek, letting her lips linger there for longer than is really necessary.

"Call me if you need me, sweetie," she says in the most ridiculous seductive voice I've ever heard.

Jesse stiffens from head to toe and looks at me, all wide eyed and alarmed. He's right to be anxious, especially after the barrel of shit he's just thrown at me because of a male client and an ex-boyfriend. Matt and Mikael would be a mass of body parts if the boot was on the other foot.

I grab his office door and open it wide before fixing my eyes on the blonde, larger-than-life tramp. "Good-bye, Sarah," I say with optimum finality.

She looks at me with a self-assured face and slides off Jesse's desk, sauntering across his office at a leisurely pace while giving me the eyeball. I hold her cocky face with my own take-no-prisoners stare, all the way to the door that I'm holding open for her, and as soon as her six-inch platform heels are over the threshold, I slam it behind her and silently hope it collided with her toned arse.

Now, let's deal with my challenging man. Seeing him sitting there with Sarah has made something perfectly clear to me.

He's mine...end of.

I turn to face him. He hasn't moved from his chair, the bottle of vodka is still in the middle of his desk, and he's chewing his bloody lip, cogs steaming.

I nod at the bottle. "Why is that there?"

"I don't know." His face is tortured and it kills me to be on the other side of the room from him.

"Do you want to drink it?"

"Not now you're here." His quiet words register loud and clear.

"You walked out on me," I remind him.

"I know."

"What if I hadn't come?" That's the operative question here. I'm revisiting the same thing over and over in my mind. He behaves like this is a piece of cake, but then I find him keeping company with a woman and a bottle of vodka because we've had words. I can't worry like this every time we quarrel.

"I wouldn't have drunk it." He pushes it away.

"Then why is it there?"

He shrugs casually. It makes me mad. My fear was warranted

and he expects me to accept his vague answers and shoulder shrugs? "I wasn't going to drink it, Ava." His voice is slightly irritated.

"Would you drink it if I leave?"

His eyes fly to mine, panic invading his handsome face. "Are you going to leave me?"

"You need to give me some answers." I'm threatening him, but I feel like it's my only option. There are some things he needs to tell me. "Why is Mikael so interested in our relationship?"

"His wife left him," he spits the words out quickly.

"Because you slept with her."

"Yes."

"When?"

"Months ago, Ava." He looks at me, sincerity in his eyes. "She was the woman who turned up at Lusso. I'll tell you before you threaten to leave me again." There's a dash of sarcasm in his tone, which I ignore.

"She wasn't worried about you, was she?"

"Yes, probably, but she wants me, too."

"Who wouldn't?" I feel incredibly calm.

He nods mildly. "I've made it clear, Ava. I slept with her months ago, and she'd gone back to Denmark. I don't know why she's decided to pursue me now."

I believe him, and anyway, Mikael has been sorting his divorce out, and divorcing someone takes time. It must have been some months ago.

"So he wants to take me away from you, like you took his wife from him."

He drops his head to his hands. "I didn't take her away, Ava. She left of her own accord, but yes, he does want to take you away from me."

"But you were all friendly, you bought Lusso." My head is hurting.

"It's just a front, Ava—on his part. He had nothing on me, nothing he could hurt me with because I didn't care about anything. But now I have you." He looks up at me. "Now, he knows where to stick the knife in."

My eyes start to prickle, and I watch as his face falls, his own eyes glazing over. That's as much as I can take being this far away from him. I walk over to his chair and he opens his arms to me. I ignore his swollen hand and crawl onto his lap, letting him swamp me in his arms and invade all of my senses. His touch and his smell settle me immediately, and the inevitable happens when we unite with each other like this—all of the issues causing us turmoil seem inconsequential and of no importance. It's just us in our own little sphere of contentment, soothing each other, settling each other.

"I'll die loving you. I can't let you go to Sweden."

I sigh. "I know."

"And you should have let me deal with your things. I didn't want you seeing him," he adds.

I'm submitting to him now, but I don't care. "I know. He knows about you."

I feel him stiffen under me. "Knows about me?"

"He told me you're a raving alcoholic."

He relaxes and laughs. "I'm a raving alcoholic?"

I look up at him, shocked by his blasé reaction to something so detrimental. "It's not funny. How does he know?"

"Ava, I honestly have no idea." He sighs. "Anyway, he's misinformed because I'm not an alcoholic."

"Yes, I know," I relent, but I'm pretty sure that Jesse's issue with drink would register somewhere on the alcoholic scale. "Jesse, what am I going to do? Mikael is an important client." I suddenly have a horribly unpleasant thought. "Did he rehire me for the Life Building just because of you?"

He smiles. "No, Ava. He didn't even know about us until yes-

terday. He hired you because you're a talented designer. The fact
that you're also stunningly beautiful was an additional benefit.
And the fact that I happened to fall in love with you was an even
bigger bonus for him."

"You exposed yourself," I say quietly. "If you hadn't trampled
my meeting, then he might never have made the connection."

"I acted on impulse when I saw your diary." He shrugs. "Anyway, he would have pursued you whether he knew you were
mine or not. Like I said, he's relentless."

I remember his eyes bulging and his jaw ticking when he
clocked my diary. It wasn't because I've replaced it. It's because
Mikael's name was plastered all over it. "How do you know? He's
married. Well, was married."

"That never stopped him before, Ava."

I'm in absolute mental meltdown. I can't possibly work
with Mikael now—not after discovering this. I don't want to
be anywhere near him. Oh God, I'm supposed to be meeting
him on Monday. This is going to get horribly messy. I want
to yell at Jesse for not keeping it in his pants. I think back
to that nasty creature John ejected from The Manor the day I
discovered what it really was. He was bawling on about husbands and conscience not getting in Jesse's way. How many
marriages has Jesse broken? How many husbands out there
want revenge?

I'm snapped from my unwelcome thoughts when Jesse cups
my face with his hand. "How did you get here?"

I grin. "I distracted your appointed guard."

His eyes sparkle, his lips twitch. "I shall have to sack him.
How did you manage that?"

I lose my grin when I consider the repair bill Jesse will be
getting. "Jesse, he's sixty, if a day. I disconnected his telephone
system so he couldn't advise you of my escape from your tower
in the sky."

"Our tower. Disconnected?" His frown line is light across his forehead.

I bury my face back in his chest. "I ripped the wires out."

"Oh," he says flatly, but I know he's suppressing a laugh.

"What are you playing at, getting a pensioner to try and keep me indoors?" I ask accusingly. I could have outrun Clive, even in my heels.

He strokes my hair softly. "I didn't want you to leave."

"Well, you should've stayed yourself then." I pull his shirt out of his trousers and slide my hands up to get my fix of his warm chest. He tightens his hold of me, and I feel his beating heart under my palms. It's so comforting.

"I was crazy mad." He sighs. "You make me crazy mad." He kisses my temple and burrows deeply into my hair.

"How's your hand?"

"It would be fine, if I didn't keep smashing it into things," he answers dryly.

I wriggle free of his embrace. "Let me see." I sit up on his lap and he pulls his hand from behind me to rest between our bodies. I gingerly take it. He doesn't wince, but I flick him a quick glance to check his face isn't pained. The glass door of the elevator was in a million pieces and I expected his hand to be.

"I'm fine."

"You smashed the elevator door," I say, stroking his recovering fist.

"I was really mad."

"You already told me that. What about the hijacking of my office this afternoon? Were you crazy mad then?"

"Yes, I was." He narrows his eyes on me, but then he grins. "A bit like you were just now."

"I wasn't mad, Jesse.' I look at his damaged hand with the pity I feel for the pathetic woman I've just evicted from his office. "I was marking what's mine. She wants you. She couldn't have been more obvious if she'd straddled you and thrust her tits in your face." I screw my face up in disgust at her desperation, looking up to find his grin has broken out into a full-on, Hollywood-worthy beam. This smile is a step up from his one reserved only for women. This smile is reserved only for me. I can't help the little smile tickling the corners of my mouth.

"You look very happy with yourself." He brushes me away from fussing over his hand.

"Oh, I am. I like it when you're all possessive and protective. It tells me you're crazy in love with me."

"I am, even though you are stupidly challenging. And don't be calling Sarah *sweetie*," I mock.

He circles our noses and pushes his lips onto mine. "I won't."

"You've slept with her." It's a statement, not a question. He recoils, his green pools all wide and wary. I roll my eyes. "A dabble?" I ask.

His eyes drop down slightly. "Yeah." His expression and body language scream uncomfortable. He's not happy with this line of conversation.

I bloody knew it. Okay, that's fine. I can cope with this as long as he keeps the hussy at arm's length—or farther. That might be bloody hard when the woman works for him and follows him around like a lost puppy.

"I just want to say one thing," I press. I need to make this clear if I'm ever going to keep company, both socially and professionally, with any men in future, although I'm fully aware that Jesse's possessive streak is never going to go away completely. "It's all about you." I drop a kiss onto his lips to reinforce my declaration.

"It's all about me," he mumbles against me.

I grin. "Good boy."

He pulls back and runs his fingers down my neck, his eyes full of satisfaction. "I love you, Ava."

I rest my cheek on his shoulder. "I know."

"Take the day off work tomorrow."

I've not even advised Patrick of my afternoon appointment with Mr. Ward, but I need a break and a long weekend with Jesse is hard to turn down. I've no appointments and I'm ridiculously up to date with everything else. Patrick owes me a few days in lieu. He won't mind.

I pull myself away from his chest. "Okay."

He frowns, like I'm going to retract my answer or add a *but* to it. "Really?" His eyes twinkle as his lips tip at the edges. "You're being very reasonable. That's not like you."

My eyes bulge at his comment. I know he knows that *he's* the unreasonable one. He's playing on it. I don't bite. "I'm ignoring you," I grumble.

"Not for long. I'm taking you home to *our* tower in the sky. I've not been inside you for way too long." He stands and props me on my feet. "Shall we?" He cocks his arm out and I link it with mine, my stomach clenching at the prospects awaiting me when we get home.

"I fancy a bit of rowing," I flip casually.

He raises a sardonic eyebrow at me. "We'll row another day, baby. I want to make love," he says softly, looking down at me. I smile.

He leads me through the summer room, to the entrance hall, and I ignore the disappointed faces on all of the women we pass, all obviously hoping we would be leaving separately. John meets us at the door and gives me his distinguished smile.

"I'll see you tomorrow," Jesse informs him as he opens the door for me.

"S'all good." He slaps Jesse on the shoulder and walks off in the direction of the bar.

Jesse places his hand in the small of my back to guide me out, and as I turn, I catch a glimpse of Sarah standing in the doorway of the bar. She greets John, but her eyes are fixed firmly on me and Jesse leaving The Manor. There is no mistaking the look of bitterness on her pouty face. I predict handbags at dawn.

"Leave your car, we'll get it tomorrow," he says as he opens the passenger door to his Aston Martin.

I don't argue.

As we make our way down the long driveway, we pass Sam's Porsche headed toward The Manor. I bolt upright in my seat. "Hey, there's Kate!" I blurt. Sam honks his horn and puts his thumb up to Jesse, and I crane my neck as we pass them. Kate puts a reluctant hand up to me. "What's she doing here?" I look at Jesse, who keeps his eyes on the road. Oh good God! "She's a member, isn't she?" I ask accusingly.

"I don't discuss members. Confidentiality." He's deadpan.

"So she *is* a member!"

He shrugs and presses a button to open the gates. The little minx! Why hasn't she told me? Is she here for all things kinky in general, or is she here for Sam specifically? Christ, just when I thought my fiery friend couldn't surprise me more.

Jesse roars off down the road and plays with a few buttons on the steering wheel, the stereo kicking in and surrounding us with a distinct male voice.

"Who's this?"

He starts tapping the steering wheel. "John Legend. You like?"

Oh, I do. I reach over to the steering wheel and Jesse slides his hands down to give me access to the controls. I locate the right one and turn it up more.

"I'll take that as a yes." He smirks and reaches over to place his hand on my knee. I cover it with mine.

"Is your hand okay?"

"Fine, unravel your knickers, lady."

"I need to text Patrick."

"Yes, do. I'm looking forward to having you all to myself to-morrow and all weekend." He removes his hand from my knee and replaces it on the steering wheel.

I fire a quick text over to Patrick and, as expected, he replies speedily, telling me to have a well-deserved day off.

Perfect. Three days straight of undisturbed time on Central Jesse Cloud Nine.

Chapter Sixteen

We stroll into Lusso hand in hand, and Clive gives me a disapproving glare. My apologetic look doesn't seem to wash.

"Mr. Ward," he says cautiously, still eyeing me.

"Clive." Jesse nods and leads me to the elevator without another word.

As the doors close, I'm not surprised to be thrust up against the wall, the full length of his body cocooning mine. The powerful throb I'm so familiar with these days drops straight into my groin and has my veins heating immediately. He slips his leg between my thighs and raises it, brushing over my core and, just like that, I'm panting.

"You've upset the concierge," he breathes, his lips close to mine.

"Damn." I force the word out through my strangled breaths, and he crashes his lips to mine, taking them with conviction and purpose, while grinding his beating erection against me. Oh Lord, I want to rip his clothes off, but this most certainly isn't making love, not that I would even dream of complaining.

"Why aren't you wearing a dress?" he asks irritably, between plunging his tongue in and out urgently.

I'm asking myself the very same question. It would be around my waist by now and he would be inside me. "I'm running out of dresses."

He moans into my mouth. "Tomorrow, we buy only dresses." He thrusts his hips forward and upward, colliding with and rubbing against my core.

I sigh in pure, uninhibited pleasure. "Tomorrow we buy one dress." I reach down between us and unfasten his belt as he breaks away from my lips and rolls his damp forehead over mine, his eyes shining with approval, his lips parted. I rub the back of my palm over his trousers, feeling him twitch and jerk beneath my touch while I run a trail across his bottom lip with my tongue. Then I unzip him and reach in to free his raging hard-on, taking a firm grip at the base, squeezing lightly.

He closes his eyes tight. "Mouth," he commands gently.

The elevator doors open onto the penthouse foyer, and I've never been more relieved that it's the only lift that comes up to the top floor. I slide my back down the wall until I'm crouched in front of him, but his hot, throbbing cock is not the only thing that has my interest. His angry scar catches my attention. I've made a pact with myself to not ask anymore, but I can't help my curiosity, especially after what John said about Jesse being self-destructive. I look up at him, finding his arms rigid and braced against the wall above my head, his eyes on me.

"What are you waiting for?" he asks me, thrusting his hips forward impatiently. All thoughts of mystery scars are expelled as I remember the last time I took him like this—how brutal he was. Will he be like that again?

I drag my eyes away from his carnal stare and flex my grip on his throbbing cock, then reaching forward, I lap up the leaking bead of cum from his swollen crown and slowly draw my hand forward, hearing him moan low in his throat, his hips shaking slightly. His breathing quickens with each lazy stroke I draw, his lower abdomen rising and falling before my eyes and when I hear him curse, I wickedly lap at his balls before gliding my tongue slowly but firmly up the underside, rising on my legs slightly to ensure I reach the very tip.

"All the way, Ava," he pants.

I'm aware of the door on the elevator closing again and Jesse reaching over, slamming his fist against the button before returning his hand to the wall behind me.

Wrapping my lips around his head, I circle my tongue slowly, delicately. He shudders. I love doing this to him. I love instigating these sounds from his mouth and the reactions from his body.

I wait for his surge forward, but it doesn't come. He's struggling. I can feel his tension seeping into my body from our contact; I can see his hips shaking slightly in front of me. I put him out of his misery and take him deep into my mouth until he hits the back of my throat. He feels like velvet on my tongue. Perfect. Right. The suppressed bark he releases as I pull back, lap slowly, and take him again fills me with satisfaction and confidence. This time, his hips surge forward, and with my head against the wall, there is no retreating space. He moves his hands to cup the back of my head, padding me as he powers forward on a shout, throwing his head back and driving in and out of my mouth purposefully.

I remember to relax, my gag reflex working hard, and let my hands drift around his hips to find his tight arse. Then I bury my fingernails into his toned flesh.

"Harder!" His voice is severe and animalistic. I dig in harder. "Oh fuck." He continues with his drives, and I know he's close. I pry one hand off a cheek and reach between his thighs to wrap my fist around his balls. It's his undoing.

"Holy shit!" he yelps, pulling out to wrap his own fist around the base. "Keep hold and open your mouth." His eyes drill into me.

I do what I'm told, keeping my tight grip of his heavy sac and opening my mouth, maintaining our eye contact. He pistons his fist back and forth, the muscles in his neck bulging, and on a stifled cry, he rests the broad head of his cock on my lower lip and releases into me, hot, creamy liquid hitting the back of my throat and coating the inside of my mouth. I swallow impulsively.

His strokes slowly and I loosen my vise lock around his sac, dragging my hand, palm up, between his thighs until I meet his slow caresses. Curling my hand around his fist, we work him down together as I lap up the salty essence of him pouring into my mouth.

"I want one of those every day for the rest of my life." His face is poker straight, his voice deadly serious, and I hope he means from me. "From you," he adds, as if reading my mind.

I smile and return my attention to his steel length, which is still contracting through both of our hands. I circle and lick, ensuring I've got every last bit of him, and then drop a tender kiss on the very tip.

His fingers flex and I release him. "Come here." He reaches down and pulls me up against his chest. "I love you and your filthy mouth," he says quietly as he nuzzles my nose with his.

"I know you do." I reach down to start tucking him back in and refastening his trousers.

He lets me finish securing him and then grabs my hand, pulling me out of the elevator toward the penthouse door. "That was a complete waste of time. They'll be off as soon as I get you inside."

He lets us in and the smell of something lovely invades my nostrils. "Oh, dinner!" I'd completely forgotten about that. Thank God I turned the oven off, or we might have returned to fire engines and yet more damage bills.

He leads me into the kitchen and releases my hand to grab an oven glove, putting it on and pulling out an overcooked lasagna. He dumps it on the side, shaking his head. "I employ a housekeeper and a cook and you still manage to burn dinner."

What with our screaming match and subsequent makeup, I had forgotten about the poor woman whom I was so inexcusably rude to. I will have to make amends with her. She probably thinks I'm a total bitch. "Will she come back?"

He laughs. "I hope so." He pokes the crusty top layer of the lasagna. "Cathy's lasagna is delicious." He focuses his eyes back on me. "It looks like I'll have to find something else to eat."

Slowly stalking toward me, his green eyes full of promise and pleasure, he wraps his arm around my back and carries me tightly against his chest. I reach up and fan my fingers through his soft, messy mop and frown when he bypasses the stairs, heading for the terrace.

"Where are we going?" I ask as I watch the stairs pass.

"An alfresco fuck." He pushes his lips to mine. "It's a pleasant evening. Let's not waste it."

He carries me onto the terrace, the sounds of London by night clear in the cool evening air, and I'm placed on my feet before he starts unbuttoning my blouse, his big fingers struggling with the tiny gold buttons, his concentration frown tickling his forehead. I reach for his trousers and start undoing his belt and fly. Then, starting at the bottom of his shirt, I undo each button slowly until his delicious chest is warm and firm under my palms. I circle his nipples with my thumbs as he reaches the final button of my blouse before moving to my trousers.

"Show-off," he mutters, his lips finding mine as he starts feeling for my trouser fastening. It's cruel, but I let him search. He feels around the front and then moves his hands to the back, and when he has no luck there either, he growls. "Where's the zipper?" he moans against my lips.

I collect his hands from my back, guiding them to the side

fastening of my trousers, and he makes swift work of getting it down and lifting me so I can kick my shoes off. He drags my trousers down. "Yet another reason for dresses only," he complains as he pushes my blouse off my shoulders. "Anything that stops me from getting to you fast has to go."

I smile to myself. Now he's trampling my wardrobe?

The cool air attacks my skin, puckering my already-solid nipples further. He steps back from me and kicks his Grensons off before removing his socks, trousers, and the rest of his shirt while running his shimmering eyes up and down my body.

"Lace," he says approvingly, and then he slowly drags his boxers down his thighs, his cock springing free and ready. I want to drop to my knees and take his deliciousness in my mouth all over again, but the urgent thump in my own groin is demanding attention. I reach around my back and unclasp my bra, letting it fall to the wooden floor, and within a second, his body is pressed up against mine and he's breathing in my face.

I feel him slip a finger into the seam of my underwear and brush across my clitoris, prompting my head to drop to his chest and my hands to grab his arms, steadying myself as his touch sends electric shocks to every nerve ending.

"Wet," he says, all low and rough, extending the word as he rolls the tip of his finger around and around, applying a little pressure when he reaches the top. "Just for me?"

"Just for you," I pant.

The satisfying rumble that escapes his lips vibrates in the evening air. I will always be his.

My head lifts and his lips skim against mine, coaxing my mouth to part as my knickers are pushed down my thighs and his tongue slips between my lips on a shallow moan. The taste of him is addictive, and I return every lap, lick, and stroke with my own, until he pulls away and kneels before me, dragging my underwear off my legs. He wastes no time burying his nose in the hair at the apex of my thighs, and then draws a long, hot, excruciating stroke straight up the center of my core.

I moan, my knees buckle, and an almost painful buzzing starts at the very tip of my sex.

"Ohhhh."

His grip strengthens around my hips as he continues his hot trail straight up the center of my body until he's at my neck and then in my mouth, taking it with respect and passion, humming into me.

Releasing my lips, he locks eyes with me, his green gaze seeping into me. "You are my life." His clear words stab at my heart as he returns to worshipping my mouth delicately, running his palm over my bum and down the back of my thigh. He tugs gently to pull my leg up, so my inner leg cradles his hip. Then he pulls back. "Do you love me?" His eyes search mine.

"You know I do," I whisper.

"Say it. I need to hear it." His voice is laced with desperation.

I don't hesitate. "I love you." I kiss his moist, full mouth and wrap my arms around his neck, and then gracefully lift myself up his body to straddle him. "I'll always love you." I stare him square in his beautiful, cloudy green eyes as he positions himself at my entrance. He hovers there, and I struggle to resist sinking down onto him.

"Do you need me?" he asks.

"I need you." I know this satisfies him as much, if not more, as "I love you."

"Always," he confirms, and then he pushes slowly and with control into me in one patient motion, both of us sucking in sharp breaths as we unite.

He holds me to him while we stabilize our breathing, and then walks over to the lounger and lowers me onto it, bringing his body down with me so the connection isn't broken. He stares down at me with the most incredible amount of sincerity gushing from his eyes.

"Feel how perfect we are together?" He slowly withdraws and sinks back in, setting a smooth, steady foundation for what's to come. He wants to *really* make love. "Do you feel it?" he asks softly, repeating the scorching motion, accelerating my need for him.

"I do," I confirm quietly. From the very first time we connected I felt it, probably even from the very first time our eyes met.

He continues with his slow, restrained strokes, and I shift my hands down to his back, trailing soft flicks over his firm flesh. "Me too," he whispers. "Let's make love."

I concentrate on absorbing him into me as he seeps back and forth, swiveling his hips each time and carrying me closer to climax. He's looking at me with complete awe and devotion, our eyes burning into each other, his patience and willpower to maintain his steady, luscious pace making me love him all the more. He really does make sweet love.

His frown line swims with moisture that shimmers on his brow, even in the cool air surrounding us. Unable to resist, I cup the side of his face, desperate to feel him, as he stares down at me, his shaking body vibrating all over me. He's pulsating inside me, and I instinctively contract around him as he lets out a rush of breath.

"Oh God, Ava," he breathes, sinking in and grinding down hard. The exact strokes of my inner wall are wreaking havoc with my need to thrust up and capture the orgasm that's moving forward.

"I can't hold on to it anymore," I pant.

"Together," he gasps, and I tense my thighs as he jerks forward again, this time with less control. He puffs uncontrolled spurts of air and rests his forehead on mine as he regains control with another delicious plunge.

"I'm there, Jesse," I whimper, feeling my self-control pang and dissipate.

I shatter underneath him on a loud cry.

He quickens his last few drives, sending himself over the edge with me. "Oh Jesus," he yells, thrusting one last time and holding himself deep inside me before collapsing on top of me to join me in my aftermath. His erection jumps and jacks as he comes inside me, filling me, heating me, completing me.

"Fuckkkkkkkkk," I muse quietly, my eyes closing in relaxed satisfaction. This man has a direct link to my release switch.

"Mouth," he murmurs into my neck through exhausted breaths. "Do you think you will ever stop swearing?"

"I only swear when you challenge me or pleasure me," I defend myself and trail the word *fuck* across his back with my fingertip. He pushes himself up on his elbow, slipping out of me so he can look down into my eyes. Then he takes his finger and slowly trails the word *mouth* across my breasts before dropping a kiss on each nipple. I grin when he flicks his eyes up to me. They are dancing with mischief as he clamps his teeth lightly on my tight bud.

"Ouch!" I laugh.

He releases and laps a wet circle around my breast and then grabs my hip. I jump under him on a yelp as he clamps his teeth back down over my nipple. My body stills in a heartbeat as I catch onto his game immediately.

"You can't!" I cry, as he slowly starts massaging my hip with the tips of his fingers while he remains locked onto my nipple. I clench my eyes shut and wiggle my feet to try and prevent the reflex reaction of bucking him off me. "Jesse, please stop!" I hear him chuckle and increase the pressure on my hip and nipple. "Please!" I squeal through a giggle. My nipple would probably hurt if I weren't being distracted by the unbearable hip torture. He's driving me insane!

My lungs scream a thank-you as I release a rush of air and muster up the strength to blank out his torture. I still under him, and after what seems like forever, he eases off my hip bone and starts sucking the life back into my nipple.

I sigh. "You'll be the one getting a retribution fuck."

He grabs my hip again. "Ava!" he scorns me tiredly before returning his attention to my breasts. I heave a huge contented exhale and close my eyes while Jesse lavishes me with his tongue.

"You're shivering," he says against my chest. "Let me get you inside." He lifts up, and I grumble an audible objection, yanking him back down onto me, making him chuckle. "Comfy?"

"Hmmm." I can't talk.

"Bed." He pulls me up so I can wrap myself around him, which I do without delay, sinking my nose into the comfort of his neck.

Once he's carried me up to the master suite, I'm lowered into bed, and as soon as Jesse slips in beside me, I crawl onto his chest. He kisses my hair before smoothing his palm up and down my back. I shift closer to him; I can't get near enough. As always, there is no space welcome between us.

CHAPTER SEVENTEEN

I wake up with Jesse buried deep inside me, his chest to my back as he holds my waist and pumps forward. My brain isn't the only thing woken up. My body jumps to attention, and I reach back and curl my fingers into his hair, arching my back and tilting my head back to find his lips.

I let him take my mouth, our tongues delving wildly as he pistons forward. I push myself back onto him with each surge, every one cranking me up further and further.

"Ava, I can't get enough of you," he gasps against my mouth. "Promise you'll never leave me?"

"I won't." I fist my hands in his hair and yank his lips back down to mine. I love his mouth, even when he's being challenging and I want to sew it shut. Will he always make me swear to stay? I'll always comply, without a shadow of a doubt, but what I really want is for him to know this without having to ask me to repeatedly swear on it.

I pull away to look at my uncertain man. He shows such confidence in everything except this. "Please believe me." He maintains his firm, powerful drives as he looks at me, offers a small smile, then bangs our mouths back together, increasing the tempo of his thrusts further.

I try hard, but I can't keep my mouth to his when he's thundering forward with such intensity. I release him and face forward, gripping the edge of the mattress to keep myself in position as I'm yanked back onto him repeatedly.

The coil snaps and I jerk as we both yell at the same time and he charges forward manically, throwing me into a bottomless abyss of utter pleasure. I try and catch my breath, my heart fighting to gain control and my body convulsing of its own accord. Jesse swears and bucks forward one last frenzied time, and then the warm sensation of his release floods me.

"Oh my fucking God," he puffs, slipping out of me and falling onto his back.

I roll over and climb onto his body, straddling his hips and lying on his chest, nuzzling my face in his neck. "That wasn't sleepy sex."

"No?" he pants.

"No. That was a sleepy fuck." I wince, immediately realizing that I just swore and we haven't even gotten out of bed yet.

"For God's sake, Ava. Stop swearing!"

"Sorry." I bite his neck and suck a little.

"Are you trying to mark me?" he asks, but he doesn't stop me.

"No, just tasting." He lets me have my way, and I spend forever skimming my lips all over his face, his neck, his chest.

He sighs deeply. "Ava?"

"Hmmm?"

"I knew you were the one the second I laid eyes on you."

"The one?" I try to lift, but I'm pushed back into his neck. He turns his face and begins nuzzling at my ear.

"The one to bring me back to life," he says in that matter-of-fact tone, the one that basically means he's saying something only he understands.

I make it out of his embrace this time and find his gaze. "How did you know?"

He rolls me onto my back, coating me completely, and looks me straight in the eyes. His greens are bursting with meaning. "Because my heart started beating again."

A lump jumps into my throat. That is some serious deep, and I'm totally overwhelmed by it. I don't know what to say. He's looking down at me, this devastating man, like I'm the only thing that exists.

I pull at his grip on my wrists until he lets go and throw my arms around his body, my legs around his waist, holding on to him like *he* is the only thing that exists.

He is, for me.

I don't know the whys and wherefores of that statement, but the power of those words really does say it all. He can't live without me. Well, I couldn't live without him either. This man is my world.

He lies still over me and lets me squeeze him until my muscles ache. "Can I feed you?" I ask when my thigh muscles start to scream in protest. He lifts me from the bed, still coiled around his body, and carries me from the bedroom and down the stairs. "I'm going to forget how to use my legs," I say as he reaches the bottom and heads for the kitchen.

"Then I'll carry you everywhere."

"You would like that, wouldn't you?" It would be a perfect excuse for him to have me nailed to him.

"I would love it." He smirks at me and parks me on the marble, the coldness radiating through my backside reminding me that we're both stark, bollock naked. I admire his perfect arse as he walks over to the fridge and collects an assortment of breakfast things and a jar of peanut butter.

I slide off the island. "I'm supposed to be making *you* breakfast." I shove him out of the way. "Sit," I command in my most demanding tone. He grins and grabs the jar of peanut butter before tweaking my nipple and doing a runner to the stool. "What

do you want?" I ask as I shove some bread in the toaster. I turn
and see him diving into his fresh jar.

"Fried eggs," he says around a finger, blatantly trying to suppress a grin.

I look down at my naked form. I might have to get dressed
if he wants fried anything. Looking back up to him, I find he
has lost the battle and is grinning, his face delighted. "I'll cook
yours, if you cook mine." I run my eyes down his naked chest
and raise my eyebrows.

"Savage," he says, removing his finger from his mouth.

Both of our heads snap toward the kitchen archway when we
hear the front door opening. My wide eyes flick back to Jesse,
who has a finger suspended in midair on its way to his mouth.
He is looking as equally who-the-fuck?

Jumping up, he knocks his jar of peanut butter flying off the
island, sending it crashing to the floor, where it smashes, scatter-
ing glass everywhere. I'm panicking now.

"Fucking hell!" He looks at me, all wide eyed. "It's Cathy!"

Oh good God help me!

I ripped her head off last night and now I'm going to flash
her! And to top it off, her burned lasagna is sitting on the side,
bold as brass. She's going to hate me. There is no way out of this
kitchen without going toward the source of our distress. I stare
at Jesse. He's frozen on the spot, looking as torn as I am. Cathy
probably won't mind copping a load of him. I smile, but then
snap back to the here and now. I finish ogling my finely tuned
man and peg it across the kitchen.

"Shit!" A stab of pain shoots through my foot. "Ouch ouch
ouch!" I carry on my way, trying to ignore the pain.

Jesse is not far behind me, laughing uncontrollably as we run
up the stairs. "Mouth!" he splutters, and smacks my arse.

"Goodness gracious!"

I hear the distressed voice as we reach the top. Oh, what must we look like? I run full pelt to the bedroom and throw my-self under the covers. I feel Jesse land on the bed. "Where are you?" He works his way through the covers until he locates me with my head buried in the pillow. "There you are." He flips me over and submerges his face in my breasts. "You've upset the concierge, and now you've *really* upset my housekeeper."

"Don't!" I throw my arms over my face in complete despair.

He laughs. "Let me see your foot.' He shifts himself onto his heels and clasps my foot in his hand.

"It hurts," I complain when I feel his fingertip run lightly over my heel.

"Baby, you've got a piece of glass stuck." He kisses the heel of my foot and jumps up from the bed. "Tweezers?"

I throw one arm off my face and point to the bathroom. "Makeup bag," I grumble. I can't believe I've just flashed Jesse's housekeeper. This is horrible—mortifying. I need a dressing gown.

I feel the bed sink under his weight again and he clasps my foot. "Hold still."

I hold my breath and reposition my arms so my palms are flat on my burning red face, but all embarrassment is momen-tarily eliminated when I feel the warm wetness of his tongue dragging up my instep, licking the trail of blood away. I shiver under his tongue's stroke and remove my hands to look down at him, shifting a little, my thighs tightening. He smiles knowingly, his eyes sparkling, before he wraps his lips around the offending shard.

"What are you doing?"

"I'm getting it out," he says against my heel. He sucks on my heel and pulls away before taking the tweezers and getting up close and personal with the heel of my foot.

I grin as I watch his concentration frown appear across his brow.

"There." He kisses my foot and releases it. It was pretty pain-free, actually. "What are you grinning at?" He looks at me in amusement.

"Your frown line."

"I don't have a frown line." He's offended.

"You do."

He crawls up the bed and lays himself over me. "Miss O'Shea, are you saying I have wrinkles?"

My grin widens. "No. It only pops up when you're concentrating, or if you're concerned."

"It does?"

"It does."

"Oh." He frowns. "Is it there now?"

I laugh and he bites my boob, sending me on a little buck under him.

"Get ready." He lands me with a hard kiss. "I'll go and see if Cathy's run out screaming."

My laughing abates at the reminder of Jesse's poor housekeeper, who has just copped a load of my bare arse. "Okay."

"I'll see you downstairs." He leans back down and plants a molten lasting kiss on my mouth. "Don't be long."

He jumps up and pulls on a pair of checkered lounge pants, and then leaves me so he can go and placate his housekeeper.

I distract myself from my despair by having a shower and getting myself ready, slipping on a floral tea dress—probably too short—and my flat sandals. I pull my hair up into a ponytail. I'll do.

* * *

As I walk into the kitchen like a timid waif, all fidgety and nervous, Jesse looks up from his salmon and scrambled egg bagel and gives me one of my smiles. His bare chest distracts me fleetingly from my embarrassment, and I don't miss his slight scowl when he registers the length of my dress. I ignore him.

"Here she is." He pats the stool next to him as Cathy turns from the fridge to look at me. "Cathy, this is Ava, love of my life." My cheeks burn and I offer her a small, apologetic smile. I feel much better when I detect a red flush in her cheeks. I've been so worried about my own mortification, I hadn't considered how embarrassed she might be. I take a seat next to Jesse and he pours me some orange juice.

"I like your dress," he smirks. "Too short but excellent access. It can stay."

I look at him in horror and give him a kick under the island. He laughs and sinks his teeth into his bagel. I'm shocked by his behavior but pleasantly surprised he's not marched me back upstairs in disgrace.

"Ava, it's a pleasure to meet you. Would you like some breakfast?" Cathy's voice is friendly and warm. I deserve neither.

"You, too, Cathy, I would love some breakfast, thank you."

"What would you like?" She smiles at me. She has the kindest face.

"I'll have the same as Jesse, please." I wouldn't be surprised if she turned around and told me to stuff it up my arse, but she doesn't. She just nods and carries on about her business.

I pick up my glass of juice and glance at Jesse, finding he's looking unapologetically smug. I'm glad he finds my discomfort amusing, but I can't imagine he'd be so tickled about the situation if Cathy were a man. Reaching over to his lap, I slip my hand into his lounge pants and grab his cock loosely. He jumps, smacking his knee on the marble, and starts coughing around his mouthful of food. Cathy turns around, startled at Jesse choking, and fetches him a glass of water, passing it over the counter to him. He holds his hand up in a thank-you gesture.

"You okay?" I ask, all concerned, as I start to stroke his hardened length slowly.

"Fine." His voice is all high pitched and stressed.

Cathy returns to preparing my breakfast, and I continue wickedly playing havoc with Jesse's sanities. He drops his bagel and takes a silent, controlled inhale, looking at me with wide eyes.

Ignoring his shock, I roll my thumb slowly over his moist tip before drawing down again to his base. I feel the incessant throb under my grasp and the wetness of cum escaping the tip. Gathering the moisture, I glide smoothly up and down his iron-stiff erection.

I turn my eyes on him. "Good?" I mouth, and he shakes his head in desperation.

I'm in my element. This has never happened. He must have a lot of respect for Cathy because I know for sure that with anyone else, I would have been hauled out of the kitchen by now.

"There you are, Ava." Cathy slides a plate over the island to me.

I drop Jesse like a hot potato and slip my thumb into my mouth before pulling my plate toward me, hearing a sharp intake of breath, and feeling his eyes burning into me.

"Thanks, Cathy," I say cheerfully. I pick my bagel up and take a big bite. "Cathy, this is delicious," I inform her as she starts loading the dishwasher. She looks at me and smiles.

I'm aware of scorching eyes still burning into my face as I enjoy my bagel, so I slowly turn to look at him, finding a face full of shock and horror.

He raises his eyebrows at me and then flicks his head to the kitchen exit. "Upstairs, now," he says quietly as he gets up. "Thanks for breakfast, Cathy. I'm going for a shower." He eyes me. I nod.

"You're welcome, boy. Can we go through what you would

like me to do today? I'm all out of sync and I can see that you have done absolutely zero, except break doors and make holes in walls." She dries her hands on a tea towel and gives Jesse's back a disapproving look.

He doesn't turn around to face her, because he's concealing the huge arousal tenting the front of his lounge pants. I mentally chalk a tally for me on a smirk.

"Ava can sort that out with you as soon as she's helped me with something upstairs," he shouts over his shoulder as he disappears.

Can I? I don't know what Cathy does or what he wants her to do today, and I have absolutely no intention of following him upstairs to finish what I've started.

I sit exactly where I am, taking a deep breath of confidence. "Cathy, I just wanted to apologize for yesterday and this morning."

She rolls her eyes. "Don't worry, darling, honestly."

"I was so rude to you, and then this morning . . . well, I wasn't expecting company." I feel my cheeks burning up again as I pick at the last bits of my bagel.

"Ava, really, it's fine. Jesse told me you had a bad day and he failed to notify you of my return. I understand." She smiles at me as she dusts down her apron. It's a sincere smile. I like Cathy. With her gray bob, friendly face, and floral skirts, she is typically wholesome.

"It won't happen again." I take my plate to the dishwasher and go to open it, but the plate is whipped from my hand before I have a chance to see through my chore.

"I'll take that. You better go and help my boy with whatever it is he needs you for."

I know exactly what he needs me for, and I'm not going anywhere. It's killing me to deny him, but his face was just brilliant. "Oh, he'll manage."

"Okay, shall we go through what I should get on with? I have a roster, but being away for so long, it's all gone to cock!" She takes a pad and pen from the front of her apron and gets ready to take notes. "I should probably start with the washing and ironing."

"Urm, I'm not sure," I shrug. "I don't even really live here," I whisper, wanting to add that I've been moved in against my will.

"You don't?" Her face is puzzled "My boy said you did."

"Well, it's a conversation yet to be had," I explain. "He doesn't like the word *no*. Well, not from me, anyway."

Her shiny forehead furrows. "What, my easygoing boy?"

I scoff. "Yes, so I'm told." If anyone else says he's easygoing, I might just trample them.

"Well, it's nice to have a lady in the house," she says, collecting some cleaner from under the sink. "My boy needs a girl."

I smile at Cathy's affectionate referral to Jesse and wonder how long she has worked for him. Jesse had said that she was the only woman he couldn't live without, although I suspect that has changed now.

She sprays the worktop down with antibacterial spray and starts wiping. "I'll wait for Jesse then, if you would prefer."

"Yes, thank you. I'm just going to make a few calls." I notice my phone charging on the side but no bag. "Have you seen my bag?"

"I popped it in the cloakroom, darling. Oh, and I've had Clive sort out the elevator door."

I cringe. "Oh, thank you." I grab my phone and make my way out of the kitchen to retrieve my bag. She probably thinks that I'm a slob, as well as a rude cow, a vandal, and a flasher. I glance down at my phone, noting two missed calls from my mum and a text from Matt. My shoulders sag. I should delete it, but curiosity gets the better of me.

I don't know what got into me. I'm sorry x.

I bristle from head to toe and delete the message. The last thing I need is Jesse finding it. Matt's been sorry before, and it's still bothering me how he knows about Jesse. I should ring my mum first, but I have a friend with some explaining to do. She takes a while, but she eventually answers. I knew she'd be looking down at her screen, wondering what to say.

"You're a member!" I blurt accusingly when she finally picks up.

"And?" She's aiming for nonchalance, but I'm detecting irritation.

"Why didn't you tell me?"

"It's none of your business."

"Thanks!" I'm completely offended. We tell each other everything.

"It's just a bit of fun, Ava," she huffs impatiently.

"You keep saying that," I grate down the phone. "Why won't you admit there is more to it?"

"Like what?" Her tone indicates surprise—surprise that I've come right out and asked the million-dollar question.

"Like you really like him."

She scoffs. "I do not!"

"Oh, you're hopeless," I snap. Why can't she just swallow her pride and admit it? What harm would it do, especially to me?

"Talking of hopeless, how's Jesse? Fuck me, Ava. That man can lose the plot!"

I laugh. "Yes, he can. Matt tried to jump my bones before Jesse ambushed the flat. He proceeded to tell Jesse that we had a little snog. I think Matt might be nursing a black eye this morning."

"Ha, good!" She laughs, and I can't help the small smile of satisfaction developing on my face. He deserved it.

"He knows about Jesse's little drink issue," I add. I'm not laughing now.

"How?" Her shock matches mine.

"I have no idea. Anyway, I've got to ring my mother. I guess I'll see you later."

"Oh yes!" she chirps excitedly. I can't match her excitement for the anniversary dinner tonight. "See you there!"

"Bye." I hang up and dial my mother before she sends out the search party.

"Ava?" Her shrill voice assaults my eardrums.

"Mum, not so loud!"

"Sorry. Matt's called again."

I take myself across to the main open area and sit down. Any hopes of being cheered up by my mother have been well and truly dashed with that little statement.

"Ava, he said you've moved in with a raving alcoholic who has a terrible temper. He beat Matt up!"

I fall back in a chair and look up to the ceiling in total mental exasperation. Why can't the prick just crawl into the dark hole he came from and die? "Mum, please don't speak to him any-more," I plead. What a lowlife he really is, dumping this shit on my parents. It just reinforces my conclusions about the deceit-ful, nasty snake.

"Is it true?" she asks tentatively. I can see her in my mind's eye flicking a worried glare at my dad.

"Not exactly," I can't completely lie to her. She'll have to find out where I am eventually. "It's nothing like Matt says, Mum."

"Well, what is it then?"

Oh, I can't do this over the phone. There is far too much to explain, and I don't want her passing judgment on Jesse. I could kill Matt. "Mum, listen. I've got to get to work." A little white lie won't hurt.

"Ava, I'm so worried about you."

I can sense her despair. I hate Matt for doing this. He said he was sorry. Was that before or after he called my parents to give them an update on my love life? I should send Jesse around to trample all over him. "Please, don't be. Matt wanted me back. He pounced on me when I went to collect the last of my things and turned nasty when I rebuffed him. Jesse was just protecting me." I try to cut a long story short and purposely leave out any parts that could tarnish Jesse. There are a few.

"Jesse? Was that the man you were with when I called last weekend?"

"Yes."

"So, he's not just a friend?" Her tone is scornful. She's rumbled me and my white lie, and she won't be happy about it.

"I'm just seeing him. It's nothing serious." I try and play it down and laugh in my head. I can't believe I just said that.

"And he's an alcoholic?"

I let out a tired breath that I know she won't appreciate. "He's not an alcoholic, Mum. Matt's being spiteful, ignore him. And don't answer any more of his calls."

"I'm not happy about this. There is no smoke without fire, Ava." She really doesn't sound happy, and I can't blame her. I've never been so glad that they live so far away. I don't think I could face her. "Your brother will be back in London soon," she adds threateningly. I know for sure she'll be hanging up with me and ringing Dan immediately to give him the lowdown.

"I know. I've got to go."

"Fine, I'll speak to you over the weekend," she says on a huff. "Take care of yourself." She adds the last bit a little more softly. She never ends a conversation on a bad note.

"I will, I love you."

"You, too, Ava."

I close my eyes and try to dispel all thoughts of hideous ex-boyfriends and worrying parents. It doesn't work and as soon as

I open them, Jesse's face is floating above mine, a hand braced on each arm of the chair as he leans over me.

His big smile disappears when he registers my expression. "What's up?" he asks, all concerned. I don't want to tell him. The last thing I need is to rile him after yesterday's events. "Hey, tell me."

"Okay," I say as he crouches in front of me so our eyes are level.

He takes my hands in his. "Come on then," he prompts when I don't elaborate. I don't want to start the day on a Jesse rage.

"Matt phoned my parents and told them I'm shacked up with a raving alcoholic who beat him up." I blurt it out fast and brace myself for the storm. I can see the color rising in his face already as he chews his bottom lip. I've changed my mind; I don't think I want to send Jesse around to sort Matt out. By the look of his face, he would probably kill him. I sit and wait for him to ponder whatever it is that he's pondering.

"I'm not an alcoholic," he eventually grates.

"I know." I give him my most reassuring voice, but I fear I just sound patronizing. He really doesn't like being called an alcoholic, and now I'm wondering if he's right or if he's in denial. He looks so angry. I wish I had kept my mouth shut.

"Jesse, how does he know?"

He stands up straight. "I don't know, Ava. We need to have a chat with Cathy."

Is that it? Isn't he going to try and find out? "Why do we need a chat with Cathy?" I ask shortly.

"She's been away. She needs to know stuff." He puts his hand out to me, and I let him pull me up.

"Like what?"

"I don't know," he answers on a huff. "That's why we need to talk to her." He tries to tug me toward the kitchen, but I pull my hand away.

"No. *You*, Jesse. This is *your* place, she is *your* housekeeper."
I shake my head. That little comment has just earned me an
almighty growl and a glare.

"Ours!" He reaches around me, grabs my bum and yanks me
to his body. "You really know how to rub me up the wrong way.
Which reminds me," he rolls his groin into me, "that was cruel
and unreasonable." He arches his brow. "I waited upstairs and
you didn't show."

A small chuckle escapes my mouth. "What did you do?"

"What do you think I did?"

I burst into fits of laughter at the thought of my poor man
resorting to a quick wank because I'm a tease. I'm soon shut up,
though, when I feel him grind into me again. I catch his eyes.
They are dancing in delight. I know his game, and with Cathy
in the kitchen, I also know he has no intention of seeing me
through to the end. I wriggle out of his arms and straighten myself out.

"I'm sorry," I say on a grin. I'm not.

He narrows his dazzling greens on me. All of the anger has
gone, thank God. "You will be." He makes a grab for me and
positions me back in front of him. "Don't do it again." He kisses
me hard, grinds his hips, and then removes himself from me,
leaving me dazed and disorientated. The bastard.

*   *   *

After Jesse has a quick chat with Cathy while I make peace with
Clive, collecting some post and stuffing it in my bag, Jesse and I
take off toward the city, the morning rush-hour traffic not bothering Jesse in the slightest. Oasis sings "Morning Glory," and
I watch Jesse as he hums along. He looks so trouble-free and
happy with himself. This is the easygoing Jesse who everyone
keeps telling me about. I know he has a history, and a pretty sor-

did one at that, but it's in his past. He loves me. I don't doubt it for a minute.

"What?" He glances across, catching me studying him.

"I was just thinking about how much I love you."

"I know you do." He reaches over and grasps my bare knee. "Where am I heading then?"

"Oxford Street. All of the stores I like are on Oxford Street."

His face screws up disapprovingly. "All of the stores?"

"Yes."

"Isn't there just one shop you go to?"

"I want some new shoes as well. And maybe a bag. I won't find it all in one store."

"I would!"

I can't imagine Jesse shopping for clothes. Men's shopping is a lot simpler than women's. If he's expecting a similar experience then he's in for a shock.

"Where do *you* go?" I ask.

"Harrods. Zoe sorts me out every time. It's quick and pain-free."

"Yes, that's because you pay for the service you get."

"The service is second to none and worth every penny. They're the best at what they do," he says firmly. "Anyway, you're not buying the dresses, so I get to choose the shopping style."

My head snaps up. "One dress, Jesse, you owe me one dress," I remind him. He shrugs, completely ignoring me. "One dress."

"Lots of dresses," he counters quietly.

"You are not buying my clothes!"

He looks at me like I've just grown another head. "I fucking am!"

"No, you're not."

"Ava, this is not up for discussion. End of." He removes his hand from my knee to change gear.

"No, you're right, it's not. I buy my own clothes." I turn Oasis up to drown out any counterattack. I'm not budging on this. I will buy my own clothes. End of!

We travel the rest of the way with only Oasis filling the silence. I catch him chewing his bottom lip, and the cogs are turning so fast I can almost hear them. I smile because if we were not in public, I would be having a sense fuck right about now. Instead, though, he's thinking about how else he can go about getting his way.

He parks the car then turns to face me. "I have a proposition for you."

Ah, the cogs at work. I've no doubt the end result of this proposition will be Jesse getting his own way. "I don't care what you propose. You're not buying my clothes," I say haughtily, getting out of the car. "And there's no scope for a sense fuck here, is there?"

"Mouth! You've not even heard me out," he complains, jumping out and joining me on the pavement. "You already owe me a retribution fuck."

"Do I?"

"Yes, another for your little performance at breakfast." He arches a smug eyebrow. "You'll like what I'm going to propose." He grins. His confident persona is back, and I'm intrigued. I study him for a second and his grin widens. He knows he's got my attention.

"What?"

His eyes twinkle in satisfaction. "You let me spoil you," he tips his finger under my chin to shut my mouth when I try to object, "and I will tell you how old I am." He lowers his mouth to mine and seals his deal with a deep kiss.

What?

I allow him to kiss all of my obstinacy right out of me on the busy London pavement, as he moans into my mouth and tips me back, holding me suspended in his arms.

"I know how old you are," I say against his lips.

He pulls back and gazes down at me. "Do you?"

I gape at him. "You lied?" He's not thirty-seven? How old is he then? Bloody hell, is he older? "Tell me," I demand on a scowl.

"Oh no. Spoil first, age confession later. You might turn me over. I know my beautiful girl can play dirty." He grins and returns me to a standing position.

"I won't," I scoff. I will! "I can't believe you lied to me."

He gives me an inquiring eye. "I can't believe you handcuffed me to the bed."

No, I can't believe I did that either, but it seems the whole episode was fruitless after all.

He takes my hand and leads me across the road and into the store.

Chapter Eighteen

My eyes are immediately blessed with masses of drool-worthy handbags, but I'm not given the opportunity to look. He walks with purpose and meaning as he drags me along behind him, and when we get in the elevator, he presses the button for the first floor. I scan the store guide.

"Hey, I want the fourth floor." I'd like to avoid the international collections of the first floor. They scream expensive, but he completely ignores me. "Jesse?" I look at him and find his face is completely impassive as he keeps a firm grip of my hand. The elevator door opens and I'm pulled out behind him.

"This way," he says, pulling me through the incredible displays of designer clothes and couture gowns. I'm glad he's bypassing those.

But my heart quickly sinks when I spot the sign for personal shopping. "No, Jesse, no, no, no." I try to stop him, but he presses forward, pulling me toward the entrance of the department. "Jesse, please," I plead, but again, he completely ignores me.

I want to kick him in the shins. I hate fuss and attention in stores. They kiss your arse and tell you everything looks fabulous and the whole thing makes you feel like you *have* to buy something. The pressure will be immense, and I dare not even think about the cost.

"I have an appointment with Zoe," he advises the smartly suited and booted chap who greets us. Why did he ask me where we were heading if he already knew? I want to wring his neck.

"Mr. Ward?" the assistant asks.

"Yes," Jesse says, still refusing to look at me, even though he knows damn well I'm scowling heavily at him and I'm mighty uncomfortable with this.

"Please, this way. Can I get you any drinks? Champagne, perhaps?" he asks politely.

Jesse looks at me, and I shake my head. I want to cut and run straight to House of Fraser, where I can shop in peace with a can of coke and minimum fuss.

"No, thank you," Jesse replies. The young man leads us into a luxurious private area and Jesse pulls me over to a big leather sofa. I sit down next to him and pull my hand out of his. This is quite possibly my worst nightmare.

"What's up?" he asks as he makes a grab for my hand again.

I look at him accusingly. "Why did you ask me where I wanted to go if you'd already made an appointment?"

He shrugs. "I don't understand why you would want to trail around a dozen stores when you can have everything brought to you here."

Before I have a chance to respond, a young blonde-haired girl appears and beams at Jesse. She's pretty and kitted out in a Ralph Lauren cream suit.

"Jesse!" she sings at him. "How are you?"

He gets up and she kisses him continental style. "Zoe, I'm good. You?" He smiles at her. It's one of his knockout smiles—the kind that reduces women to a mass of hormones at his feet.

"Great, this must be Ava. It's a pleasure to meet you." She puts her hand out to me, and I stand to take it, offering a small smile. She's friendly enough, but I'm still not comfortable here. She sits in the chair opposite us. "So, Ava, Jesse tells me we're looking for something special for an important party," she says excitedly. Something special sounds like it's going to have a special price tag, too.

"Something *very* special," Jesse reiterates as he pulls me back down to the couch. I suddenly feel like I'm overheating, and I'm all claustrophobic in this massive room.

"Okay, what's your style, Ava? Give me an idea of what you like." She places her hands in her lap and looks at me expectedly.

I don't know what my style is. If I like something and I feel good in it, I buy it. "I don't have a style really." I shrug, and her eyes light up. That must have been a good answer.

"Lots of dresses," Jesse interrupts. "She likes dresses."

"*You* like dresses," I mutter, earning myself a nudge of his knee.

She smiles, revealing a perfect set of Hollywood, too-white teeth. "You're about a ten, yes?"

"Yes," I confirm.

"Not too short," Jesse spits quickly.

I look at him with my mouth agape. This is what I knew would happen. I'm not generally a short-dress person, but he's turning me into one with his caveman attitude.

Zoe laughs. "Jesse, she has fantastic legs. It would be a shame to waste them. What shoe size are you, Ava?"

I like her. "I'm a five."

"Great, let's go." She stands, and I join her. Jesse gets up, too.

"I can't believe you've done this to me," I whine as he dips and kisses me on the cheek. I like Zoe, but I would much prefer to be left to my own devices.

He sighs. "Ava, let me have my fun." He leans in and crowds me. "I get my own little fashion show with my favorite lady modeling." He pouts.

"Who gets to pick the dress, Jesse?"

He nuzzles my nose. "You do. I'm just observing. I promise. Go on, knock your self out." He sits back down on the sofa and starts making a call. I'm relieved. I don't think I could bear him following us around the store, trampling everything I give a second look at.

Zoe leads me through the department. "So, you're being spoiled today?" she asks on a friendly smile. She is lovely, but those teeth are really very white.

"I am, under duress." I return her smile.

"You don't want to be spoiled?" She laughs, picking up a long, green gown and presenting it to me. It's lovely but more Kate's color than mine. I give a little apologetic shake of my head. She mirrors it. "No, I agree. What about this one?" She places a hand on a lovely Grecian-style dress.

"That's lovely," I admit, but it also looks very expensive.

"It is. We'll try it. What about this?"

"Wow!" I blurt at the cream, tight number with a thigh-high slash up the leg. "Jesse can be a bit uptight with overexposure." I laugh as I hold the slit open. You would have to shave everything off!

"He can?" She looks at me curiously. If she says... "He's so laid-back," she adds.

I release the dress and move on to a red satin one. "Not with me," I mutter. "I like this one."

Zoe replaces her curious stare with a smile. "Good choice. And this one?" She walks across the way and strokes a stunning cream, strapless affair. Is strapless allowed?

"It's lovely," I agree. I can try it. I'm sure he will make it known if it's a no-go. My attention is seized across the department, and I'm wandering over before I realize my legs are moving.

I run my finger lightly down the front of the black, delicate lace gown. It's beautiful.

"You absolutely must try that one," Zoe says, joining me in front of the gown. She takes it down and turns it gently. It's attached to a security wire, which can only mean one thing. "Isn't it wonderful?" she asks dreamily.

Oh, it is. It is also in the realm of ridiculously expensive if the store feels the need to wire it up. Plus there is no price on the tag—another telltale sign that I'll pass out at the cost. I run my eyes down the back of the fitted dress, which splays midthigh to pool on the floor slightly. The design is simple, with a plunged V-shaped back, dainty capped sleeves that fall slightly off the shoulder, and a flattering deep neckline. It absolutely screams couture.

"Jesse loves me in lace," I muse quietly. He also loves me in black.

"Then we should definitely try," Zoe hangs it back up. "How long have you been seeing Jesse?"

The question instantly puts me on guard. What do I say? The truth is, I've been seeing him for a month-ish, and a week of that was spent with Jesse drunk and me nursing a broken heart. A sudden nasty thought invades my mushy brain.

"Not long," I try to sound as casual as Zoe when I follow it up with, "Does he bring all of the women he dates here?"

She actually starts laughing. I don't know if that's a good thing. "God, no! He would be bankrupt!"

It's definitely a bad thing.

She must catch my expression because she pales a little. "Ava, I'm sorry. That came out all wrong." She shifts uncomfortably on her heels. "What I meant to say was if he brought all of the women he had slept..." She halts and pales further. I feel slightly sick. "Shit!" she exclaims.

"Zoe, don't worry about it." I turn my attention to another dress. Who am I kidding? I know he put himself about.

"Ava, he's never actually dated anyone. As far as I know, anyway. He's quite a catch. You'll be fighting the women of The Manor off, that's for sure."

"Yeah." I laugh lightly. I need to get away from this line of conversation. That thought—the one of Jesse with another woman—pops into my head again. Zoe clearly knows his business. "Where to next?" I plaster on a nonjealous, unaffected face, if there's such a thing. I'm bubbling on the inside and bristling on the out. Why did he have to be such a slut?

"Shoes!" Zoe sings, leading me off toward the Egyptian escalators.

* * *

An hour later, we return to the plush personal shopping area with a young guy pulling a rail of dresses and shoes. Jesse is still sitting on the sofa with his phone to his ear.

He smiles brightly and disconnects the call. "Have fun?" he asks as he gets up and smothers my face with his lips. "I missed you."

"I've been gone an hour." I laugh, and grip his shoulders as he pushes me back.

"Too long," he grumbles. "What have you got?" He brings me back up to vertical.

"Too much to choose from," I say. I managed to convince Zoe to abandon the lace gown. In fact, I avoided anything that was attached to a security wire.

"Go try." He slaps my bum, and I turn to follow Zoe and the rail into a large fitting room. Zoe's admiring face doesn't escape my notice.

For the next few hours, I'm trussed into dress after dress. I count twenty dresses, all of which are stunning and all of which Jesse approves of.

Zoe disappears for a while, leaving me to sit and wonder which bloody dress I'm going to choose. They are all too nice. My head jumps up when she walks back in with another rail of dresses, but these are more day dresses and evening dresses, not gowns. I look at her, completely confused.

She shrugs. "I'm under strict orders to make you try on lots of dresses, so I got these," she says as she goes to the back of the rail. She comes back to the front holding the lace gown. "And this, too."

"What?" I blurt, pushing myself to my feet. I'm in my underwear and gaping like a goldfish.

"Well," she starts toward me, "he didn't say to try this gown in particular, but he did say you must have what you want." She smiles brightly. "And I know you really want this one."

"Zoe, I can't," I stutter, trying to convince my brain that the dress is hideous—disgusting. Damn right awful. It's not bloody working.

"If it's the price that's bothering you, then don't worry. It's within the budget." She hangs the dress on the wall hook.

"There's a budget? What's the budget?" I ask hesitantly.

She turns and grins. "The budget is: there is no budget."

I groan and collapse back into the chair. "Can I ask how much it is?"

"No," she replies cheerily. "Put this on." She hands me a black lace bodice. I start to get myself into it and Zoe turns me around to fasten the row of hook and eyes trailing up the back. I'm distracted from my hesitancy with the thought of Jesse's face and all this lace. I smile. He'll orgasm on the spot.

I'm helped into the gown by Zoe and presented to the oversized mirror. "Holy shit!" she exclaims, and then slaps her hand over her mouth. "I'm sorry. That was so unprofessional of me."

Holy shit, indeed. I turn slightly to view the back and gasp a little. It clings to every curve I have perfectly and skims the floor when I raise on tiptoes. The lining under the lace is matte, giving the delicate, intricate pattern a shimmery effect, and the deep neckline is perfect with the cap sleeves sitting just off my shoulders, revealing my collarbone. I hear Zoe scuttle off and return.

She kneels before me. "Put these on," she instructs. I pull my eyes from the mirror and look down to find a pair of black slingback Dior heels at my feet. I feel a faint coming on. I slip them on and Zoe stands back. "Ava, you have to have this dress," she says, deadly serious. "Go and show Jesse."

"No!" I blurt rudely. "Sorry, I know he'll love it." It's lace and it's black. He'll pool at my feet, I know he will, but what about the slight exposure of flesh? Will that be cause for my neurotic control freak to tackle me to the ground and wrap me in his body to stop anyone from seeing my skin? And, finally, how much does the damn thing cost?

I quickly battle with my conscience over the bloody dress as Zoe hands me a clutch to match the shoes. I want to cry. I knew I shouldn't have tried it on. "Did he see it?" I turn to face Zoe, and she looks at me all confused. "This dress, did he see it on the rail when you came back?" I ask.

"No, I think he's gone to the gents'."

I raise my hand to my mouth and start frantically tapping my front tooth with my nail.

"Okay, I'm having the dress, but I don't want Jesse to know." I'm taking a risk with this. Zoe claps her hands together, and I smile at her delighted face. "What's all this?" I point to the additional rail she's dragged in.

"He wants you to have lots of dresses." She shrugs.

I laugh. He's taking the instant access rule way too far. I get myself out of the gown and have another stab of uncertainty as

Zoe takes it and gives strict instructions to a young girl not to let Jesse see it. I start on the other dresses. I'm having three maximum, and he better not argue with me.

I work off a million calories getting myself in and out of dozens of dresses. We build up a "like," "no," and a "maybe" pile, and I'm surprised that I'm enjoying myself. Jesse sprawls back on the sofa and watches as I appear and disappear, wearing a different dress each time.

"She's like a clotheshorse, isn't she?" Zoe muses to Jesse when I appear in a very short, gray Chloé dress. I love it, but like all of the other dresses that have a price tag of over three hundred pounds, it will go on the "no" pile.

I watch as his face turns to shock when his eyes reach my legs and he registers the length. "Get it off!" he spits, and I return to the changing room laughing. He's right, I love it, but it is way too short. It could pass for an undergarment.

I'm whacked when I'm finally finished trying everything on. I've changed more times in a couple of hours than I have this month. I go through the "yes" pile with Zoe and get a bit anxious when I realize just how many "yes" items there are. I flick through the rail and try to narrow it down.

"What have we got then?" I hear him approach. I cringe.

"Oh, she's got some fabulous pieces. I'm very jealous," Zoe says. "I'm just going to get this all wrapped and bagged for you."

Oh hell!

I'm even more mortified when Jesse hands Zoe a credit card. She takes it and leaves us alone.

"Jesse, I'm really not comfortable with this." I take his hands and stand in front of him so I have his full attention.

His shoulders sag disappointedly. "Why?" His voice is genuinely hurt.

I watch Zoe disappear with all of my "yeses."

"Please, I don't want you spending all of this money on me."

"It's not all that much," he tries to reason with me, but I saw the price tags. It's way too much, and I don't even know how much the gown is.

I look down at the floor. I don't want to get into a row in Harrods over this. "Just buy me a dress for tonight. That would be acceptable to me."

"Just one dress?" he asks unhappily. "Another five dresses and you've got a deal."

I'm pleasantly surprised by this. "Two," I counter anyway, returning my eyes to his.

"Five," he tosses back at me. "This wasn't part of the deal."

No, it wasn't, but I don't care how old he is anymore, and I've done this meeting-in-the-middle scenario before. I've learned that while I maneuver, Jesse sticks exactly where he started.

I narrow my eyes on him. "I don't care how old you are. Keep your silly little age secret."

"Okay, but it's still five," he says acceptingly. I suspect he was never going to keep his end of the deal, anyway. "I've got to make a phone call." He drops a kiss on my lips. "You go and pick five dresses. Zoe has my card. My pin is one, nine, seven, four."

I recoil. "I can't believe you've just told me your pin number."

"No secrets?"

No secrets? Is he kidding me? He strolls off, and I have a sudden, delighted moment of comprehension. I do a quick mental calculation. "You *are* thirty-seven," I shout to his back. He stops. "Your pin number. You were born in seventy-four." I can't help the triumph in my voice. I've totally rumbled him. Men are so predictable. "You didn't lie at all, did you?"

He slowly turns and flashes me his signature smile, reserved only for me, before blowing me a kiss and leaving me to go and pick my five dresses.

*   *   *

I walk out of the personal shopping area and find Jesse waiting for me. I hand him his card and plant a kiss on his cheek. "Thank you." I'm not sure whether I'm most grateful for the dresses or for his slipup in revealing that he's actually thirty-seven. Either way, I'm a very happy girl.

"You are more than welcome." He takes my bags from me. "Do I get another show?" He raises his eyebrows.

"Of course." I can't deny him for how reasonable he's being. "But you don't get to see the gown."

"Which one did you pick?" he asks curiously. He liked all of them, but he didn't see *the* gown, which is safely out of view in a suit bag.

"You'll find out later." I inhale him into me as he nestles his face in my neck. "So, my man really is knocking on forty," I rib.

He pulls away and rolls his eyes before taking my hand and leading me through the store. "Does it bother you?" he asks casually, but I know he's worried that it does.

"Not at all. Why does it bother you, though?"

"Ava, do you remember one of the very first things you said to me?" He looks down at me.

How could I forget? And I still don't know where the question about his age came from. "Why did you lie?"

He shrugs. "Because you wouldn't have asked if it wasn't a problem."

I smile. "It doesn't bother me in the slightest how old you are. Is that a gray hair?" I ask deadpan as we board the Egyptian escalators.

He stands on the step below and turns around to face me. We're pretty much at eye level. "Do you think you're funny?"

I can't keep a straight face, and when he dips and tips me over his shoulder, I barely suppress a squeal. He can't behave like this in Harrods! I correct myself. Jesse has no regard for public opinion on his behavior. He'll pick me up, ravish me, or even be blood-boiling mad with me wherever he pleases. He doesn't give a toss and, quite frankly, neither do I.

He carries me out of the store and onto Knightsbridge, setting me on my feet outside, where I straighten my dress, take his offered hand, and we start walking back toward the car. I don't even scorn him. It's fast becoming an everyday occurrence for him to hoof me about, whether it's in private or in public.

"We'll grab some lunch at The Manor," he says as he puts my bags in the boot and then me in the car. He slides in beside me and gives me my smile before slipping his Wayfarers on. "Enjoying your day so far?"

I was, until he reminded me about our need to go to The Manor. I've got to endure a whole night there, too. "Absolutely." I can't complain, though, as long as I'm with him.

"Me too. Put your belt on." He starts the car and roars into the lunchtime traffic, cranking up the stereo and letting his window down so the whole of Knightsbridge gets a little listen of the Stereophonics's "Dakota."

Chapter Nineteen

Jesse skids to a halt outside The Manor where John is waiting for us on the steps. There are only a few cars, mine included. I forgot it was here.

"Come on. I want to get done and get home so I can have a few hours of you all to myself." He grasps my hand and leads on.

"Take me home now then," I grumble, earning myself a mild scowl.

"I'm ignoring you," he mutters.

"Ava," John nods as we pass, and then follows us in.

"Is everything okay?" Jesse asks as he leads me to the bar. It's empty, except for the staff flying around in a fluster. He sits me down on a barstool and takes one opposite me, resting my hand in his lap. I spot Mario polishing the optics.

"S'all good," John rumbles. "Caterers are in the kitchen and the band will be here at five to set up. Sarah has it all under control." He waves Mario over, and I bristle at the mention of *her* name.

"Great, where is she?" Jesse asks.

"She's in your office sorting out the gift bags."

Gift bags? What would you put in a gift bag for a party at a sex club? Oh God, I don't even want to know.

Mario approaches and swings his tea towel over his shoulder. His warm smile makes me return one automatically. He's the sweetest man.

"Do you want a drink?" Jesse squeezes my hand in his lap.

"Just some water, please."

"Make that two, Mario." He turns back to me. "What would you like to eat?"

Well, that's easy. "Steak," I say, all wide eyed and enthusiastically. That was the best steak I've ever had.

He smiles. "Mario, tell Pete we'll have the steak twice with new potatoes and salad, both medium. We'll eat at the bar."

"Of course, Mr. Ward," Mario chirps happily, placing two bottles of water and a glass on the bar.

"Are you happy to stay here while I go and check on a few things?" Jesse asks as he drops my hand in his lap and takes a bottle, pouring some water into my glass.

I arch an eyebrow at him. "Are you going to have Mario guard me?"

"No," he says slowly, flicking a cautious eye at me. I hear John's low, rumbling laugh. "There's no need now, is there?"

"I suppose not." I shrug and look around the bar. "Where is everyone?"

He stands and places my hand in my own lap. "We close during the day on anniversary night. There's a lot to get ready." He kisses my forehead and picks up his own bottle of water. "John?"

"Ready when you are," John replies.

He brushes a hair away from my face. "I'll be as quick as I can. Are you sure you're okay here?"

"I'm fine." I shoo him away.

They leave me at the bar among the chaos of staff frantically polishing glasses and restocking the fridges. I feel like I should help, but then I hear my phone shouting from my bag and I pull it out, finding Ruth Quinn's name illuminating my screen.

I should let it go to voicemail, it is my day off, but this could be my opportunity to get out of drinks with her.

"Hi, Ruth."

"Ava, how are you?"

She's so friendly—too friendly. "I'm good, and you?"

"Lovely. I received your fee structure and designs. They're wonderful!"

"I'm glad you like them, Ruth." Her enthusiasm will be a pleasure to work with, I suppose.

"So, now you've shown me how amazing my dire downstairs can look, I'm eager to start."

"Okay, well, if you could settle the consultation fee, I'm assuming you've received the invoice, then we can crack on."

"Yes, I did. I'll sort a transfer. Do you have the company bank details?"

"I don't, Ruth. Could I ask you to ring the office? It's my day off so I can't lay my hands on them at the moment."

"Oh? I'm sorry. I didn't realize."

"It was a last-minute thing. It's not a problem, really."

"Are you doing anything nice?"

I smile. "Yes, I am, actually. Some quality time with my boyfriend." That sounds weird.

"Oh."

Silence falls down the phone. "Ruth? Are you there?' I glance at my phone to see if my service has dropped. It hasn't. "Hello?"

"Yes, sorry. It's just that you said there was no man." She laughs.

"No man trouble. I meant to say there's no man trouble."

"I see! Well, I'll let you get back to your quality time."

"Thank you. I'll call you next week and we can proceed."

"Great. Bye, Ava." She hangs up, and I instantly realize that I didn't pull out of drinks. She didn't confirm either, though.

I put my phone back in my bag and spot Mario on his way

over with a box full of cocktail ingredients and fresh fruit. "Ava, are you well?"

"I'm very well, Mario. And you?"

He heaves the big box onto the bar and I help him by pulling it toward me. "Very well, too. Would you be..." He frowns. "How you say...guinea pig?"

"Oh, yes!" I sound way too eager. I love all that mixing, shaking, and tasting business.

He chuckles and passes me a small chopping board and a paring knife. "You cut," he instructs, handing me a basket of various fruits from the box. I collect a strawberry, hull it, and chop it in half. "Yes, this is good." Mario nods at me as he starts pouring various liquids into a large silver container.

I work my way through the whole pile of strawberries, then start on the lemons. Mario sings some Italian opera–style song softly as we sit at the bar, me chopping and watching with interest as he measures, pours, and faffs around with various cocktail equipment.

"Now we do the good part." He smiles, slamming the lid on the silver container and proceeding to shake it. He flips it up and grabs it and then tosses it over his head, before spinning quickly to catch it. I'm stunned on the spot as he knocks the container on the side of the bar and pours the dark pink liquid into a long glass with some mint and a strawberry. "Voilà!" he sings, presenting me with the glass.

"Wow!" I gasp at the sugared-rim glass. "What's it called?"

"This is Mario's Most Marvelous!' His voice gets higher toward the end of the name. He's proud of it. "You try." He pushes the glass toward me, and I lean in to take a sniff.

It smells lovely, but I remember the last time Mario insisted I try one of his drinks; it burned my throat. I take the glass tentatively as Mario nods eagerly at me. I shrug and take a little sip.

"It is good, yes?" He dazzles me with his happy face and starts putting the lids on all the tubs of fruit.

"Yes!" I take a longer sip. It's delicious. "What's in it?"

He starts laughing and shaking his head. "Ah, no, no. This, I tell no person."

"What have you got there?" Jesse's husky tone invades my ears from behind, and I swing around on my stool to see him standing behind me with his frown line firmly in place.

I hold the glass out and smile. "You should try. Oh my God!"

He recoils slightly, his frown deepening. "No thanks, I'll take your word for it." He sits down next to me. "Don't drink too much." He gives the glass a disapproving look, and my brain quickly engages.

"I'm sorry!" I blurt. "I wasn't thinking." I mentally throw myself over the bar and into the waste disposal unit.

Mario must sense the tension because he soon disappears, leaving me and Jesse alone. I put the drink down and turn back toward the bar. The delicious cocktail doesn't taste so sweet now.

"Hey." He pulls me off my stool and onto his lap, and I bury my face under his chin. I can't look at him. I feel so stupid. "It's fine. Unravel your knickers, lady." He laughs. His facial expression didn't say it was fine. Or was that because *I* was drinking it? He leans back to look down at me and pulls my chin up with his finger. His eyes soften. "Stop it and kiss me."

I oblige immediately, finding the back of his neck to pull him down. I relax completely in his arms and soak him up, humming into his mouth. I feel him smile around my kiss. "I'm sorry," I repeat myself. I feel so stupid.

"I said stop it," he warns. "I don't know what your concern is."

My concern? My concern is his reproachful glare at the alcohol. "Did you get everything sorted?" I ask.

"I did. Now we eat, and then we go home to bathe and snuggle for a while, deal?"

"Deal."

"Good girl." He gives me a chaste kiss and shifts me back onto my stool. "Here's our lunch." He nods across the bar, and I see Pete carrying a tray in our direction. He places it down. "Thank you, Pete," Jesse says.

"It's my pleasure, as always. Enjoy." He gives me a pleasant smile. He's so nice. In fact, everyone who works for Jesse is lovely, with the exception of one person, but I won't let her ruin my day on Central Jesse Cloud Nine.

I unroll my knife and fork and plunge straight in to the colorful salad doused in that yummy dressing. I need to find out what it is.

"Good?"

I look up around a forkful of salad and see Jesse pop his own fork into his mouth. I moan my appreciation. I could eat this every day for the rest of my life. He smiles at me.

"Jesse, are you happy for the band to set up in the far corner of the summer room?"

My shoulders tense as Sarah's shrill voice washes over me.

"Fine. I thought we agreed on that?" Jesse turns slightly on his stool to acknowledge her. I don't. I stay facing the bar and start poking at my salad with my fork.

"We did, I was just checking. How are you, Ava?" she asks.

I scowl at my plate. Does she really want to know because I'll happily tell her. I feel Jesse's eyes on me, waiting for me to be decent and answer the witch. I swivel on my stool and plaster a big, insincere smile on my face. "I'm good, thank you, Sarah. And you?"

Her smile is as phony as mine, and I wonder if Jesse is picking up on the clear animosity. "I'm fine. Are you looking forward to tonight?"

"Yes, I am." I lie. I might be looking more forward to it if she wasn't going to be here.

Jesse pipes up, relieving me of strained pleasantries. "I'm heading off. I'll be back at six. Make sure everything is in order upstairs. The suites and communal room remain locked until ten thirty," Jesse points his fork toward the bar entrance. "No exceptions," he adds sternly.

Any hope I had of finishing my lunch has completely diminished at the mention of the communal room. I'm going to be watching people drift off upstairs all night.

"Of course," Sarah agrees. "I'll leave you to it. See you later, Ava."

"Bye." I smile and she returns it, but after last night there is no escaping the fact that we dislike each other, so all of this pretending is pretty senseless. I swivel back to face the bar as soon as I can and recommence poking at my salad. I have no doubt she's playing all friendly for Jesse's benefit. Surely he must see her for what she is.

"Why are you not looking forward to this evening?" Jesse asks quietly as he continues with his lunch.

"I am," I say without looking at him.

I hear him sigh heavily. "Ava, stop twiddling your hair. You did it when Sarah asked you and you're doing it now." He nudges my knee with his, prompting me to freeze midtwiddle and drop my hair.

I put my fork down. "I'm sorry if I can't get excited about attending a party where every time someone looks at me or speaks to me, I'll be thinking they might want to drag me upstairs and fuck me."

I jump as Jesse's knife and fork clatter against his plate. "For fuck's sake!" He pushes his plate away aggressively and in my peripheral vision I see him reach up and rub calming circles into his temples. "Watch your mouth, Ava." My jaw is grabbed and yanked to face him. His green eyes are brimming with anger. "No one will be doing any such thing, because they all know you're mine. Don't say things that make me crazy mad."

I shrink a little under his stern tone. "Sorry." I sound grumpy, but it's the truth. They could be thinking anything. How would he know?

"Please try and show a bit more willingness." He shifts his grip on my jaw and cups my cheek. "I want you to enjoy yourself."

His beseeching face makes me want to slap my loser arse all over the bar. He's spent God only knows how much money on a stunning gown and dresses for me and this is a special night for him. I'm such an ungrateful cow. I crawl across to straddle his lap. He, of course, doesn't give a shit that my legs are wrapped tightly around his waist at the bar.

"Forgive me?" I bite his bottom lip cheekily and circle his nose with mine.

"You're adorable when you sulk." He sighs.

"You're adorable all of the time," I toss back at him, and seal our lips together. "Take me home," I say into his mouth.

He moans. "Deal. Up you get." He stands with me, and I release my thighs' iron grip on his hips.

"What about my car?"

"I'll get one of the staff to drop it off." He dismisses my concern and starts guiding me to his car. I'm looking forward to some tub-time.

* * *

I'm relieved when we finally get back to Lusso.

"Will Cathy be here still?" I ask. I hope not. I want to crawl inside Jesse and stay put for a while.

"No, I told her to get off as soon as she's done." We exit the elevator and Jesse balances my bags as he negotiates the key in the lock. He opens the door and I follow him in before taking the bags from him.

"What are you doing?' he asks on a furrowed brow.

"I'm taking these upstairs to the spare room. You can't see my dress." I make my way to the stairs.

"Put them in our room," he shouts after me.

"No can do," I call, disappearing into my favorite spare bedroom.

I immediately unpack my dress from the suit bag and hang it on the back of the door, sighing as I stand back to get the full view. He's either going to come on the spot or disintegrate on the spot.

I set about unpacking my corset, shoes, and bag and leave the other dresses until later, and it's not long before I hear a small knock at the door. "Don't come in!" I blurt, and run to the door, opening it slightly. I find a smirking Jesse with his hands shoved in his pockets.

"Are we getting married?" he asks.

"I want it to be a surprise." I wave him away. "I need to paint my nails. Go." He wanted willing, so he better not complain.

He holds his hands up. "Fine, I'll wait for you in the bath. Don't be long," he grumbles, walking off across the landing.

I shut the door and retrieve my makeup bag from my handbag, finding the post that Clive handed me this morning. I put it on the chest near the door before settling on the bed to paint my nails.

*   *   *

Walking into the bathroom, I find Jesse submerged in bubbly water with a disgusted look on his face. I pull my dress over my head and remove my bra and knickers, his expression changing from affronted to approving as I climb in the bath.

"Where have you been?"

"I was waiting for my nails to dry." I settle between his legs and lie back against his firm chest.

He hums happily and tangles our legs together, wrapping his arms around me and sinking his nose into my hair.

"Oh, I forgot. Clive gave me some post for you this morning. I shoved it in my bag and forgot about it. Sorry."

"No problem," he dismisses my concern. "I love, love, love you wet and sliding all over me." He palms my boobs and bites my neck. "Tomorrow, we stay in bed all day long."

I smile to myself, silently wishing we could do exactly that right now, but then I feel his heart beating against my back and it has me thinking about his beating heart comment. "What was the first thing you thought when you saw me?"

He's silent for a few moments, before he growls, "Mine," and bites my ear.

I squirm above him, laughing. "You didn't!"

"I fucking did, and now you are." He turns my face to his and kisses me gently. "I love you."

"I know you do. Did it ever occur to you to ask me to dinner instead of stalking me, asking inappropriate questions, and cornering me in one of your torture chambers?"

He glances away thoughtfully. "No, it didn't. I wasn't thinking straight. You made me crazy confused."

"Confused about what?"

"I don't know. You triggered something in me. It was very disturbing." He leans back and I rest my head back again.

Triggered what? A heartbeat? I would think that a strange statement, but he triggered something in me, too, and that was also very disturbing. "You gave me a flower," I say quietly.

"Yeah, I was trying to be a gentleman."

I smile. "So the next time you saw me, you asked me how loud I would scream when you fuck me?"

"Mouth, Ava." He laughs. "I didn't know what to do. I only usually have to smile to get what I want."

"You should have tried to be less arrogant." I don't relish the thought of Jesse smiling and getting what he wants. How many women has he *smiled* at?

"Maybe. Tell me what you thought." He nudges me, and I smile to myself. We could be here a very long time. "Tell me," he presses impatiently.

"What, so your head can swell further?" I scoff, earning myself a dig in the hip. I jerk, sending water flying over the edge of the bath. "Stop!"

"Tell me, I want to know."

I take a deep breath. "I nearly passed out," I admit. "And then you kissed me. Why did you kiss me?" I ask in disbelief, performing a little shudder.

"I don't know. It just happened. You nearly passed out?" he asks. I can't see his face, but I would put my life on the likelihood of his roguish grin being firmly fixed on his lush face.

I crane my head back. Yes, as I thought. I roll my eyes. "I thought you were an arrogant arse, with your touching, tactless comments and inappropriate manners. But I was so affected by you." I still can't believe how blind I was to The Manor. I was too wrapped up in fighting off the unwanted reactions I was having to him—then giving in, then fighting again.

He starts circling my nipples with his fingertips. "I needed to keep touching you to see if I was imagining things."

"What things?"

"My whole body buzzed every time I laid a finger on you. It still does."

"Me too," I agree quietly. It's the most incredible feeling. "Do you realize the effect you have on women?" I spread my palms over the tops of his thighs.

"Is it similar to the one you have on me?" He laces his fingers through mine. "Do they stop breathing for a few seconds every time they see me?" He presses his lips onto my temple and inhales deeply. "Do they want to keep me in a glass box so nothing and no one can hurt me?"

I almost stop breathing.

He sighs heavily, and I rise and fall on his chest. "Do they think their life would be over if I wasn't here?" he finishes softly.

Tears jump into my eyes and I struggle to catch my breath. Okay, the first one for sure, but the other two I think are probably reserved only for me. They are pretty strong words, considering we've known each other for a month. This man was relentless, and now I'm so thankful he was. His business and drink issue are irrelevant now. He's still Jesse, and he's still mine.

I turn myself over to my front and slide up his chest, his eyes following mine until they are level with his. "You stole my lines," I say softly. I need him to know that he isn't the only one in this relationship who feels unbelievably possessive and protective. It's crazy, this big domineering man, who has completely and utterly taken me, who has me surrendering to him without question or without much doubt. I've given him the power to completely destroy me. He's as important to me as I know I am to him. It just is. "I love you so much," I say firmly. "You have to promise me that *you'll* never leave *me*."

He scoffs. "Baby, you're stuck with me forever."

"Good. Kiss me."

"Are you making demands?" His lips twitch, his eyes twinkle.

"Yes. Kiss me."

He parts his lips in invitation as he closes the gap between our mouths, and I'm soon savoring the heat of his minty breath and meeting his circling tongue with equal sentiment as he slides his palms all over my wet back.

"I know it would make you very happy to stay here all night, but we need to think about getting a move on." He palms my bum and pulls upward so I slide higher and he has access to my neck.

"Let's stay," I plead unreasonably. I slide back down and catch a perfect rub of him against my entrance.

He sucks in a sharp breath. "Oh, you have to let me out because if I stay, we'll be going nowhere." He kisses me urgently and pushes me up so I'm sitting on my heels in front of him.

"Stay then." I pout, pushing against him, wrapping my arms around his neck, and sitting myself on his lap. He makes a poor effort to stop me. "I want to mark you." I grin and latch on to his pec with my lips.

He groans and lies back. "Ava, we'll be late," he says with zero concern. I clamp my teeth around his flesh and suck. "Fuck, I can't say no to you," he moans, lifting me to position himself underneath me.

He lets me sink down on a united sigh, and I clamp down a little harder with my teeth, starting to work myself into a slow, controlled rhythm, up and down. He circles my waist with his palms and lifts and lowers me onto his body in time to my set tempo.

"Let me see your face," he demands. I release my bite and kiss it, before bringing my head up to his level. "Better." He smiles.

I brush his wet hair from his forehead and thread my fingers at the back of his head. Our movements remain synchronized as water laps around us and we watch each other closely, the pressure in my groin simmering gently until he flicks his hips up suddenly and my hands fly out to grip the edge of the bath. My cheeks puff out and he smirks at me before repeating the move.

"Again," I demand impulsively as the rush of my imminent climax hurdles forward. I cry out and throw my head back when he complies. One hand shifts from my waist and drifts upward until his palm rests on my neck.

"More?" he asks on a low husk.

My head falls back down. "Yes." I manage to gasp the word before he snaps his hips up. I close my eyes.

"Eyes, baby," he warns gently, sliding his hand back down my front to my waist.

I open my eyes, finding Jesse's jaw tensed, his neck veins bulging. I'm lifted again and brought down to meet his rising hips. I cry out, fighting the impulse to close my eyes.

"Does that feel good?" he asks, rewarding me with another flick of his hips.

"Yes!" My knuckles whiten from my fierce grip on the bath.

"Don't come, Ava. I'm not ready."

I concentrate on controlling the climax pushing forward, Jesse's steady, controlled movements not helping me in my attempts. His head falls back, but he keeps his eyes firmly on mine, lifting me, yanking me back down, and grinding hard, time and time again. Together, we moan, my head becoming heavy from maintaining eye contact. I just want to throw it back and let go, but I've got to wait for the okay. I don't know how much longer I can.

"Good girl," he praises me, gripping my waist harder and guiding me around on his hips. "Can you feel me, Ava?"

"You're going to come." I gasp, feeling his cock expanding inside me.

He smiles. "Get your fingers around those nipples."

I release the edge of the bath and pinch my nipples into stiffer nubs, rolling my fingers under his watchful eyes.

"Harder, Ava," he demands, punishing me with another hard blow of his hips. I cry out, clamping down further, the stabs of pain shooting straight down to my sex. "Harder!" he shouts, digging his thumbs into my waist.

"Jesse!"

"Not yet, baby. Not yet. Control it."

I swallow hard, tensing, every muscle in my body going completely rigid above him. I don't know how he's doing this. I can see the strain in his face and his tense jaw, and I can feel it in his throbbing cock. His control is incredible. I'm hurdling toward a furious climax, the pressure of my own grip on my nipples getting harder the closer I get. Then he slides his hand down to my inside thigh and moves it across to stroke lightly, the rise and fall of his hips causing the friction of his fingers to rub in time to his unhurried drives.

I start shaking my head in desperation. "Jesse, please!"

"You want to come?"

"Yes!"

He pushes his thumb to the top of my clitoris. "Come," he commands, with another thrust upward, sending me delirious as my body explodes and I scream, the desperate cry echoing around the bathroom.

On a loud curse, he lifts me back up and yanks me down onto himself, again and again and again. I yell at the shock of punishing blows, and fall forward onto his chest, shaking uncontrollably. I feel him lift my dead weight slightly and bring me back down as he plunges up, holding himself into me, his solid thighs beneath me feeling severe against my limp body.

"Oh Jesus!" He exhales loudly, water splashing around us. "Ava, tomorrow I'm handcuffing *you* to the bed," he pants. "Kiss me now."

Dragging my head from his chest, I find his lips as he slowly circles his hips, wheedling every last bit of pleasure from us. I could go to sleep right here on his wet chest.

"Take me to bed," I mumble around his mouth.

"I'm ignoring you," he replies sternly.

I clamp my palms on his cheeks to hold him in place while I smother his face with my lips in a desperate attempt to convince him that we should stay. "Let me love you," I whisper, moving my hands to the back of his head to grasp his hair. I just want to stay, but I know I haven't a hope of getting my way.

"Baby, don't. I hate saying no to you. Off you get." He pushes me away from him so he slides out, and I grumble moodily as he lifts himself from the bath.

He hates saying no to me? Yes, only when I'm offering my body to him.

"Wear your hair down tonight," he says, grabbing a towel.

I get myself out of the bath and turn the shower on. "I might want to wear it up," I retort, getting under the water to start shampooing my hair. As it happens, I am wearing it down, but I'm being insolent for the sake of it.

I yelp when his palm connects with my bum on a harsh sting, and I quickly rinse the shampoo from my hair, opening my eyes to be confronted with a glowering, extremely displeased man. "Shut up." It's that tone that dares me to object. "You will wear your hair down." He skims his lips over mine. "Won't you?"

"I will."

"I know you will." He removes himself from the shower. "You get ready in here, I'll use another room."

"Not the cream room!" I shout in a panic. "Don't go in the cream room!"

"Unravel your knickers, lady."

I watch his wet-beaded shoulders leave the bathroom and me to finish my shower.

Chapter Twenty

I'm standing in front of the floor-length mirror gazing at my-self, my stomach in absolute knots. My hair has been blow-dried into glossy, tumbling waves, my makeup is delicate and natural, and I'm in the dress. It feels incredible, but my nerves are all over the place. I'm not sure if it's because of where I'm going, or if it's because I'm having an unreasonable pang of anxiety that Jesse won't like the dress.

I turn in the mirror to see the plunging back, which seems so much more revealing than it did in the store. Will he go mad? He nearly had heart failure over a cutout panel in a summer dress.

Blowing my hair out of my face, I put my simple white gold studs in—the lace won't allow for anything more—and transfer my gloss and powder into my clutch with my phone. The door knocks and my heart joins my stomach in the knots department.

"Ava? Baby, we need to go," he says quietly through the door. He makes no attempt to come in, and that small gesture, accom-panied by his soft, unsure voice, tells me he might be nervous, too. Why? Normally he would barge in, no gentle knock or sweet coaxing.

"Two minutes," I call. My voice is high and shaky as I spritz myself with my favorite Calvin Klein scent. There is no growling or impatient voice demanding I should get my arse in gear. He just leaves me to sort my nerves out.

I take a few calming breaths, grab my clutch, and roll my shoulders back. It's no good. I'm stupidly nervous. I've got to face all the members of The Manor. Those women have made it clear that I'm a gate-crasher, and I can't imagine their opinion will change just because I'm wearing a couture gown or am officially Jesse's girlfriend.

Taking a deep breath and gathering the bottom of my gown up a little to admire my shoes, I make my way to the bedroom door and to the top of the stairs.

As the huge open-plan area comes into view, I hear the low mesmerizing tones of the Moody Blues's "Nights in White Satin" falling over me from the integrated speakers. I smile to myself. And then I see him.

I halt in my tracks at the top step and try to catch my breath. It's like seeing him for the first time all over again. He looks devastating in his black suit, crisp white shirt, and black tie. He's freshly shaved so I can see him in all of his loveliness, and his hair has been persuaded to the side with some wax. Oh God, I'm going to be doing some serious trampling tonight.

He hasn't seen me yet. He's pacing slowly, hands in his trouser pockets, watching his feet. He's nervous. My confident, domineering ex-playboy is nervous. I watch in silence as he sits down, clasping his hands together, circling his thumbs briefly, before getting up and commencing pacing. I smile to myself, and like he has sensed I'm nearby, his head snaps up to me and I get a full frontal impact of my stunning man in all of his glory. My breath hitches, and I clasp the handrail on the stairs to steady myself.

His eyes widen a touch. "Oh Jesus," he mouths, and I shift on my heels under his intense gaze. Our eyes lock and he starts walking slowly toward the stairs. I would start down to meet him, but my stupid legs are frozen firmly in place, and no amount of mental encouragement is convincing them to move. He might need to carry me down the stairs.

He takes the steps, all the time keeping his eyes firmly set on mine, and when he reaches me, he holds his hand out on a small smile. I take a deep breath and grasp my dress, placing my hand in his, letting him lead me down the stairs, my legs more solid now that he has hold of me.

When we reach the bottom, he stops and turns to face me, running his eyes up and down my lace-clad body. He takes a slow walk around to my back, and I clench my eyes shut, praying that I've not made a mammoth error with my brave choice of a plunged back. I hear him inhale sharply, and then his warm fingertip meets the nape of my neck. He trails a slow, languid path down the center of my spine, setting off a flurry of pins and needles all over my bare flesh, and finishes at the base of my spine. Then there's the unmistakable heat of his mouth on my skin as he drops a kiss on the center of my back. I physically relax under the warmth of his lips.

He slowly makes his way back around to my front and locates my eyes. "I can't find my breath," he murmurs, snaking his hand around my waist and pulling me into him. He takes my mouth tenderly, like I've become as delicate as the lace encasing me.

All knots and nerves have been chased away. Now all I have to worry about are the endless women who'll be throwing themselves at his feet. He pulls away and pushes his hips into my lower stomach, the evidence of a raging erection clear and present. He would never make me undress—not now, surely?

"I *really* like your dress," he says on a small smile. "You didn't try this one. I would have remembered this one." He looks down at the dress in awe.

"Always in lace," I repeat his words, and his eyes fly back up to mine.

"You chose this dress for me?"

I nod mildly as he steps back and puts his hands back in his pockets. He starts chewing that lip, the cogs whirling around as he nods knowingly... approvingly.

His eyes climb back up my body to reach mine. "Like I chose this for you?" He pulls his hand from his pocket, and I see a delicate, platinum, layered chain hanging from his finger.

I nearly choke on my own tongue as my eyes take in the piece. I saw it in a glass cabinet as I passed through the jewelry department with Zoe this morning. She pointed it out and it had me spellbound immediately, displayed all on its own, with layers of delicate linked platinum and a chunky square-cut diamond suspended on the end. I nearly had heart failure when I read the small card displayed next to it detailing the price.

My eyes jump to his. "Jesse, that necklace was sixty grand!" I sputter. I won't ever forget. I counted the zeros repeatedly.

I start to get really hot all of a sudden as I flick my eyes from Jesse's to the swinging diamond that's still dangling from his finger. He smiles and walks around to the back of me, gathering my hair and placing it over my shoulder. My heart is performing jumping jacks in my chest as he brings the necklace over my head and it rests on my breastbone. It feels like a huge burden on my chest. I'm starting to shake.

His hands skim my back as he fastens the clasp, then he slides his palms onto my shoulders and rests his lips on the nape of my neck. "You like?" he whispers in my ear.

"You know I do, but..." I reach up and feel the diamond, then instantly want to get a velvet cloth and polish my fingerprint from it. "Did Zoe tell you?" I feel sick. I know she is technically in sales, but to tell Jesse that I was completely rapt by an obscenely expensive diamond necklace is taking advantage. Sixty grand? Oh heck!

"No, I asked Zoe to show it to *you*." He turns me around in his arms and runs his fingertips over the necklace and down the center of my chest. "You are crazy beautiful." He kisses my lips softly.

He asked her? I laugh a nervous laugh. "Are you talking to me or the diamond?"

"It's all about you," he says on a raised brow. "As it always will be."

My laughter abates instantly. "Jesse, what if I lose it, what if..." I'm silenced by his lips.

"Ava, shut up." He replaces my hair down my back. "It's insured and it's a gift from me. If you don't wear it, I'll be crazy mad. Understand?"

His tone suggests I'm not to argue with him on this, but I'm completely overwhelmed and even more nervous than before.

I take a deep breath and rest my hands on his chest. "I really don't know what to say." My voice is slightly shaky, matching my body.

"You could say you love it." His lips tip at the corner. "You could say thank you."

"I do love it. Thank you." I reach up and kiss him.

"You are more than welcome, baby. It's not as beautiful as you, though. Nothing is." He takes my hands from his chest. "My work here is done. Come on, you've made your god late." He leads me to the front door and flicks the music off before grabbing his keys and taking us out to the elevator. I notice that the glass has been fixed.

The doors open, we step inside, and I watch him punch in the code before standing back. He glances down at me and winks.

"You're crazy handsome," I say wistfully, reaching up and dragging my thumb across his bottom lip to wipe the remnants of my lipstick away. "And all mine."

He grabs my hand and kisses the tip of my finger. "Just yours, baby."

As we walk through the foyer of Lusso, Clive does a double take and gapes slightly. Jesse's arm goes firmly around my shoulder, and I know this is a sign of things to come tonight, which is fine because I don't plan on leaving his side all evening.

He helps me into the DBS and we travel to The Manor at high speed. I've made him late for his own anniversary party, but he doesn't seem that bothered. He tosses his eyes over to me every so often and half-smiles when I catch him looking at me.

I rest my palm on his firm thigh and relax completely when he places his hand on mine, giving it a reassuring squeeze. I am so in love with him right now and, unexpectedly, I'm looking forward to this evening for the first time. Fun-loving Jesse is out to play tonight and it is these little snippets of time when I can see the laid-back character whom everyone keeps telling me about, but it's plainly obvious that he is only like this when things are going his way, when I'm doing what I'm told and he's getting what he wants. But I'm at my happiest, my most content when he's like this. I am well and truly in my element on Central Jesse Cloud Nine.

*　*　*

I'm not surprised to see John on the steps of The Manor when we pull up. Jesse collects me from the car and leads me to the entrance where John is briefing a dozen men in full valet attire. Jesse chucks his keys at John, who catches them and passes them to one of the valets with strict instructions to only move the Aston Martin if absolutely necessary.

I put my hand up to John, and he smiles broadly at me as we pass, flashing me his gold tooth. He is in his usual black suit, except he has replaced the black shirt in favor of a white one with a black bow tie. The shades are firmly in position, though, and he still absolutely oozes coolness.

"There you are!" Sarah's panicked voice is the first thing to attack my ears as we enter The Manor. She is scuttling toward us, her legs restricted to small shifting movements due to the tight red satin dress that could qualify as a second skin. She must have poured herself into the thing. If there was previously any doubt regarding the status of her breasts, it has just been completely eradicated. They are hoisted up in the strapless dress, and if she lowered her lips, she could kiss them.

She halts her hasty advance on Jesse and gives me the once-over, her eyes finishing and remaining on my neck, which is hardly surprising, you can hardly miss it, but she isn't dazzled by the beauty. Not a chance. She's weighing up the likelihood of who's given it to me, and judging by her screwed-up, Botox-pumped face, she's hit the nail right on the head. I instinctively reach up and clasp the diamond, almost like I'm protecting it from her beady eyes. She flicks a begrudging stare at me and then runs her eyes down my lace-clad body. I straighten my shoulders and smile sweetly.

"I'm here now," Jesse grumbles, as he pulls me along beside him. We enter the bar and find Mario dishing out firm instructions to the bar staff. The bar has tripled in size, and I realize that the folding doors dividing the bar and restaurant have been opened and tall bar tables and stools have been scattered between the rooms.

"Here, sit." He lifts me onto a stool at the bar and calls Mario over before sitting himself opposite me.

Sarah points at a spreadsheet in her hand. "Can we just go through—"

"Sarah, give me a minute," Jesse cuts her off without taking his eyes from me. I could kiss him. "What would you like to drink?"

I can feel the ice emanating from Sarah as she stands there like a plum and waits for Jesse to tend to me before he gives her the attention she's demanding. I might take a while to decide. Can I have alcohol? He did say I can drink if he's around.

Mario appears, looking rather dapper in his white waistcoat and bow tie, his hair combed precisely to the side and his moustache neatly trimmed. He smiles brightly and I remember the lush cocktail he made for me earlier today. "I'll have a Mario's Most Marvelous, please." I grin at Mario.

He laughs loudly. "Yes!" He starts faffing at the bar. "Mr. Ward?"

"Just a water, please, Mario," Jesse replies, leaning toward me for a kiss. I can feel Sarah's eyes drilling into me, so, of course, I oblige and let him have his way. Not that I need Sarah around to do that. He has his way wherever and whenever he chooses.

"Sloe gin, Mario," she snaps petulantly, and then proceeds to huff while Jesse gets his fix of me. He really doesn't have any regard for this woman, and I feel all the more comfortable for it. She's not even really a threat.

"Jesse, I could really do with you in the office," she presses.

He growls, and I'm mentally willing him to trample all over her. "Sarah, please!" he grates, standing up in front of me. "Baby, do you want to stay here or would you like to come with me?"

I'm not looking at her, but I know she has just rolled her eyes, and while I would love to piss her off more, I'm quite happy to sit with happy Mario and drink my Most Marvelous. "I'm good here. You go."

He grabs his water and pushes his lips to my forehead. "I'll be quick." He stalks off, leaving Sarah to virtually jog on her eight-inch heels in order to keep up with him, but not before she leans across me to retrieve her gin from the bar on a snarl. I ignore it and accept my drink from a smiling Mario.

"Thank you, Mario." I return his smile and take a sip, gasping in gratitude.

"Miss Ava, may I say how magnificent you are looking this evening?" He smiles fondly, and I blush slightly.

"Mario, may I say how devilishly handsome *you* look this evening?" I raise my glass to the small Italian man, whom I have become rather fond of.

He slaps the bar on a sharp burst of laughter, and then his eyes fall onto the diamond that's suspended around my neck before he tips his eyes back up to me with a high raised eyebrow. "He loves you very much, yes?"

I give a little embarrassed shrug, feeling suddenly uncomfortable with the friendly Italian. I don't want everyone thinking the inevitable, just like Sarah did. "It's just a necklace, Mario." A sixty-grand necklace, yes, but no one has to know that. I reach up to grasp it again. I have to keep checking it's there, even though I can feel the weight perfectly.

"I see that you love Mr. Ward very much, too." He smiles and tops my glass up. "It makes me happy."

He gets distracted by a smashed glass and goes stalking off, waving his arms around and shouting in Italian.

I sit happily at the bar watching the staff prepare for the evening. Champagne is poured into glasses, the bar is repeatedly wiped down, and Mario shouts instructions, pointing here and there to guide his staff. The little Italian is a perfectionist, making everything just so. The huge room looks stunningly made up, everything arranged precisely and with the utmost attention to detail. The low-hanging chandeliers are shimmering subtly, giving off a soft apricot glow of light—the words *sensuous* and *invigorating* springing to mind immediately, words I've heard before.

Pete appears with a tray of canapés. "Ava, you look wonderful." He presents me with the tray. "Would you like one?"

I take in the glorious smell of smoked salmon and spy the small flatbreads caked in cream cheese. "Ah, Pete," I place my hand on my stomach, "I'm still full from lunch." I have no idea how I'm going to manage a three-course meal. I'll burst out of this dress.

"Ava, you hardly ate your lunch." He gives me a disapproving look and carries on his way. "Enjoy your evening."

"You, too, Pete," I reply, feeling immediately silly for telling a member of Jesse's staff to enjoy their evening of working hard. But he's right. I didn't eat my lunch and that's because I lost my appetite when Sarah rocked up, and it's probably why I'm not hungry now.

I turn back to the bar and find my glass has been filled again. I search Mario out and spot him across the bar repositioning some stools. He catches my eye and gives me a cheeky grin, and I hold my glass up and give him a frown. He ignores it and carries on moving stools around. I'll have to be careful. I've had two glasses of this Most Marvelous concoction already, and I have no idea what's in it. I can't be falling about all over the place when people start arriving.

"Ava!"

I jump into standing position as Kate's excited shriek hammers me from the side.

"Whoa!" She skids to a stop in front of me, her eyes popping out of her head. "Fucking hell!"

"I know," I grumble. "I'm petrified of the damn thing. It should be in a safe." I reach up and fiddle with it again, and Kate bats my hand away to cop a feel herself.

"Wow! That is some serious special." She drops the diamond and stands back to eye me up. "Look at you! Someone has been thoroughly spoiled today."

I laugh. I think what I have been today is way past spoiled. "What about you?" I grab her hands and hold them out to the side. "I love the dress." I send her on a little twirl. She looks fabulous, as always, in a long green gown, her red locks vibrant and piled high on her head. "Do you want a drink? You have to try this stuff." I grasp my glass from the bar and hold it up. "Here, sit. Where's Sam?"

She pushes herself onto the stool and rolls her eyes. "He wouldn't let any of the valets park his car. He thinks they're all driving morons who can't handle the power of a Carrera." She laughs. "Where's Jesse?"

My smile disappears. "Sarah dragged him off somewhere." I glance at the clock and note he's been gone for over an hour. "Anyway, I couldn't help but notice a certain Carrera, with a certain redhead in it, pulling into The Manor yesterday evening," I say casually as I sip my drink, eyeing her reaction over the rim of my glass.

My fiery redheaded friend fires me a glare. "Yes, Ava. You've already pointed that out," she says haughtily. "Get me that drink."

I shake my head, but I don't press her. "Mario?" I call, and he waves his acknowledgment as he walks over. "This is my friend Kate. Kate, this is Mario."

"Yes, we've met." Kate smiles at Mario.

"How are you this evening, Kate?" Mario blesses her with one of his lovely, warm smiles.

"I'll be better when you get me one of those." She points to my glass, and Mario laughs before going to fetch his glass jug of the Most Marvelous stuff.

Of course they've met. But how many times? Mario returns with his jug and I slap my hand over my glass when he tries to fill mine again, throwing him a playful warning look. He shrugs, muttering something in Italian and fighting a smile, clearly trying to pretend he's offended.

"Where's the love?"

We both turn and see Sam standing, legs spread and arms extended, in the entrance of the bar. He looks unusually smart, compared to his traditional baggy jeans and T-shirt combo. He straightens his suit jacket and waltzes to the bar confidently, shouting for a bottle of beer as he approaches. He may be dressed smartly, but his hair is its usual mop of brown, messy waves, and his cheeky grin and dimple are ever present.

"Ladies! May I say how damn fine you're both looking this pleasant evening?" He kisses my cheek and then lavishes Kate with a dramatic sloppy one. She bats him away, laughing. "Where's my man?" he asks, glancing around the bar.

I want to correct him and inform him that Jesse is, in fact, my man, but I fear I might be falling into trampling territory. "He's in his office," I say, taking another sip of my drink. I'm pacing myself, but this stuff is delicious and going down a treat.

* * *

An hour later, the bar is crammed full and Jesse is still nowhere to be seen. Soft jazz is playing in the background and the sound of happy chatter is prominent in the air. The men all look fine in tuxes and suits, and the woman have all gone to town in various gowns and cocktail dresses. I'm not ignorant of the fact that I seem to be the choice of conversation for many groups of people, particularly women, who make a rubbish job at hiding their interest. The thing that is bothering me the most, though, is my unreasonable, inquiring mind wondering just how many of them Jesse has slept with. It's a depressing thought and one I don't think I'll ever shake off.

I'm sipping cautiously on my third glass of Most Marvelous. Drew has arrived and looks no different from normal, all well groomed and precise. I exhale and relax when I feel two big palms rest on my hips and fresh-water, minty loveliness drift into my nose.

His chin rests on my shoulder. "I've neglected you."

I crane my neck to see him. "Yes, you have. Where have you been?"

"I couldn't get two yards without someone making a play for me. I'm all yours now, I promise." He pushes his front into my back and leans over to shake hands with the boys before leaning toward Kate so she can kiss his cheek. I can guarantee that all of the *someones* who he couldn't get two yards past were women. "Is everyone good?" he asks as he waves Mario for some water.

"We will be when dinner is out of the way." Sam grins and chinks bottles with Drew.

"Ten thirty," Jesse says sternly. He pulls me off the stool and sits there himself before pulling me down onto his lap and burying his face into my neck. Sam and Drew throw each other disapproving looks, and Kate refuses to look at me, heightening my suspicion *and* my concern.

"I want to lay you on that bar and take my time peeling all of this lace off," he whispers in my ear, pushing his groin up into my backside. I stiffen, silently willing him to shut up before I oblige and climb onto the bar for him. "What's under the dress?"

"More lace," I say quietly on a smile, and he groans in my ear.

"You're fucking killing me." He nips my ear, causing shivers to bolt through me.

"You have to stop," I warn, rather unconvincingly. It would take him a week to get me out of this dress and back in it again. Actually, it probably wouldn't take him that long at all. He'd lose his patience and rip it off, in which case, I wouldn't be putting it back on.

"Never." His tongue dips into my ear, and I close my eyes on a sigh.

"You guys!" Kate playfully slaps Jesse's shoulder. "Put her down!"

"Yeah, you're restraining our sexual needs, but it's okay for you to sit there and fondle your girl," Sam complains.

Jesse lands Sam with a reproachful glare. "Try and stop me. I'll shut up shop now and take her home."

"You're trampling your mates now." I laugh, and they all start laughing with me. I feel Jesse resume nibbling at my nape, but my attention is captured by a woman at the entrance of the bar wearing a cream dress. "Who's that?" I ask.

"Who's who?" His head comes up from my neck, and I nod toward the woman. She's probably early thirties, with black bobbed hair and pretty features. I wouldn't have paid much attention, but she is staring straight at us and she's alone.

She starts walking toward us, and I feel Jesse tense under me. Sam and Drew shut up immediately, which only serves to make me even more wary. Who the hell is she?

When she reaches our group, she stops, keeping her eyes on Jesse. The tension is tangible, and I glance at Kate to find a heavy frown on her face. Then I'm suddenly standing myself and being positioned back on the stool, minus one Jesse beneath me.

"Coral, do you want to come to my office?" Jesse asks, way too softly and gently for my liking. She nods, and I can see her eyes brimming with tears. "Come on." He turns to me, offering an apologetic smile before leading her away with his hand placed at the bottom of her back, leaving me sitting wondering what the hell is going on and mentally demanding him to remove his hand from her.

John gives him a nod as they pass at the bar entrance and then proceeds to notify everyone that dinner will be served imminently. There is a bustle of bodies that make for the summer room, the women flicking me curious stares as they pass. I ignore them; I'm too busy wondering what Jesse is doing with the mystery woman.

The silence that has fallen in our little group is broken by Kate. "Who was that?" She helps me down from my stool.

I glance at Drew and Sam, who both shrug denial of any knowledge, but I can tell by their sudden discomfort that they know exactly who Coral is.

"I don't know. I've never seen her before," I say on a frown, following the mass of people into the summer room. "Jesse seems to know her, though," I add dryly.

We find our table, and I'm beyond relieved to find myself sitting with Kate, Sam, Drew, and John. I'm not so pleased that Sarah is also with us, though. Another man, whom I've not met, joins us. He's introduced as Niles—a cute, floppy-haired posh schoolboy type, not the kind of man I would expect to find at The Manor at all. But what is The Manor's type?

The summer room has been completely emptied of sofas and occasional tables, and in their place are masses of round tables, seating between eight and ten people. I try to count them but lose track at table thirty. The color scheme is black and gold. I wonder if that's an accident.

Candles are burning everywhere, enhancing the key ingredient: sensuality. It was on Jesse's specification for the extension, and at the time, when I was oblivious to The Manor's activities, it was a weird request. Now it makes perfect sense

A band is set up in the corner, but it's four men with saxophones who are providing the music throughout dinner. The chair next to me is still empty, and the one next to that has Sarah perched neatly on it. I'm guessing she arranged the seating plan and was most pissed off when she had no choice but to sit me on the other side of Jesse.

Where is he?

Kate picks up a gold, structured satin bag and waves it in the air at me. They must be the gift bags, and I decide that I'm not even going to peek, my decision only reinforced when Kate shoves her nose in and then snaps the bag shut with wide blue eyes. Sam tries to snatch it from her, but she bats him away and he grumbles, grabbing the men's black equivalent that's positioned at his place setting. He does the same little rendition as Kate, but instead of a wide-eyed, stunned look, he looks at Kate and grins from ear to ear, prompting her to make a grab for his bag. He pushes her away.

A starter of scallops is served, and I'm momentarily distracted from my speculating by the divine dish. The Manor really does do food very well.

"So, Ava, I'm told you carried out the works at Lusso," Niles says across the table. "Quite a feat." He smiles, raising his glass to me.

"It didn't hurt the portfolio," I reply casually.

"You're modest." He laughs.

"She's good," Kate pipes up. "She's working on the extension upstairs." Kate points her fork toward the ceiling of the summer room in the most unladylike manner.

"I see. Is that how you met Jesse?" Niles asks, a little surprised.

"It is," I confirm politely but elaborate no further. I'm not comfortable talking about me and Jesse, especially with a stone-faced Sarah within touching distance. And Niles's question has just reminded me that Jesse still isn't here. "What do you do?" I ask to steer the conversation away from Jesse and my curious mind.

He puts his fork down and wipes his mouth with his napkin. "I supply Jesse's stock," he says on a small smile.

I manage to stop myself from asking the most stupid question I ever could. He doesn't supply food or drink to The Manor. No, Niles supplies other essentials—essentials for the top floors of The Manor. I nod my acknowledgment, not wanting to push that line of chat any further.

Sarah jumps into the gap of conversation, asking Niles how his recent trip to Amsterdam went. I'm thankful, even though

I quickly turn my attention away from where *that* discussion is heading, too.

I look over at Kate, who tosses me a filthy look, and then nods toward Sarah while cupping her breasts on a grin. I try not to smile, but I can't help the corners of my mouth tweaking at her brashness. She is so unaffected by everything. I love her.

I finish my Most Marvelous and accept the glass of white wine the waiter offers, taking an immediate sip and laughing when Drew stabs at his last scallop with his fork and it flies into the middle of the table. He gets rather mad with the slippery culprit as he tries to retrieve it, grumbling sulkily as he stabs at it, eventually giving up and grabbing it with his hand. He throws it on his plate in a mood, then glances up at the rest of the table who, with the exception of Sarah, are all delighting in his little performance. He relents and stands to bow, restoring his refined character. His fun, lighthearted performance is a mile away from the standoffish Drew I know.

Starters are swiftly removed from the table and replaced with salmon and an array of colorful vegetables. I'm thankful dinner is relatively light. I couldn't stomach much more with Sarah next to me. She hasn't said one word to me during dinner and has not inquired as to Jesse's whereabouts, so I assume that she knows. She advises the waiter to remove Jesse's untouched starter and hold off on his main for the meantime. If Kate weren't here, I would be getting really cranky now.

"You didn't bring Victoria?" Kate tosses the question at Drew and he catches it without an ounce of shock or surprise.

"No, she's sweet but hard work." He takes a swig of wine and sits back in his chair. "I'm happy exactly where I am at the moment." He raises his glass and everyone joins him, including me, even though I'm not particularly happy about where I am right now. "Anyway, she wouldn't let me lay a hand on her without the lights off."

I nearly spit my wine all over the table, then proceed to laugh—really hard.

Kate throws a napkin over the table at me, and I grab it, mopping up the wine dripping down my chin, still laughing.

Drew looks at me and Kate in turn, a smirk breaking the corners of his serious face. "You kind of need to see what you're doing for what I had in mind."

"Stop!" I howl, trying desperately to rein in my chuckles. I glance across at Sarah, and I'm met with a filthy glare. I resist the killing temptation to smash her face into her salmon.

I sit bolt upright—as does Sarah—when I spot Jesse and the mystery woman emerging from the corridor that leads down to his office. John must catch our sharp reaction because he jumps up from the table and makes his way over. They have an exchange of quiet words before John takes over responsibility of the woman and leads her out of the summer room.

Jesse looks across the room until he finds my eyes, and then starts making his way over. He's stopped a dozen times by various men and women as he passes tables, but he doesn't hang about for conversation. He just shakes hands with the men and leans down to kiss the women, smiling politely before searching me out again. He eventually makes it to me and sits himself down, grabbing my knee under the table. Sam cheers his arrival and pours some water into Jesse's wine glass, Kate frowns at me, and Sarah drops all conversation with Niles in favor of Jesse.

He turns into me and gives me very sorry eyes. "Forgive me?"

"Who was that?" I ask quietly.

"No one for you to be concerned about." He nods at my half-empty plate. "How is the food?"

No one for me to be concerned about? Well, that just makes me all the more concerned. "It's good, you should eat," I say shortly, looking for a waiter, but I'm a bit slow on the uptake. It seems Sarah has taken care of that already. His salmon lands in front of him and he tucks in, keeping his palm firmly on my knee, chopping and forking with one hand. When John returns and does his signature nod at Jesse, I throw him a curious stare, which Jesse catches and tramples all over by leaning in and lavishing me with his lips. I only halfheartedly return his kiss, fully aware that he's trying to distract me again.

He pulls back, giving me an inquiring eye. "Are you holding back on me?"

"Are you?" I toss back.

"Hey," he grates, quite loudly, considering the close proximity of our company. "Who do you think you're talking to?" he asks on a scowl, his grip on my knee tightening.

I shake my head. "Let's see what your reaction would be if a mystery man pulled me away from you for over an hour." I look him straight in the eye, noticing Sarah's sly smile behind him. She can fuck off. I'm in no mood for her.

His eyes soften, his tense jaw easing up a bit as he releases his grip of my knee and strokes up to the juncture of my thighs. I tense. He knows what he's doing. "Ava, please don't say things that will make me crazy mad." His voice has softened, but I can still detect the slight anger in his tone. "I've told you not to worry, so you shouldn't. End of."

I turn back toward the table, ignoring his hot touch through my dress. I'm simmering on the inside with possessiveness. I'm getting as bad as him, and this conversation is going to get us nowhere—not here and now, anyway.

Chapter Twenty-one

When dessert and coffee have been served and my cheeks hurt from Kate and Sam's antics at the table, John stands and announces, in his usual booming voice, that everyone should clear the room so it can be readied for the rest of the evening.

Jesse stands and helps me up from my chair, making a meal of showering me with attention, which I petulantly brush off. I'm stopped from walking away from the table when he grabs my elbow and whirls me around so we're front on front.

He burns a hole into me with pools of green displeasure. "Are you going to behave like a spoiled brat for the rest of the evening, or have I got to take you upstairs and fuck some sense into you?"

I recoil at his animosity as he looks past me and smiles, obviously acknowledging someone who is behind me. He returns his eyes to mine, his smile disappearing instantly. Reaching around me, he places a firm palm on my bum, pushing me into his groin and circling those damn hips, hard and slow. I curse my treacherous body for tensing, and my hands for instinctively flying up to grab his shoulders.

He leans into my ear. "Do you feel that?" He grinds hard again.

I lose the battle to restrain my moan of pleasure. I do not want to be getting horny here, because there is not a chance in hell I'm going to let him take me while we're in this place. Not ever.

"Answer the question, Ava." He clamps onto my earlobe and drags it through his teeth.

My grip of his shoulders tightens. "I feel it." My voice is broken and low.

"Good. It's yours. All of it." He pushes harder, further into me. "So stop with the fucking sulks. Do you understand me?"

"Yes." I exhale into his shoulder.

He releases me and stands back, raising expectant eyebrows at me, and I nod, trying to gather myself together. Will he always have this influence on me? I'm trembling and seriously rethinking my vow to avoid sex at The Manor. I could, quite easily, drag him upstairs to one of the private suites and let him eat me alive.

I glance past him and catch the viper glare of Sarah, and in a pathetic stamp of ownership, I put myself into Jesse's chest again and look up at him with sorry eyes.

He gives an approving nod of his head and leans down to rest his lips on mine. "That's better," he says into my mouth. He turns me around and starts guiding me out of the summer room. "I'm struggling to deal with all of the admiring stares you're attracting," he says, placing his hand firmly at my lower back.

I scoff. "You're attracting quite a bit of attention yourself," I muse, just as we pass an attractive brunette.

She smiles brightly at Jesse and strokes his arm. "Jesse, you're looking as delicious as ever."

I can't help the small shocked burst of laughter that flies from my mouth. She's got some front, and I'm hugely offended that she clearly thinks I'll just take her brazen flirting without so much as a word. I'm about to stop and put her in her place, but Jesse pushes me on, preventing me from following through on my intent to confront the shameless hussy.

"Natasha, you are an intolerable flirt, as ever," Jesse retorts wryly, draping his arm over my shoulder and landing me with a chaste kiss, obviously sensing my irritation. She smiles slyly and narrows easy eyes on me.

Has he slept with her, too? I feel my newfound possessiveness simmering steadily inside me. I can't imagine that I'm going to be spending much time here if this is the response I'll receive whenever I do. Not that I particularly want to be here, but with it being Jesse's place of work, it would be handy if I could come here and feel comfortable, rather than feeling like I'm stepping on a million attractive women's toes. And that's another point. Does Jesse only offer membership to women of an eight or above on the good-looks scale? Retirement is looking more likely by the day. I want to stay stuck to Jesse so I can fight off all these women.

As we walk into the bar, we find that the stool I always seem to get positioned on is taken by a man. He soon makes way when he sees us approaching, raising his glass in greeting. I'm lifted onto the stool, and Mario appears without delay, leaving the members of The Manor to be served by one of the other bar staff.

"What would you like to drink?" Jesse perches on his stool opposite me and takes my hand in his. "Most Marvelous?" He raises his eyebrows.

I turn to a waiting Mario. "Please, Mario," I say, and he smiles his usual fond smile, but looks a little more flustered than he did earlier. I'm not surprised; he's being run off his feet.

"I'll have one of those." Kate joins us and leans on Jesse's shoulder with a huff. "These shoes are killing me!" she exclaims with a look of true pain on her pale face. "Seriously. A man categorically devised the high heel, and he did it in an attempt to make it easier for you dudes to rugby tackle us womenfolk to the ground and haul us back to your beds."

Jesse throws his head back and laughs a proper belly laugh as Sam and Drew find us.

"What's the score?" Sam asks as he eyes Jesse laughing hard. He looks at me and Kate and we both shrug on wide smirks. Kate slaps Jesse's shoulder affectionately. I can't help but share in Jesse's amusement at Kate's dry comment. When he laughs like that, faint lines spring from his twinkling greens and fan his temples. He looks so handsome.

"I'm sorry, drinks?" he asks, getting his laughter under control and giving me a wink.

I pool on the stool, sending him a telepathic message to take me home immediately. Basking in the sun on Central Jesse Cloud Nine has resumed.

Drew and Sam throw their orders at Mario, but he's already halfway to the fridge to collect their beers. I scoop up our cocktails and pass one to Kate, catching her nodding over my shoulder. I frown at her, so she repeats the jig of her head, and I realize what she is signaling. I lean into Jesse, and he drops his conversation with the boys, instantly turning his face to me.

"What's up, baby?" He looks worried.

"Nothing, I'm just going to use the ladies'." I lower myself from the stool and grab my clutch from the bar. "I won't be long."

"Okay." He kisses my hand.

I walk away and join Kate. "I need a fag," she spits urgently.

"Really? I thought you wanted to drag me upstairs," I flip as she leads me out. "I'm going to the toilet quickly, I'll meet you outside."

"The front," she calls, making her way to the entrance hall, while I head in the other direction toward the toilets.

I find the ladies' empty and let myself into a cubicle before quickly negotiating the dress up to my waist. I'm not alone for long. I hear the door open and a few voices chatting happily.

"Have you seen her? She is young for our Jesse."

I freeze mid-wee and hold my breath. Our Jesse? What? Did they share him? I collapse on the toilet and release my bladder. I've started now. I can't stop.

"He's all over her. Fucking hell, did you see the diamond around her neck?" voice number two gushes.

"You can hardly miss it. It's obvious what she's after," voice number three pipes up.

How many of them are there out there? I finish up and start pulling my dress back down while contemplating what I should do. What I want to do is go out there and put them straight on the whole money business.

"Ah, come on, Natasha. Jesse is beyond a fucking god. The money is just a bonus." That's voice number two, and now I know that voice number three is Natasha, the incorrigible flirt. And he's *my* fucking god!

"Well, it looks like we've made all this effort for nothing. I had heard, but I didn't believe, not until I saw it with my own eyes. It looks like our Jesse has been whipped from under our feet." Voice number one laughs.

I stand in the cubicle willing them to leave so I can escape, but I can hear the pops of lips from the reapplication of lipstick and the spray of perfume going on.

"It's a shame, he's the best I've had and I'm never going to get to try it again," voice number three—aka Natasha—muses.

My hackles rise. He *has* slept with her. I look up at the ceiling, trying desperately to gather some calming thoughts, but it's impossible, especially with three tarts out there having a good old chinwag about my god's sexual capabilities.

"Oh, me too," voice number one adds, and I stand with my jaw on the floor, waiting for voice number three to pipe up and make it a clean sweep.

"Well, I don't know about you two, but he was too good to give up trying." Voice number two totally finishes me off.

I can't listen to this shit. I flush the chain, silencing all three, and make sure my dress isn't tucked into my bodice before I swing the door open and walk casually out of the cubicle. I smile politely at the three women, all with some sort of makeup suspended in front of their faces, staring completely flummoxed at me as I make my way to a mirror at the other end of the bathroom. I calmly wash my hands and dry them before topping up my gloss, all in silence and under the wary eyes of the three brazen hussies at the other end of the ladies'. I waltz past and leave the bathroom without a word, my dignity still firmly intact.

My heart is jumping and my legs are slightly shaky, but I make it to the entrance hall still standing. That was horrific. Hearing those women talk about Jesse like that has me more upset than mad. He really has put it about...everywhere...with a lot of women. I think I need a cigarette, too.

I know I audibly groan when Sarah steps out from the doorway that usually serves the restaurant. She's been waiting for this moment all night, and after what I've just endured, I'm feeling even less tolerant of her than usual. I'm facing the fourth woman in as many minutes—no, probably seconds—who Jesse has fucked. My stomach is turning, I feel sick and in no mood for Sarah and her viper gob. "Sarah, you've done an amazing job tonight," I say courteously. I'll get in first with the pleasantries so there is no mistaking my attempt to keep things civil, even though it is taking every ounce of strength I have.

She folds an arm under her chest, boosting it even further while holding her sloe gin in front of her mouth. Her body language screams superiority. "Did you collect your gift bag from the table?" she asks on a smile.

It throws me. I thought we were past faking pleasantries when Jesse isn't around. "No, I didn't," I answer warily. After seeing Kate's face, I really didn't want it.

She broadens her smile. "Oh, that's a shame. There was something in there that may have been of use to you."

"Like what?" I can't help the curiosity in my voice. What's her game?

"The vibrator. I noticed yours was left in a million pieces on Jesse's bedroom floor."

"Pardon?" I blurt on a laugh.

She smiles slyly, and I dread the words I know she's about to say. "Yes, when I rescued him on Wednesday morning after you left him handcuffed to his bed." She shakes her head. "Not a wise move."

My stomach falls into my heels as I watch her weighing up my reaction to her information overload. Jesse called Sarah? When he was bollock naked, handcuffed to the bed and with a vibrator next to him, he chose Sarah to come and release him?

I thought John freed him. Why did I think that? I can't even reflect that far back. At the moment, I'm just looking at the nasty creature standing in front of me, smugly delighting in my misery. I'm going to kill him, but first I'm going to wipe that sly smile off of her Botox-pumped face.

"Have you ever heard of tit tape, Sarah?" I ask coolly. Her face drops, as do her eyes to her chest. I start walking forward. Oh, she is so getting trampled!

"Excuse me?" She laughs.

"Tit tape. It's widely known to keep breasts secure, or..." I shake my head. "Of course, it's your intention to assault people's eyes with your overinflated chest." I stop in front of her. "Less is more, Sarah. Have you ever heard that saying? You would do well to remember it, especially at your age."

"Ava?"

No!

I turn and find Jesse standing with his frown line perfectly in place. Good, because he should be really concerned. And then

I hear Sarah's heels disappear off into the restaurant. Yes, she's dropped her bombshell and has now fucked off to avoid being hit by the shrapnel.

"What's going on?" he asks, his handsome face full of confusion and concern.

I don't even know what to say. I glance around the entrance hall of The Manor and see many members making their way upstairs. It must be past ten thirty.

"Ava?"

I return my eyes to Jesse as he starts walking toward me, but I step back and he stops in his tracks. "I'm leaving." My tone is completely resolute. I can't stay here and listen to women boast about their sexual encounters with Jesse and listen to them pass judgment on why I'm with him. Neither am I watching as he disappears with another woman with no explanation. And I'm certainly not setting myself up for humiliation by Sarah. I turn and walk with purpose to the huge, double doors that will take me out of this hellhole, my heart hammering and tears of frustration brimming.

"Ava!" I hear him yell, and then the telltale sign of his thumping footsteps coming after me.

I have no idea what I plan on doing when I get outside. I know he will catch me, and I know he won't let me leave. I'll steal a car. I don't care that I'm way over the limit. I can't subject myself to this torture anymore. It's rotting my reasonableness, turning me into a jealous, resentful monster. I shouldn't have come here.

"Ava, get your fucking arse here!"

I make it to the steps and bump into Kate. "Where have you been?" she asks shortly, her eyes widening when she obviously catches sight of Jesse in pursuit of me.

"I'm going," I blurt, gathering my dress up, ready to take the steps. She watches me hastily pass her with a what-the-hell look coated all over her pale face. I fly down the steps stupidly fast and collide with his solid, suit-covered chest. That fucking chest! I'm hoofed up and slung over his shoulder with no effort at all.

"You're not fucking going anywhere, lady," he growls, and starts back up the steps to The Manor.

I flick my hair out of my face and push my hands into his lower back to try and break free. "Let go of me!" I yell frantically as I wriggle, but he has a tight hold, and I know he would die before letting me go. "Jesse!"

Kate watches with an open mouth as we pass her, before throwing her cigarette butt on the ground and following us in. "What's going on?"

"He's an arsehole! That's what is going on!" I yell, attracting the attention of all the valet staff, who halt all duties and quietly observe me being jostled back into The Manor. "Jesse, put me down!"

"No!" He continues through the entrance hall and toward the summer room. "It's fine, Kate. I just need a little chat with Ava," he says calmly, increasing his grip on me as I continue to battle his hold.

Looking up, I see Kate stop at the bar entrance and shrug at me. I want to scream at her, but I know she'll be of little use in trying to pry Jesse off me. I'm carried through the summer room, where all of the tables have been cleared and a dance floor set up, and the band stops their sound check to watch as Jesse strides through with me draped across his shoulder. I crane my neck around and spot John coming from the direction of Jesse's office, and he laughs as he shakes his head. It's not bloody funny. We pass him in the corridor, but he says nothing. He just moves to let us by before carrying on his way, like this is an everyday, normal occurrence. I suppose it is.

Jesse kicks his office door shut and dumps me on my feet, his face contorted with rage, which only boosts my own fury. He points his finger in my face. "Don't you *ever* walk away from me!" he roars.

I flinch.

He throws his arms up in frustration and walks over to the drinks cabinet as I make for the door again. Will he have a drink if I leave? At the moment, I'm too mad to care. I grab the handle of the door, but make no further progress. I'm grabbed and yanked back before he places me on my feet again and practically kicks a cabinet until it blocks the exit.

"What the fuck are you playing at?" He grasps my shoulders and shakes me ever so slightly. "What's going on?"

I regain possession of my body and walk away from him. He growls but leaves me. It's not like I can go anywhere now.

I swing around and throw him the filthiest look I can muster. "I can't believe you trample all over any man who so much as looks at me, yet you think it's perfectly okay for you to have another woman in your bedroom while you are lying naked on the bed!" My voice is getting higher. I'm so mad! "I thought John freed you!"

His face drops slightly as he takes on board what I have just screeched at him. "Well, he didn't!" he yells. "He was at The Manor, Sam was unobtainable, and Sarah was nearby. What did you want me to do?"

I gape at him. How can he be mad with me? "Well, I wouldn't want you calling another woman!"

"Well, you shouldn't have left me handcuffed to our fucking bed!"

"It's your bed!" I'm poking.

His eyes widen. *"Ours!"*

"Yours!"

He throws his head back and curses at the ceiling. I don't care. He is not turning this around on me.

"And, while we're at it, I've just had the pleasure of listening to three women compare notes on your sexual abilities. That, I really enjoyed. And who the hell was that woman?" I try and regain a bit of composure. I'm struggling. The constant thoughts and mental images of Jesse entertaining another woman are poisoning my mind. It's ridiculous. He's thirty-seven years old.

He walks toward me. "You know I have a history, Ava," he says impatiently.

"Yes, but have you fucked every female member of The Manor?"

"Watch your fucking mouth!"

"*No!*' I walk over to the drinks cabinet and grab the first bottle of alcohol I can lay my hands on—which happens to be vodka—and pour some into a tumbler. My hands are shaking as I lift the glass and tip the neat contents down my throat. It's only now I wonder why he keeps alcohol in his office if he wants to avoid drinking it. My throat burns and I shudder as I slam the glass down on the polished wooden counter. I'm not stupid enough to pour another. I stand with my hands braced on the cabinet, staring at the wall.

He's silent.

My throat is sore and gravelly and I feel completely out of control, consumed by jealousy and hatred. "How would you feel if another man laid his eyes all over my naked body while I was handcuffed to a bed?"

The heavy breath that travels the short distance between us and warms my back tells me my answer. "Murderous," he snarls.

"How would you feel listening to someone voice their opinions on my bedroom manner? Saying they weren't going to give up trying to get me in bed."

"Don't!"

I turn to find him watching me closely, his jaw ticking wildly. "My work here is done," I quip, and make my way to the door. That sideboard looks heavy, but I don't get the opportunity to try and move it. Jesse steps in my way, halting my progress. I take a calming breath and look up at him. "You should know, I'm not leaving, but only because I can't. I'm going out there and I'm going to have a drink, and tomorrow night I'm going out with Kate. And you are not going to stop me."

"We'll see about that," he fires confidently.

"Yes, we will."

He starts chewing his lip, his eyes burning into mine. "I can't change my past, Ava."

"I know. And it doesn't look like I'm going to be able to forget about it either. Will you move the cabinet, please?"

"I love you."

"Move the cabinet, please."

"We need to make friends." His face is deadpan, while my eyes have just widened.

"No!"

He takes a step forward, and I take one back. "I'll trample, Ava," he warns calmly. I take another step back, watching as he regards me carefully. "Are you going to deny me?" He arches a cautionary eyebrow, and I carry on stepping back until I'm pushed up against the drinks cabinet. If he gets his hands on me, I'm completely done for, and I want to stay mad. I need to stay mad! He reaches me and places his hands over mine. My face is level with his neck and jaw, and I try to block off my sense of smell. I fail miserably.

"Tomorrow I'm going back to Kate's," I say bravely. I need time to try and sort out my unreasonable jealous frame of mind. It would seem that Jesse Ward has brought out some rather nasty qualities in me, too.

"That's never going to happen, Ava. But just you saying it makes me really fucking mad."

"I am," I retort. I'm being stupidly daring, but I need him to know how much this is bothering me.

He bends so he's at my eye level. "Crazy mad, Ava," he warns softly. "Look at me," he breathes in my face.

I whimper slightly. "No."

"I said, look at me."

I shake my head faintly and he heaves a sigh.

"Three." My eyes instinctively fly up to his, but not because he's started the countdown and I don't want him to reach zero. It's because I'm shocked. I've unwittingly complied with his command, and I'm now staring into dark green pools of lust.

"Kiss me," he demands.

I purse my lips and shake my head, attempting to pull my arms free.

"Three," he begins again and I freeze, my mouth dropping open in shock. He brushes his lips gently over mine. "Two."

This isn't fair. He could kiss me, but I know he won't. He wants me to submit and I'm desperately trying to resist, even though my treacherous body is screaming for him.

"One." His lips meet mine again.

I snap my head away and wriggle under his hold, desperately fighting him off. "No, you're not distracting me, Jesse."

He shouts a frustrated yell, releases his grip, and my hands fly up to his chest to push him away. We battle, my flailing hands beating him away from me as he tries to grab at my wrists.

"Ava!" he yells, securing me and spinning me around. I don't know why I'm doing this. I could never win, even though he's obviously handling me with care. "Fucking stop it, you crazy woman!"

I ignore him, rage and adrenaline spiking my stamina to continue fighting him off.

"For fuck's sake!" he shouts, taking me down to the floor and securing me under his body. "Pack it in!"

I heave under him, every muscle aching, my hammering heart jumping from my chest. I open my eyes, finding a perplexed look on his face. He doesn't know what to do with me. I'm losing complete control.

We stare at each other, both of us panting from the exertion of our physical battle. And then we both move forward fast, our mouths crashing together, our tongues dueling urgently.

It's a tally for Jesse. He moans, releasing his grip of my wrists and fisting my hair in his hands as he tackles my mouth with as much force as I'm taking his. This is a possessive kiss. I'm reinforcing my claim on him, trying to make him see how strongly I feel about him, how the thought of other women and Jesse makes me just as crazy mad as him. His hand finds my breast and grabs me hard through the material of my dress, kneading and squeezing as he groans.

My tongue aches, my lips are becoming sore, but neither one of us is letting up. We're both trying to make a point here. My hands move from his biceps to his head, and I yank his hair before applying pressure, pushing him into me. I'm fizzing all over, burning up completely as I writhe on the floor beneath him, making a damn successful point of ownership. And then he rolls us over and my lips leave his, drifting down his suit-covered torso until I reach the zipper of his trousers. I yank it down and make quick work of releasing him, his cock slipping free, my hand wrapping around his shaft without delay.

In a complete frenzied mess, my mouth coats him and I take him all of the way, no soft caressing, no light licks or teasing strokes. I attack him, frantic and desperate.

"Fuck!" he barks, as I feel him hit the back of my throat. "Fuck, fuck, fuck!"

I don't gag or heave. I thrust him into my mouth repeatedly, tirelessly, squeezing his base and reaching between his thighs to grasp his heavy sacs. Hard.

"Jesus!" His hips fly up. "Ava!" His hands find my head and yank at my hair. I don't know if he's begging me or scolding me.

I concentrate on reinforcing my desperation for him, working him fast and harshly, his flesh feeling silky on the insides of my mouth, the friction from the speed of my strokes heating us both.

"Keep me in your mouth, Ava," he orders, his hips meeting my every advance. My cheeks are aching, but I power on.

And then I recognize the sign of him expanding in my mouth, his breathing becoming disjointed, and his fists tightening in my hair. I moan around him, increasing my iron grip on his balls and moving my other hand under his shirt. I grab his nipple, squeezing hard.

He bellows, his groin shoots up and he pushes my head down onto him, his tip pushing against the back of my throat.

He comes.

I swallow.

We both moan.

"Fucking hell, woman," he pants, withdrawing from my mouth and pulling me up his body. "Fucking, fucking hell." He takes my lips again, sweeping his tongue through my mouth, sharing his salty essence. "I take it that means you're sorry," he puffs between firm lashes of his tongue.

I have unwittingly just given him an apology fuck. Am I sorry? For being a complete, unreasonable, possessive fool . . . just like him? "No, I'm not," I affirm. I'm really not. Our tongues keep up together, both of our groans and shifting hands working all over each other's bodies.

I reach back down and wrap my hand around his semierect length, relentlessly working him while we both tackle each other's mouths hard . . . aggressively. I'm not prepared to stop. He pulls away, panting, his chest heaving, but I don't give up. I push my abused lips back to his, plunging my tongue in, continuing with my frantic handling of his cock.

"Ava, stop." He grabs my hand from his groin and turns his face to break our lip contact.

I don't give up, even now. I fight him, urgently smothering him with my mouth. He's never refused me before.

"Ava! Please!" He loses his patience and pushes me over onto my back, pinning me under his body.

I feel tears stabbing at my eyes. I'm more desperate than any of those women. I'm not dealing with this well at all. A sob slips through my lips and I turn away from him, completely ashamed.

"Baby, don't," he pleads softly, pulling my face back to his and brushing my wild hair from my face. He gazes down at me, almost in sympathy. "I understand," he whispers, wiping his thumb under my eye. "Don't cry." He skims my lips with his. "It's always just you."

I blink back my tears. "I'm not coping with this." I reach up to touch his face. "I feel violent," I admit. I can't believe I just openly volunteered that information, and I'm stunned I really do feel like that. "Mine," I say quietly.

He nods. He gets it. "Always just yours." He pulls my palm to his lips and kisses it firmly. "Please, ignore them. They're shocked, that's all. Their noses have been put firmly out of joint by a young, dark-eyed, breathtaking beauty. My beauty."

"You're my beauty," I affirm harshly.

"All of me, Ava. Every single piece." Shifting his body, he rests himself all over me, completely coating me. He grasps my face in his palms, his green eyes staring down at me. "Ava, you own me." He places his lips on mine. "Do you understand me?"

I nod in his hold, feeling weak and needy.

"Good girl," he whispers. "You are mine and I am yours."

I nod again for fear of wailing if I open my mouth. I didn't think I could love him more.

He runs his palms over my cheeks and his eyes scan every inch of my face. "I know this is hard for you, but believe me, I don't see them. Only you."

"I love you." I just about manage to get the words out.

"I know you do. And I you." He sits up and secures himself before helping me up. "We'll make friends properly later. I don't want to trample your dress." He smiles a little and spins me around. "It looks like it needs a bit of patience, and we all know how little of that I have when it comes to you." He turns me back and rubs his nose over mine. "Better?"

"Yes."

"Good. Let's go." He takes my hand and leads me to the door, dropping it briefly to shift the sideboard back, before reclaiming it and leading me back to the party. He understands.

CHAPTER TWENTY-TWO

The band has started and people have filtered into the summer room.

"Motown?" I ask, a little surprised, as I'm pulled through the few tables left set up.

"They're a great band. You want to dance?" He glances down at me with a half-smile, and I'm reminded that my man has some serious moves.

"Later." I'm conscious that Kate is probably wondering what has happened and where I am. He nods and takes me through to the bar.

My stool is free and I'm lifted onto it. Kate, Drew, and Sam are all holding position at the bar and all seem to be lit up, the alcohol flowing well.

"Where have you been?" Kate inquires, flicking a cautious glare at Jesse.

"In Jesse's office discussing a certain female who he called to free him after I left him handcuffed to the bed," I blurt it all out quietly while I keep my eye on Jesse to ensure he's not listening. He's too busy ordering drinks with Mario.

"You left him there?" She's trying not to laugh. I didn't mention that before.

"He was really mad."

Her lips purse. "And he called Sarah to free him?"

"Yes," I grate. "And he's slept with her."

"Oh." Kate's eyes widen. "Why would he call her?" She comes in closer, wedging herself between me and Jesse so she is standing in front of me.

"He couldn't get hold of anyone else. John was here and Sam was otherwise engaged."

"What day was this again?"

"Wednesday." I raise my eyebrows and watch as she mentally casts her mind back to Wednesday morning. The penny obviously drops because a guilty look washes over her face. I won't even ask why Sam couldn't get to Jesse. "Sarah took great delight in advising me. That and the pleasurable experience of listening to three women compare notes on Jesse's bedroom skills sent me over the edge," I grumble.

"Oh dear." Kate gives me a sympathetic face. "History, Ava."

"I know." I shake my head disgustedly. "Kate, I've got so much to tell you. Can we go out tomorrow night? I need to let off some steam."

She nods and then lets out a small yelp as she's lifted from her feet and placed to the side by Jesse, giving him access to me. She slaps him on the shoulder playfully and giggles.

"Drink." He thrusts a glass of water under my nose, and I take it without complaint, watching him smile as I down it and hand him the empty glass. He nods in surprised approval, then replaces the empty with a glass of Mario's Most Marvelous stuff. "See how much easier things are when you do as you're told?"

I narrow playful eyes on him and shake my head at his impertinence. Yes, they are, but his demands are not always as simple as drinking a glass of water. He turns away to catch up with Drew and Sam, but keeps a firm hand on my knee.

"Oh look," Kate whispers.

I follow her gaze and see Sarah with a group of men, laughing, stroking, touching, and generally feeling up every single one of them at every opportunity. Her beady eyes land on me, and she stares with a smug, satisfied look on her face—until I feel Jesse's lips on my cheek. I leave her seething in the knowledge that her little plan hasn't worked and turn my attention to Jesse. He winks at me and, standing me up, he collects my arms and drapes them over his shoulders before sweeping his hands around my back and pulling me close, his forehead resting on mine. It's a gesture of reassurance. I'm grateful.

"You okay?"

I smile, pulling back to get an eyeful of his beautiful face. "Perfect."

"Good."

We both jump at a flash of light and turn to see Kate with a camera pointing at us. Jesse grabs me and suspends me in his arms, my head flying back on a laugh as I register the continuous clicks and flashes of the camera.

His mouth rests on my throat. "Smile for me, baby."

I pull my head back up and find his green eyes shimmering with contentment... with happiness. I make him happy. I make him determined to live. I make him want to leave this lifestyle behind. I smile, lacing my fingers through his hair and pulling his lips down to mine.

"Okay," Kate shouts, "that's enough!"

Jesse has me, taking what he wants with no regard for our audience or concern of our location, before I'm returned to a standing position and placed back on the stool. My drink is handed to me, and he returns to the male conversation, like he hasn't just silenced the room with his out of character display of affection. I glance across the bar, finding Sarah spitting nails. "She really doesn't like me, Kate."

"Oh, fuck her!" Kate spits nastily. "Do you care?"

"No, I don't. But I'm pissed that I have no choice but to suck up the fact that Jesse will be coming here daily and she'll be here." Would he sack her if I asked him to?

Kate disappears from in front of me when Sam makes a grab for her and hauls her out of the bar. "Ava, dance!" she shouts, as she vanishes from view.

I'm distracted when a man approaches Jesse with his hand outstretched. I recognize him. Jesse takes it, shaking it mildly as he shifts and flicks his eyes to me. They chat briefly and the guy tips his drink in my direction, prompting Jesse to glance toward me and step forward with him. He's probably midforties and looks a little tipsy.

"Ava, this is Chris," Jesse's tone suggests he would rather not be introducing me to Chris. "He was the estate agent of Lusso."

Of course. I knew I recognized him. He smiles a slimy smile, and I immediately dislike him. "Hi." I put my hand out reluctantly, and he takes it. His palm is sweaty. "It's nice to meet you." I fake a sincere smile and notice Jesse watching my coiled fingers in my hair on a fond smile.

"It's an absolute pleasure," he drawls. I flick nervous eyes to Jesse when Chris moves in closer, keeping a firm hold of my hand. "I love this dress." He runs his eyes down my front, prompting me to lean back slightly.

This is one brave man—either that or extremely stupid. Jesse is at his side in a nanosecond, jaw muscles going into overdrive. He's physically twitching and Chris is soon removed from my personal space by a short, sharp yank of his shoulder. He stands back, where Jesse has put him, and watches as Jesse moves in, picking me up and taking my seat before resting me back down on his thighs.

"Chris, you'll do well to keep your hands and your eyes to

yourself. Do that and I might not break your fucking legs, understand?" Jesse says it so calmly, but there is no denying the cutting edge to his tone.

I watch as Chris backs off with a justifiably worried look on his face. "Jesse, I apologize. I assumed she was fair game."

"Excuse me?" I cough.

I feel Jesse tense beneath me and in a panic, I place my hand on his leg and squeeze slightly. The heat is pouring from him and his heart is stabbing my back. I would love to set him on this cheeky swine, but I also want to see the night through without having to put an ice pack on Jesse's abused fist. Chris here will be slayed if I don't hold him back.

He lifts from the stool slightly and pulls me to his chest. "I suggest you fuck off now," he snarls maliciously.

I push back against him and throw Chris a fuck-off-if-you-know-what's-good-for-you look. He backs away vigilantly, and I doubt very much that he'll be back any time soon.

I crane my head around and give Jesse an inquiring look. "Murderous?"

I get my very own scowl followed by a smothered face. "Deadly."

"Are all the women fair game?" This is news.

He shrugs. "You don't join The Manor if you aren't sexually adventurous."

Oh, lovely. I look around the bar, which has thinned out since the band started and the upstairs opened. The people I'm sharing company with look like any other people, but they are all here for one reason and that has nothing to do with the posh sports facilities that The Manor boasts. One thing is certain, judging by all of the prestigious cars that are often parked outside—they are all very rich people.

"How much is the membership?" My curiosity is getting the better of me.

He works his face right into my neck. "Why, do you want to join?"

"I might."

He bites my neck. "Sarcasm doesn't suit you, lady." He pulls me up further onto his lap. "Forty-five."

"A month?" That's not bad.

He laughs. "No, grand a year."

"Shit!"

He clamps his teeth on my ear and then rolls his hips into my bum. "Mouth."

I moan a little at his evident hard state. Forty-five thousand a year is ridiculous money. These people must all be stupid or desperate, but as I look around, there are no particularly ugly men and women. They all look like they could get some if they wanted to.

"Hey, does Kate pay that?" I know she's not short of a few quid, but she is very shrewd with her cash.

"What do you think?" he asks on a little laugh. I don't know? Did Jesse waive the membership fee because she's my friend? Would he do that?

"Sam," I say in realization. "Sam paid."

"At mates' rates, of course.'

He applies mates' rates for membership to his sex haven? I'm on another planet at the moment. This sort of thing is way past my comprehension and here I am, dining and drinking with these people and dating the owner.

"I wish you had refused," I grumble. Kate might be laid-back, but I can't help thinking that she is coasting toward complete disaster.

"Ava, what Sam and Kate do is their business."

I scowl to myself. "How many members are there?"

He brings his palm up to my forehead and applies a little pressure until the back of my head rests on his shoulder.

"Someone is very nosey, considering she hates the place." He kisses my cheek.

"I'm not nosey." I shrug casually, but I *am* interested. It's made him a very rich man, even if it's down to Uncle Carmichael.

He laughs lightly. "At the last count, I think Sarah said fifteen hundred-ish, but they're not all active at the moment. Some we don't see from one month to the next, some of them meet people and start a relationship, and others take a break from the whole scene."

I do a quick mental calculation in my head and come up with a whole lot of millions. "Is the restaurant and bar included?"

"No!" he says shocked. I don't know why. For forty-five thousand pounds a year I would want more than an open invitation to have sex with anyone and everyone. "The bar and restaurant are a separate entity. Some members eat breakfast, lunch, and dinner here four or five times a week. I wouldn't be making much money if I included all meals and drinks in with their memberships. They have accounts they settle on a monthly basis. Turn around, I need to see you." He nudges me to get up and positions me between his thighs. He brushes my hair over my shoulder and straightens my diamond before taking my hands in his. "Would you like to see upstairs?" he asks, and then commences chomping his lip.

I withdraw slightly. I know he doesn't mean the suites, I've seen them, or I've seen one of them. He means the communal room. Do I want to see it?

Fucking hell!

I bloody well do. I don't know if it's Mario's Most Marvelous giving me a bit of spunk, or if it is just pure curiosity, but I really want to be in the know. "Okay." I utter the word quietly before I talk my way out of it, and he nods ever so slightly, almost thoughtfully.

He stands and I let him lead me into the entrance hall and to the bottom of the stairs. I gaze up to the massive gallery landing, hearing the comings and goings of people in and out of rooms. Then I let Jesse slowly tug me up the stairs. I know he's taking it leisurely to give me time to retract my decision, and I want to tell him to hurry up before I do. We reach the top and start circling the landing until we arrive at the stained-glass window. There are people milling around everywhere, all fully dressed, some outside rooms, some just chatting. It's bizarre.

"We need to get cracking on those next week," Jesse says, pointing through the archway to the extension. I can see now why he needs to. "Ready?"

I know he's watching me as I stare up at the double doors that lead into the communal room, and my eyes are pulled to his like the magnets they absolutely are. His deep greens pierce me. He knows everything about this place makes me immensely uncomfortable, but he doesn't seem offended. It's like he almost approves of my reaction and aversion.

He moves closer, preserving the eye contact, until we're standing chest to chest. "You're curious."

"Yes," I confess.

"You don't have to be so apprehensive. I'll be with you, guiding you through. If you want to leave, say the word and you're out of there." His attempt at reassuring me is weirdly working. He squeezes my hand and I'm calmer, more comfortable and at ease as he gives me a gentle tug toward the stairs. I kick my feet into gear and let him lead me up, my heart jumping a little harder as we get closer.

"There will be various acts in progression. Some will be mild, some not so much. It's important for you to remember that everything transpiring is because all parties have agreed. Just being in this room doesn't necessary show your desire to participate in any of the acts." He looks down and grins. "Not that you ever will. I'm making it my mission objective to ensure that every man knows what the consequences will be if they approach you." He returns his eyes forward. "I might send a memo out."

A small laugh escapes my mouth. He probably would as well. He flicks me mischievous eyes and a soft smile, and my love for him intensifies further.

I let him lead me through the open, dark-wood double doors and into the communal room.

CHAPTER TWENTY-THREE

As the full room comes into view, I concentrate on maintaining my steady breathing. It's hard. The overwhelming background music is the absolute essence of sex and only increases my heartbeat further.

The vast room is as beautiful as I remember it, with all of the exposed beams prominent and the gold chandeliers dimly lit. The Austrian blinds are all drawn at the Georgian sash windows and that, mixed with the dusky light from the chandeliers, makes the mood sensual and erotic, but not sleazy. I can't put my finger on exactly what it is. How ironic that I'm surrounded by naked people and I'm admiring the décor and ambiance. Jesse acknowledges numerous *naked* people as we make our way through the room, the women swooning and straightening their backs when they spot his presence, even though he has a firm hold of my hand. I feel so out of place, mainly because I'm fully dressed. I look up at him and see how unperturbed he is by the surroundings. Why would he be? This is normal for him. Unfolding before my eyes are various scenes, all of which muddle my mind, but at the same time totally captivate me. It's difficult not to look.

He glances down at me and smiles, giving my hand a little

squeeze. "Okay?' he asks, as he comes to a stop and turns to face me.

I nod and offer him a small smile and look down at our joined hands when I feel him run his thumb over the top of mine. He has literally drawn all of the anxiety out of me with his touch, and as I gaze back up at him, I find his eyes are watching our hands, too. He continues to smooth his thumb over my skin as he turns to face a young woman who is probably late twenties and trussed up on a suspended frame, just like the one in the extension. She's blindfolded with black satin and her mouth is slightly agape.

A man, naked from the waist up with legs slightly spread, stands before her holding a crop in his hand. The look in his eyes is one of pure lust and appreciation as he slowly, deliberately traces the curves of her breasts with the tip. She's rippling under its touch.

Jesse's hand shifts slightly in mine, and I look up at him, but his gaze is set firmly on the scene before us. I return my eyes to the bound woman as the man slowly draws the crop down her front, between her breasts, and toward her abdomen, circling the tip around her belly button in meticulous, measured movements. She's whimpering.

I shift on my heels and Jesse flicks me a curious glance, but I ignore him and watch as the man continues his descent until the crop meets the juncture of her thighs, and as she lets out a loud moan, he crashes his mouth against hers to swallow her sounds. He discards the crop and replaces it with his fingers, separating her and beginning a slow friction, up and down, building up her pleasure and her moans. Her body arches, pulling the restraints that are holding her hands secure to the frame, a signal that she's close.

I'm sweating, feeling slightly claustrophobic, and my heart rate has accelerated further. Her partner responds to her sounds by speeding up his strokes and hardening his kiss, the sound of tongues knotting and dueling becoming desperate, and in one stifled cry, she reaches climax and her body holds the bonds rigid as he slows his strokes down to work every last bit of pleasure from her. She slumps, dropping her chin to her chest. I involuntarily gasp, feeling Jesse's hand squeeze mine in agreement. This is intense, and I'm surprised by it all. We're not the only ones watching the erotic scene in front of us. It has captured the interest of quite a few people, who have gathered around the couple. I look around and recognize various people from the bar and dinner, except now they are all semiclothed or naked. You have to be bloody confident to frequent the communal room.

Jesse tugs my hand to get my attention. I look up at him, but he just nods toward the scene, and I look to find the man kissing her in gratitude. He recovers the crop from the floor and saunters slowly around to the back of her, dragging it on the floor as he goes. She's blind to his movements, but her sudden awareness is apparent as her body solidifies and she raises her head, panting. He starts to stroke her back, running his fingertips up and down the center of her spine and then down to the cheeks of her backside. She hums in satisfaction, and I think I might have as well. I feel Jesse's eyes on me. He heard me, too.

He caresses her perfect, firm cheeks, rubbing and kneading with the palm of his hand, and he groans as she arches her back and loosens again. After a few minutes of manipulating and stroking her pert bum, he withdraws his hand and I see the woman tense.

She knows what's coming. I know what's coming. Jesse's increased pressure around my hand confirms it, too, but I can't drag my eyes away. He raises the crop and in one hard, fast stroke, he brings it down to meet one of her cheeks. She cries out, and I flinch at the sharp snap, turning my head away from the scene and into the hard vastness of Jesse's chest. Before I'm aware, his free hand is cradling my head, pushing my face into his shoulder and pulling me closer to his body. The pressure of his hand around mine increases further, as I hear another crack. My hand is released and he wraps his arm around my back to join his other, my own arms bunched up in between our torsos. I'm completely cocooned by his body, and despite my surroundings and what is taking place in it, this is the most comforting place I have ever been.

"This is not your thing, let's move on," he whispers in my ear.

Move on to what? Will that be my thing? I resent the exposure when Jesse releases me from his body, hearing the crack of the crop again and again as I let him take my hand and lead me away. I snap my eyes shut each time, holding my breath. I can't grasp what I've just witnessed. But then I remember being handcuffed and Jesse's hard slaps across my backside as he slammed into me. I'm not even going to pretend I didn't enjoy my retribution fuck.

"What is this music?" I ask as we round a corner and approach a group of people.

He looks down at me with a smile. "Enigma. Is it making you horny?"

"No," I scoff. It is! All of this is, but I'm not going to admit it, although my finger twiddling wildly in my hair is a dead giveaway. He laughs and bats my hand down as he stops me in front of one woman and three men.

Jesse bends his body so our eyes are level. "Just for the record, none of this will ever happen with us."

I look at him and he winks. It's bitterly endearing, and I'm grateful for the clarification because I wouldn't share him either. "What about the other stuff?" I try to sound casual and not hopeful. I think I pull it off.

His eyes snap to mine. "I don't share you with anyone, Ava. Not even their eyes." He sounds affronted and I smile, but I didn't mean in here specifically. There are private suites. Bloody hell, what's gotten into me? I turn my attention back to the scene before us.

A woman is laid out on a cushioned fur throw, her hands bound loosely with a strip of soft leather. Her eyes flick to Jesse's and she licks her lips. I actually let out a little laugh at her shamelessness. Not another one? She is completely naked, and her eyes are full of want as she drags her stare from Jesse and diverts it to the three naked men looming over her. She wants Jesse, too, and I'm certain that what I'm about to see is going to be for his benefit.

The three men all take position, kneeling at various places around her strewn body and placing their hands on her in different positions. None of them go for the same area; they all know their place on her body. One slowly lowers his head to her breast and begins swirling his tongue around one of her nipples, bringing it to a stiff peak before sealing his mouth around her areola and sucking while massaging the mound under his mouth.

Another man is performing the same sensual routine on her other breast, working in unison with his fellow member, like they know how best to pleasure her. The woman's answering sighs and exhalations suggest they are succeeding in their endeavors. I can't help my own nipples tingling and puckering as I shift on the spot, feeling Jesse's eyes on me. I look up at him, and he quickly looks away, but he has a smirk tipping the corners of his lips. He knows I'm affected. I cringe and look back to the scene, willing my body to behave. Now the third man has joined in and is stroking and rubbing between her thighs.

The slickness of her is making his fingers slide with ease over the outer edges of her entrance. He withdraws his hand to reach up and run his wet fingers across her bottom lip, and her tongue darts out, lapping up the wetness. His fingers fall to her chin and then begin a slow trail down the center of her body before reaching her sex. She bucks in response to his touch, letting out a cry of frustration as he removes his hand and lays his free arm across her stomach to prevent her movements. Then he plunges two fingers into her, smiling at her attempts to struggle free.

I'm watching, completely rapt, as she laps up the attention with intermittent moans, telling them they are making her a very happy woman. I'm shocked to feel hugely turned on. She's being showered with attention from these men, and their only pleasure is her pleasure.

I know Jesse's eyes are on me again; I can't look at him.

Just then, the guy at her thighs nods to the two men on her breasts—a silent signal—and they all release her from their touch. She yells at the loss of contact, but then cries out as her legs are pushed up, her knees parted and a mouth is slammed on her swelling folds. I cross my legs as I stand, then feel Jesse's hand relax around mine before squeezing hard.

Another of the men takes her mouth in a greedy claim while the last man goes back to her breasts. His hands cup both mounds, teasing and petting, while his tongue runs a trail between them, before he finally divides the attention of his tongue between both of them at steady interludes. Each of the men frequently gaze up to her face, and each time they are rewarded with a look of pure satisfaction, which seems to embolden them. She's being worshipped by three magnificent males, and you would have to be a nun for it not to turn you on.

Swiftly, her body noticeably tenses—a visual display that she is about to orgasm. I tense on the spot, too. The attention increases as they get the signal she is close and everything suddenly becomes urgent. The man at her mouth catches her moans with his hard kiss, and her knees spread farther to give the man between her thighs better access. They're working as a team, building her up for explosion.

And then she falls apart on a loud cry that is only slightly stifled by one male's mouth. They work her through her orgasm, slowing the friction and speed of their strokes and licks. She relaxes and goes quiet as the men return to gently caressing her body with their mouths and hands. The man at her mouth releases her lips and reaches up to unbind her hands from the leather bond. He smiles as she rubs her wrists lightly, and after a few minutes, she stretches out on the fur throw, her actions symbolic of satisfaction personified. Her gaze falls on Jesse again.

I shake my head in disbelief. Does she want to stand up and take a bow? Despite her brashness, though, it was pretty incredible and I was enthralled, but now I've got the inevitable niggling feeling of inadequacy. Jesse has been up here, he has done these things and he has done it with plenty of woman, some of whom are in this room. How many and to what extent? I suddenly feel the flex of Jesse's hand between mine and realize that I have a vise hold on him. I gaze up at him and loosen my grip.

He's watching me carefully, trying to work out my thoughts and then he turns his full body to face me and takes my other hand. "You're not an exhibitionist, Ava, and I love you all the more for it. You are mine and mine only, and I am only yours. Do you understand me?" His voice is laced with concern. He knew what I was thinking.

My bones turn to mush, my heart misses too many beats, and I stagger forward slightly. He pulls me into him, my forehead meeting his shoulder. He is solid and warm and all mine.

"Fucking hell," he whispers on a deep breath. "I can't tell you how much I love you." He kisses the top of my head. "Come on, I want to dance with you." He breaks away and tucks me under his arm to head for the door. After watching all of that, he wants to dance with me? He leans down. "I bet if I checked, you'd be wet." My breath catches and I hear him laugh quietly. "Only for me," he reminds me. Not that I need reminding.

I glance over my shoulder and come to an abrupt, shocked halt, watching as the woman is flipped over onto her hands and knees and one man slams into the back of her as another one of the men kneels in front of her. He thrusts himself straight into her mouth, silencing her shocked yelps. My eyes widen at the sudden change in approach. They both pump into her, one at each end of her body, and the third man starts circling the kneeling mass of bodies. What the hell is he going to do?

I watch as the third man collects something from the nearby cabinet and then lowers himself to the floor on his knees at the back of her. The other man pulls out and spreads her cheeks, giving him access to her arse. I need to walk away. I need to leave now, but I'm transfixed as I watch him insert something. I have no idea what, but it's big and it's only half-submerged when he's finished. I can't rip my eyes away. He then leaves to allow the other man to reenter her on a yell before he positions himself on his back under the woman. He grabs a breast with one hand, lifts his head, and takes the other in his mouth, and then wraps his spare hand around his cock.

Oh good Lord. I feel Jesse tug my hand, and I look up at him, finding a cautious face. There must be no denying the look on mine. Please don't tell me he has done this sort of stuff.

"Come on, you've seen enough." He pulls me toward the doors that will take me away from all of this. Jesus, the reality of this place has just slammed right into my poor, innocent brain.

"Jesse?"

"Don't, Ava." He shakes his head without looking at me. He knows what I'm thinking. The inadequacy has returned, harder, more forcefully than before. "I just need you."

"Have..."

"I said, don't!" he repeats, still refusing to look at me. I choose not to push it. I can't think of Jesse like that.

As we reach the door, Natasha intercepts our escape. She's

naked, except for a microscopic pair of satin knickers, her boobs jiggling all over the place as she comes to a stop in front of us. I don't know where to look.

"You're a bit overdressed, Jesse," she purrs.

After what I've just endured, this is a surefire way to tip me over the edge. I could slap her. My hand balls into a fist and my jaw tenses, but Jesse diverts us, taking us around to the side. "Have some fucking respect, Natasha," he snaps.

My simmering anger transforms into smugness at Jesse's curt retort as we leave the communal room and an undoubtedly sour-faced Natasha behind.

"I would like to send a memo, too," I say sardonically as he guides me down the stairs.

"Whatever you want, Ava." He laughs as we approach the bar. "Do you want a drink?"

"Please." I'm trying not to sound hurt, but I know I'm failing miserably. I'll never be able to wipe those sights from my mind, but I don't see strange men up there kneeling or pleasuring. All I see is Jesse. I feel sick, but I asked for it. He's looking at me thoughtfully, and I can tell he's regretting taking me up there, too.

"You want me to be more open," he says quietly.

He's right and I'm regretting that. "I never want to go up there again."

"Then you won't," he answers immediately.

"And I never want you to go up there either." I'm being unreasonable by asking him to avoid the epicenter of his business.

He studies me carefully. "I've no need to go up there. Everything I need is standing within touching distance, and I plan on keeping her that close."

I nod my head, my eyes darting across his body. "Thank you," I say quietly, feeling guilty for making such a demand and even guiltier that he's submitted with no questions, arguments, or challenging.

He pushes my hair from my face gently. "You find Kate and I'll get the drinks."

"Okay."

"Go." He turns me around, sending me on my way.

I make my way through to the summer room, finding the dance floor is busy, and I spy Kate immediately, her red hair a beacon in the crowd. I step onto the dance floor as Otis Redding's "Love Man" kicks in, and Kate screams, thrilled at my arrival and the track.

"Where have you been?' she yells over the music.

"A tour of the communal room." I shrug, but then the hideous thought of Kate up there stamps all over my mind. Oh God no!

Her big blues widen in astonishment, and then her pale face breaks out in a big grin. This does not assist in ridding my head of such unbearably awful thoughts. She grabs my hand and I grasp my dress so I can join her. Sam and Drew are very well oiled and performing some pretty criminal moves as they attract the attention of many women on the dance floor, but Kate doesn't seem to mind. She keeps her hand in mine and rolls her eyes at her wayward fellow and his cheeky grin. She is as laid-back and unthreatened as ever, but Sam, it would seem, is not so. He soon yanks her away from a man dancing a bit too close for his liking.

I jump and have a mild panic attack when a back presses up against mine, but his smell soon invades me and I turn my face into the chin that's resting on my shoulder.

"Hey, my beautiful girl."

"You made me jump."

He smiles. "I'm going to dirty you up."

He is? He reaches down and shifts my dress up ever so

slightly, and then hunkers down behind me, taking me with him. He starts slowly circling his hips, placing his palm on my lower stomach and guiding me around with him. My rotating hips soon catch on to his tempo and we're in sync and in time to the band, who are doing an amazing rendition of the famous track. I throw my head back on a laugh when his arm appears suspended at the side, drifting up and down as he grinds his hips into mine, our circling speeding up and slowing in unison to the beat as I'm swayed from side to side and back and forth. Kate and Sam are in a tight clinch, and Drew makes a grab for a woman who's blatantly asking for it.

I place my hand over Jesse's on my stomach and let him do his thing, with no reservations and no concern for the dozens of women around us, who are all suddenly well aware of Jesse's presence on the floor and have all upped their game in the danc-ing department. Their attempts to catch his eye will be totally in vain. It's all about me.

"Oh God, I love you," he says in my ear, kissing my temple, then clasping my hand and sending me out on a little spin be-fore returning me to his waiting chest. The dancers applaud, and the band kicks into Stevie Wonder's "Superstition." I hear Kate squeal from behind me. "More dancing?" His eyebrow arches on a confident grin as he slowly sways me from side to side.

"Drink," I plead.

"You can't keep up with your god, sweet temptress." His voice is husky.

We're the only ones in an embrace as everyone around us gets down to the current offering from the band. Jesse's right; they are really very good.

He runs his nose up the side of my face and then circles it slowly. "Are you happy?"

"Deliriously." I don't hesitate. That is the easiest question I've ever had to answer. I pull him closer to me. There is too much space between us.

"Then my work here is done." He pushes his face into my neck and breathes in deeply, and I smile in pure and utter bliss as he holds me tight, cocooning me in his arms. I've never been so happy, and I know I never will be. I can deal with his past.

"Your temptress is dying of thirst," I say quietly.

I feel him grin against my neck. "God forbid," he says, releasing me under duress. "Come on, I don't want to be accused of neglecting you." He turns me in his arms and starts guiding me from the dance floor, back to the bar.

"There." He places me on my customary stool and waves Mario over, who produces my drink immediately from behind the bar, along with two bottles of water.

I pick a bottle up and start swigging the water willingly before Jesse has the opportunity to demand it.

He perches on the stool opposite and reaches over to straighten my diamond. "You okay?"

I stifle a yawn as I nod. "Fine."

He smiles. "I'm taking you home. It's been a long day."

John walks into the bar, claps Jesse on the shoulder and nods at me. "You good, girl?" he rumbles, and I nod at him, too. I've suddenly lost the power of speech. I'm absolutely exhausted.

"I'm taking her home. Everything okay upstairs?"

"S'all good," John confirms. He nods at me, and I'm yawning again. "I'll call for your car. Take her home." He gets his phone out and gives a few short, precise instructions before giving Jesse the nod.

"I need to see Kate," I manage to mumble through my tired state.

John performs that deep baritone laugh that reverberates through my entire being. "I think I may have just seen her disappear upstairs with Sam."

Jesse joins John in his amused state. "Do you want to go and say good-bye?"

"No!" I know my face is screwed up in disgust and they laugh harder. Oh God, will anyone else be joining them? Where's Drew? I frantically shake my stray, uninvited thoughts away. "Take me home." I shudder and drop onto my tired feet.

Jesse and John exchange a few words, but my brain won't allow my ears to listen. I do, however, home in on him telling John not to expect him in tomorrow, which means I'm getting my lie-in with him, and I'll be performing an Oscar-worthy hissy fit if he wakes me up with the dawn chorus and presents me with my running kit.

I say good-bye to Mario and John and let my head fall onto Jesse's shoulder as he leads me out of The Manor and puts me in his car before sliding in behind the wheel.

"I've had the best day," I murmur dreamily, as my body molds into the cool, soft leather. I really have, brazen hussies aside.

I feel his palm fall lightly onto my thigh and circle lazily. "Baby, I've had the best day, thank you."

"What are you thanking me for?" I yawn again, my eyes getting heavy. It's me who's been spoiled and lavished with attention.

"For letting me remind you," he says quietly.

I turn sleepy eyes onto him and smile, watching as he starts the car and pulls out hastily. I close my eyes and give in to my exhaustion. He's reminded me all right, and I'm so glad I let him.

"Tomorrow, we get all of your things from Kate's," he says as we drive away from The Manor. "On Monday, we tell Patrick. And I think you should be letting your parents know that I'm more than just a friend."

I mumble an inaudible acknowledgment of his words. Moving in officially doesn't seem like such a concern now, but I'm

mindful that Patrick and my parents might be a completely different scenario. To the outside world, Jesse might seem like a
controlling tyrant, and he is to a certain extent, but he is also a
whole heap of other things. I'm not sure my mum and dad will
see past his obvious need to smother me and control me. They
will see it as unhealthy, but is it unhealthy if you accept it? Not
because you're frightened or vulnerable, but because you love
them immeasurably, and the times when you want to scream
with frustration, and maybe even strangle them, are trumped by
the times like this. He's challenging all right, and I fight him to
a certain extent, but I'm not deluded enough to think that I'm
the one wearing the trousers in this relationship. I know exactly
why he is like this with me. I know he lives in fear of me being
taken away from him, but I live with the same fear. And I'm not
sure that Jesse's fear is an unreasonable one—not with my developing knowledge of his history.

CHAPTER TWENTY-FOUR

Good morning."

I open my eyes to an invasion of natural light, the erotic music from the communal room playing in the background. Jesse's handsome face is floating above mine and he has his morning stubble. He looks delicious.

I shift my arms in an attempt to grab hold of him, but they go nowhere.

What the hell?

His face breaks out into his dark, roguish grin, and I know immediately what he's done. I lift my eyes and find my hands are cuffed to the headboard of the bed.

"Were you planning on going somewhere?" he asks.

I return my eyes to his and find them hooded, his long lashes fanned. I should have anticipated this. "What are you going to do?" My morning voice is husky for more reasons than one.

"We're going to make friends," he says on a half-smile. "You want to make friends, don't you?' His eyebrows rise expectantly.

"Sleepy sex?" I try feebly.

"No, not sleepy sex. I haven't thought of a name for this one yet," he says, reaching over to the bedside table and picking up my gold satin gift bag from the anniversary dinner.

I don't remember bringing that home, but then again, I don't remember bringing myself home either.

He straddles his naked body over my hips and sits the bag on my stomach. "What have we got in here then?"

Jesse pulls out a gold vibrator. "We don't need that." He looks at it with disgust before tossing it over his shoulder. It lands with a thump on the bedroom floor. "What else is there?" He pulls out a small box and throws that over his shoulder, too, with an even more disgusted look on his face. "We don't need those either."

"What?" I ask, but he completely ignores me and carries on rummaging through the bag.

He pulls out a silver satin thong and gives it a thorough inspection before that gets tossed over his shoulder, too. "Not lace," he mutters, returning to the bag.

I look at him in slight amusement, straddling my hips, a scowl firmly in place. He's not impressed. He pulls out a card, reads it, and scoffs before tearing it up and throwing it to join the other offenders on the floor.

"What was that?" I ask, completely intrigued.

He glances up at me briefly. "Nothing you'll ever need."

"What?"

"A voucher for Botox," he mutters.

I laugh and he flicks me a devilish grin. Sarah definitely organized the party bags. I wish he hadn't torn it up; I would have donated it to her.

"These bags are crap," he spits, before taking one last thing out and tossing the bag on the floor with the other criminal contents. "Though this looks interesting." He holds up a black rubber ring attached to a small, metal, bullet-type contraption.

"What the hell is that?" I blurt.

He holds it up and runs his eyes over it before returning them to me. He smiles knowingly and leans forward, plumping a pillow under my head and kissing me chastely on the lips, "I want you to have a good view," he whispers, before returning to his position over my hips and lifting himself up to his knees.

He takes the black rubber loop and starts to slide it over his erection, and it all, very swiftly, becomes *very* clear.

"Oh no! If I don't get battery-operated devices, neither do you!" I yell, but he ignores me. He keeps his eyes on his hands as he rolls the loop to the base of his arousal and positions the bullet on his shaft. I huff and throw my head back onto the pillow, looking up at the ceiling.

"Look at me," he demands, but I keep my eyes firmly pointing upward. I feel the mattress sink next to my head from his fist resting in it, then his other hand clasping my jaw. "Look."

His tone dares me to disobey.

He shakes my jaw lightly, and I find my eyes falling down to his. They are bright pools of green lust and his lips are parted. "Kiss me now, Ava." He lowers his head and I raise mine to meet him.

He attacks my mouth with urgency, delving in with his tongue and moaning in satisfaction. I know I'm going to be left panting and squirming and there will be nothing I can do about it. His hard animalistic kiss has my senses saturated with need for more and just like that, he pulls away. I whimper.

"You'll watch," he says, biting my lip.

"Turn the music off!" I buck a little in defiance.

He grasps my hipbone sharply, throwing me a warning look. "Why? Are you feeling horny?"

Oh, this is going to be hell. He lifts away from my face and latches onto my nipple, sucking it hard. My body arches on a moan as I close my eyes and look for somewhere to bury my face. There is nowhere.

"Open!" he barks, and gives my hip a dig again. My lids fly

open as he moves to my other breast and mirrors his sucking, lapping, and biting, elongating my nipples to their maximum. I fight to keep my eyes from clenching shut, my legs from tensing. I want to bend them, but his lower legs are clamped on the outside of mine, preventing movement.

"You're cruel," I moan as I look up into a very satisfied stare. He's getting revenge all right.

He rises to his knees and grabs his erection with one hand, flicking the switch of the bulletlike contraption with the other. I hear the steady pulse of a vibration kick in and his mouth parts. "Wow," he mouths.

I close my eyes for the briefest of seconds before I'm grabbed on my sensitive hip and they fly open again. I take a deep breath and run my eyes from his, down his hard chest, past his scar, and to the mass of hair at his groin. I find him slowly working himself back and forth, the muscles in his thighs tense and bulging. I cry out in desperation to touch him. Now I know how he felt and it isn't bloody nice. I want to touch him, feel him, and I can't. I'm helpless.

His fist flexes as he draws back, his moist head glistening. "This feels good, baby." His voice is husky and it spikes at my groin. "Do you want to help me out?"

My gaze travels back up his body to his eyes. "Fuck you," I say quietly and calmly. I don't care about my blue language. It's not like he can punish me any worse than this.

"Mouth," he forces the word out on a moan, and I wriggle with the cuffs. "You'll mark yourself, Ava. Stop fighting," he hisses through a broken voice, his fist still slowly gliding over his solid length.

I wriggle some more.

"Still!" he barks, and suddenly his strokes are picking up speed. This is absolutely killing me, but good God does he look incredible on his knees above me, working himself. I watch as every muscle on his chest, his arms, and his thighs tense further and the vein in his neck jumps out.

"Please," I beg. I need to touch him.

"It's not nice, is it?" he asks. "Think of this the next time you stop me from touching you."

"I will! Jesse, please, let me go." I clench my eyes shut, screaming in my head to block the loud music out.

"Open your fucking eyes, Ava!"

"No!' My head starts thrashing from side to side. This is the worst torture. I'm never going to stop him from accessing me again. Not ever. I feel his fingers slide down my sex, gathering some moisture and then spreading it, his finger surging into me harshly. My eyes fly open. "Please!"

His face strains as he continues working himself. "You'll watch," he affirms, his fist suddenly becoming faster, more urgent. "Fuck!" All of a sudden, he's moving and his knees are braced on either side of my head, his groin in my face. "Open your mouth," he roars, and I do as I'm bid without a second's hesitation. He braces his free hand on the headboard and pistons back and forth with his fist. "Oh Jesus!" His head drops as he guides himself into my waiting mouth and spills himself all over my tongue, the saltiness of him sliding down my throat. I take the opportunity to wrap my lips around him and get some contact.

Jesse's chest heaves as he slowly works himself down, the vibrations from the bullet traveling down his length and tickling my lips as I lick and lap at him. His cock twitches on my tongue and I roll, lap, and suck to my heart's content while he shakes above me, attempting to stabilize his breathing. Dragging his eyes open, he looks down at me before his body is shifting and the vibrating stops, the little ping of elastic and small thud telling me the contraption has been relegated to the floor.

He cradles himself between my thighs and gazes down at me,

his face thoughtful as he strokes the exposed underside of my arms. Isn't he going to let me go? The erotic tones of Enigma are still flooding my hearing and it's not helping with my pre-exploded state.

"I might keep you like this forever." He drops his lips to mine and sweeps his tongue through my mouth. "This way, I will know where you are all of the time."

"I think that might be falling dangerously close to sex slave territory," I mumble into his mouth.

"And that's a problem because?"

"Because I would like to think that you want me for more than my body."

"Oh, I want you for more." He trails his lips up my face and back down, plunging his tongue back into my mouth. "Like my wife."

What?

I very nearly bite his tongue off in shock while he continues to take my mouth, like he hasn't just said that after ejaculating into my mouth with me restrained.

He eventually pulls back and looks down at my stunned face. "Marry me," he demands softly.

"You can't ask me that when I'm handcuffed to the bed!"

"Does someone need some sense fucked into them?" he asks quietly, and then takes my lips again.

I'm completely stunned. He can't fuck a yes out of me for this! I inwardly laugh because he absolutely could and he probably would.

He pulls back, drops his eyes, and sighs. "That was a joke, a very bad joke." He starts chewing his lip and the cogs start whirling in that beautiful mind of his. "You completely consume me, Ava. I can't function without you. I'm totally addicted to you, baby." His voice is soft and unsure. My confident, domineering ex-playboy is nervous. "You own me. Marry me."

I stare up into his painfully handsome face, still in complete shock. I didn't see that coming, not in a million years. I
only really decided last night that I would move in, although
Jesse, in that crazy mind of his, had me moved in a week
ago. He's frantically chewing his lip while he watches me try
to figure out what is happening. I'm twenty-six years old,
he's thirty-seven. Why am I thinking about our age difference now? It's never mattered before. What I should be more
concerned about is his challenging ways. I'm not even going
to consider that he will change if I agree to marry him. He's
never going to change, but that's who he is; that is part of the
man I love.

"Okay." The whispered word falls out of my mouth without
much thought at all. This is the natural progression for us.
Whether he asks me now or in a year, the answer will always be
the same. I want to be stuck to him forever, even with all of his
challenging ways. I love him. I need him.

The stunned expression that was riddling my face has now
worked its way onto Jesse's, the cogs spinning so fast I'm beginning to see them smoke. "Yes?" he asks quietly.

"It's instinctive." I shrug and then realize that I'm still handcuffed to the bed. "No sense fuck required. Can you let me go
now?"

He flies into a panic and jumps up to retrieve the key from
the bedside table, making quick work of undoing the cuffs. I
grasp my wrists to rub some life back into them, but I'm soon
disturbed when I'm dragged up from under him and completely
engulfed in his body as he squeezes me to him.

Holy fucking shit! I've just agreed to marry this controlling,
neurotic ex-playboy, and I've known him for a matter of weeks.
Oh God, my parents are going to burst a blood vessel.

He falls back onto the bed, taking me with him, and buries
his face in my neck. He has a vise grip on me, and I haven't

got the heart *or* inclination to tell him to ease up. I'm not going anywhere—not ever now.

"I'm going to make you so happy." His voice is broken.

I wriggle a little to free myself, but he keeps his face exactly where it is, so I work harder, prying myself from him until I find his eyes. They're glazed. "You already make me happy." I smooth his face and wipe my thumb under his eye, collecting a stray tear. "Why are you crying?" I battle the quiver in my own voice.

He shakes his head mildly and rubs frantic palms over his face. "See what you do to me?" He reaches up to clasp my face and brings it down to his, resting his forehead on mine. "I can't believe you're in my life, I can't believe you're mine. You are so, so precious to me, baby." His eyes dart across my face and his hands smooth across my cheeks, as if ensuring I'm real.

"You're precious to me, too," I say quietly. I hope he comprehends how precious. He's everything...my complete world.

He smiles mildly. "Are we friends?"

"Always." I return his smile.

"Good, my work here is done." He rolls us over so he's cradled between my thighs, and then slowly sinks into me. "Now, we have sleepy celebration sex." He reaches for the remote control and turns the music off. "I only want to hear *you* when you come for me." He drops his mouth and moans as I accept his lips and he grabs my hands, holding them above my head. He rears back and pushes forward.

"That was a proposal fuck," I say around his mouth, feeling him smile against my lips, but he doesn't say anything, or reprimand me on my language. He just seeps in and out at the most dreamy pace, plunging deeply, swiveling his hips gently and pulling back.

My earlier blissful state is recaptured as the coils reload and prepare to release, his leisurely drives and grinding hips working their usual magic on my body.

He pulls back from my mouth, carrying on with his luscious thrusts. "You'll be Mrs. Ward." His minty breath heats my face as he gazes down at me.

"I will." That will be strange.

"You'll be mine forever."

"I already am." That ship has long sailed.

He clenches his eyes shut as I feel the hints of his imminent orgasm thumping inside me, pushing my own climax forward. "I'm going to worship you every day for the rest of my life." He shoots forward. "Jesus!"

"Oh God." I breathe, stiffening beneath him, my quivering core accelerating into fast, continuous pulsations.

He pumps forward again and again, kissing me desperately and growling on his forceful grinds, keeping my hands above my head as he plunges incessantly into me. He snaps on a yell, and I wrap my legs around his hips, pulling him in closer, which pushes me into a free fall of intense trembling as lightning attacks my whole body, leaving me panting and sweating underneath him. His head drops into my neck, his breathing erratic and shallow.

"I can't breathe," he says, releasing my hands. They immediately wrap around his warm, solid back and I liquefy under him. I feel his head lift, creeping up the side of my face until he finds my lips. "I crazy love you, baby. I'm glad we're friends."

I smile as he rolls us over and I'm astride his waist. I place my hands on his chest, and he covers them with his as I lazily circle my hips on him. "I know you do. If I'm going to marry you, you have to answer some questions." I use an assertive voice that's the equivalent of his *dare to defy me* tone. I don't know if it will work, but it's worth a shot.

His eyebrows jump up. "I do, do I?"

"Yes, you do," I say haughtily.

"Come on then, spit it out. What do you want to know?" He sighs heavily, and I scowl at him. "Sorry." He has the decency to look apologetic. He keeps his hands over mine, resting on his chest.

"Who was that woman last night?"

"Coral," he says flatly, with no hesitation, like he completely expected the question.

I roll my eyes. "I know her name is Coral. Who is she?"

"She's the wife of the nasty little fucker who got ejected from The Manor the day you found the communal room."

Oh? I cast my mind back to that wretched day and remember the snide, spiteful creature hurling harsh words at Jesse.

"You had an affair with her?"

"No." He shakes his head on a frown. "They came to me to source someone to participate in a threesome."

I recoil slightly. He doesn't need to tell me any more than that. "You?" I whisper. He nods, almost ashamed. "Why would you do that?"

"She asked me to."

"She fell in love with you."

His eyes widen a little at my conclusion. It's obvious. He shifts uncomfortably beneath me. "I guess she did."

Oh, this has opened a whole new can of further questions. I'm not so surprised that she fell in love with him. It's her surprise visit to The Manor last night and the amount of time Jesse was in his office with her that I want to know about.

"What did she want yesterday? You were gone for a long time."

He takes a deep breath and pins me with determined eyes. "She left Mike . . . for me. I don't know why. I never gave her any reason to believe I wanted her like that." He pauses momentarily to assess my reaction. I'm not quite sure how I feel. He sighs.

"He's thrown her out, taken her car, and seized her cards. She has nothing."

"She came to you for help?"

"Yes."

"And what did you say?" I'm not sure I'm going to like the answer to this question.

"I said I would do what I can." He starts chewing that bloody lip.

I was right. I don't like the answer. What can he do? Helping her will only encourage her and fill her with hope that things could progress. I cock my head slightly. "Has this got anything to do with the police?"

He laughs a little. I don't know why, it's not funny. "Mike's playing games. He advised the immigration police that half of my staff are illegal immigrants. It was cleared up quite quickly, no harm done. It was just a bit of an inconvenience."

"Why didn't you just tell me all of this instead of letting my mind race?"

He frowns. "Why would I trouble you with that trivial shit?"

I can see his point, but nevertheless, I should know, especially if it involves another woman wanting my challenging man. I hold his eyes as he continues to circle his thumbs over the tops of my hands. "So, you took part in the threesome and that was it?"

"Yes." He shifts, avoiding my eyes.

"You're lying to me." My teeth clench together. "That wasn't it, was it?"

"Not exactly, no." He shifts again, still avoiding my eyes. "Do we need to go on with this?" he asks irritably. "She was under the wrong impression that I wanted more, I didn't. End of."

"So you did have an affair with her?"

"Yes! Okay, yes I did, but it was just sex, nothing more." His green eyes are fierce. "Now, let's drop it."

"You told me once that you've never wanted to fuck a woman

more than once, only me." I will never forget that comment, and as stupid as it undoubtedly sounds, given how many notches Jesse has tallied up on his bedpost because of it, I like the thought of him only having me more than once.

"I never said I didn't have a woman more than once. I said I've never *wanted* a woman more than once. It was a means to an end, that's all. She offered it on a plate."

"So, you haven't only fucked me more than once?" I sound hurt. How ridiculous. He was a pleasure-seeking playboy before he met me. And now I'm delving into territory that is, without doubt, going to send my jealous mind into overdrive.

"Ava, watch your mouth!"

"No, not when we're talking about you fucking other women! You've not just fucked me more than once, have you?"

He growls at me, and I scowl at him. "No, I've not," he admits, rubbing extra-fast circles on my hands. "But you have to understand, none of them meant anything to me. I used them, treated them like objects. I'm not proud, but that's just the way it was. They would take me whatever way I came, Ava. They all wanted more, but they certainly never expected it. Now, though, they've seen I can be a one-woman man."

I feel slightly nauseous. This conversation was a guaranteed stomach turner. How many of them can I expect to come seeking out my neurotic control freak? Mikael's wife already has, and now Coral.

"She's still in love with you," I say quietly. That's another reason why Coral was at The Manor last night. "She can't have you," I say. "None of them can," I add, just so he's aware that I know there'll be more. I feel like I'm preparing for war.

His eyes soften and he half smiles. "She can't, I told her that. None of them can. It's all about you."

"I don't want you helping Coral, either. It's unfair for you to expect me to be okay with that."

"Ava, I can't turn my back on her." He looks truly shocked by my demand.

"Okay, I'll keep working for Mikael then." I have no idea why I just said that. How stupid of me. The look on his face has gone from soft and reassuring to black and hard. Will I ever learn?

"You had better retract that statement." His chest is heaving beneath me and his jaw tenses to snapping point. That's exactly how I feel about him helping Coral.

"No," I blurt, aware that I'm pushing my luck.

"Three," he begins.

"Oh no you don't!" I go to climb off him, but his grip tightens on my hands, clenching down fiercely.

"Two."

"No! You are not giving me the countdown on this! No way, Ward. You can take your zero and shove it up your fucking *arse*!" I fight with his grip of me, getting angrier the harder he holds me.

"Mouth!" He flips me over so I'm facedown and he is blanketing me with his body. "One."

"Get lost!" I'm not backing down on this.

"Zero, baby." His fingers move straight to my hip and dig right in . . . hard.

I scream, being tossed into hell by his unrelenting digs. Oh, he's really going for it, and my bladder suddenly feels like a punch balloon. "Okay! Okay, I'm sorry! I'm sorry! I'm sorry!" I can't bear it.

He stops immediately, and I'm spun over, his body pinning me to the bed. "Kiss me," he orders, leaning down a little so his lips hover over mine.

"I'm not doing anything until you accept you're being unfair." I can see my words sinking in, those cogs spinning as he considers my words. So I continue before he can interject. "She wants to take you away from me, and I'll never let that happen.

If I'm going to marry you, you have to appreciate and respect my feelings. I don't want you seeing or speaking to her. I feel pity for her, but not enough to let it impact us, and I hope you feel the same."

"Of course I feel the same." He sighs.

"Then it shouldn't be hard to fulfill my request."

"It won't be. I'm sorry." He rubs our noses together. "I was thoughtless. I won't see her again. Forgive me."

"Forgiven. Kiss me."

He wastes no time joining our mouths and kissing the life out of me as he hums into my mouth, a throaty sound of pure satisfaction.

"Tell me you love me," he demands.

"I love you."

His green eyes twinkle and a smile tickles his lips. "Tell me you'll marry me."

"I'll marry you."

"And I can't wait. Now *you* kiss *me*." His husky tone is making my head spin. I throw my hands around his neck and land him with an adoring kiss, feeling his smile under my lips as he rises from the bed with my arms wrapped around him, my thighs finding his hips and curling around. I keep my kiss up as he walks me into the bathroom and uses a free hand to peel my legs from around himself. I grumble in disgust, and he laughs. "You brush your teeth, I'll start breakfast." He reaches behind his neck and peels my arms away, placing me in front of the mirror, dropping a kiss on my shoulder before slapping my arse and stalking out of the bathroom.

So, I'm getting married then? I stare at my reflection in the mirror, seeing my dark hair is a mass of ruffled waves, my eyes bright, lips pink, and cheeks flushed. I look well.

I absentmindedly grab my toothbrush and slap some paste on it while considering how well I feel, too. I've never felt so refreshed and alive, and there is only one reason why that is and it's called Mr. Challenging. Bloody hell, Kate's going to have kittens, and I can't even begin to think what my parents are going to make of all this.

I lift my toothbrush up to my mouth and start brushing happily, flicking a stray tendril of hair from my face with my spare hand. But something catches my immediate attention.

What the fucking hell is that?

CHAPTER TWENTY-FIVE

I spit toothpaste all over the mirror on a shocked gasp, and the toothbrush clatters into the sink. I stare down at my left hand which suddenly feels like lead, and clench the edge of the vanity unit to steady myself. Then I blink a few times and shake my head, like it might go away, like it's a hallucination or something. But no, I'm face to face and being blinded by a dirty great big diamond sitting loud and proud on my ring finger.

"Jesse!" I screech, and then start feeling my way along the edge of the vanity unit until I'm close enough to the chaise longue to stagger and collapse onto it. My head goes between my legs as I try to control my breathing and my sprinting heart. I think I'm going to pass out.

I hear him fly through the bathroom door, but I can't persuade my heavy head to lift from between my legs. "Ava, baby. What's wrong?" His voice is freaked as he collapses to his knees in front of me, spreading his hands on my thighs.

I can't speak. There's a lump in my throat the size of the diamond that's weighing my left hand down.

"Ava, God help me! What's happened?" He gently pulls my head up and searches out my eyes. His are flooded with despair while mine are flooded with tears. "Please! Tell me."

I swallow in an attempt to spit out some words, but it's not working so I hold my hand up. Oh God, it feels so heavy.

I watch through glazed eyes as his frown line jumps into position and he flicks his confused eyes from mine to my hand. "You found it then?" he says dryly. "You took your bloody time. Jesus, Ava. I had a thousand heart attacks." He takes my hand and presses his lips to the top of it, right next to my new friend. "Do you like it?"

"Oh God!" I cry incredulously. I'm not even going to ask how much it cost. This is too much responsibility. A rush of breath escapes my lips as I quickly lift my hand up to my chest in search of my other friend.

"It's in the safe." He grabs my hand and pulls it down to join my other in my naked lap. I sag in relief as he rubs his thumbs over the tops of my hands and smiles. "Tell me, do you like it?"

"You know I do." I look down at the ring. It's platinum, the flat band loaded with a dazzling square-cut diamond. I look up at him. I know my brow is wrinkled in confusion. I might need that Botox voucher after all. "When did you put this on my finger?"

His lips form a straight line. "Right after I cuffed you."

My eyes widen. "That's rather confident of you."

He shrugs. "A man can be optimistic."

"You call it optimistic; I call it pigheadedness."

He grins. "Call it whatever the fuck you like. She said yes." He dives on me and tackles my naked body down to the cold, hard bathroom floor, rolling me onto my back and burying his face between my boobs. I laugh as he ravishes me.

"Stop!"

"No!" He bites my boob and sucks it into his mouth. "I'm marking you."

Even if I could stop him, I wouldn't. He's the only one who will see me. I let him do his thing and thread my fingers through his hair, gaping again when my eyes fall on the ring. I can't believe he put it on before he asked me, the arrogant arse. How did I not notice it?

Distracted...challenged.

"There," he kisses his mark chastely. "Now we match."

I look down at the perfect circle he has made on my breast and then to Jesse, who's studying his handiwork with satisfaction.

"Happy?" I ask.

"I am. You?"

"Delighted."

"Good, my work here is done. Next job: feed my temptress. Up you get." He pulls me up to my feet. "Are you coming down anytime soon?"

"I'll be five minutes-ish."

"Ish." He leans in to bite my ear. "Be quick." He slaps my bum and leaves me again.

A huge smile spreads across my flushed face. I said yes. I have absolutely no doubts, none at all. I belong with Jesse.

I have a quick shower before grabbing his dress shirt from the floor and putting it on with some jersey shorts. I cross the landing and remember the post that I've still not given to Jesse, so taking a quick detour to the cream room, I grab the post from the unit before taking the stairs, ignoring the fact that I have been away from him for twenty minutes-ish and I miss him already.

I find him in the kitchen with his finger in a jar of peanut butter and looking intently at the screen of his laptop. I sigh at his beautiful face concentrating hard, then wrinkle my nose in distaste as he pops his goo-covered finger in his mouth.

"Here, I forgot to give you these." I hand him the post and pour myself some orange juice.

"You open them."

I spot my car keys on the worktop. "My car's back?"

"John dropped it off," he says, continuing to study whatever he has on the screen of his computer. I smile to myself at the image of big John driving my little Mini.

"Are you religious?" he asks casually.

I frown into my juice. "No."

"Me either. Do you have any preference on dates?"

"What for?" I sound confused, which is fine because I am.

He looks up at me with a heavy frown. "Is there any particular date you would like to become Mrs. Ava Ward?"

"I don't know." I shrug. "Next year, the year after." I grab some toast and start buttering. He only asked me half an hour ago. I need a chance to wake up properly. There is plenty of time for all of that, and I need to speak to my parents, for a start.

He drops his jar of peanut butter on the marble island, making me jump. "Next year?" he exclaims, with a look of pure disgust.

"Okay, the year after." Next year is a bit soon, I suppose. I cut my toast in half and wrap my teeth around a corner.

"The year after?"

I look at him and find his handsome face contorted in total disbelief. I really don't mind. The year after that then, it's no bother to me. I shrug and carry on chewing my toast.

His expression morphs into a scowl. "We get married next month." He picks up his jar and shoves his finger in aggressively.

I nearly choke on my toast, and then chew frantically to rid my mouth of it. Next month? Is he mad? "Jesse, I can't marry you next month!"

"Yes you can and you will," he snaps without looking at me.

I withdraw slightly. I've not even told my mum and dad that I'm living with him, let alone marrying him. I need time. "No I can't," I half laugh.

His fierce eyes fly to mine and he smacks his jar down. It

makes me jump again. "Excuse me?" he says, his voice genuinely shocked.

"Jesse, my parents don't even really know about you. You can't expect me to call them up and break this sort of news down the phone." I silently beg for him to be reasonable. I've seen that face plenty of times and it always suggests that he's not budging.

"We'll go and see them. I'm not pussyfooting around, Ava."

I take a nervous sip of my orange juice while he drills displeased eyes into me. The thought of introducing Jesse to my parents fills me with dread.

I'm wilting under his fierce gaze, but I have to hold my own here. "You're being unreasonable. We can't organize a wedding in a month, anyway." I take another bite of my toast and soak up the resentment emanating from every pore of my challenging man.

"Do you love me?" he asks sharply.

I look at him with narrowed eyes. "Don't ask stupid questions."

"Good." He grunts with utter finality, returning his attention to his laptop. "I love you, too. We get married next month."

I drop my toast in exasperation. "Jesse, I'm not marrying you next month." I get up from my stool and take my plate to the bin to get rid of my half-eaten breakfast. I've completely lost my appetite.

"Come here," he growls to my back.

I swing around to face him, finding the fierceness is back. "No," I toss at him. His eyes widen. "And you are not going to be fucking an agreement out of me. Forget it."

"Watch your fucking mouth, Ava." His face screws up and his lips press into a straight line as he pins me in place with his glare. "Three."

"Oh no!" I laugh. "Don't even think about it!"

"Two."

"No!"

"One."

"Jesse, you can fuck right off!" I scorn myself for my bad language, which has probably just heightened his annoyance.

"Mouth!" he barks. "Zero." He starts making his way around the island to me, and I instinctively start circling the other way.

"Come here." He grinds the words out.

I ensure I remain on the other side of the island from him. "No, what's the rush? I'm not going anywhere."

"Damn right you're not. Why are you delaying it?" He continues calmly coming at me.

"I'm not delaying. It takes a good year to organize a wedding."

"Not our wedding." He thrusts his body forward threateningly, and I dive in the opposite direction. "Stop running from me, Ava. You know it makes me crazy mad."

"Then stop being unreasonable!" I almost laugh when he suddenly changes direction and I dive off the other way.

"Ava!"

"Jesse!" I mock, weighing up the likelihood of making it through the arch and up the stairs before he catches me. I don't fancy my chances.

He sprints toward me and I screech, darting off toward the archway. I know I'll never make it up the stairs, so I fly into the gym and try to shut the glass door. He's up against the other side, pushing against me, but I know he's holding back so he doesn't hurt me. "Let go of the door," he yells.

"What are you going to do?"

He immediately lets up on the pressure and looks at me through the glass with slight concern etched on his face. "What do you think I'm going to do?"

"I don't know," I lie. I know damn well what he's going to do.

He's going to hit me with a sense fuck, but my busy hands pushing up against the door prevent my fingers from delving into my hair. His trepidation seems to intensify and the pressure on the door lessens further. I take advantage and slam it shut, flipping the lock.

His mouth drops open. "You didn't just do that!" He tries the handle of the door. I step back. "Ava, open the door."

I shake my head. His bare chest starts heaving violently.

"Ava, you know how it makes me feel if I can't lay my hands on you. Open the door."

"No, tell me we can discuss *our* wedding reasonably."

"We were." He tries the handle again and the door shakes. "Ava, please, open the door."

"No, we weren't discussing it, Jesse. You were telling me how it's going to be. You've really never had a relationship, have you?"

"No. I've told you this."

"I can tell. You're shit at it."

His anxious, green eyes flip to mine. "I love you," he says softly, like that explains everything. "Please, open the door."

"Do you agree?" I know how much he hates not being able to get to me and this is taking advantage of his weakness. But it's the only weakness I know, so if I have to use it, then I will, especially for something of this magnitude.

His teeth are going ten to the dozen on his bottom lip as he mulls over my demand. "I agree. Open the door." He grasps the handle, but then I think of something else—something that will have cause for another countdown later. I may as well kill two birds with one stone.

"I'm going out with Kate later," I say daringly.

His eyes bulge, as I knew they would. "What?"

"Last night, I told you that I was going out with Kate," I remind him.

"And? Open the door."

"You can't stop me from seeing my friend. If I'm going to marry you, it's not so you can control my every move. I'm going out with Kate later, and you're going to let me...without a fuss." My voice is calm and assertive, although inside I'm bracing myself for a sense fucking to rival all those that have come before.

"You're pushing your luck, lady." His jaw clenches, and I exhale a weary breath.

I'm pushing my luck because I want to go out with my friend? I turn my back on him and take myself to the weights bench, sitting down and making myself comfortable. I'm not opening that door until he relents, so I might be here a while.

"Ava, what are you doing? Open the fucking door." I watch as he shakes the door frantically. God, I love him, but he's got to ease up on the unreasonable demands and protectiveness.

"I'm not opening that door until you start being more reasonable. If you want to marry me, then you need to loosen up."

He looks at me like I'm stupid. "It's not unreasonable to worry about you."

"You don't worry, Jesse, you torture yourself."

"Open the door." He jiggles the handle again.

"I'm going out with Kate later."

"Fine, but you're not drinking. Open the fucking door!"

Oh yes, I should be challenging him on that, too, but I think I have probably given him enough heart attacks for one morning. He looks beside himself, which is ridiculous. I'm right here. On a sigh, I stand up and walk to the door, flipping the lock and standing back before I put him in an early grave. He barrels in and yanks me to his chest, taking us to the floor on one of the cushioned mats.

He completely smothers me with his body and breathes heav-

ily into my hair. "Please don't do that to me again," he pleads.
His anxiety on this matter is one of his most unreasonable parts.
"Promise me."

"It's the only way I can get you to listen to me." I try and
placate him as I stroke his back, feeling his heart hammering
against my chest.

"I'll listen. Just don't put anything between us again."

"You can't be with me all of the time."

"I know, but it will be on my terms when I can't be."

I laugh and throw my arms over my head. "What about me?"

He pulls his head back and scowls at me. "I'll listen," he mutters grumpily. "You're being very challenging, wife-to-be." He
buries his face in my neck on a sulk.

Oh, he is so thick-skinned. I don't bother arguing with him
on that, though. I had expected to be thrust up against the wall
and fucked to within an inch of my life after my delinquencies,
so the fact he is just holding me is a bit of a surprise. Maybe I've
found my bargaining tool.

He sits up and drags me onto his lap. "Why don't you go to
The Manor for a drink?"

"Absolutely not!"

"Why?" He looks insulted.

"So you can keep an eye on me?"

"It's logical. You can have a drink, I can make sure you're safe,
and then I can bring you home."

He really does make it sound logical, but I'm not making a rod
for my own back. I'll never set foot in the bar again. "No. End of."

He pouts, and I shake my head to affirm my answer. And
anyway, she will be there, throwing her looks and nasty little
comments about. Not a chance.

"Impossible woman," he sulks, standing with me in his arms.
I'm placed on my feet and given a chaste kiss. "I'm going to get
a shower, you'll come." He arches a suggestive eyebrow and hits

me with his roguish grin. I don't mind so much when he demands things like that.

"I'll be up in a minute. I need to call Kate." I pull myself from his grip and make my way back to the kitchen. "Where's my phone?"

"Charging on the side. Don't be long."

I find my phone and ring Kate.

"Hello?" Her croaky voice comes over the phone. She sounds hungover.

"Hey, feeling bad?"

"No, tired. What time is it?"

I glance at the oven. "Eleven."

"Shit!" she exclaims, and I hear a commotion in the background. "Samuel, you loser. I'm late! Ava, I'm supposed to be in Chelsea delivering a cake! I'll call you later."

"Hey, are we still out tonight?" I shout before she hangs up on me.

"Of course. Are you still allowed?"

"Yes! I'll be at yours at seven."

"Brill! See you then."

I hang up and my phone immediately alerts me of a text message. I open it as the penthouse monitor system starts bleeping at me, and walking over to the cordless device that will connect me to Clive, I glance down to my screen.

My blood runs cold. It's Mikael.

I don't want to look at it, but my thumb presses down on the open button before I can convince my brain to delete it without reading it.

I can't make Monday. I'm back in Denmark temporarily. I will be in touch upon my return to rearrange our meeting.

My stomach flies up to my mouth, choking me, and my phone starts to shake in my hand. What the hell am I going to do? I delete the message immediately, knowing Jesse's bad phone manners will have him finding it. I don't reply either. At least I've got a bit more time to figure this out and to speak to Patrick. How long will he be gone? How long have I got to prepare for that meeting? I contemplate texting him back to tell him I already know about his wife and Jesse, but then the intercom shrieks again, startling me.

I answer to Clive. "Ava, there's a delivery here for you. I'll be up in a minute."

I don't have a chance to ask what it is or whom it's from. Clive hangs up. I walk back into the kitchen, apprehensive and nervous, and start scrolling through my phone, searching for the PIN feature so I can prevent Jesse from intercepting any more messages that Mikael might send. He's going to get so suspicious when he finds it's got a lock on it, but I would rather deal with his slighted state than deal with a six-foot three-inch whirlwind flying through the penthouse. I open the door and hear the elevator arrive, then the unmistakable sound of Clive grumbling. Curiously walking toward the elevator, I find Clive heaving box after box and bag after bag.

"Ava, you have a serious problem. I think you are what they call a shopaholic. Do you want it all inside?' he huffs.

"Urh, yeah." I look and see Harrods bags and gift boxes everywhere. What the hell? I'm like a spare part, holding the door open, mouth gaped, as Clive hoofs them all through and dumps them in the penthouse.

I can't believe he's done this. Why didn't I suspect something was amiss when he so willingly let me have my way when bargaining with him? Or let me think I got my way, more to the point. The man must have blown a ridiculous amount of money yesterday.

Clive dumps the last bag and starts making his way back to the door. "That's your lot. Was there anything left?"

I look bewilderedly up at Clive's back. "Pardon?"

He turns and frowns. "At the store, did you buy them out?"

"Urhhh, yeah. Thanks, Clive."

"Oh, a young lady stopped by," Clive informs me, but then instantly clamps his mouth shut, obviously realizing his error.

That soon snaps me from my dazed state. "Really?"

His old eyes are wide. "Urm...I don't know..." He starts walking back. "Actually, maybe it was for a different resident. Can't be sure." He laughs nervously. "It's my age."

"Short, black hair?' I ask. He said *mature* when referring to the blonde wavy one, who I now know to be Mikael's wife—or ex-wife.

"Can't be sure, Ava."

I actually feel a little sorry for him. The poor man shouldn't have to deal with this. "Let's keep this quiet, shall we?"

"Oh?" He looks relieved.

"Yes, you don't tell Jesse about the *young* woman, and I won't tell anyone about our neighbors' habits."

He sucks in a sharp gasp. Oh yes. I play dirty, old man. I walk over and shut the door in his face. Can my poor brain cope with much more? I'm not telling Jesse. I don't want him contacting Coral, helping her, seeing her. I'm brimming with uncertainties and fear, battling raging jealousy, and I've just set myself up for a lifetime of this. I agreed to marry him. Am I stupid?

Jesse's phone starts screaming from the kitchen, and I find myself following the ringtone until I'm standing at the island looking down at the screen. Rightly or wrongly, I answer it, disregarding my conscience that is currently advising me I'm a hypocrite.

"Coral?" I say, evenly and clearly. There is silence, but she doesn't hang up. "Coral, what do you want?"

"Is Jesse there?" Her voice is small, and I'm a touch surprised that she hasn't hung up. "He's in the shower. Can I help you?" I sound polite, but with an edge of irritation.

"No, I need to speak to him." She doesn't sound polite. She sounds affronted.

"Coral, you need to stop bothering him." I need to make myself clear here, as Jesse seems to have grown a conscience.

"Ava, isn't it?"

I'm not sure I like her tone. "That's right."

"Ava, he'll make you need him, then abandon you. Walk away while you still can." She hangs up.

I stand with Jesse's phone suspended at my ear, my eyes darting around the kitchen, my mind swamped again, and try to convince my brain that she is just envious. All of these women are jealous and slighted because Jesse played them all off, used them and tossed them away when he was bored or finished with them. I know how I felt when I was without him, so if that is how all of these women feel, then I completely get it. I feel very sorry for them, but it's not my fault they can't stand the fact that he has changed his ways for me—not for any one of them...for me. He has stopped drinking for me. He has stopped his dabbling for me. It's his history, a nasty history, but history nevertheless. I straighten my shoulders in my own little private display of determination. I will never walk away from him. He *has* made me need him, but I know he needs me, too. I'm going nowhere.

Sliding his phone on the counter, I walk back into the living space and stand with my arms hugging my body, looking at the mountain of shopping bags and boxes before me. I don't know whether to be excited or furious. He disregards my opinions and wishes at every turn, with his neurotic, challenging ways, and now I fear I'm becoming neurotic and challenging as well. I kneel on the floor and gingerly poke one of the bags, peeking inside cautiously, like something could jump out and attack me.

Huh? That wasn't in my like pile. I pull out a navy silk Calvin Klein dress. That was in my maybe pile. I open a box and find a structured, cream and black Chloé dress. That was in the no pile. It was way over my set price threshold.

Oh no. They've mixed it all up. I pull another bag toward me and find a pair of baggy-fitting Diesel jeans. Okay, they weren't in *any* pile. I work my way through all of the bags and boxes, also finding lace underwear in every design and color you could imagine.

God only knows how long later, I'm sitting in the middle of the floor, surrounded by a mass of clothes, shoes, bags, and accessories. Every single item I tried on is here, except for the gown—all of the likes, the no's, the maybes, and a whole lot more that I didn't try. I know there must be a mistake because even the slate Chloé dress is here, and Jesse would *never* have willingly bought that for me. I do love it, though.

I flop back onto the floor and gaze up at the high ceilings of the penthouse. This is just way too much—the gown, the necklace, the ring—and now all of this. I'm completely overwhelmed and feeling a bit suffocated. I don't want all of this stuff. I just want him, without the history, without the other women, and without the complication of Mikael.

"Hey, baby." Jesse's wet, handsome face appears, floating above me. "I've been waiting for you. What's up?" I scoff and signal in the general direction of the designer jumble sale surrounding me. Can he not see it all? He looks around, completely unfazed by the piles and piles of women's wear flanking me.

"It arrived then?" I make a dramatic display of throwing my arms back in exasperation, and he exhales to match my drama before lying down next to me. "Look at me," he orders softly. I turn my face to his and get an injection of his fresh, minty breath. "What's the problem?"

"This is too much," I complain. "I just want you."

He smiles, his eyes twinkling with pleasure. "I'm glad, but I've never had anyone to share my money with, Ava. Please humor me."

"People will think I'm marrying you for your money." I say it how it is. I've already faced the accusation.

"I couldn't give a fuck what people think. It's all about us." He twists onto his side and pulls at my hip so I'm mirroring him. "Now, shut up."

"You won't have any money left if you spend like you did yesterday," I grumble quietly.

"Ava, I said shut up."

"Make me," I counter on a half-smile.

And he does. He eats me alive amongst half of the Harrods women's department.

CHAPTER TWENTY-SIX

I walk into the bedroom after a fresh shower and shake my head at Jesse, who's sprawled on his back across the bed wearing only his tight white boxer shorts and making a damn effective point of letting me know he's not happy. I sit myself in front of the floor-length mirror and start drying my hair. We've spent all day carting the obscene amount of clothes and accessories up the stairs. I now have my own side of the colossal walk-in wardrobe and had a very happy man—until I started to get myself ready for my night out with Kate. His contented mood soon dulled, but with Tom and Victoria joining us and a whole heap of shit to dump on Kate, I'm looking forward to it, and Jesse has got to learn to share. I finish my hair and turn the dryer off to hear heaving, huffing, and puffing coming from the bed. He's behaving like a schoolboy, so I ignore him and make my way into the bathroom to cream up and get my makeup on. I'm mid-mascara application when he walks in, all casual, and lies himself down on the chaise longue with an almighty exhale of air, his lean body reclining coolly and his arms draping over his head, accentuating every fine muscle on his torso. I try to ignore him, but Jesse prancing around in a pair of white, tight Armani boxer shorts is very distracting. He's doing this on purpose.

I make a hasty retreat from the bathroom to find my underwear and something to wear. That could take some time, especially with Jesse's critical eyes watching over me, but I don't even make it to my newly appointed underwear drawer before I'm seized and slung onto the bed, minus one towel. I should have known. He's going to trample me, mark me, and send me out with his scent all over me, the bloody neurotic control freak.

I'm flipped over onto my hands and knees, and my legs spread as he grasps my waist, efficiently restraining me. "You won't come," he growls as he plunges two fingers into me, stretching me and preparing me.

The sudden invasion has me burying my face in the bedding to stifle my cry. He's going to leave me pre-orgasm, I know he is. "This is for my pleasure, not yours," he grates firmly. He starts circling my entrance, and I moan into the bed in desolation. This is ultimate torture. He knows exactly what he's doing. I stiffen all over in response to his touch.

"Relax, Ava. I don't want to hurt you." He pushes into me with his fingers, my natural instinct having me tensing my muscles in an attempt to prevent his invasion.

I cry out.

"Relax!" he yells, and I will my body to obey his command, but it's not having any of it. I'm fighting the inevitable, which will be Jesse abandoning me before I explode. I don't want to go out this evening full of pent-up pressure in my groin. I want to be sated and relaxed, and he can do that. The bloody arse! I feel him position himself at my opening.

I whimper.

"Damn it, Ava." His tone is full of aggravation "Stop fighting me."

"You're going to desert me, aren't you? You're not going to see me through."

"That's my call, baby." He slaps my backside. "Relax!"

"I can't!" The sting radiates through me from his swift collide, and he yells in frustration at my nonconformity as he reaches underneath me to brush his fingers over my pulsing center.

"Ohhhhhhhh!" I relax instantly as the connection of his heated touch blasts my senses and rockets me forward, flicking the switch that he has a direct link to. A sea of intense pleasure drowns me, and I start a hasty buildup toward a furious climax. I try and grab it and keep hold, but he withdraws his fingers. "No!" I shout, completely frustrated.

"Oh yes." His fingers reenter me, sweeping through me, his thumb skimming across the very tip of my clitoris, prompting me to push back in a desperate attempt to try and capture more friction. He pulls out, spreading the moisture up my crease.

"No, Jesse!" I feel his solid cock pushing against my opening. "Please!"

"You love it, Ava." He advances, breaching me, slowly and with control. "Oh *fuck*."

I could cry with fury and frustration, but it doesn't stop me from pushing back, taking him all of the way. I know I'm not going to come, but I can't help myself.

He yells, grabs my waist, and then thunders forward, knocking every scrap of air from my lungs.

"Oh God!" I scream as he fills me completely. He charges forward, giving me no time to adjust to him. He means business.

"Oh Ava," he pants, holding himself inside me. "You feel fucking amazing, baby." He grinds himself against me on a long, drawn-out moan, and I concentrate on getting my ragged breaths under control. "Brace yourself on the headboard."

I take a deep breath and reach up to wrap my hands around one of the wooden planks, crying out as the change in position has him penetrating me deeper. He holds still as I follow through on his orders, running his palm down my spine gently. The fireworks crackling at my core are bordering painful.

"Do you have a good grip?"

"Yes!" I spit shortly, earning myself a swift slap across my backside. I'm going to scream and he's not even done with me yet. Why the hell am I not stopping this?

I hear him suck in a sharp breath as he starts withdrawing from me, the fullness alleviating slightly, but then I'm thrust forward as he reenters me on a punishing drive. I scream again.

"Brace your arms, Ava!" He repeats the delectable move, and I stiffen my arms and rest my sweating forehead on my forearm.

"Jesse, please," I beg.

"It's feels good, doesn't it?" he asks, his voice carnal and hungry.

"Yes."

"You love me taking you hard, don't you, Ava?"

"Yes!"

"I know you do." He shifts his grip from my hips and hooks his hands over my shoulders before he crashes forward again and again, yelling in fulfillment each and every time. He reaches under me and glides over my quivering clit with his fingers.

I scream and sink my teeth into my arm in desperation as my head starts to spin with a mixture of incredible pleasure and sharp stabbing pains. I can feel my climax approaching, and in a fraught attempt to seize it, I push back against him on each of his incessant blows.

"Oh no you don't," he growls, removing his fingers and withdrawing his cock.

I cry out in anger as he yanks my hands from the headboard and spins me around, pushing me down on the bed. He straddles my stomach, trapping my arms by my side with his knees and starts lashing his fist back and forth over his pulsing cock. I close my eyes.

"Open your eyes, Ava!" he shouts, and grabs my hip bone, prompting me to scream and buck under him.

"You're a bastard!" I throw him my evilest look. "I'm going to get so drunk tonight!"

"No, you're not." He continues working himself over me as I press my lips together. He falls forward, bracing his free hand on the bed and spills himself over my breasts on a loud yell that resounds around the whole bedroom. Panting above me, he slows his strokes as I wriggle futilely. My breasts are coated in his warn cum, my hair is all over the place, my makeup probably needs redoing, and I'm fit to burst with the immense pressure in my groin. I am not a happy girl.

"Do you want to come?" he asks, looking down at me, sweat coating his forehead.

"I'm going out!" I bark, just to make it clear that I am not bargaining with him on this. No way!

"Stubborn woman." He reaches down and wipes his palm all over my chest, spreading himself over every square inch of my torso. "My work here is done," he says on a half-smile, before leaning down and pressing his lips hard on mine.

My lips part involuntarily, and I soak up the greedy lashes of his tongue, moaning, begging for more, but then he pulls back and I thrash my head from side to side, flipping myself onto my front. I hear him laugh, and then he slaps my arse hard before he gets off the bed. "Don't shower."

"I've not got time!" I jump off the bed and set about sorting myself out. My blow-dried waves are now more of a tousled array of brunette and my cheeks are flushed. I look well and truly fucked, which is ironic because I'm not. I clench my thighs together on a groan and grab a washcloth to wipe the remnants of Jesse from my chest. There is no wiping away the huge love bite on my boob. There will be no low-cut anything for me tonight, and not just because of the bruise on my chest.

* * *

After refreshing my makeup and getting dressed, I walk down the stairs as quietly as possible. He is nowhere to be seen as I scan the vastness of the penthouse, so I tiptoe to the kitchen and poke my head around the archway.

"You're not fucking wearing that!"

My legs instantly kick into gear at the sound of that fierce voice and I dash for the door, slamming it behind me to hinder his pursuit while praying the elevator is open. I thank all that is holy and dive in the lift, punching the code in frantically. The doors shut just as I see Jesse's raging face appear through the tiny gape. I give him a cheeky wave and turn to look at myself in the mirror.

Okay, so the gray Chloé number is a bit on the racy side, but my legs look incredible, if I do say so myself. He asked for this.

The elevator door opens and I scurry across the marble floor, searching for my keys as I go. He's got to get some clothes on and wait for the elevator to get back up to the penthouse, so I should be fine.

I hear him before I see him. I turn and watch as he flies out of the foyer of Lusso, looking like the Devil himself. I clench my lips shut to suppress my laugh. He looks homicidal. He tears toward me, barefoot and gloriously naked except for his fine, tight boxer shorts. I stay where I am. I knew I wouldn't be going out in this dress. Whether he caught me here or at the bar, I was always going to be hauled home in disgrace and dressed in something more suitable by Jesse's standards.

He grabs me and flings me up onto his shoulder, reaching up to hold the hem of my dress down before taking me straight back into Lusso. "It's just my fucking luck that I go and fall crazy in love with most impossible woman in the fucking world. Evening, Clive."

"Mr. Ward," Clive nods without paying much attention to us. "Hello, Ava."

"Hi, Clive!" I sing through my laughter as Jesse gets in the elevator and punches the code in while muttering under his breath.

"Have you still not gotten that code changed?"

"Shut up, Ava."

"Are we friends?" I grin to myself.

"No!" He slaps my arse hard and I yelp. "Don't fuck with me, beautiful girl. You should know by now, I always win."

"I know. I love you."

"I love you, too, but you're a fucking pain in the arse."

* * *

We pull up outside Kate's super late, after I gained Jesse's approval on a blush dress and matching heels, but I very nearly got handcuffed to the bed again when he saw my engagement ring on the bedside table. Jesse made sure it made it onto my finger, but I managed to convince him to leave the necklace in the safe. I'm not comfortable with this dirty great big rock sitting on my finger as it is. The necklace added to the equation would tip me over the edge of nervousness.

Kate comes barreling out of her house and Jesse gets out, letting her in the back of the car. "Wow! I like this better than the Porsche," she says as she gets comfortable in the back. "Don't tell Samuel I said that. Come on then, let's have a look."

"What?" I shift in my seat so I can see my fiery friend.

She freezes and throws the back of Jesse's head a fearful look. "Oh shit!"

"It's fine," Jesse assures her.

I gape at him. "She knew?"

"I needed one of your rings to make sure the size was right."

He shrugs and keeps his attention on the road. I hear Kate sigh in relief.

"Was it romantic? Show me." She gestures for me to pass her my hand.

I actually laugh—really hard, and Jesse looks at me out the corner of his eye, his lips pressed into a straight line as he weaves in and out of the traffic. "Yeah, it was romantic." I snort. If you call handcuffs and being forced to swallow romantic. I thrust my hand at her.

"Fucking hell!" She grabs my hand with both of hers and gets up close and personal with the diamond. "That is some serious special. So, when's the wedding?" She drops my hand and fishes around in her bag, pulling out her compact mirror. "Shit, Ava. Have you told your mum and dad?"

Kate has just innocently hit on two very sore subjects. "Don't know and no."

Jesse shifts in his seat and flicks me a displeased stare. I ignore it. I'm not getting into this now. I turn back around in my seat to face Kate. "Did you enjoy your evening?"

"Yes, it was fab." She keeps her eyes in her mirror.

"What time did you wrap up?"

"I can't remember." She pouts in the mirror and then flicks her big blues to me. "Is there a point to this line of inquiry?"

Jesse laughs. "I think Ava would like to know if you enjoyed yourself upstairs after I took her home."

Kate slaps him on the shoulder. "That, my friend, is none of your business. Well, it is, but it isn't." She laughs. I'm surrounded by crazy people.

* * *

Jesse pulls up outside Baroque and gets out to free Kate from the back.

"I'll get the drinks!" she declares as she dances into the bar.

Jesse waits for me to come around to the pavement. He's brooding again and it doesn't escape my notice that he has just given the doorman a nod.

He pulls me into his chest and sucks in a deep breath from my hair. "Don't drink."

"I won't."

He pulls back and rests his forehead on mine. "I mean it."

"I won't drink," I assure him. I'm not arguing. It will get me nowhere, except into his car and back at Lusso before I blink.

"I'll pick you up. Ring me." He brushes my hair out of my face and kisses me deeply, a public display of ownership. I'm wearing a colossal diamond; you don't get more claimed than that. He seems so despondent, I almost don't want to leave him, but we have got to get over this unreasonable anxiousness at me being anywhere other than with him.

I cup his face and kiss his stubbled cheek. "I'll ring you. Go for a run or something." I leave him on the pavement and mentally pray that he goes home, gets his running kit on, and does twelve laps of the Royal Parks. I smile sweetly at the doorman as I pass and he cocks his head at me, giving me a knowing smile.

I find Kate at the bar with Tom and Victoria, who are already being served. Victoria looks a little less sulky, and Tom looks delighted to see me. He's wearing a ridiculous pink-and-yellow candy-striped shirt.

"Ava!" he screeches. "Wow, fabulous dress!" he croons as he strokes me.

"Thanks." God knows what his reaction would have been to the gray number.

"What are you having, Ava?" Victoria asks over her shoulder.

"Wine!" I blurt desperately, and all three of them laugh.

We settle at a table, and I take my first relaxed sip of wine, gasping in pleasure and closing my eyes in appreciation. Oh, that is so good.

"Oh good Lord! What the hell is that?" Tom dives over the table and grabs my hand, and then proceeds to dribble all over my new friend. "The Adonis?"

I shrug. "I'm crazy in love."

"You've known him, what...a month?" Victoria's disapproving tone riles me. "And he owns a sex club?"

"And?" I spit at her, feeling defensive.

She recoils at my hostility. "And nothing, I'm just saying," she flops back on the stool.

"When did this happen? The last I knew, you were just sleeping with him," Tom mimics my own words.

"Well, now I'm marrying him." I yank my hand back and take refuge in my glass of wine. I'm conscious of the fact that I'm facing an Olympic gold-medal-worthy interrogation from my parents and Dan. I don't need it from this lot, too. Oh, Dan's back tomorrow. With all of the spectacular events of the last few days, it had slipped my mind. A wave of guilt washes over me for forgetting his return, but it's soon replaced with a twinge of excitement and then, just as quickly, replaced with dread. What will Dan make of all this?

"How's Drew?" Kate asks Victoria.

I'm not so sure that it's a sensible question, but I'm thankful for my friend's diversion tactic.

"I wouldn't know," she answers haughtily. "I'm not seeing him anymore. I have a date."

"Tonight?" Tom asks, perplexed.

"Yes."

Tom scoffs and sits back in his chair. "Well, thanks a lot! You're ditching me!"

Victoria's eyes bulge at Tom's huffiness. "You don't think twice about casting me aside if you're offered a bit of action!"

Her tone is reproachful and quite rightly. He's abandoned Victoria on plenty of occasions when a gay man has flashed him a promising stare.

"Still, there are six other days you could have picked. Who is it, anyway?" He stirs his piña colada, trying his hardest to look bored.

"Just a friend of a friend," she muses. "Oh, there he is." She jumps up. "See ya!" She heads toward an average-height, average-looking guy at the bar and they greet each other with an awkward kiss on the cheek and a handshake. She says something in his ear and he nods before they leave. That's a sensible move. We'd all be watching how the date progresses and Tom would just be a total bitch.

* * *

Over the next hour, we laugh, chat about anything and everything, and drink. It's lovely. I'm reminded why I need to battle with my challenging man on this matter. I need my friends.

"And how's Sam?" Tom turns his attention to Kate.

"Why? Do you still want to screw him?" She winks at me, and Tom flushes from head to toe, flashing Kate a dirty look

"No." He tuts and crosses his legs. "I was just being polite. How's Jesse?'

"Why? You want to screw him, too?' Kate jumps in with her tongue-in-cheek question, and I burst into laughter.

Tom looks between us in disgust. "So, it's pick on Tom night, is it?"

"Looks like it," I say, and raise my glass. "Tom, Jesse would blow...your...mind."

"Ava!" he gasps.

"Oh, please! I have to endure torturous stories of your sexual encounters."

Kate laughs. "I'm going for a fag if we're getting into Tom's sex life." She jumps down from the stool and makes her way to the smoking area.

"I need the lavatory," Tom grumbles, and clears off to the toilets, leaving me people watching, a pastime I usually enjoy, but then Matt comes into my field of vision and I find myself ducking. *Shit!*

My ring is suddenly burning through the flesh of my finger and I'm breaking out in a sweat. I didn't reply to his apology text and I know the slimy worm has been on the phone to my parents again. Just when I think I've evaded him, his beady eyes land on me like a kettlebell. I glance around the bar, mindful that the doorman could be watching out for me, and then return my eyes to Matt, catching a glimpse of a healing black eye. I mentally applaud Jesse and suddenly wish I had relented and stayed at home with him.

"Ava," he greets cheerfully, as if nothing has happened, as if he hasn't been calling my parents and feeding them duff information. Well, duff-ish.

"Matt, I think it's probably best if you leave." I maintain a steady, firm voice.

"Ava, please hear me out. I couldn't be sorrier, really. I was a complete twat. I deserved everything." He shifts uncomfortably on his feet and stares into his pint glass. "If you're with someone else now, then I accept that. I'm gutted, but I accept it."

I keep my hands under the table, the ring firmly out of sight. I have to ask, I can't help it. "How do you know about Jesse?"

His shocked eyes fly up from his pint glass. "So, you're still seeing him then?"

"That's none of your business, Matt. And why are you ringing my parents, telling them a load of crap?"

"Is it crap?"

"Who have you been talking to?"

"No one." He won't meet my eyes, but then he leans his elbows on the table and gets too close. "Ava, I still want you back."

My back straightens and I flick my eyes to the entrance to make sure I'm not being spied on. He's just told me that he has accepted it. How many times do we need to go over the same old crap? I could kiss Tom when he returns from the toilets and gives Matt his roving eye, which Matt responds to by abruptly pushing himself away from the table, knocking my bag to the floor. I jump down from my stool.

"Oh darling!" Tom crouches down to help me gather my scattered possessions. "He's still hot!" he whispers to me on the floor.

"He is not." I screw my face up and rise to find Matt walking away, holding his hand up in a catch-you-later gesture.

"Oh, where's he going?" Tom exclaims, stamping his foot.

"Hopefully, to jump off a cliff," I mutter uncharitably under my breath. I finish my wine in one foul swig. After seeing Matt, I could do with another.

"Matt's in here!" Kate throws herself on the barstool. "And he has a black eye. High five, Jesse!"

"Well, it's been a pleasure, girls, but I need some action tonight and it doesn't look like I'm going to get it in here." Tom throws a disgusted look in the general direction of all the blatantly straight men, "I'm going to Route Sixty. Want to come?" he asks hopefully.

"No!" Kate and I shout in unison, leaving us laughing and Tom stropping out of the bar in search of action.

"Did the snake speak to you?" Kate asks when she's stopped chuckling.

"He tried." I'm just about to volunteer bar duties when Tom flies back into the bar and collides with the table. He's huffing and puffing all over the place. Kate and I point frowns at him.

He gets his breathing under control. "You will not *believe* who I've just seen."

"Who?" Kate asks before I have a chance to engage my mouth.

"Sally." His face breaks out into a big grin and he glances over his shoulder before returning excited eyes to us. "Sally...wearing a miniskirt and low-cut top—a *very* tight, short miniskirt and a *very* low-cut top. She has a date!"

"Oh?" I say, a little surprised, but not because of the apparent outfit. I'm surprised because she was suicidal on Thursday.

"What? Wallflower Sally? Boring office girl Sally?" Kate asks.

"Yes," I confirm. "Tom, leave the girl alone." I return to my glass, promptly remembering that I want another.

"I might get a picture!" Tom dances out of the bar, getting his phone from his pocket.

"I'll get the drinks." I slide off the stool and grab my purse. "Same again?"

"Do you need to ask?" She rolls her eyes and waves her empty glass at me.

I fight my way to the bar and wait my turn, attracting the attention of some muscle-pumped, ponytailed slimeball, but I ignore his leering stare and order our drinks.

"Hi, can I buy you a drink?"

I glance around and smile sweetly. "No, thank you."

"Come on, just one drink," he presses, and moves in closer.

"No, really. I've got it, but thanks."

The barman places one glass of wine on the bar. "I've just got to pop down to the cellar. We're out." He leaves me at the bar with ponytailed guy dribbling all over me. I roll my eyes, not that the barman notices.

"Maybe I could take you out sometime then?" He's really close now.

"I'm involved with someone," I say over my shoulder. He can't have missed the gigantic diamond on my finger. I take a swig of my wine.

"And?"

I turn toward him. "And... I'm involved with someone." I flash my ring and he nods, but not in an accepting way. I think I've just made the challenge more interesting.

"He's not here, though, is he?"

"No, lucky for you, he's not," I reply curtly, turning back toward the bar. I'm immensely relieved when I see the barman approaching.

He places Kate's wine down and I pass him a note, willing him to be quick. My skin is prickling under the leering eyes of the overinflated man next to me, so I take another long sip of my wine and try to blank him out. I'm beyond exasperated when the barman signals no change. He walks off to the end of the bar and starts faffing about in various tills.

Ponytailed creep moves in closer. "If you were mine, you wouldn't be out of my sight."

Oh good God! "Listen, I've tried to be polite. Back off!"

"I think we could show each other a good time." He runs his fingertip down my arm.

I jump, instantly furious with myself for appearing anxious, but then I'm distracted by the barman returning. Thank God! He hands me my change and I grasp Kate's drink quickly, keen to escape this toad. Turning a bit too hastily, I drop my coins everywhere.

Fuck!

I place the glasses back on the bar and retrieve the coins within grabbing distance and leave whatever else there may have been. I'm not that desperate. I grab the drinks and catch my heel awkwardly, causing me to stagger slightly.

"Shit!" I curse. Now he'll think I'm pissed and easy.

I'm met with the twat again when I turn back around. "A bit drunk, sweetheart?"

"Fuck off!" I've tried to be patient.

"Oh, feisty." He laughs as I push my way past him, thinking how grateful he should be that Jesse isn't here. He would be flattened by now.

I make it over to Kate and place the drinks down a bit too sloppily, spilling a considerable amount. I shake my head mildly and take my position on the barstool, staggering again. Kate frowns at me.

"Shoes," I mutter.

"Are you okay?" Kate leans forward, looking all concerned.

"Yeah, I'm fine," I assure her. I'm not drunk. This is only my third glass of wine.

"Who was that idiot?" She nods in the direction of the self-proclaimed stud as she has a sip of her fresh glass of wine.

"Exactly that...an idiot," I say shortly. "Anyway, you have some explaining to do."

"I have?"

"Yes, you have, and don't you dare brush me off. What's going on?"

She glugs down more wine, refusing to meet my eyes. "What are you talking about?"

I feel myself getting a bit impatient with my fiery friend. She would never allow me to evade her questioning, and I wouldn't anyway. We tell each other everything. "I'm talking about you, Sam, and The Manor.'

"Fun!"

"No! Don't you dare!"

"I'm just having some fun, Ava. What are you? The sex police?"

"So, there's no feelings?"

"No!"

"You know, if you were me, you'd be twiddling your hair." I

take a long swig of my wine. "Okay, try and help me out. Being as you're refusing to open up, I'll dump my shit on you. I value your opinion." I smile sweetly.

She ignores my snipe, her eyebrows shooting up. "This sounds serious."

"It is. You know the developer of Lusso, the one who asked me to dinner?"

Kate nods. "Yeah, the Dane—handsome in a Scandinavian kinda way."

"Yes, Mikael. Jesse slept with his wife. He's going through a divorce at the moment."

"No!" Kate leans in.

"Yes, and now he's on some sort of revenge mission to turn Jesse over, and it looks like he's decided that I'm the best way to do this. I've got to meet him, and I know it won't be work related."

"Oh shit!"

"I know. The wife has been sniffing around, too."

"What are you going to do?"

I shake my head, taking another swig of my wine. "I don't know, just like I don't know what to do about that woman, the one who turned up at The Manor's anniversary."

"Who is she?" Kate's eyes are widening by the second. I'm not surprised. This is information overload.

"Her name is Coral. Do you remember that nasty man at The Manor the day we found the communal room?"

"Oh yes! Jesse crushed him. It was frightening, Ava."

"That's her husband. She asked Jesse to be the third in a threesome. She fell in love with him, left her husband, and now has nothing. She wants Jesse. She turned up at Lusso and also rang his phone. I've told Jesse about neither, but I answered the call. She warned me off."

"Oh my fucking God!" Kate flops back on her stool, and I take another glug of wine.

Hearing it all out loud, it sounds ridiculous, crazy, unreal.

I see Kate's face light up as she follows the path of someone approaching behind me. I don't have to turn around to see who it is.

"Ladies!"

I look up and see Sam grinning from ear to ear. What's he doing here? It's supposed to be a girls' night out, and Kate still hasn't given her verdict on my current screwed-up situation.

He shoves his tongue in Kate's ear, and I huff to myself. The old Kate would never let any man invade her girl time. I pick up my wine and down the rest, watching over the rim of my glass as Kate accepts Sam's affection willingly. If she tries to tell me tomorrow that this is just fun, then I'll challenge her...hard!

"I'm going to the toilet," I inform them.

"Okay," Kate says idly.

I stand and turn toward the entrance, reaching up to rub my temples in an attempt to soothe my thumping head. As I make my way through the roaring crowd, the sound around me dulls into a faint hum and my head starts spinning slightly. I push my way past the blurry gatherings of people and very nearly have a seizure when I clock Jesse standing a few meters ahead of me in the doorway of the bar.

Oh shit!

I freeze on the spot. I knew he wouldn't be able to leave me be, not even for a few hours to enjoy a few glasses of well-earned wine. My vision might be challenged, but there is no mistaking the pure fury that's spread across his handsome features. I don't know why. I'm not drunk. I've had a few glasses of wine, and I've enjoyed them. He's the one with the drink issue, not me.

And with that thought, I stagger slightly again.

We stand staring at each other for a few moments, then he starts stalking toward me. I make a grab for a table when I feel my legs wobble, and the change in his approaching expression, from rage to pure terror, is the last thing I see before the black sets in and I become weightless.

Chapter Twenty-seven

Jesse, calm down. She had three glasses of wine. She wasn't drunk."

My eyes are attacked by fluorescent lighting and bright white at every wall. I feel like I've been bashed over the head with an iron bar. Where the hell am I? I close my eyes again and reach up to brush away a lock of hair that's tickling my cheek, the soft contact of my hand on my head stabbing at my brain.

"Ava?" His voice is quiet and his hand clamped around mine. "Ava, baby, open your eyes."

I try my best, but it is too bloody painful. Fuck! What is wrong with me? Is this the worst hangover ever? I don't remember drinking that much.

"Will someone tell me what the *fuck* is going on!" he roars.

I snap my eyes open again and gaze around my unfamiliar surroundings. The only familiar thing is that irate voice, and it's a strange comfort to me, but, God, it's playing havoc with my sensitive head. I reach up to clasp my aching skull.

"Ava, baby?"

I squint my eyes in an attempt to focus, and I'm met with a green, grief-stricken pair. The feel of his warm palm stroking my head has me groaning in protest. It hurts. "Hi," I squeak. My throat is raspy and dry.

"Oh, thank fucking God!" He smothers my face in kisses, and I beat him away. I can't breathe.

"Ava, chick. Are you okay?"

I follow the sound of another familiar voice and find Sam leaning over me, looking the most serious I've ever seen him. What's going on?

"Does she fucking look all right?" Jesse yells in Sam's face. "For fuck's sake!"

"Calm down!"

I know that voice, too. I flick my sensitive eyes around the room and find Kate sitting in a chair opposite me. "Where am I?" I ask through my dryness. I need some water.

"You're in hospital, baby." He strokes my face and kisses my forehead again.

What on earth am I doing in hospital? I try to sit up, but I'm met with the full force of Jesse pressing down on me. I slap his persistent hands away and scramble into a sitting position, prompting my hands to fly up and grasp my head when the full force of gravity crashes in around my brain. Holy shit, this really is the worst hangover ever. I groan and cross my legs in front of myself, resting my elbows on my knees and my head in my hands. Something tugs at my arm, and I look across to see an IV line in my arm.

"Someone get the fucking doctor in here!" Jesse yells, making me wince.

Kate stays put, but Sam leaves the room.

"Ava, what happened?" Kate's voice is laced with complete concern, a rare reaction from her.

"I don't know," I reply, resting my back against the head-board. I feel incredibly sleepy again.

"I do!" Jesse exclaims, looking at me accusingly.

I use all of my depleted energy to throw him a filthy look. "I wasn't drunk!"

"You pass out from being sober often, do you?" he yells.

It makes me wince, piercing my tender ears. He has the decency to look remorseful when I reopen my eyes.

"Don't shout at her!" Kate defends me. I'm grateful. He throws her a look, stuffs his hands in his jean pockets, and starts pacing up and down the room. "She had a few glasses of wine. She's got through two bottles before and not passed out." Kate sits next to me and rubs my arm. "Did you eat?"

I cast my mind back. "Yes," I answer. Jesse fed me all day, between shipping clothes up the stairs and getting his fix of me.

Jesse stops with the pacing, his lip getting a punishing chomp from his teeth. "Are you pregnant?" he asks, watching me carefully and returning to the chomping.

"No!" I blurt, shocked at his forwardness, but then I freeze. *Oh good God!*

My pills. I've not replaced my pills! I suddenly feel faint again. I'm hot, too. Oh, what a stupid woman I am. I've been having sex like a rabbit and with no protection. How did I let that slip? I glance at Jesse and pull my best unaffected face.

He narrows his eyes on me. "Are you sure?"

"Yes!" I wince at my own shrill voice, tensing my arm to prevent my natural reflex from giving me away. Jesse will assume my tone is defensive. It's not—it's completely freaked.

"I'm just asking." He resumes pacing.

"What do you remember?" Kate asks, continuing to stroke my arm.

I reflect on the evening, but I'm struggling to remember anything now. All I can think of is how many pills I've missed and what the chances are of me being pregnant. I battle to fight off the worry and try to remember something, anything of last night. I remember Matt, but I won't be mentioning him. Then

I remember the swollen, slicked, ponytailed guy, but I won't be mentioning him either. I shrug. There isn't a lot I can say without sending Jesse into neurotic orbit.

Every head in the room turns to the door when the doctor enters, followed by Sam. "I was told you were awake." He nods. "I'm Dr. Manvi. How do you feel, Ava?'

"Fine." I sigh wearily. "My head is banging, but other than that, I'm fine."

I hear Jesse growl beside me as he sits and takes my hand in his. "Ava, it is four o'clock in the fucking morning!" He closes his eyes to regain his composure—not that he ever had it. "You've been out cold for nearly seven hours, so don't you dare say you're fine."

Seven hours?

"We'll go and get something to eat." Kate looks at Sam and he nods his agreement at her suggestion. Clearly they don't want to be around Jesse in his current mood.

Dr. Manvi shines a light in both of my eyes then pops the pencil-like contraption back in his top pocket. "Ava, what do you remember about last night?"

"Not a lot." I feel Jesse's hand lock harder around mine, the anger still evident. I feel god-awful. I don't need this.

Dr. Manvi glances at Jesse. "You are?"

"Husband," he states sharply, without taking his greens off me. My eyes widen, but he remains impassive. He forgot to add the "to-be" part.

"Oh?" The doctor flicks through my papers. "It says *Miss* O'Shea."

"We get married next month." His eyes drill into mine, daring me to challenge him. I don't have the energy. I flop my head back gingerly on the bed.

"Oh okay," Dr. Manvi seems satisfied with Jesse's explanation of who he is. I'm past caring. "We ran some routine tests." He pulls up a chair and it scrapes along the rubber floor, making me wince. "When was the date of your last period?" He looks at me with sympathetic eyes, and I want to crawl across the room and into the clinical waste bin.

"A week-ish ago," I answer quietly. I don't need to look at Jesse to know he's twitching.

"Right, well it's routine for us to do a pregnancy test to try and establish what caused the blackout episode." He pauses, and I brace myself for the hurricane that will be Jesse flying around the room in a complete frenzy. "You're not pregnant."

My head flies up. "I'm not?"

"Well, I say you're not, but if it's only been a week since your period, it may be too early to tell." He smiles kindly, but it does nothing to settle me. "Do you use the contraceptive pill, Ava?"

"Yes."

"Then I think we can safely say you're not pregnant." He gives me a reassuring smile and leans forward. "Ava, it's important that you try to remember anything of last night, who you spoke to, who you met."

Jesse's animosity travels through our joined hands, attacking me. "What?" he snaps. "What are you trying to say?"

I don't bother with scorning him for his rudeness, and Dr. Manvi continues, turning a blind eye. "We proceeded with a further test. Your symptoms prompted it."

"Symptoms? What symptoms?" I ask, completely confused.

The doctor inhales and shifts in his chair. "We found clear evidence of Rohypnol."

"*What!*" Jesse roars.

My eyes widen and my heart starts hammering in my chest. Oh fucking hell!

Jesse flies up from his sitting position, dropping my hand, and I glance up nervously to find him shaking and sweating, the anger pouring from him. "As in date rape?" he yells at the poor doctor.

"Yes," Dr. Manvi confirms my fears and Jesse's.

I spiral into panic at the doctor's diagnosis of my blackout episode. Oh, this is so bad.

Jesse flies around and throws his head back. "Jesus fucking Christ!" he cries. I see the back of his shirt rising and falling violently as he braces his arms on a nearby metal unit.

"Ava, I would advise you notify the police. You need to tell them everything you remember." Dr. Manvi turns to Jesse. "Sir, can you confirm whether she was alone at any point?"

My mind races with the evening's events, but my mind won't allow me to put anything into place. I don't think I was. I watch as Jesse's fingertips reach for his temples and start circling. He's going to explode. He'll be like a whirlwind flying through the hospital. Suddenly, telling him I could be pregnant seems so much more appealing than this.

"She wasn't alone," Jesse replies, more calmly than I expected. "I watched her hit the deck, I was there in a split second." He turns to face me, and I stare into his tortured eyes. I feel devoid of any emotion. I think I might be in shock.

"And you are sure of this?"

"Yes," Jesse all but growls.

"Ava, I would like to do an examination," he pushes, "for bruises and scratches, initially. Just to be sure."

"I've checked every square inch of her. There isn't a mark on her." Jesse stomps across the room and flings the door open. "Kate?"

I hear a brief exchange of abrupt, muffled words from outside the door, no doubt Jesse pressing for answers. The doctor flicks a confused gaze from me to Jesse, while I continue to rack my brain for something.

He's by my side again. "Baby, Kate said she went for a cigarette, but Tom was with you. Can you remember that?"

"Yes," I answer quickly. I definitely remember that. "But

Tom went to the toilet while Kate was having a cigarette," I add.

"Okay, do you remember what happened during the time you were on your own?" he pushes.

"Yes." I won't tell him why I remember. Holy shit, mentioning Matt would be a grave mistake. "Why?"

"Because I don't want anyone poking you about unless it's necessary. So please, think hard." He squeezes my hand. "Before I arrived, were you okay? Do you remember everything?"

"Yes, I do."

"That is good," Dr. Manvi interjects. "But, Ava, I would be happier if you would consent to the examination."

"No! I know nothing happened. I have no bruises, no cuts."

"If you are one hundred percent sure, Ava, I can't force you."

"Nothing happened. I remember everything until Jesse arrived." I look at Jesse. "I remember everything." My voice is shaking. I'm shaking.

He slides his palm over my cheek. "I know. I believe you."

"Okay. Well, all of your vitals are fine," Dr. Manvi says. "You'll have a sore head for a while, but other than that, you will make a full recovery. Once I've sorted your discharge papers and removed your IV, you can go home."

"How long will that take?" Jesse has reverted back to madman.

"Sir, we are in the aftermath of a Saturday night in central London. How long is a piece of string?"

"I'm taking her home now," Jesse says with utter finality. I look up at him and know immediately it's a battle not worth fighting—not if you want to live.

I lie back in a complete trance as the IV is removed and the doctor talks to Jesse. I hear nothing. It's all a muddled garble in the distance. How did this happen? I didn't once leave my drink unattended. I didn't accept a drink that was offered. I was careful and sensible. Jesus, what if I had gone to the toilet a few seconds earlier and missed Jesse at the door? I could have been unconscious and completely unaware of anything going on around me. I could have been raped. I'm attacked by unexpected tears and uncontrollable shakes as I start sobbing in my hands.

"Ava, please don't cry." I feel his warmth engulf me, holding me tight as my body jerks under him. "Baby, I'll get really crazy mad if you cry."

I sob relentlessly while he comforts me, muttering his own little curses and prayers above my head. "I'm so sorry," I heave between sobs. I don't know why I'm sorry, maybe for defying him and going out anyway. I really don't know, but I feel so remorseful.

"Ava, please shut up." He holds me tightly and strokes my hair. I'm aware of the frantic clatter of his heartbeat under my ear.

When I've finally regained a little control, I wipe away my tears and sniffle. I must look a mess. "I'm fine," I say, taking a few calming breaths and pushing him away. "I want to go home."

I start to clamber from the bed, but I'm met by the fierceness of a tall, lean, green-eyed wall. He picks me up and carries me to the door, meeting Kate on the way. "Get her stuff," he orders, striding past her.

"What's going on?" Sam jumps up from the chair outside the room.

"She was drugged." Jesse doesn't stop to give any further explanation.

"Oh shit!" The horror in Sam's voice is clear.

I hear Kate's heels trying to keep up with us. "Drugged?"

"Yes," he shouts as he proceeds down the corridor with me in his arms. "I'm taking her home."

I'm lowered into the DBS and secured in my seat belt. I flinch when the door closes, and then I hear the mumble of voices outside the car. There's a subtle tap on the window, and when I look, I see Kate giving me the call-me gesture. I nod my acknowledgment and rest my head against the window as Jesse slides in and places my shoes and bag in the foot well. I close my eyes again and drift off.

*   *   *

I'm being placed into his huge bed, and I'm vaguely aware of my dress being removed and disapproving grumbles coming from Jesse, but I ignore him, rolling over and releasing a contented exhale of breath when I'm greeted with my most favorite smell in the world; fresh water and mint. I know I'm back where I belong.

Chapter Twenty-eight

Ohhhhhhhh Godddddddd!" I stretch out and it is the most satisfying stretch I've ever executed. Propping myself up, I crane my neck and gaze around the room to find it empty of any other inhabitants, so I gingerly shift to the edge of the bed and sink my bare feet into the lush cream carpet, bracing myself for an attack of dizziness as I stand. But nothing happens. I feel surprisingly steady. I pad across the bedroom and out onto the landing to see Jesse below, sitting back in one of the huge armchairs talking quietly on his mobile. He's showered and shaved and is wearing some pale blue jeans. He's naked from the waist up.

I lower myself quietly onto the top step and watch him through the curving glass that leads down to the big open space. He looks fresh but troubled.

"I don't know," he says quietly, picking at the fabric on the arm of the chair. "I swear to God, I'll claw their fucking eyes out." He moves his hand from the arm and rubs his eyes. "I'm close, John. I really need it. Fuck, it's a mess."

Oh God, am I pushing him toward drink again?

As if he's heard my silent question, his eyes flick up and find mine. I shift uncomfortably on the top step as he studies me. "See what you can find out, John. I won't be in for a few days . . . yeah, thanks, big man." His phone slides into the center of his palm, but his hand remains by his ear, his elbow resting on the arm. I feel like a complete intruder.

He sits in his chair and I sit on the top step for the longest time, just staring at each other through the glass. I have no idea what to say to him. I wanted to prove that he was being unreasonable with his over-the-top protectiveness, but now I've just made it one hundred percent worse. He's never going to let me out of his sight.

As I'm contemplating my next move, he rises from his chair and starts walking toward the bottom of the stairs. I follow his slow climb up until he's standing a few steps below me, looking down at me. His expression is flicking from anger to sorrow, back and forth, and his frown line looks like it's been set in place for a long, long while.

"If you are going to shout at me, then I'll go now," I say through the dryness of my throat. I don't need Mr. Neurotic on my case. I just want to forget about it and think myself lucky that it wasn't worse. It could have been so much worse.

"I've shouted enough," he replies, and I detect the hoarseness of his own voice. "How do you feel?"

"Fine." I rip my eyes away from his and stare down at my bare feet. I'm naked except for my black lacy underwear, and I feel small with him towering over me like this.

"Ish?" he asks.

"No, fine." I sound stroppy.

He lowers himself to his knees so we're on a more equal level and plants his hands on the top step, on either side of my body. I glance up from my feet to look at him.

"I'm crazy mad, Ava." His voice is soft.

"I wasn't drunk," I affirm sharply. Damn it, I wasn't even remotely drunk.

"I told you not to drink at all. I knew I shouldn't have let you go out."

"I'm curious as to why you think you can dictate what I do," I challenge. "I'm a grown woman. Do you expect me to live a life with you where my every move is controlled?" My voice is quiet, but firm through my dryness. He has to see my point.

His lips form a straight line and I can hear the cogs start whirling into action. "You're mine. It's my job to keep you safe."

I drop my eyes on a sigh. "You said you were close. Close to what?" I pull my face up.

He searches my eyes. He must know that I heard. He looked directly at me after he uttered the words. "Nothing."

"Nothing?" I can't help sounding disbelieving. "You want a drink, don't you? That's what you need to deal with this fucking mess."

His eyes widen. "Will. You. Watch. Your. Fucking. Mouth! We're in this fucking mess because you went out and completely defied me." He pushes his face up close to mine. "We would not be in this situation if you'd fucking listened to me."

His insensitive words, and the tone in which he delivers them, sting painfully. "I'm sorry!" I spit. "I'm sorry for not listening." I stand up, leaving him kneeling on the stairs. "I'm sorry if you feel the need to drown in vodka because of me! I'm obviously bad for your health. I'll put you out of your misery." I pivot and stalk into the bedroom, physically shaking with anger.

"Crazy mad, Ava."

I turn and find him stalking toward me with a face like thunder. I back up slightly, and then mentally curse myself for not standing my ground. Why can't he see that it's his own unreasonable expectations that are pushing him to complete madness, not me.

He stops in front of me, his chest puffing, breathing his minty breath all over me. "Kiss me."

"No!" The bloody man is deluded!

His eyes darken and narrow. "Three."

He must be joking. "Are you mad?"

"Crazy fucking mad, Ava. Two."

He is completely serious. Oh my God!

"One," he whispers.

I know better than to try and escape this time.

"Zero."

I'm captured as if I was running and pinned on the bed in seconds, my arms held above my head by one of his. His jean-clad legs rest over my thighs, restraining me, not that I'm fighting against him. He breathes down on me, tracing the line of my stomach with his finger, and then up the center of my body to my mouth. He rests the tip on my bottom lip before letting it travel back down my body.

"Please don't have a drink." I would never forgive myself if he put his body through that again because of me.

"I'm not going to have a drink, Ava." His voice is flat and unconvincing. It makes me uncomfortable. He pushes himself up to his knees before pulling me up to straddle his lap. He brushes my hair out of my face and clasps my cheeks with his hands. "Last night in the hospital when you wouldn't come round, I felt my heart getting slower by the minute. You will never know how much I love you. If you were ever taken away from me, I wouldn't survive it, Ava. I want to rip my own head off for giving you room to defy me."

My eyes widen at his confession. His face is deadly serious, and it's very worrying. He is, in effect, saying he would kill himself, isn't he? Well, that is just crazy talk, but I don't think I would do well to point that out.

"I'm okay," I say in a futile attempt to lighten him up.

"But what if you weren't? What if I didn't come when I did?" He clenches his eyes shut. "I just came to the bar to check you were okay, and then I was going to leave. Can you imagine how it felt to see you collapse like that?" His eyes open and they're glazed and haunted. I know now, for sure, that I may as well handcuff myself to the bed forever. This isn't healthy, for him or me.

"It was a freak incident, someone playing stupid games. I was in the wrong place at the wrong time, that's all." I take his hands from my face and rest them between our bodies. "You will put yourself in a stress-induced coma at this rate, and then what will *I* do?" I ask quietly.

He shakes his head and starts chewing his lip. "You looked relieved when the doctor said you weren't pregnant."

I look anywhere but at him, instantly mortified. "I missed a pill." I feel his hand shift and close around mine, and I look up cautiously, finding his accusing eyes and an arched brow. "I missed a few. I lost them again."

"You've not replaced them?"

"I forgot." I shrug.

"Okay." He studies me for a while. "So, when did you last take your pill?"

"Only a few days ago," I answer quietly. I'm lying through my teeth, fighting my hand from delving into my hair. I can't believe it's been nearly a whole week and I've not replaced them.

"So you'll replace them?"

"Tomorrow." A funny look passes over his face. Regret? "Jesse," I pause, not knowing how to piece together what I'm about to imply.

"What?" He looks cautious and slightly guilty. He knows what I'm thinking, I know he does, and I'm super suspicious now. He can't have seriously been trying to get me pregnant? Would he do that? I'm not even sure, but if he has been hiding my pills, then he knows damn well I've not been taking them for a week. Or did he think I'd replaced them already?

"Nothing," I say, shaking my head. I know he won't admit it, so I'm playing dumb, but I'll be searching every square inch of this penthouse at the first opportunity.

"Your brother rang," he says in an obvious attempt to distract me from my drifting thoughts.

I straighten up. It's worked. "Dan?"

"Yes."

"You spoke to him?"

He gives me a dubious look. "Well, I couldn't leave it ringing constantly, he would have been worried. And why is there a lock on your phone?"

I laugh to myself. I wonder how many combinations he tried to unlock it. "It didn't stop you answering, though, did it? What did you say to my brother?" My voice is slightly panicked, which is fine because I'm panicking. Dan will be straight on the phone to Mum, and this, on top of everything else, is not something I want to be explaining.

"Well, I didn't tell him what had happened. I don't want your family thinking that I can't look after you. He said you were supposed to be seeing him." He looks at me like I've committed a serious sin for not telling him of my plans, even though there are no firm plans yet.

"You told him I'm living with you, didn't you?" My lips straighten.

"Yes." He is completely unapologetic.

I could kill him! "Jesse, what have you done?" I drop my head onto his shoulder in hopelessness.

"Hey, look at me." He sounds angry again. I drag my head away from its resting place and look at him with all the misery I feel. His frown line has joined the argument. "Don't you think he would've been worried? Get over it, Ava."

He pulls me down onto his chest, and I notice his heart bucking wildly. "I'm going for a run. You take a shower. I'll get something to eat while I'm out."

"Can't you stay?" I ask into his chest. I don't want him to go.

"No." He lifts me and directs me into the bathroom. "In the shower." He turns it on and leaves me in the bathroom feeling affronted and worried. He never wants to leave me.

Chapter Twenty-nine

A couple of hours later, I walk into the kitchen and find Jesse still in his running gear with his finger in a jar of peanut butter. I screw my face up in disgust as he glances up and gives me a small smile that doesn't quite reach his eyes.

"Cappuccino extra shot, no chocolate." He holds up a Starbucks cup, and I take it gratefully. "I got you everything," he shrugs. "They don't do salmon."

"Thank you." I smile and take a seat next to him.

"I hope you've got lace on under all of that baggy shit." He nods at my body as he plunges his finger into his mouth.

I look down at my ripped jeans and cropped Jimi Hendrix T-shirt and smile. "I have." I pull my T-shirt up to display my cream lace, and he nods his approval. "I thought you were getting dinner?" I pull over the nearest paper bag, finding a croissant, and make quick work, sinking my teeth into it.

"Technically, as you have been asleep all day, it's breakfast time." He smiles a little, "What do you want to do this evening?"

"I get to pick?" I garble around a mouthful of pastry.

He cocks his head to the side. "I told you, I have to let you have your way some of the time." He reaches up and knocks a flake of pastry from the corner of my mouth. "I'm all for give-and-take."

A burst of laughter flies out and I struggle to keep in my half-chewed croissant as I cough and slap my hand over my mouth. Give-and-take? This man is beyond crazy.

"Something funny?"

I look up to a serious face. "No, nothing, it went down the wrong way." I cough a little more and, God love him, he starts patting my back.

I regain control as the intercom starts ringing and Jesse leaves me to answer it. "Clive, yes, send him up." He replaces the phone. "Jay," he mutters without looking at me.

"Jay? Who's Jay?"

"The doorman. He's got the CCTV footage from the bar." He puts his peanut butter back in the fridge and leaves the kitchen.

Oh fucking hell!

CCTV footage that will show me talking to Matt?

I think I'm going to be sick.

I hear the muffled greetings, and a few moments later, Jesse walks back into the kitchen with Jay. The doorman gives me a small smirk, one that suggests he may have already watched the footage himself and knows what's coming.

Yeah, I'm definitely going to be sick. I get down from the stool and start to leave the kitchen.

"Where are you going?" Jesse asks me.

I don't look back. My face must display complete panic. "Toilet," I call, leaving Jesse and Jay in the kitchen. As soon as I'm out of sight, I race up the stairs and shut myself in the bathroom, where I'm safe from the hurricane that I know is coming. I should have known he wouldn't leave it. I should have known he would be on a mission to hunt down the perpetrator. Oh God, this is so bad. I sit on the toilet seat, get up, walk circles around the bathroom, and then the door handle jiggles.

"Ava?"

I stand looking at the door. "Yes?" It comes out all squeaky and nervous. I'm so nervous.

"What's up, baby. You okay?"

Perhaps I should say no, make out I'm ill so I can stay in the bathroom.

"Yes, fine. I'll be down in a minute." Saying I'm ill would be stupid. He'd break the door down to tend to me.

"Why is the door locked?"

"I didn't realize I'd locked it. I'm having a wee." I cringe. It's a good job there's a giant lump of wood between us because my finger is a knotted mess in my hair.

"Okay, don't be long."

"I won't." I hear his long, even steps take him out of the bedroom.

I'm panicking. Really panicking and I don't know why. I didn't arrange to meet Matt. It was a chance encounter, that's all. *Fuck!*

Damn him for being so fucking persistent. Why can't he just let it go instead of having the doorman lift the CCTV footage? I should go down and stamp on the thing. I yank the door open and stomp out of the bathroom, through the bedroom, and out onto the landing. He's taking this too far. I'm halted mid determined march when the gigantic flat-screen television comes into view. It lights up like a cinema screen, emphasizing everything, making it seem huge. It's not, though. It's quite blurry, the movements are disjointed and the screen keeps jumping. Jay starts fast-forwarding the footage, and the whizzing of people passing through the bar, the lights flashing here and there, all make it an even more disordered mush of activity. But then I see myself settling at the table with the others.

"Slow it," Jesse orders, and Jay puts the film to normal speed. "That's it, leave it playing."

I lower myself to the top step and watch the television as my night plays out in front of me. Nothing interesting happens, not for a long while. I watch as Tom dives across the table and seizes my hand. I watch as Victoria leaves us to join her date and then Kate leaves the table, and I know all too well what's coming. I mentally plead for the television to spontaneously combust, but no. Tom leaves, and then Matt approaches. I stiffen from top to toe and watch as Jesse's shoulders raise, kissing his earlobes. Matt's back is to the camera, but there's no mistaking it's him. I could never fob Jesse off on this.

"Pause it," Jesse instructs shortly, walking over to the television, getting way up close to have a good inspection. His head starts nodding thoughtfully. "Keep it going."

Jay continues the tape, and Jesse takes a few steps back. This is bad. I'm sitting on the top step, running through the last time Jesse found out I'd seen Matt. I really don't want a repeat of that. Why didn't I foresee this? I watch myself jump down from the stool and crouch to gather my scattered possessions with Tom.

"I need another angle," Jesse says.

"There's another camera," Jay answers swiftly.

"Get me it. Did you see her talking to him?"

"Ward, I do what I can, but if I'm called away to deal with some drunken twat or a few cat-fighting girls, then I can't watch her."

I shake my head to myself. He'll have a bodyguard flanking me next. This is ridiculous. "I don't need someone watching me," I grate. Both of their heads swing around to me, Jay suddenly looking uneasy and Jesse looking stiff and agitated. A few moments' silence lingers between us. It's uncomfortable, and I unconsciously wrap myself in my own arms as I sit, while Jesse scrutinizes me.

"Did you leave your drink unattended at any point?" Jay asks. The question shocks me. "No."

"When did you start feeling strange?" Jesse pipes up, his arms folding across his chest.

"I had a little stagger at the bar, but I put it down to my heels."

"Did you speak to anyone at the bar?"

Oh fuck! Should I lie? I've seen Jesse's reaction to a man coming on to me and it wasn't pleasant. Shit shit shit! I glance nervously at Jay. He knows what I'm deliberating.

Jesse stares at me with dark, cautionary eyes, his torso rising and falling, his arms still over his chest. "Answer the question, Ava," he says, more calmly than I know he's feeling.

"There was a guy at the bar who offered to buy me a drink. I refused," I spit the words out quickly, obviously uncomfortable and looking down at my feet, but he's going to find out for himself when he finishes watching the footage, so I may as well be upfront. "It was fine. I left the bar and returned to Kate," I try and brush it off before Jesse passes out.

"Stop saying it's fine!" he yells.

I jump and reluctantly take a glimpse at him, finding bulging neck veins and a tense jaw. And then something catches my attention on the television and I look past Jesse. I shouldn't have. I should have ignored it, and then maybe it would have passed before Jesse got a chance to see it. My blood turns to ice. At the bar is a tall, suited man. It's too late to feign ignorance. Jesse swings back toward the screen to see what has caught my abrupt attention, as does Jay.

The silence is back as we all watch the man on the screen shift out of view when I get up to go to the bar. Then there's the pumped-up, ponytailed creep getting way too close, me dropping my change and gathering it up before I stagger and make my way back to the table. Then the man comes back into view. I squint to try and focus better. Is it him? It certainly looks like it, but his text message said he was in Denmark.

I can see Jesse in my peripheral vision twitching, indicating he is having the same thoughts as I am, but I'm watching the footage with complete fascination now, also aware of Jesse's hard breathing, but too rapt by the television to look and confirm what I already know. He'll be rampant. He thinks it's Mikael, too. But Jesse doesn't know that he's supposed to be in Denmark. Or does he?

We fast-forward the video until Sam walks in, and I get up from the table. Then Jesse appears in the lower corner of the screen, and I watch as I collapse, hitting the floor hard, the flurry of people gathering around my lifeless body blocking out my view.

No one says anything— not for a long, uncomfortable time. I turn my eyes to Jesse and find him watching me. I'm not at all comfortable with the blackness in his eyes, and I can feel tears brimming in my own. Should I tell them about the text? Jesse looks sadistic already. Should I add to his obvious fury?

Jay coughs, pulling my attention back to him. "Have you seen enough?"

"Yes," Jesse answers without taking his eyes off me. It's quite obvious now that Jesse turning up was probably the best thing that could have happened.

"I'll be off then." Jay gets up and retrieves the disc from the player. "I'll see myself out."

Jesse says nothing as Jay leaves, shutting the door quietly behind himself.

I drop my eyes to my feet. This really could have been so much worse. No doubt Jesse will have something to say about my lack of honesty with regard to Matt's presence, but he can't blame me. Why would I openly offer that information? I'm not completely stupid. Well, it would appear I am. I never gave CCTV footage a thought, and I certainly didn't expect Jesse to start playing Detective Poirot.

"You didn't mention Matt before." Jesse's calm tone doesn't fool me, and why has he homed in on that instead of the more important issue at hand...the tall, suited man at the bar. I know he thinks it's him, too.

My shoulders rise anxiously, but I don't look up; I already know he's angry. I don't need visual confirmation, and I should think it's pretty obvious why I didn't mention Matt. "I didn't want to upset you."

"Upset me?" His voice is high with surprise.

"Okay, I didn't want to piss you off." I look up at him and find a completely impassive expression. I'm surprised; I was expecting boiling mad. "It was a chance meeting."

"But you had a few minutes' conversation. What did you talk about?"

"He apologized."

"And that took a few minutes?" His eyebrows are raised. He's right, an apology doesn't even take two seconds, but I can't remember every detail of the conversation. "I told you not to see him again."

I gape at him. "Jesse, I didn't plan on it. I told you, it was only by chance." What did he want me to do? Walk out of the bar? "I wanted to know how he knows about you."

"Do you care?" He's reining in his temper. I can see it.

"No, I don't."

His teeth start working his bottom lip as he watches me. I feel guilty and I don't know why. I've done nothing wrong. He's not shouting at me, but he's clearly not happy. What am I supposed to do? I know he's thinking exactly what I'm thinking about Mikael, but he can't possibly be mad at me about that, because I didn't even know he was there—if it was even him.

"Then leave it." He starts across the open space of the penthouse and up the stairs. "I'm going for a shower." He walks straight past me, leaving me stunned by his calm façade. I think

I would rather have him blow his top. At least then I would know where I am. I haul myself up and make my way toward the bedroom. I need to establish exactly what is going on in that complex mind of his. I know he's mad, so why is he holding back his temper? It's not pleasant, but I would rather he blow his top and clear the air. I feel like I'm hovering over a detonate button. I walk into the bedroom and pad across to the bathroom, finding him under the spray. Even now, I'm drawn to the mass of beauty that stands before me, quaking with anger. It's potent, but he's not letting rip.

"Will you please just rant at me and have it over with." I sit myself on the vanity unit and put my hands in my lap. I notice for the first time since I woke up that my engagement ring is missing. Did he take it off? The thought is like a stake through my heart. I don't like this, not one little bit.

He doesn't say a word. He carries on soaping himself down before stepping out and grabbing a towel to dry himself off. He leaves me sitting exactly where I am, my eyes darting around the bathroom, uncertainty plaguing me. I lower myself down and walk nervously back into the bedroom.

"Jesse?"

He completely ignores me and goes into the wardrobe, appearing a few moments later in some faded jeans. His jaw is ticking constantly, and I can see it's taking his every effort to hold on to his emotions. I never thought I would want him to fly off the handle. And where is he going, anyway?

He pulls a gray T-shirt over his head and makes his way back into the bathroom while I stand in the middle of the room, wondering what the hell to do. I follow him again and find him brushing his teeth. His eyes flick to mine in the mirror. I feel anxious . . . uncomfortable.

"Please speak to me."

He finishes brushing his teeth and splashes his face with water, before bracing himself on the edge of the vanity unit and taking a few deep breaths. I prepare myself for the storm, but it doesn't come. He walks straight past me and into the bedroom.

I follow like a desperate soul. "Where are you going?" I ask his back as he makes his way to the door.

He stops and it's a few moments before he turns dark, troubled eyes on me. "I need to sort some things out at The Manor." His voice is devoid of any emotion, whereas I'm close to wailing. I'm petrified.

"I thought we were doing something this evening," I remind him desperately.

"Something came up," he mutters, and turns to leave.

"You're mad with me," I cry frantically. I don't want him to go. He would usually insist on me going with him, and I would fight him on it, but now I *want* to go.

He shakes his head and lets it fall slightly, but he doesn't face me. I need to see his face. He walks out of the bedroom, and I collapse to the floor and cry. I feel helpless and incomplete. All of this pain because I wanted to have the final say, all of this because I insisted on going out and proving a point. The only point I've proved is that I'm at a loss without him.

I drag myself up and across the room, collapsing onto the bed and finding my way to the place that smells the most of him. It's a meager substitute for the real thing. Only he can make this better, make all of this go away. And worst of all, I know where he has gone, who will be there, and what he'll be doing. What am I supposed to do? I'm a mess, my face feels swollen and stingy with tears, and my head hurts from too many disturbing thoughts. Will he crack open a bottle of vodka? I know that if he does, I won't be seeing him anytime soon—not when he's like that. I would rather not have him at all than have the hollow beast that is Jesse drunk. I never want to see that man again.

I sit up on the bed, suddenly remembering something. He's

not here, and I am…and I'm alone. I jump up and run into the bathroom, flinging open the cosmetics unit and staring at the masses of bottles, boxes, and tubes. Starting my search, I shift the contents of the unit to the side, my shaking hands doing me no favors in executing the operation without knocking bottles over. A frustrated yell slips from my mouth, and in a temper, I sweep my hand through all of the shelves, knocking bottles all over the bathroom floor.

What am I thinking? He's not stupid enough to hide them in such an obvious place. I leave the bathroom and run into the wardrobe, shoving my hands into every pocket of his suit jackets, inside and out, tipping his shoes upside down, and searching through piles of neatly folded T-shirts. Nothing, but I'm not giving up. My pills are mysteriously disappearing and they have been since I met this man. What's he playing at?

I drop myself to the floor of the wardrobe, wiping my still-streaming tears away, and proceed to hunt through his jean pockets, tossing clothes all over the wardrobe in a frenzy but finding nothing. The gold satin gift bag slips out as I yank a suit jacket down from a hanger, the contents spilling onto the floor.

Condoms.

We don't need those.

He *is* trying to get me pregnant! Fucking hell!

I fly around the penthouse like a madwoman, searching every drawer and cupboard, anywhere he could possibly hide them, but an hour later, still no pills. I halt when I hear my phone ringing in the distance, and I track the sound until it cuts off. "Fuck!" I curse to myself, but then the text message tone starts bleeping and I follow it to the armchair where I found Jesse sitting earlier. I grope down the side and find my phone. The missed call is from my mum. Oh God, has Dan been on to her already? I really cannot be talking to her now, a really uncharitable thought, but I don't even know where I am myself to be able to tell her. My heart sinks when I see the text is from John.

He's fine, but you should probably come.

My heart lifts a little at the first part of the message and then sinks just as quickly. I should probably go? Is John playing tug-of-war with Jesse and a bottle of vodka? I fly up the stairs and run into the bathroom to scrub my face and attempt to generally sort myself out. It's no good, I look like I've been wailing and no amount of makeup or washing will help. After retrieving my keys, I make a hasty run for my car.

*   *   *

I make the drive to The Manor in record time, and I'm not at all surprised when I pull up to the gates and they open immediately. John must be looking out for me. My pace up the driveway is fast and frantic in my desperation to get to him. I find The Manor's door open and run through the entrance hall, ignoring the noise coming from the bar and restaurant. All conversation halts when I run through the summer room. I'm sure if I paid attention, there would be many vicious, scowling faces pointed straight at me, but I don't have the time or inclination to stop and soak up the resentment.

As I approach the door to Jesse's office, I hear a thundering crack that makes me jump. What the hell was that? I hold the door handle and look behind me, but find the corridor empty. I turn the handle of the door and push it open.

"Ava!" Big John's loud rumble travels down the corridor, halting my progression, but I can't see him. "Fucking, moth-erfucker! Ava, wait!" He appears, moving faster than I would think possible for such a mountain of a man, his glasses in place as he hurdles toward me like a steam train. "Jesus, woman, don't go in there!"

. I look at the frantic beast rocketing toward me in slow motion and jump at the sound of another ear-piercing snap. It pulls my attention from John's booming voice and toward Jesse's office. What is that? I push the door open a little farther until the full room comes into view. And I choke.

Oh Jesus Christ!

CHAPTER THIRTY

I stagger back on a loss of a few dozen beats of my heart. What the fucking hell is going on?

"No!" John crashes into me and grasps me around the waist.

I lose all feeling as I stare at the hideousness before me, and then fight with the incredible strength of John, who's trying to haul me out of the room. I don't know how, adrenaline perhaps, but I break free from John and fall into the room as Sarah raises the evil-looking whip that she's holding and brings it thrashing down on Jesse's back. My stomach jumps into my throat, and I feel John's warm palm wrap around the top of my arm.

"Ava, darling," John's voice is the softest I've ever heard it, "you don't need to see this."

I shrug him off and stand, trying to piece together the scene unfolding before me. It's hard, even though time has slowed and every tiny detail is perfectly clear to me. Jesse is shirtless and kneeling on the floor, his head dropped limply. He hasn't even looked up. Sarah is standing behind him, kitted out in black leather trousers, a leather bodice, and thigh-high leather boots, looking as evil as the whip in her hand.

I can't move. I'm completely rooted to the spot. My legs are shaking, my heart beating so fast it might escape my chest, and I can't open my mouth. What's happening?

Sarah glances up at me, a look of deep satisfaction on her face as she slowly raises the whip again. I want to scream, tell her to stop, but my mouth is dry and not responding to my brain's commands. Her pouty face screams pleasure at subjecting Jesse to this wicked torture and, no doubt, having me here to bear witness to it.

She brings the whip crashing down on Jesse's bare flesh again, and he arches his back, throwing his head back, but he doesn't make a sound.

The loud scream echoing around the room is me.

His head snaps up as my cry seeps into his ears. I'm struggling against John again, who has regained his hold on me. "Let go of me!" I fight harder, twisting my body in his grip, clawing and hitting him.

"Ava?" Jesse's voice stills me. It's weak and broken as his head turns in my direction.

A desperate cry escapes my mouth as our eyes meet and all I find are empty, glazed holes. He doesn't look completely with-it. He looks drugged and hollow. He makes to stand but staggers forward slightly in complete disorientation. My eyes fall onto his back, finding at least ten angry welts spread from one side of his back to the other, overlapping and seeping with beads of blood.

I feel sick. My stomach starts to heave, and as Sarah raises the whip again, I hear John in the distance bellowing her name. My knees give out and I crumble to the floor at John's feet.

"Ava?" Jesse makes it to a standing position, but he is nowhere near stable. He shakes his head as if trying to regain his focus, his confused face becoming stricken as he registers my presence. "Jesus, no!" Fear floods his handsome features. Even his voice is unstable. He goes to walk forward, but he's stopped by Sarah, who's grabbing at his arm. "Get the fuck off me!" he roars, knocking her backward. "Ava, baby. What are you doing here?" He rushes forward and drops to his knees in front of me, grabbing at my face and searching for my eyes.

He's a complete blur through my tears. I can't speak. I'm just shaking my head frantically, trying to rid my brain of what I have just witnessed. Is this a nightmare? He wasn't fighting her off at all. He knelt there waiting for the blows in a total trance. I throw my arms out to bat him away from me and scramble to my feet.

"Ava, please!" he pleads, as I push his grabbing hands from me. I need to get out of here.

I turn, knocking John out of the way, and run in blind shock down the corridor, emerging into the massive summer room. As I hurry through, I'm vaguely aware of shocked gasps, and I turn to see Jesse and John in pursuit of me. I slap my hand over my mouth as I feel the bile rising in my throat. Oh God, I'm going to throw up. I fall through the toilet door and into a cubicle, slamming the door behind me, and just make it over the bowl before I proceed to evacuate the contents of my stomach on loud, painful retches, my face wet with sweat and tears. I'm in the lowest level of hell.

The sound of the toilet door crashing into the tiled wall rings out around the ladies' washroom. "Ava!" He bangs on the door behind me, and I sink to my bum as I feel another round of violent heaves coming on. "Ava! Open the door!"

I can't answer him through my persistent retching, even if I wanted to. What the hell am I supposed to say? I've just watched him accept a thrashing from a woman I despise—a woman who I know wants Jesse and hates me. My imagination doesn't stretch to this kind of callousness. I throw up again and fumble for some toilet paper to wipe my mouth as the door continues to bang behind me.

"Please," he begs, and a dull thud meets the door. I know it's his forehead. "Ava, please, open the door."

My tears gather force again at the sound of him begging. I can't possibly look into the eyes of the man I love, knowing he has done this to himself.

"Who let her in?" His tone has turned fierce, and he punches the door. "Fuck! Who the fucking hell let her in?"

"Jesse, I didn't let her in. I would never have let her in." John's low hum is soothing. I want to jump to his defense. He didn't let me in. John's fretful voice, his attempts to stop me from entering Jesse's office, it all brings me to one conclusion. He didn't text me. He didn't open the gates. She's done it again. I've underestimated her hatred of me. She has more than succeeded in her attempt to shock me, but that doesn't detract from the fact that Jesse was actively, willingly participating in the appalling activity. Why?

"What's going on?" The familiar sound of Kate's voice gives me hope of escaping this horror scene. "Fuck! Jesse, what the hell has happened to your back?"

"Nothing!" he snaps.

"Don't fucking talk to me like that. Where's Ava? What the hell is going on? Ava?" She calls my name, and I'm desperate to answer her, but I know if I open the door, Jesse will be in. I can't see him.

"She's in there. She won't come out. Ava?" he calls. "Please, Kate, get her out." He bangs the door again. He sounds desperate and frantic.

"Hey! Tell me why she's locked in there and why you're out here bleeding all over the place?" Kate's voice is fierce.

"Ava walked in on something she shouldn't have seen. She's freaked out. I need to see her." His talking is strained through his heavy breathing.

I want to scream exactly why I've freaked out, but I'm attacked by another succession of retches, rendering me incapable of speech.

"If you've fucked her over, Jesse!" Kate shouts. "Ava?"

He's fucked me over all right, but not in the way she's thinking. It's almost worse. It *is* worse.

"No!" Jesse's voice is full of defense. "It's not like that!"

"Well, what is it like then? She's in there throwing up. Ava?" The subtle knock of Kate's fist starts drumming on the door. "Ava, come on. Open the door."

"Ava!" Jesse shouts frantically.

"Jesse, just go," Kate yells.

"No!"

"She's obviously not going to come out with you here. Hey, big guy. Get him out of here."

"Jesse?" John rumbles, and I pray that Jesse listens to him and leaves. I'm not going anywhere with him out there. "Let's get you sorted out, you stupid motherfucker."

I sit with my head in my hands while I listen to the back and forth coaxing of Jesse from the bathroom.

I eventually hear the door open and close again and then Kate's subtle knocking on the door. "Ava, he's gone," Kate assures me through the door. I lift up and slide the lock across to let my friend into the toilet with me. She pushes through the small gap and screws her face up at the vomit-splattered bowl. "What the hell's going on?" She crouches on the other side of the cubicle so we're knee to knee.

I take a few controlled breaths through my sobs and try to steady my vocal cords. "He had himself whipped." The sound of those words has me throwing my head back over the toilet pan, but all I'm achieving is choking myself on dry heaves. I feel Kate rubbing my back.

"He what?"

I push myself away from the toilet and find Kate's jaw

dropped in shock. Who would believe it? But I saw the evidence plain and clear and plastered all over Jesse's back. "I walked in on him being whipped by Sarah."

Her eyes widen. "The mega bitch?"

"Yes." I nod in case the word didn't make it out of my mouth. "He was on his knees, Kate, like some sort of submissive slave." My tears start again and my mind is invaded with the horrible images of my strong, self-assured man being willingly beaten.

"Oh fuck." She rests her hand on my knee. "Ava, his back is a mess."

"I know!" I cry. "I saw it!" That was no kinky kicks. There was no pleasure element in it. Not on Jesse's part, anyway. Sarah could be a different story, though. Jesse wanted to be hurt. My stomach convulses. "Kate, I need to leave. He won't let me. I know he won't let me go."

A look of determination invades her pretty, pale features and she rises to her feet. "Wait here."

"Where are you going?" My voice sounds panicky. He'll barrel back in here as soon as Kate exits. I know he will.

"John's taken Jesse to his office. I'm just going to check, though." She opens the door and shuffles past my slumped body.

I hold my breath, waiting for a commotion, but it doesn't come. The door opens and closes, and then there's silence. I'm alone. I stand myself up, but my legs are weak and shaky as I attempt to wipe the toilet down, and then the toilet door opens and I freeze, holding my breath.

"Ava?" Kate whispers, tapping the door gently. "Jesse's in his office with John. Sam will get the gates."

I open the door and catch a glimpse of myself in the mirror before I'm pulled out of the toilet cubicle and yanked toward the door. I look god-awful. "Wait, I need some water." I shake Kate off and take myself to the sink, leaning over to splash my face and swill my mouth.

"Here, have some gum." Kate shoves a stick in my mouth.

I'm now weighing up the merits of alcohol. Would I have preferred to have found him drunk? Yes, without a doubt, I would have faced that merciful creature rather than witness him being beaten. He really is self-destructive. Grief turns into anger as I consider his reactions to a few bruises on my backside when I took a trip in Margo senior, and his face when he clocked my bruised arm after my run-in with Mr. Baldy Jag—how over-the-top he was.

Before I have a chance to declare my intention of tracking Jesse down and demanding some answers, he comes barging back into the toilets in a blind panic. I notice his eyes have cleared of the glaze as they land on me, his chest damp, his dirty blond hair dark with sweat. I can feel Kate's eyes passing between us as she assesses the situation.

He starts toward me, and I make no attempt to stop him from doing what I know he's going to do. He leans down, scoops me up into his arms, and strides out of the toilets toward his office. He keeps his line of sight firmly forward as he walks with purpose, back through the summer room under the watchful eyes of some members, who are still floating around soaking up the spectacle. I'm aware of whispers and pointing as tears invade my eyes and start trailing down my cheeks. I'm in absolute agony, I feel sick to my stomach, and my heart feels like it's been sliced straight down the center.

He kicks the door of his office shut and walks straight to the couch, lowering himself down on a wince. My stomach turns. His arms immerse me and his head falls straight into my neck. He's silent, holding me as close as he can get me while I try to control myself, try to control the shakes that are attacking my body. But it's a battle I can't win. My beautiful man has deep issues, and just when I thought I was figuring him out, I'm hit with the worst kind of wake-up call. I don't know him at all, and I certainly don't understand him.

"Please don't cry." His muffled voice reaches my ringing ears. "It's killing me."

"Why?" I ask. It's the only thing I can think to say. It's all I want to know. Why would he do this to himself?

"I promised you I wouldn't have a drink."

What?

He had himself beaten rather than have a drink because he promised me he wouldn't. "You wanted a drink?"

"I wanted to block it out."

"Look at me," I demand, but he makes no attempt to lift his head from its secluded location. "Damn it, Jesse, look at me!" I wriggle to try and get a grip of his head and pull it up, but he hisses in pain, and I still immediately. "Three." I say calmly, not knowing what else to do. I feel him tense under me, but he still doesn't look. "Two."

"What happens on zero?" he asks quietly.

"I leave," I say calmly.

His head flies up, and I whimper at the sight of him, his green eyes clouded, pain spilling out of them, his chin trembling. He gazes straight into my eyes. They are pleading silently to me. "Please don't."

Any ounce of strength that was keeping me marginally to-gether is shredded at the sight and sound of him. I clasp his face in my hands and put my lips on him, but I'm not close enough. I gingerly shift so I'm astride his lap, and then pull him as close as I can get him without hurting him. "Tell me what you were blocking out."

"Hurting you."

"I don't understand." Doesn't he think that this is hurting me? "I would rather you had a drink."

"You wouldn't." He says it on a slight laugh that sends a nervous twinge through me.

I pull back and search his eyes out. "I would rather face you with half a vodka distillery inside you than see what I just saw."

He drops his head in shame. "Trust me, Ava, you wouldn't."

"Trust you? Jesse, I feel sick with betrayal." I've not even thought about what I'm going to do to Sarah when I get my hands on her. She has marked my neurotic god, and the more all of this sinks in, the angrier I'm getting.

I lift myself from his lap and bat him away when he tries to grasp me. "I'm not leaving," I say a bit too harshly. His panicked expression has me even madder. I start pacing his office, tapping my fingernail on my front tooth under the intense gaze of my challenging man, who just keeps delivering on fucking challenges. God, I thrashed a belt at him on the launch night of Lusso.

Lowering myself on the sofa opposite him, I rest my aching head in my palms. I can hear him repeatedly drawing breath, as if he wants to say something. I exhale wearily and massage my temples. "Is there anything else I need to know?"

"Like what?" he asks guardedly. I don't appreciate it, and how the hell would I know? He knocked me for six with this place, the drinking, and now this.

"I don't know, you tell me." I throw my arms up in annoyance. I desperately want to comfort him. Keeping myself away from him is hurting almost as much as bearing witness to his beating. "Why would I prefer this to drunken Jesse?"

He leans forward delicately on a clenched jaw, resting his elbows on his knees, rubbing his temples thoughtfully. "Drink and sex go hand in hand for me."

"What does that mean?" My voice is high and edgy.

"Ava, I inherited The Manor when I was twenty-one. Can you

imagine a young lad with this place and a whole lot of women ready and willing?" He looks ashamed.

My mind starts racing. Oh, I can imagine all right, and it's no wonder the women were ready and willing. They still are. "You drank and dabbled?"

He exhales. "Yes, like I said, drink and sex go hand in hand. But it's all behind me." He sits forward on a wince. "Now, it's all about you."

He reaches across the big table that's positioned between us, but I pull back. His hand drops and he looks down at the floor. I still don't understand, and it still doesn't explain why he has just accepted a thrashing from Sarah.

"So you didn't have a drink because you would have wanted to have sex?" My forehead must look like a road map because I am thoroughly confused.

"I don't trust myself with alcohol, Ava."

"Because you think you will jump the nearest woman?"

He laughs nervously and runs his hands through his hair. "I don't think so. I couldn't do that to you."

"You don't think so?" I'm shocked.

"It's not a risk I'm willing to take, Ava. I drink too much, lose reason, and women throw themselves at me willingly. You've seen it." He gives me an embarrassed smile.

I scoff. "You didn't look very capable of anything last Friday!"

"Yeah, that's not my normal level of intemperance, Ava. I was on a mind-numbing mission."

"So, you usually maintain a steady level of drinking and then have lots of sex with lots of willing women?" I think I'm getting my head around this. "You've never had a drink when you've slept with me?"

He gets up and shifts the table so he can kneel in front of me and rest his hands on my thighs. He looks straight into my eyes. "No, Ava. I have never been under the influence of alcohol when I've had you. I don't need it. Alcohol blocked things out for me, made me forget how hollow my life was. I didn't give a fuck about any of the women I slept with, not one. And then you fell into my life and things changed completely. You brought me back to life, Ava. I never want to touch the drink because if I start, I might not stop, and I never want to miss a moment with you."

Tears start to prick at my eyes at his confession. "Have you had sleepy sex with anyone else?" I hold my breath. Of all the things to ask, I ask this?

He sighs heavily. "No."

I narrow my eyes on him. "What about a sense fuck?"

"Ava, no! I've never cared about anyone else enough to need or want to fuck any sense into them." He squeezes my thighs. "Only you."

I push his hands away from my thighs and get up, leaving him crouched by the sofa looking lost. "So on Thursday in your office, are you telling me that if you had drunk the vodka, I would've found you nailing Sarah on your desk, not just looking cozy with her on your desk?"

He gets up and stalks over to me, grabbing my hips to immobilize me before bending down to get into my line of sight. "No! Don't be so stupid."

"I don't think I'm being stupid," I scathe. "It's bad enough worrying about you drinking. I don't know if I can cope with the additional worry of you being drunk and wanting to fuck other women!" I'm screeching, but I can't help it.

He recoils. "Will you watch your fucking mouth? It doesn't make me want to fuck other women. It just makes me want to fuck!"

"So I had better ensure that I'm with you when you have a drink then, hadn't I?"

"I won't be having a drink! When will you listen to me,

woman?" he shouts. "I don't need drink." He releases me harshly and stomps off toward the window and then back again. He points at me. "I need you!"

And we're back to that. I slap his finger out of my face. "You need me to replace drink and screwing." I want to cry. All he needs is to remove himself from a lifestyle that would kill him if he kept it up for much longer. I'm his escape from a certain premature death by alcohol poisoning. I think I might throw up again. He really is scared of me leaving, but it has nothing to do with how much he loves me. It's because he is scared of returning to a hollow life. "You manipulate me."

"I don't manipulate you!" He actually looks offended.

"Yes, you do! With sex! Sense fucking, reminder fucking. It's all manipulation. I need you, and you use it against me!"

"No!" he roars, and then swipes his arms straight across the top of the drinks cabinet, sending dozens of liquor bottles and glasses crashing to the floor, the sound of broken glass thundering around us.

I jump back, but he stalks forward and grabs the tops of my arms. "I need you to need me, Ava. It doesn't get any simpler than that. How many times have I got to tell you? As long as you need me, I look after myself...simple."

"How is having yourself whipped looking after yourself?!" I scream in his face.

He drops me and grabs at his hair, virtually pulling it out. "I don't fucking know!"

I look to the heavens above. This is hopeless. "I do need you, but not like this."

He takes my hands. "Look at me," he demands harshly. I drop my head back down so we're at eye level again. "Tell me, how do I make you feel? I know how you make me feel. Yes, I've had a lot of women, but it was all just sex. Mindless sex. No feelings. Ava, I need you."

I look at my handsome, troubled, neurotic rogue, looking me straight in the eyes, and I want to scream at him, bang his head against a wall, and knock some sense into him the conventional way.

"How can you need me if I make you do this to yourself?" I ask tiredly. "You're more self-destructive now than you were before me. I've made you *need* alcohol, not want it. I've made you into an unreasonable, crazy man, and *I'm* certainly not stable anymore. Don't you see what we're doing to each other?"

"Ava," his tone is warning. He knows where I'm headed. "Don't."

"And for the record, I hate the fact that you've slept around." I need him to know this, but then the most horrific thought slams into my head.

I gasp.

"When you disappeared for four days..." I can't even finish. My heart has just jumped into my throat and exploded.

His eyes widen at my obvious conclusion, his mouth tightening, the muscles in his jaw ticking. "They. Meant. Nothing. I love you. I need you."

"Oh God!" I fall to my knees. He hasn't denied it. "You were fucking other women." My palms find my face as the tears start again, and a massive hole is punched straight through my stomach.

He joins me on the floor, clenching my arms, shaking me. "Ava, listen to me. They meant nothing. I was falling in love with you. I knew I would hurt you. I didn't want to hurt you."

"You said you couldn't do it to me. You forgot to add *again*. You should have said you couldn't do it to me *again*."

"I didn't want to hurt you," he whispers.

My defeated face comes up. "So to remedy that, you fucked other women?" My stomach is turning. I can't breathe. "How many?"

"Ava, please don't. I hate myself."

"I hate you, too!" I cry, my shoulders jerking as I sob relentlessly. "How could you?"

"Ava, why are you not listening to me?"

"I am, and I don't like what I'm hearing!" I scramble to my feet, but he grabs my waist to prevent me from walking away.

He rests his forehead on my stomach, and I watch through my hazy vision as his own shoulders start jerking. "I'm sorry. I love you. Please, I beg you, don't leave me. Marry me."

"What?" I cry. We've not even spoken of the issue at hand and I'm already balancing on the edge of a complete breakdown. This is the death blow. "I can't marry someone who I don't understand." I utter the words quietly through my heaves and feel him sag before me on a sharp intake on breath. I can see the angry welts and beads of blood across his back. I feel sick again. "I thought I was working you out." My voice is trembling. "You've destroyed me again, Jesse."

"Ava, please. I was a mess. I lost control. I thought I could fight you out of my head."

"By getting pissed and fucking other women?"

"I didn't know what to do," he says quietly.

"You could have talked to me."

"Ava, you would have run away from me again."

"All of the apologies you've been giving me were because your conscience was eating away at you. It wasn't because you were drunk or because of The Manor. It's because you screwed around on me. You said you hadn't dabbled since way before me. You've lied to me. Every time I think we've made progress, more bombshells. I can't cope with this anymore. I don't know who you are, Jesse."

"Ava, you do know me." He looks up at me with pleading eyes. "I've fucked up. I've really fucked up, but no one knows me better than you, no one."

"Sarah might do. She seems to know you very well," I say with zero emotion. "Why?"

He collapses onto his heels and drops his head. "I've let you down. I wanted a drink, but I promised you I wouldn't, and I know what's likely to happen if I do."

I wince at his admission. "So you had yourself whipped?"

"Yes."

My stomach joins my heart in my throat. "I don't understand."

His head remains dropped. "Ava, you know I've led a colorful life." His voice is quiet. He's ashamed. "I've broken marriages, treated women like objects, and taken what's not mine. I've damaged people, and I feel like all of this is my penance. I've found my little piece of heaven, and I feel like everyone is going out of their way to take it away from me."

The lump in my throat grows further. "*You* are the only one who's going to fuck this up. Just you. You drinking, you being a control freak, you fucking other women. *You!*"

"I could have stopped it all. I can't believe I've got you, Ava. I'm terrified you're going to be taken away from me."

"So you ask a woman I despise, a woman who wants to take *you* away from *me*, to whip you?"

He frowns as he looks up to me. "Sarah doesn't want to take me away from you."

I shake my head in frustration. "Yes, Jesse, she does! You doing this to yourself is agony for me. You are punishing me, not you." I'm desperate for him to see this. "I love you, despite all of the shit you keep landing on me, but I can't watch you do this to yourself."

"Don't leave me," he grinds the words out, reaching up and grabbing at my hands. "I'll die before I'm without you, Ava."

"Don't say that!" I shout at him. "That's crazy talk."

He yanks me back down to my knees. "It's not crazy. That

nightmare I had when you were gone. Just like that—gone. It gave me a clue of what it would be like without you." He's in such a state. "Ava, it killed me."

His repeated apologies in his sleep make sense now. "If I leave, it would be because I can't watch you hurt yourself—I can't watch you torture yourself anymore."

"You could never understand how much I love you." He reaches for my face, and I pull away. That statement just makes me fuming mad. "Let me touch you," he demands, trying to grab at me. He's becoming frantic and panicked, and it's ripping my insides out.

"I do understand, Jesse, because I feel the same!" I yell. "Even though you've fucked me over completely, I still fucking love you, and I fucking hate myself for it. So don't you dare tell me I don't understand!"

"It's not possible." He grasps the tops of my arms and pulls me forward on a hiss. "It's just not fucking possible!" His voice is severe. He really does believe that.

I let him pull me into his chest and smother me, but I can't even put my arms around him. I'm emotionally drained and completely numb. My strong, dominant playboy is reduced to a frightened, desperate soul. I want my fierce Jesse back.

"I'm going to get something to clean you up with." I struggle from his fighting arms. "Jesse, I need to clean you up."

"Don't walk away from me."

I break free and stand myself up. "I said I would never leave you. I meant it." I turn and leave him on his knees, walking from his office in a complete daze.

I'm not going to get anything to clean him up. A bit of attention on his wounds isn't going to prove anything. There is only one way I can get him to comprehend that I understand how he feels. And if that's what it takes, then I'll do it.

CHAPTER THIRTY-ONE

I bypass the toilets, the busy bar, and the restaurant quickly. It won't be long before he comes looking for me, so I need to be quick.

I reach the entrance hall and take the stairs two at a time, walking quickly around the gallery landing and ignoring the women's harsh stares.

But then I spot her.

She's chatting to a few female members, no doubt filling them in on the events of the past hour. She's still kitted out in her leather gear, whip still in hand. I approach and stop behind her, and the other women silence immediately. Obviously curious about the sudden halt in conversation, she turns to face me. Her expression is superior, with a little sick satisfaction mixed in there, too. It makes my blood boil further as she stands in front of me, relaxed in her pose, twirling the whip in her grasp.

"You sent me a text from John's phone," I accuse calmly.

She almost laughs. "I don't know what you're talking about."

"Of course you don't." I shake my head disbelievingly. "You also let me into The Manor when I discovered the communal room."

"Now, why would I do that?" she asks cockily.

"Because you want him." My voice is amazingly calm, considering I feel lethal and I'm physically shaking. The other women's stares are burning through my skin as I spread my gaze over all of them. "You all want him."

None of them say a word. They just all stand there watching me, probably anticipating my next move.

Sarah can't keep her trap shut, though. "No, little girl, we've all had him."

I snap.

My fist bunches and flies out, cracking her clean across her Botox-pumped face, sending her staggering back on her heels and to her arse. I don't stop there. I grab her hair in the most unladylike, cattish fashion and haul her up, pinning her against the wall by her throat. Shocked gasps ring out through the air before silence falls, and the only sound is Sarah's stunned breathing.

"You *ever* lay a finger on him again, requested or not, and I won't stop until I've snapped every bone in your fucking body. Do you understand me?"

Her eyes are wide. I can feel her shaking under my hold.

"*Do you understand me?*" I scream the words in her face. I've lost control.

"Yes," she squeaks quietly, shifting under my vise grip on her throat. I'm restricting her breathing.

I release her and she crumbles to the floor in a heap of leather, gasping and gripping at her neck. I'm shaking with anger as I turn and absorb the shocked expressions of many witnesses, all standing in stunned silence. I don't need to say any more. I've made my point pretty clear to Sarah and every other person standing observing my meltdown. I leave them all and carry on my way to my original destination, shaking violently, breathing heavily. As I reach the bottom of the stairs to the communal room, I waver for a few seconds, but as soon as I remember Jesse's words, I race up the stairs with nothing but adrenaline and determination coursing through my veins.

I enter the dimly lit room, ignoring the few scenes playing out in front of me, while trying to blank out the erotic music drowning my hearing. I'm not here to be turned on. I head to the right and find myself where I want to be.

Two men are talking quietly while a woman puts her underwear back on and as I approach the scene, they all turn their attention on me, the conversation ceasing as I get closer. One of the men watches me cautiously while the other eyes me approvingly, his face breaking out into a dark smile. I kick my shoes off and pull my T-shirt up over my head before throwing it to the floor and unfastening my jeans.

"Come to play, sweetness?" one of the men drawls as he starts toward me.

"Steve, leave her," the other guy warns. He clearly recognizes me. I throw him a filthy look, and he shakes his head.

"She wants to play, don't you, sweetness?" His eyes are dark but sparkling at me.

"She's Jesse's girl, Steve. It's not worth it." His friend tries to reason with Steve, but he looks like he's on a mission and doesn't like being told what to do, which is just what I need.

"All's fair in sex and The Manor," Steve quips on a smirk. "What can I give you, sweetness?"

"Seriously, Steve, she's special to him."

"She's special all right. Now she can be special for me, too. Ward has never had an issue with sharing before."

His words stir the bile that's coating my throat, and I watch as the sensible man grasps the woman's arm and pulls her away with a cautious look all over his face. This Steve, though, he's cocky and confident, but not in an attractive way. Not that it matters. I'm not planning on kissing him.

I walk over to the stand by the wall and pick out the

fiercest-looking whip I can find before turning and handing it to him with steady hands. Any reluctance will foil me, and this is the only way that I can demonstrate to Jesse how crazy all of this shit is. His face spreads into a wide smile as he accepts the whip and runs his eyes down my seminakedness. I remove my jeans and walk over to stand myself under the suspended gold frame and hold my hands above my head. "No contact, just the whip. Hard." My voice is clear and totally resolute. I feel resolute. I have no fear or hesitations at all.

"Hard?" he asks.

"Very hard."

"What about your bra?" His eyes are fixed firmly on my chest.

"The bra stays."

"Fair enough." He nods and saunters over, tucking the handle of the whip in his back pocket, before reaching up to secure my hands in the manacles on the gold suspended frame.

"Steve, you need to stop," another voice calls.

"It's none of your business," I grate.

"You heard her, she wants this." Steve looks up at me with hooded eyes filled with lust before he starts walking around the back of me.

My heart starts a heavy, steady thump in my chest, and I close my eyes, reciting Jesse's words over and over.

It's not possible. It's not possible. It's not possible.

I blank my mind of everything, except those words, the music fades, and I brace myself for my own punishment—my punishment for reducing Jesse to a fraught mess of a man, for making him need alcohol, not just want it, for turning him into an uptight, neurotic freak . . . for making him do this to himself.

I hear it before I feel it. A fast, sharp whip though the air before it connects with my back. I cry out.

Holy fucking shit!

The thrash sends a continuous stabbing pain radiating

throughout my entire body, and my legs turn to jelly. I keep my eyes firmly shut. It's only now I realize that we didn't agree on a number of strikes. I hold my breath and grit my teeth as a second lash falls across my back, and mentally plead with myself to keep quiet and accept the beating.

I tense myself, waiting for the next hit, and when it comes, I release my body and hang helplessly from the frame. I'm at the complete mercy of this stranger. The fourth, fifth, and sixth thrashes connect at even intervals, until I'm familiar with when to expect the strikes, and I've completely numbed out what I'm doing. I'm unaware of my surroundings, the music is dull in the distance, and the voices around me are quiet. The only thing I'm alert to is the timing between each lash and the air whipping before the leather connects with my flesh. I might be unconscious. I'm not sure. I'm not even tensing anymore.

Another thrash connects with my back and I jerk again, my back arching, my head flying back.

"Noooooooooo!"

The roar I know so well snaps me to the here and now as another burning snap spreads across my back. I buck in shock, the metal restraints clanking loudly above my head. I can't open my eyes. My head is heavy, my body lifeless, and my arms are lacking any blood and feeling in them.

"Jesus! Ava, no!" His voice is loud but broken. My body starts swinging slightly, and I feel his warm hands all over me. "John, release her hands! Oh God, no, no, no, no, no, no!"

"Motherfucker!"

"John, fucking hell, get her down! Ava?" He sounds terrified. I'm grabbed and stroked all over as I feel the tampering of big, clumsy hands on mine. It feels like forever, but it's probably only a few seconds before my body falls down like lead. I'm limp in his arms. "Ava? Oh God, please! Ava?" I'm vaguely aware of being moved.

And then the pain kicks in.

Oh good God!

My flesh feels like it's on fire, pain emanating from every single nerve ending across my back and beyond. I'm being shuffled about, and I can't even speak to tell him to stop. I've never felt pain like it.

"Don't let him go anywhere!" Jesse's voice is muffled, but I know who he is talking about, and through my haze, I realize that I've probably just sent Steve to his death.

I need to stop that. I asked him to do this, although I'm wondering why the hell I did right now. I really am completely crazy, but then I remind myself of the reasons behind this. He might not be so willing to do this to himself if he is faced with me following suit.

My crazy side and my sane side are having an argument in my head, and I can hear Jesse's thundering footsteps and many shocked gasps as I'm carried through The Manor.

"What the fuck!" Kate's shocked voice is distant. "Jesse?"

He doesn't answer. All I hear is John's low rumble fading into the background along with all the commotion that I have caused. I don't care. A door slams and a few moments later, I feel the sofa beneath his thighs as I'm cradled in his lap.

"You stupid, stupid girl," he sobs on a cracked voice. I feel him buried in my neck, inhaling into my hair, and frantically stroking my head. "You crazy, stupid girl."

I drag my eyes open and stare blankly across his chest. I'm in so much pain, but I have no desire to move or voice my discomfort. I feel sedated, like I'm floating on the outside, observing this shocking scene from afar. What if my attempts to make Jesse see my point of view fail? What if he does punish himself again? I couldn't bear to go through this again, and not just because I'm in absolute agony—I couldn't bear to see Jesse on his knees, accepting lashes dished out by Sarah, or by anyone, for that matter. Not that I'll ever be able to scratch that image from my mind. It'll be etched there forever.

I don't know how long we sit in silence, me staring into the distance, completely detached from the circumstances, and Jesse sobbing into my hair. It feels like hours, maybe longer. I've lost all sense of time and reality.

There's a knock at the door.

"What?" Jesse's voice is fragmented and low, and he sniffs a few times.

The door opens, but I don't know who it is. My eyes have been staring into space for such a long time, I think they may have set in place. I hear some movement close by and something being put on the table in front of us, but whoever it is doesn't speak. They leave just as quietly, the office door shutting almost silently.

Jesse moves slightly under me, and I inhale on a sharp, painful hiss. He stills. "Oh Jesus." He sounds fraught. "Baby, I need to move you, I need to see your back."

I shake my head mildly and press my face into his bare chest. It's going to hurt like hell when he moves me. I want to delay it for as long as possible. His own back is a bloodied mess, and he's leaning back on the sofa with me on his lap pressing into him. He must be in some serious pain himself.

He sighs and rests his chin on the top of my head. "Why?" he croaks, kissing my head. "I don't understand."

If I could talk, I would be throwing that back at him.

"Ava, I need to see your back." He makes to move again and pain slices through me, but I clench my dry eyes shut and let him move me until I'm sitting up on his lap.

The gravity smacks right into my stomach and I'm suddenly heaving, my stomach convulsing, my body jerking, which only serves to increase the pain further. I double over on his lap.

"Oh God, Ava!" He places his hand on my back in an instinctive move to soothe me. The hot contact of his hand has me jolting forward on a cry and my stomach deciding that yes, there is something left to evacuate. I throw up all over his office floor.

"Shit! Ava, I'm sorry. Oh fuck!" He pulls my hair from my face and tentatively moves to get better access to me. "Fuck! Fuck, Ava, what have you done?" His traumatized voice tells me my back must look as bad as it feels. I'm desperately trying to get a handle on the retching in an attempt to minimize the pain. "I'm going to move you now, okay?" He grasps me under my arms and stands. I cry out. "I can't lift you without touching you." He grunts a few frustrated curses as he tries to maneuver me to the other couch without catching my back.

My legs are still wobbly and unsteady. I never imagined this.

"Get on your front." He lowers me to the sofa on my stomach, and I put my arms under my head as a pillow. "Ava, I can't believe you've done this." He kneels by the sofa and pulls over a glass bowl of water with a bottle of purple liquid. He squirts the liquid into the water and takes the roll of cotton wool, tearing some off before dipping it in the solution and squeezing off the excess. "This is going to sting, baby. I'll be gentle, okay?" He puts his face in my field of vision, and my eyes lift with some effort, finding green pools of total anguish.

I stare blankly at him, all muscles refusing to work.

He lowers his lips to mine and kisses me gently, and it's the first time ever that I don't have to fight my body's reaction to his touch. He shakes his head, returning his attention to my back, and I pull in a severe, distressed breath as he unclasps my bra gently, letting the straps fall to the sides. Then I feel the soft cotton wool skimming over my skin. It feels like he is dragging barbed wire across my back. I sob.

"I'm sorry," he blurts. "I'm so sorry."

I turn my face into my arms and clench my teeth as he attempts to coat me in the solution, refreshing the cotton wool repeatedly and reloading it with the warm mixture for each painful swipe. He curses with each one of my flinches.

When I hear the bowl scrape across the table, I let out a long, thankful lungful of air. I turn my face back outward and see the purple-tinged water is now stained red, with used cotton wool balls piled in, soaking up the liquid. He gets up from beside me and returns swiftly with a bottle of water and crouches in front of me.

"Can you sit up?"

I nod and start the painful process of getting myself up into a sitting position on the couch with Jesse flapping and cursing in front of me. My bra falls onto my lap and I halfheartedly attempt to pull it back on.

"Leave it." He pushes my hands away and puts the water into my grasp. "Open your mouth." I comply without thought, accepting the two pills he puts on my tongue. "Drink."

The bottle feels like an iron weight as I lift it to my mouth. He must see me struggling because he places his fingers on the base to alleviate the weight and I welcome the ice water into my dry mouth. Jesse walks over to his desk and grabs his keys and phone, stuffing them in various pockets, before pulling his T-shirt over his head and walking back toward me.

He gets my clothes from the back of the sofa and crouches back in front of me. "I'm taking you home." He opens my jeans at my feet and taps my ankle, then helps me pull them up my legs.

He looks from the T-shirt, to my exposed breasts, and then to me with a slight frown. The thought of anything resting on my skin makes me want to vomit, but I can't be walking out of here and into Lusso naked from the waist up.

"Can we try?" He stretches the neck of my T-shirt and pulls my dangling bra from my arms before easing the shirt over my head.

I start lifting my arms to accommodate Jesse's hold on the T-shirt, but tears start to stab at my eyes with the effort and painful stings. I shake my head frantically. It hurts too much.

"Ava, I don't know what to do." He sounds desperate as he holds the material away from my body. "Please, don't cry." He kisses my forehead as tears stream down my face. "Oh fuck it!" He pulls the T-shirt back over my head and throws it on the sofa. "Come here." Bending, he curls his arm under my bum and lifts me up with one arm. "Wrap your legs around my waist, arms around my neck. Be careful." I do as I'm told slowly and carefully. "Are you okay?" he asks.

I nod into his shoulder and link my ankles around the small of his back, feeling him pull my hair over my shoulder and rest his palm on the nape of my neck, holding me as tight as he can without inflicting further pain. My boobs are squished to his chest, my back completely exposed, but I couldn't care less. He strides to the door and releases my neck to open it, before replacing his hand securely on my nape.

"Okay, baby?" he asks, walking down the corridor into the summer room. I nod into his neck, but I'm far from okay. I feel like I've been lying directly on the sun, all of my skin burned away, exposing raw flesh. "John!" he yells. There's a succession of shocked gasps, all sounding more shocked than when I was carried in.

"How's the girl?" John's low voice is close by.

"How does she fucking look? Get a cotton sheet from the cleaning quarters."

"Ava?" Kate's fretting tone assaults my ears. "Oh, fucking hell. What have you done, you stupid cow!"

"I'm taking her home." Jesse's not stopping for anyone, not even Kate. "She's fine, I'll call you."

"Jesse, she's bleeding!"

"I know, Kate. I fucking know!" I feel his chest rise under me.

"I'll call you." I don't hear her again, but I do hear Sam soothing her, his usual chirpy voice layered with concern.

I know we're getting close to the entrance hall because the cool air starts to slowly spread across my back. It's a welcome sensation.

"Jesse, mate, I didn't know."

We halt abruptly and silence falls, all concerned chatter coming to a complete stop as I hear Steve's voice drift into my ears. I squeeze Jesse's body with what little strength I can find, and he nuzzles my neck.

"Steve, you want to be thanking all that's fucking holy I've got my girl in my arms, because if I didn't, the cleaners would be scooping up your remains for a fucking year." Jesse's voice is acidic, his heart pounding wildly.

"I...I..." Steve stammers and stutters over his words. "I didn't know."

"No one told you she was mine?" Jesse asks, clearly shocked.

"I...I assumed...I..."

"She's *mine!*" Jesse roars, jolting me in his arms. I whimper from the flash of searing pain that his movement instigates, and he tenses, pushing his face into the crook of my neck. "I'm sorry," he whispers. I feel his jaw ticking against me. "You're a fucking dead man, Steve." He stands still for a few moments, and I know he's glaring at Steve with murder carved all over his face. I feel responsible.

"Jesse?" John's rumble breaks the screaming silence. "S'all good. Priorities, yeah?"

"Yeah." Jesse picks up his feet again and the slow-building cool air is suddenly sharp and pelting at my back. He walks slowly down the steps.

"I'll get the door." Kate's heels clatter down the steps.

"I've got it, Kate."

"Jesse, stop being such a pigheaded twat and accept the fucking help! You're not the only one who cares about her."

I'm squeezed against him. "My keys are in my back pocket."

Kate's hand brushes over my jeans as she negotiates the keys out of Jesse's pocket, and I smile on the inside at my fiery friend living up to her reputation. My eyes open and catch Kate's.

"Oh, Ava." She shakes her head and bleeps Jesse's car open.

Jesse turns back toward The Manor. "Everyone needs to fuck off back inside." He doesn't want anyone to see me. I hear the crunching of gravel under footsteps as Jesse waits with me in his arms, ensuring everyone has gone before he releases me from his body. "Ava, I'm going to ease you down, you need to turn onto your side and face the driver's seat. Can you do that?" he asks softly. I loosen my grip on his neck to show my willingness, and he begins slowly lowering me down into the car. "Don't lean back."

I shift slowly on the soft leather until my shoulder is resting against the seat and I'm facing the driver's side. Fucking hell, it hurts. He then lays a light sheet over me before shutting the door softly without even attempting to get the seat belt over me. My head falls against the seat, my eyes close, and in no time at all, the driver door shuts and Jesse's scent invades my nose. I open my eyes and adjust my vision until I'm confronted with green, pitiful eyes.

He reaches over and brushes my cheek with his knuckles. "Stop," he orders, wiping another tear away, but I'm not crying with pain anymore. I'm crying in desperation.

Turning the engine over, he drives slowly down the driveway, the rushed roar and madcap driving skills that I've fast become accustomed to sidelined for a sensible purr of the DBS's engine. He takes corners carefully, accelerates and brakes gently, and flicks his eyes to me at regular intervals.

I remain still and stare blankly at the profile of my handsome, troubled man and wonder whether I could be classed as troubled now, too. My sanity is certainly questionable, but I'm sane enough to admit that. I was a normal, sound-minded girl. I definitely don't qualify for that anymore.

The silence of the journey home is filled only by the humming of the car and the background sound of Snow Patrol's "Run."

CHAPTER THIRTY-TWO

I know if I stretch, I'll yelp really loud. The overwhelming need to spread myself out is playing havoc with my natural instinct to remain still and curtail the aching and stinging. All of the previous day's events come crashing into my head before my eyes open—all of the hideousness, all of the sounds of whips, the flashes of pain, the anguish and torment. It has all landed in my waking brain with a spectacular wallop followed by a little greeting curtsey. My eyes open and I spy Jesse. His hand is resting on my cheek, his face close to mine, his lips parted and breathing steady, peaceful breaths onto my face. He looks so serene, his long lashes fanning his face, his hair its usual morning disheveled mop of dirty blond. He has his morning stubble, and his untroubled, handsome face close to mine brings a small smile to me. Past all of his annoying, challenging ways is a deeply messed-up man, who drinks, fucks, and has himself whipped to punish himself. And I'm a huge contributing factor to his sorry state.

I watch as his eyelids flicker and slowly open, blinking a few times before he focuses in on me. It takes a few silent moments, but he eventually sighs and inches himself closer to me until we are nose to nose. I don't feel close enough. I pull my arms from under the pillow and shift myself on a few winces. His hand rests on my hip to steady me, and he moves until our bodies are pressed together.

"It is possible," I whisper through the incredible dryness of my throat, "to understand how you feel about me, it is possible."

"You did this to yourself to prove you love me?"

"No, you know I love you. I did it to show you what it feels like."

His brow furrows deeply. "I don't understand. I know what it feels like to be whipped."

"I don't mean that. I mean the agony of seeing the man I love hurting himself." I bring my hand up and stroke his stubble, and I see him begin to grasp my point. "Nothing will ever hurt me as much as seeing you doing that to yourself. That will kill me, nothing else. If you punish yourself again, then I will, too." My voice is slightly shaky, just at the thought of ever having to face another day like yesterday. But if he loves me like he claims he does, then my request should be a very easy one for him to fulfill.

His eyes dart around a bit, and he chews his lip as he starts shaking his head ever so faintly. His eyes fall back onto mine. "You love me."

"I do. And I need you. I need you strong and healthy. I need you to understand how much I love you. I need you to know that I can't be without you either. I would die before losing you."

"I don't deserve you, Ava. Not after the life I've lived. I've never had anything I've valued or wanted to protect. Now I have, and it's a bizarre mixture of total happiness and complete fucking fear." His eyes scan every inch of my face. "I crave control with you, Ava. I can't help it. I really can't."

"I know." I sigh. "I know you can't." I move into his chest and soak up his heat. For once, I feel like I completely understand him. He's had a life of not caring, of unfeeling, and complete disorder. He doesn't know what to do with all of this newfound emotion.

"You're hurting because of me," he says into my hair.

"And you are because of me. We deal with the past. As long as I have you, the strong you, then we deal with it. It's not your history that's hurting me. It's you. The things you are doing now." I'm pulled from his chest.

"You're crazy mad," he says softly, pushing his lips to mine "Crazy, crazy mad."

I welcome his soft lips onto mine. It's the only part of me I can move without pain slicing me. "I'm crazy in love with you. Please don't do that to yourself again. My back hurts."

He pulls back on a mild scowl. "I'm still furious with you."

"I'm not very happy with you either."

"I can't touch you," he grumbles, kissing me again, all over my face.

"I know. How's your back?"

He scoffs and continues covering my face with his lips. "I'm fine. I'm just pissed at you. We need to get you moving or you'll seize up."

"I'm happy to seize up," I argue. I'm happy to lie here and have him kiss me from head to toe.

"Not a chance, lady. You need a lavender bath and some cream on your back. I can't believe out of all of my members, you picked the most unstable one."

"I did?" I wasn't to know. I just handed the whip to the first man who would take it.

"You did." He drags his mouth away from my face and narrows displeased eyes on me. "John and I were due to have a meeting today to discuss revoking his membership. We've been monitoring him for a while. His behavior has become a little erratic lately, and while some of the women welcome the rough side of his sexual exploits, others not so much. He makes some women uncomfortable and that's a problem." A look of regret washes over his face, and I know he's thinking that he should have kicked Steve out sooner. "He hadn't done anything to warrant us getting rid of him until last night."

"I asked him." I try and ease Jesse's guilt. I don't want a repeat of all this.

"There are rules, Ava." He kisses me, biting my bottom lip lightly. "Did you discuss limits?"

"No." I realize how stupid I was now.

"He's broken a lot of rules. He's got to go."

"I don't remember him. He wasn't at the anniversary party." I would have remembered that cocky face.

"No, he was on duty."

"Duty?"

Jesse smiles. It's a welcome sight. "He's a cop."

I cough and then wince. "What?"

"He's a copper."

"You threatened to kill a cop?"

"I was crazy mad." He pushes my hair from my face and gazes at me thoughtfully. "I've been thinking."

I don't like the sound of that. He doesn't look like he does either. "What about?"

"Well, about a lot of things. But the first thing is that I need to talk to Patrick about Van Der Haus."

I knew I wasn't going to like what he said, but I can't see any way around this. Mikael is probably the equivalent of Patrick's retirement fund, and I know he's going to pass out with shock when I tell him that I can't work with Mikael anymore. Oh God! "It's Monday!" I blurt, shifting a little in an attempt to get myself up.

His hands swiftly press into my shoulders, pushing me back down. "Do you honestly think I'm letting you go anywhere?"

He shakes his head. "Listen, that's not the only thing I've been thinking about." He commences to chomp on his lip.

Oh no. "What?"

He pushes himself in closer to me. "I can't ever be without you."

"I know that."

"But it's not because I'm worried about reverting back to my old ways. I love you because you give me purpose. You've filled a massive hole with your beautiful face and your spirit, and while I might be making your life a little more difficult with my challenging ways..." He raises a sarcastic eyebrow. "I want to throw that right back at you."

I laugh hard and wince immediately afterward, but Jesse doesn't join me in my hysterics. His lips purse and his grip increases on my hip.

"I am not challenging, Jesse Ward." His eyebrows jump higher. He obviously disagrees, but I slap my hand over his mouth to halt his counterattack. "You just said that I've filled a massive hole with my spirit..."

"And your beautiful face," he mumbles into my hand.

I roll my eyes. "Part of that spirit is my incessant need to challenge *your* challenging ways. You'll never get rid of that tiny part of me that rebels against you, and you wouldn't want to. That's what makes me different from all the women of The Manor, who've licked your boots for far too long." It's me who raises a sarcastic eyebrow now, and his eyes narrow slightly in return. "I've given myself to you completely. Every part of me is yours. No one will ever take me away from you. Not ever. And I know part of your issue is keeping me as far away from what the other women in your life represent."

"There have been no other women in my life!" he argues through my hand.

I push it harder to his lips. "But I need to know something."

His eyebrows rise. He can't answer, because my hand is too tight on his lips.

"You want to keep me as far away from the women of The Manor, but what about the sex?" I ask, feeling him grinning against my palm. I take my hand away from his mouth. Yes, he's grinning that roguish grin. It's a beautiful sight, even if I'm not happy about his amusement at my question. He goes out of his way to dress me suitably, according to him, makes me wear lace—that request is suddenly very obvious—and he doesn't want me to drink.

Oh God!

The reason for that has just landed with an enormous smack in my brain. "You don't like me drinking because you think I'm going to do what you used to do when you were drunk. You think I'm going to want to fuck everything in sight!" I practically screech the words at him, and his grin soon disappears. I've not even given him a chance to answer my previous question and I'm lobbing him another. Well, not a question, more of a conclusion.

"Will you stop fucking swearing?" He rolls onto his back without so much as a hiss or spit of pain.

Oh no. I scramble up, ignoring my own pain, and straddle him. "That's it, isn't it? That's the reason."

I watch as he absorbs my words. He can't possibly argue with it, I know I've got him here. He takes a deep breath and opens his mouth to talk, but nothing comes out. He takes another, but still, nothing comes out. He does this three times before he eventually speaks. "It's not just that, Ava. You're vulnerable when you're drunk."

"But it is part of the reason, isn't it?" I know the other is men assuming I'm fair game.

"Yes, I guess so," he admits.

"Okay, what about the sex?" This I really need to know. He

wants to make me the opposite of all things Manor-ish, yet he fucks me stupid.

The grin is back.

"I already told you this. I can't get close enough to you."

"Sleepy sex achieves that."

"Yes, it does, but we have an incredible chemistry. I've never felt it before."

My heart gallops in my chest and for the first time in nearly a day, it's with happiness. He's never felt it before. But he's slept with dozens of women. Or is it hundreds? My smile disappears. "What feelings?"

His hands rest on my thighs. "It's pure bliss, baby. Total gratification. Absolute, complete, earth-shifting, universe-shaking love."

My smile is back. "Yeah?"

"Oh yeah. Complete heaven."

I fall forward onto his chest. "Ouch!"

"Careful." He pushes me back up. "Does it hurt bad?" A flash of anger flies through his eyes as he waits for my answer, and I pray that John has sent Steve packing before Jesse gets hold of him.

"It's fine." I shift. "What am I going to do about work?" Where has this weekend gone? I inwardly laugh. It's gone on lavish shopping trips, lavish food, lavish jewelry, lavish lace, a lavish party, a peculiar marriage proposal, lots of incredible sex, a drugging, whippings...

I groan. It's been one hell of a weekend.

"Unravel your knickers. I've spoken to Patrick." Jesse sits up and shifts us to the edge of the bed.

"Is there anyone in my life who you haven't trampled?" I ask dryly.

He stands and places me on my feet, his wonderful nakedness right in front of me. "Don't be cheeky," he warns with total seriousness. "There are no whip marks on your arse, lady. Anyway, why does our home look like it's been ransacked by burglars?"

Oh, I forgot about that. "I was looking for something."

He frowns. "What?" he asks, but I detect a hint of cautiousness.

I study him, assessing his expression and his body language. I can't fathom it at all. "Nothing."

He turns me away from himself and starts walking me to the bathroom with one hand on my elbow and another cupping my bum. His lack of curiosity as to what I was looking for has only heightened my suspicions. He would never usually accept such a vague answer to one of his questions.

"What did you tell Patrick?" I ask as he lifts me onto the vanity unit.

"I told him that you passed out on Saturday and put your back out."

Good thinking. "Did he not think it strange that you called him?"

"I don't know and I don't really care." He starts drawing a bath and comes back over to me. "Look what you've done to your beautiful body," he says quietly, gazing over my shoulder to my bare back in the reflection of the mirror. "I won't be taking you on your back for a while."

A wave of disappointment travels through me as I glance over my shoulder. "Is that it?" I blurt incredulously. I feel like I've been skinned alive, and all I've got to show for my torture are a few long, red welts and one with a sliver of dried blood.

"What do you mean, 'Is that it'?"

I drag my eyes away from my pitiful wounds on a scowl and look at Jesse, who is displaying a similar expression to mine, but fiercer. I grab his hips. "Turn around," I order as I push him to guide his reluctant, lean body away from me. His back comes into view and I gasp. He has double the amount of lash marks, more blood, and generally more to show for the shitty day we had yesterday. "See, yours are better than mine."

He flies back around and pins me with an incensed stare, grabbing the tops of my arms, shaking me slightly. "Shut up, Ava!"

"Sorry!" Why am I talking such rubbish? "It just hurts so much. I thought it would look a lot worse than that."

"It's fucking bad enough!" He drops me and returns to the bath, pouring in some lavender oil and swishing the water with his hand.

I cock my head to the side and admire his firm nakedness as I swing my legs and roll my shoulders in an attempt to work some flex back into them. I need to relax. I can feel my muscles knotting across my shoulders. I sit patiently on the vanity unit while Jesse goes about getting towels and collecting up the mess I've made. He does it all in complete silence, not looking at me once. He knows what I've been looking for.

"Off." He offers his hand and an expectant face, but I decline and slide off the unit with care, removing my knickers and taking myself to the bath. I step in and gingerly lower myself into the stinging water.

Jesse climbs in and sinks down behind me without so much as a huff of discomfort as the water coats his back. He clasps his hands over my shoulders and gently tugs, easing me back against him. "Don't fight me." He bites my ear, and I squirm. His legs bend up and he wraps his arms around my neck so I'm completely swathed in him.

Right then. Now for the tub-talk.

I rest my head against his shoulder and relish his morning stubble grazing the side of my face. "So, Steve is out on his arse?"

"Gone."

"No questions asked?"

"Not one, except whether he would prefer burial or cremation." His answer, although brutal and a tad over-the-top, is just the response I was hoping for. "Am I hurting you?"

"No, I'm fine," I assure him. "So, does the same apply to Sarah?"

Boom!

He pauses mid-nuzzle, and I continue my slow, feathery circles of his thighs with my index fingers, like I haven't just asked what I know will be a sensitive question. Steve had no sexual interest in me, not long-term anyway, but Sarah clearly has, and as my thick-skinned man seems oblivious to her romantic pursuit, it's down to me to instigate damage control.

"What has Sarah got to do with this?"

"She hurt you."

"I asked her to."

"I asked Steve to," I counter calmly.

"Yes, but Steve knew you were off-limits, that you are mine. He crossed a clear line that I drew, and not just with who he practiced his shit on, but also how he carried it out. Although the former is my ultimate bone of contention." He bites my earlobe to make sure I know he means me. Who else? "He accepted a whip from someone he hadn't met before and never even clarified the limits. You could have been mentally unstable for all he knew."

"I probably was at that specific moment," I mutter. "And anyway, you're mine. You're off-limits, too, you know."

"I know," he says softly. "I know, baby. Never again, but I think you've demonstrated your grievance with Sarah," he adds sarcastically.

I smile smugly. Yes, I have, but I still want her out on her arse. "So, you're not getting rid of her?"

"She's an employee and a close friend. I can't sack her for doing something I asked her to, Ava."

I sigh heavily, blatantly wanting him to be aware that I'm

not happy about this. A friend? A close friend? "She planned it, Jesse."

"What do you mean, she planned it?"

"The text I got from John."

"What text?"

"The one she sent from John's phone saying I should go to The Manor."

"You think Sarah lifted John's phone and sent you a text?"

"Yes!"

"Don't be daft!"

"I'm not being daft!" I screech. "I have it on my phone, I'll show you."

"Ava, Sarah wouldn't do that."

Oh please! She's supposed to be a friend, but he obviously doesn't know her very well. I had the pleasure of her company for only a few seconds before I worked her out. "Do you think I imagined it?"

"No, I'm thinking that you were drugged on Saturday night and maybe you've made a mistake."

"I'll show you." I sound like a stroppy teenager. "She wants you."

"Well, she can't have me, she knows that. I belong to you." He presses his lips to the side of my face.

"You do." I push my cheek onto his lips, thinking how difficult this is.

Jesse is right; he can't dismiss her from his employment for doing something that he asked her to do, which stinks because I can't imagine Jesse would be of the same opinion if the boot was on the other foot. My only comfort is the knowledge that Jesse has absolutely no interest in her. And of that, I am completely sure.

"Lean forward so I can bathe your back." He encourages me to sit up. "I'll be gentle."

"I like you rough," I whisper cheekily.

"Ava, don't say things like that when I'm in no position to violate you."

I smile as he takes his time bathing me, sweeping the sponge gently over my back, dropping kisses whenever and wherever he can. My hair is washed and I'm wrapped in a towel and carried to the bedroom where he lays me gently on the bed. "This might be a bit cold." He straddles my bum and squeezes some cream onto my back. My shoulder blades fly up and tense. "Shhhhh," he hushes me. "You won't be doing this again, will you?"

"I will if you do," I grumble, burying my face in the pillow, sending a small prayer to God that he won't.

He starts small, tender strokes across my back, getting me used to the friction before working the cream into the welts once I've relaxed a bit more. The warm fluidity of his big hands gliding all over my back soon becomes hypnotizing, and I'm more than aware of something hard and moist probing at my lower back. I smile to myself. He will never keep his hands off me for long, and I hope he doesn't. But he'll be wearing a condom. I'm massaged until all of the tightness has been rubbed away and my back feels something close to normalcy.

"Hello?"

Both of our heads snap up at the sound of Cathy's voice drifting into the room.

"Shit!" Jesse curses, jumping up from my body. "I forgot to call Cathy." He disappears into the wardrobe and reappears in some jeans and a pale blue T-shirt. "Up you get." He grasps my waist and pulls me from the mattress. "I need to feed you."

"I'm not hungry."

"You'll eat." It's that tone. "Your stomach must be completely empty after you emptied it all over my office floor."

I cringe. "Sorry."

"Don't be. Get some clothes on. I'll meet you in the kitchen." He kisses me chastely and leaves me to sort myself out.

*　*　*

"Good morning, Ava." Cathy smiles kindly as she looks up from loading the dishwasher.

Wearing my old, soft, ripped jeans and a white oversized T-shirt that doesn't grip my back too much, I lift myself up on the stool next to Jesse as he leans over to inhale my freshly washed hair. "Hi, Cathy, how are you?" I beat him away, and he growls at me before wiping a blob of peanut butter across my bottom lip. My tongue automatically sets about clearing it away. "Oh God!" I screw my face up in distaste, and he laughs before pulling me closer and licking it away for me.

"Yum." He smiles and plants a wet peanut butter–flavored kiss on my lips. I wipe my mouth and return my attention to Cathy, finding her regarding our little exchange with a small smile on her thin lips. I blush profusely.

"I'm very well, Ava. Would you like some breakfast? Salmon?"

"Oh yes, please," I say gratefully, and she nods her head, wipes her hands on her crisp white apron and heads for the fridge. I glance around the kitchen and see all of my mess has been cleared up.

"We have some news, Cathy," Jesse chirps up.

We do?

I turn a frown on him, but he ignores me. "Ava will soon be Mrs. Ward."

My mouth falls open, but he still ignores me. I'd forgotten about that, what with everything else we've dealt with over the past couple of days. How could I?

"Oh, how wonderful!" Cathy places the eggs and salmon

on the island and makes her way around to clench me into a tight squeeze. "Oh, I'm so happy," she sings in my ear. I clench my teeth as she makes a meal of rubbing my back while I'm still sitting on the stool. She pulls back and wraps her palms around my face. "I can't tell you how happy that makes me. He's a good boy." She lands a sloppy kiss on my cheek and releases me. "Come here, you." She takes Jesse in an equally enthusiastic hug, and he accepts willingly, with no flinch or hiss of pain, while he watches me over Cathy's shoulder gaping at him.

After the events of last night, I had—quite mistakenly, it would seem—assumed *that* matter was up for review. My ring has disappeared from my finger, and when he asked me if I would still marry him, I had said I couldn't. Don't we need to figure out the boatload of shit that has developed over the weekend? Our insecurities, Sarah, Coral, Mikael...

He's completely disregarded me. I've not even spoken to my parents yet. If I am marrying this challenging arse, then they should know first.

"My boy is finally settling down." Cathy squeezes his cheeks and lands him with a kiss to match my own. She is behaving like a proud mother. It makes me wonder about the history of Cathy and Jesse's relationship. It seems to be more than an employee-employer concern. She releases Jesse from her slightly wrinkled hands and pulls her apron up to wipe her eyes on a sniffle.

"Cathy, stop that!" Jesse admonishes her.

"I'm sorry." She composes herself and returns to preparing breakfast with a wide smile on her face. "So, where and when?"

I cringe and reach over for the coffeepot. This is where the fireworks might start flying.

"Next month at The Manor," Jesse informs her confidently.

I clank the coffeepot against the side of the mug and then swing my eyes onto Jesse. "Really?"

"Really," he counters coolly. It hasn't taken long for the challenging arse who drives me insane to return.

"How lovely," Cathy chirps.

My eyes fly from Jesse to her. Does she know what The Manor is?

"It will be." Jesse screws the lid of the peanut butter back onto the jar and starts picking at the label, ignoring my stunned expression, which is firmly rooted on his profile. I watch as he looks at me out of the corner of his eye and starts chewing his lip as he rolls up a piece of the label and flicks it onto the worktop.

I exhale slowly in an attempt to cool my fraying patience and grab the small piece of rubbish from the marble. What happened to discussing our wedding together?

Lowering myself from the stool, I head for the bin, just for something to do other than kick him in the shins. I pause behind him and push my mouth to his ear. "Who are you marrying?" I ask quietly, before I carry on my way to the bin.

He growls. "I'll trample, Ava."

"Pardon?" Cathy turns from the hob.

"Nothing," we say in unison, before our scowls collide in the space between us. The hostility emanating from his body is palpable. This weekend has just proved that we need to be focusing our attentions on other more important issues, like filling each other with the reassurance that we both obviously need.

I stamp on the bin pedal and throw my minuscule piece of rubbish in, but something glimmers at me from the dark depths, catching my eye. I reach in on a frown and pull out one half of a silver-and-white card. It's a wedding invitation. I turn it around and tilt my head before looking back into the bin. I retrieve the other half and hold them together.

Mr. & Mrs. Henry Ward request the pleasure of your company at the wedding of their daughter, Miss Amalie Ward, to Dr. David Garcia.

Oh God!

The invitation is swiped from my grasp and stuffed back in the bin, and I'm yanked back over to the kitchen island in a complete daze. "Sit," he demands in that tone—the one that I know not to ignore. I'm lifted onto a stool with care, and I look up to find a ticking jaw and bulging neck muscles.

"Your sister?" I ask quietly.

"Leave it," he warns without looking at me.

My mind starts racing. We haven't spoken about his parents much, but what I *do* know is that he hasn't seen them for years. Is that their choice or Jesse's? If they are sending him an invitation to his sister's wedding, then I'm guessing it must be Jesse's. I study his profile, but dare not say a word.

"Here you are." Cathy presents me and Jesse with our breakfast and then stuffs a duster in the front of her apron. "I'll leave you to eat in peace."

"Thank you, Cathy," Jesse says with zero gratitude.

I can't even speak. I start picking at the edges of my salmon bagel in awkward silence, and after an eternity of quiet, I finally relent and lower myself from my stool.

"Where are you going?" he asks shortly.

"Upstairs." I make my way from the kitchen, leaving my breakfast untouched. Jesse and the constant challenges surrounding him are doing my appetite no favors.

"Ava, don't walk away from me," he threatens. I ignore him. "Ava!"

I swing around. "You are more than crazy mad if you think I'm marrying you, Jesse," I say calmly before leaving a face full of hurt in the kitchen. I half expect to get tackled to the ground, but much to my complete surprise—and worry—I'm allowed to leave the kitchen, taking myself up to the master suite without so much as a countdown or a Jesse-style sense fuck. I'm delicate at the moment, so no manhandling is possible.

I see Cathy in my favorite spare room, dusting to her heart's content while singing "Valerie." She brings a small smile to my face. Shutting the bedroom door softly behind me, I go and brush my teeth. I'll go to work. I'm not hanging around the tower all day like a spare part, and my back feels all right, if I don't make too many sudden movements. I would rather face my boss and his certain questioning about my and Jesse's relationship.

I flick through the rails and rails of new dresses and settle on one of my old ones. I get changed and slip on my heels before presenting myself to the mirror to put on some makeup.

The bedroom door opens. "Where are you going?" he asks, with a hint of apprehension in his voice.

"I'm going to work."

"No, you're not."

"Yes, I am." I carry on with my makeup, ignoring his imposing body behind me. The no touching will be killing him, especially now when he wants to restrain me.

"How's your back?"

I flick my eyes to his. "Sore," I reply, loading my voice with warning. I take my attention back to the mirror and weep on the inside for the man standing behind me, who really doesn't know what to do with himself. His way of dealing with my defiance is off-limits. He's truly stumped. I finish up with my makeup and start putting my bag together. "Where's my phone?" I ask as he lingers behind me.

"It's charging in my office."

I'm surprised he volunteered that information. "Thank you." I pick my bag up and walk to the door but jump back when Jesse lands in front of me, blocking my path.

"Let's talk." He spits the words out like they are garbage in his mouth. "Please, don't go. I'll talk."

"You want to talk?"

He shrugs sheepishly. "Well, I can't fuck any sense into you, so I guess I'll have to talk some into you."

"That is the conventional way of dealing with things, Jesse."

"Yes, but my way is much more fun." He gives me that roguish grin, and I fight to keep the smile from twitching the corners of my lips. I need to keep this serious. He takes my hand and moves into me. "I've never had to explain my life to anyone, Ava. It's not something I relish the thought of talking about."

"I'm not marrying someone who refuses to open up. You keep holding information back and then we end up in a huge mess."

"I know." He sighs. "Ava, you know more about me than any other living soul. I've never been close to anyone, not like you. You don't tend to get caught up in conversation and life stories when you're just fucking someone."

I wince at the reminder of his dabbling days, which have only recently ended. "Don't say things like that."

He tugs me toward the bed. "Sit," he orders, pulling me down. He takes a steadying breath. "The last time I saw my parents it didn't go particularly well. My sister was a bit underhanded and set us up to meet. My father had a rant, my mother got upset, and I got very drunk, so you can imagine how it ended."

"So your sister obviously wants you to make amends." My voice is small but hopeful.

"Amalie is a bit stubborn." He sighs, and I laugh on the inside. Like brother like sister! "She won't accept that too much has happened, too many harsh words exchanged over the years." He looks up at me and I see anguish in his eyes. "It's not fixable, Ava."

"But they're your parents." I can't imagine my life without my mum and dad. "You're their son."

He offers me a half-smile, a smile that suggests I just don't get it, which is fine because I absolutely don't.

He sighs. "That invitation only arrived because my sister sent it behind my parents' backs. They don't want me there. Their address was scrubbed off and replaced with Amalie's."

"But Amalie obviously wants you there. Don't you want to see her get married?"

"I would love to see my little sister get married, but I also don't want her wedding ruined. If I go, it will end only one way. Trust me."

"What happened to make it like this?"

His shoulders drop spectacularly and he starts circling his thumbs over my hands. I can see this is painful for him, which makes it all the more frustrating to me because it shows that he *does* care.

"You already know that my Uncle Carmichael left me The Manor when he died. Things were already strained after my parents moved to Spain and I chose to stay with Carmichael. I was eighteen and living at The Manor. I understand that it was any parents' worst nightmare." He laughs lightly. "I slipped into a playboy lifestyle and fell harder when Carmichael died. If it wasn't for John, there probably wouldn't be a Manor. He practically ran it while I gorged on too much drink and too many women."

"Oh," I whisper. He gorged? I prefer dabbled.

"I calmed it down, but my parents offered me an ultimatum: The Manor or them. I chose The Manor. Carmichael was my hero, I couldn't sell up." He finishes his little speech with utter finality.

"Your parents knew you were carrying on…" I clear my dry throat. "Well, like you were?" I can't say it. It makes me feel sick.

"Yes, and they predicted it, so you see, they were right and they've never let me forget it. I've lived a pretty sordid lifestyle, I admit that. Carmichael was the family black sheep. No one spoke to him and the family disowned him. They were embarrassed of him and then he died and I filled his shoes. My parents are ashamed of me. That's it."

I recoil at the last part. "They shouldn't be ashamed of you."

"It's just the way it is."

"So you've known John a long time?" If he helped run The Manor in the early days, we're talking sixteen-ish years.

"Yes, a long time." He smiles fondly. "He was great friends with Carmichael."

"How old is he?"

He looks up and frowns. "Fifty-ish, I think."

"Well, how old was Carmichael?"

"When he died? Thirty-one."

"That young?" I blurt. I imagined him to be a long silver-haired, tanned, smarmy type.

He laughs at my stunned face. "There were ten years between my father and Carmichael. He was an afterthought on my grandparents' part."

"Oh." I do a quick mental calculation. "So, there were only ten years between you and Carmichael, too."

"He was more like a brother."

"How did he die?" I'm probably pushing my luck now, but I'm intrigued. I'm beginning to build a picture of Jesse's history, and now I'm like a dog with a bone.

Sadness washes over Jesse's face. "In a car accident."

"Oh," I whisper, but then realization dawns, and my eyes drift down his stomach, lingering in the area where I know his scar to be. Jesse was in the car with Carmichael. All of those times I've probed him and badgered him about it, he said it was too painful to talk about and it really is.

"Don't go to work." He pulls me over onto his lap with care and nuzzles my nose with his. "Stay at home and let me love you. I want to take you out for dinner this evening. I owe you some special time."

I melt all over him. My newfound knowledge, coupled with his reasonableness, refuses to let me say no. "I go back to work tomorrow," I say assertively. I need to resolve some work-related issues, namely Mikael.

"Fine." He rolls his eyes. "Right, I'm going for a run to alleviate some of the pressure that my challenging temptress presents me with, and then we snuggle all afternoon and go out for dinner. Deal?"

"Deal, but I challenge the middle part of that statement and trump it with a deluded god."

He gives me his smile, reserved only for me, and falls back onto the bed cautiously. "Kiss me, now," he demands, and I dive straight in with an appreciation kiss. He's opened up, and I feel so much better. Basking on Central Jesse Cloud Nine has resumed.

CHAPTER THIRTY-THREE

Good morning, baby."

I open my eyes wide in alarm. Morning? "It's not, is it?"

"No, it's five o'clock. You've been asleep all afternoon. How does your back feel?" He crawls up the bed, completely naked, until he is lying flush with me, and I marvel at the beads of water glimmering on his firm shoulders and chest. He's shaved. He smells divine.

I wriggle a little. "It feels okay." I turn into his chest to get a hit of his yummy scent.

"Just think, if you gave up work, you could do this every day. How perfect would that be?"

"For you," I grumble. "Perfect for you because you'll know where I am all the time." I push my lips into his chest, contemplating that he might just get his way. I know Patrick well, but not well enough to be confident that he would send Mikael packing when I tell him what's going on.

"Exactly." He threads his fingers through my hair. "You could come to work with me and we would never have to be apart."

"You would get sick of me."

"Not possible. Are you going to let me take you out for dinner?"

"Or we could just stay right here." I slide my hand over his stomach and brush over his scar.

"Nothing would please me more, but I would like to take you out. Do you mind?" he asks, rather reasonably.

That's not like him at all. And him turning down the opportunity to keep me in bed? I'm suspicious.

"But then again," he whispers, "I've not been inside you for way too long. That is not acceptable." He eases me over onto my back gently. "Baby, sleepy sex is off the menu for a while, so I'm just going to fuck you. Any objections?" He rests his body half on mine, his eyes instantly smoking out. That, mixed with his lurid words, has me whipped into a lustful frenzy.

"You're asking if you can fuck me?" I'm full of suspicion.

His eyes dance with mischief as he kisses the corner of my mouth and then the other corner. "Watch your mouth. I'm trying to be reasonable." He circles his groin and hits me in just the right spot.

"Don't be!" I blurt.

He pulls back, his perfect frown line perfectly in place. He ponders my demand for a few seconds. "You don't want me to be reasonable?"

"No." I'm getting a little breathy. He knows exactly what he's doing.

"So, let me clarify. I'm a little confused." He rolls his hips into me, unearthing a persistent thump in my groin. "You really don't want me to be reasonable?"

Thrust!

"No!"

"I see." He slips his finger into the edge of my knickers and skims my tight bud of nerves lightly, sending me through the roof. "Carte blanche?"

"Yes!"

"Well, now you're just giving me mixed signals," he says, all controlled as he slips his thumb across my flesh. "I love how wet you are for me."

My spine bows, all of the discomfort of my back replaced with sexual anticipation. I'm bubbling. He inserts one long finger and pushes up on the front wall of my entrance. "Soft, hot, and made just for me." He yanks the cup of my bra down with his spare hand and flicks my already stiff nipple into a bullet. "My mark's fading," he muses as he latches onto my breast, biting and sucking. "We don't want you forgetting who you belong to, do we?"

I moan as he replaces one finger with two.

"Do we, Ava?"

"No." I breathe.

He clamps down on my nipple and scrapes his teeth over the end, sending shots of pleasure straight down to my core. "I love how receptive you are to my touch. It gives me the power." Two fingers turn into three, and with his back in such a mess, I resort to grasping the sheets. "Does that feel good?" He works his fingers in and out of me, circling and thrusting as he watches me undulate under him.

"So good." My voice is quivering, just like my body. I really need this.

"Open your eyes, Ava. Let me see them when you come for me."

I peel my eyes open and locate his gaze as he continues to work me up into a despairing mess. "Kiss me," I order, my hips meeting his hand thrusts. I'm going to fall apart and I need his mouth on me.

"Who has the power, Ava?" he asks under half-hooded eyes. "Tell me who has the power."

"You do."

"Good girl." He lifts up and smashes his lips to mine, circling his thumb on my tight knot of nerves, prompting my hands to fly to his hair and grab on for dear life as he kisses me hard, working me to climax. His tongue rolls around my mouth, firm but slow, harsh but worshipfully. He's reminding me.

His firm chest pressed into my side, his wonderful mouth all over mine, and his long, talented fingers working me has my body solidifying, my mind going blank, and my soul reinstated. I'm complete again. A long rippling wave whips through me, and I gasp into his mouth, my body shaking uncontrollably as I hit my climax.

"Only for me." He growls the words I know he absolutely means, his carnal possession of my body making me weak with lust. "Only ever for me, do you understand?"

"Yes." I sigh, and go lax beneath him, the roaring blood starting to clear from my ears.

"Up you get." He links my arms around his neck. "Get those fabulous legs around my waist."

I conform and wrap myself around him, letting him lift me from the bed. He strides toward the bedroom door. "Where are we going?" I ask, hope blossoming at the potential of a Jesse-style row.

"My office."

"Wait!" I shout abruptly.

He halts instantly. "What's the matter?"

"Take me to the wardrobe."

"Why?"

"Because we need a condom."

"What?"

"We need a condom," I repeat, even though I know damn well he heard me right.

"I don't have any."

"You do. In the wardrobe." I should be flying off the handle at him; his tense body suggests he is fully expecting it. He knows that I know.

"Ava, I don't do condoms with you."

"Then we don't have sex." I shrug against him. He's so digging himself a hole.

"Excuse me?" He pulls back and hits me with a disgusted look.

I'm fighting to maintain a straight face when I should be furious at the potential of him hiding my pills. "You heard."

His disgusted look transforms into a mighty scowl. "For fuck's sake." He makes for the wardrobe with me in his tight clinch, releasing one arm and locating the condoms he claimed he didn't have while grumbling the whole time.

"You know, my mark is fading, too," I say, looking down at his pec as he takes us from the bedroom.

His scowl disappears and he smirks at me "It is?"

"It needs freshening up." I raise my eyebrows and watch in lustful delight as his eyes darken further.

"My girl is possessive. Knock yourself out, baby."

I grin and sink my teeth into his pec, and a small moan escapes his lips as I'm carted downstairs and straight into his office. "I want to take you right here, so whenever I have to work, I will see you spread naked on my desk." He lowers me onto his big wooden desk and chucks the box of condoms down before sinking himself into his leather office chair. He's completely naked and hard as steel, and my eyes are thrilled as I drag my stare down the full length of him. His fingers hook into the top of my knickers and I brace myself on the edge of the desk to lift my bum so he can draw them down my legs. He opens the top drawer of his desk and drops them in before shutting it again and returning his eyes to mine.

"You've just come all over them." He rests his palms on my thighs. "I want to be able to smell you, too. Spread your legs."

Oh good Lord!

I pull my thighs apart as far as I can, completely exposing myself to him. It's nothing he hasn't seen a million times before, but like this, I feel completely laid bare. The chair rolls forward, and he reaches behind me, gently unclasping my bra strap and pulling it down my arms. My breathing has quickened; I'm ready to go again, but I can tell from his mood and approach that this will be on his terms. He has the power, and seated in that chair, entirely naked, his abdominals tight, his mammoth erection resting on his lower stomach, he looks mighty powerful, too.

"Lean back on your hands." He puts my matching bra in the drawer with my knickers and sits back in his chair.

I lean back, pushing my chest forward. I'm nervous, and I don't know why. He has taken me in all ways, shapes, and forms, in every Jesse temperament I know, but today I'm a little uneasy. He runs his eyes from mine, slowly and leisurely down my body until he comes to rest on my sex. His eyes stay there and he sinks farther into his chair, the reclining mechanism giving under his weight. He's making himself really comfortable. Me? Not so much.

I'm sitting here, as naked as he is, and my heart is hammering out of my chest as I watch him stare at my cleft, utterly rapt. "Why are you nervous?" he asks without lifting his eyes, his deep rolling voice doing nothing to settle me.

"I'm not." It's a feeble reply. I feel wide open and scrutinized, which is ridiculous. There's not a part of me that hasn't had him on it, in it, or over it.

He lifts his eyes to mine and the hardness softens immediately. "I love you."

My entire being relaxes with those three words. "I love you, too."

"Don't ever doubt it."

"I won't. Have you finished with your observations?" I raise a sardonic eyebrow.

"No." He reaches forward and respreads my thighs. I hadn't

realized I had partly closed them. "I'm evaluating my assets." He sits back and resumes his viewing of my most private place.

"I'm an asset?"

"No, you're *my* asset." He keeps his eyes right where they are, and I decide that I may as well drink in my own asset. His flawlessness still makes me salivate. "Would you like to hear my verdict?" he asks.

"I would."

Up come his eyes, and the corner of his mouth lifts. "I'm a very rich man." He rolls his chair forward and picks up my legs by my ankles, resting the soles of my feet on his shoulders. If I was laid bare before, then I have no idea what I would be now. "Don't hold back on me," he chides me on a slight frown. He rests his palms over the tops of my feet and turns his lips onto my anklebone, the hot connection catapulting a pulse up my leg to settle deep in my core.

A small groan seeps from my mouth.

"Push your hair over your shoulders," he commands quietly. I prop myself on one hand and gather my hair from my front, releasing it down my back. "Better. Now I can see *all* of my assets." He nips at my ankle.

I spasm.

"Seeing you turned on and knowing it's me who makes you like this is the most gratifying feeling." He reaches his hand out and runs his middle finger up my center, finishing with a light pressure at the top of my clit.

My lips part, and tiny, shallow breaths slip from my mouth repeatedly. I shift with the overwhelming need to clamp my legs shut.

"Keep them open, Ava. I want to see your flesh pulsating under my touch when you come for me." His throaty tone spikes my want of explosion under his intense touch and equally intense eyes.

He trades one finger for two and scissors my clit slowly. My head drops back. I moan. I know I'm committing a massive transgression.

"Eyes, baby. Keep your eyes on me."

"I'm close," I whimper.

"I know, but I'll stop unless you get your eyes back on me. Listen to me, Ava. Show me those beautiful eyes."

I pull my heavy head back up with a massive effort as I tremble under his touch. Our eyes lock, and he increases his strokes, his lust-filled eyes and parted lips relaxing my body and escalating my pleasure. The only movements coming from him are his fingers at my core gliding up and down, his pulsing cock, and the sharp rise of his chest. And then he turns his lips onto my ankle and grazes his teeth across the surface.

I'm a goner.

I bite back a scream and push into Jesse's shoulders with my feet as I'm assaulted from every angle by a surge of pressure that explodes and turns my body into a nonresponsive mass of twitching nerves.

"There it is." He breathes, kissing my foot and sliding his finger up my cleft. "Ava, you're throbbing. It's fucking perfect."

My breasts are rising and falling, my skin clammy, and my muscles are contracting harshly. He's watching me ride out my climax, sitting back with his stare firmly in place at my entrance. The appreciation in his eyes is something else.

"Come here." He puts his hands out and I take them, releasing my feet from his shoulders, my legs folding under me so I straddle his lap and hold on to the back of the chair. "Lift," he speaks quietly.

"Condom." I'm panting.

"Ava, don't ask me to wear a condom." He's almost begging.

"Jesse, do you realize how lucky we are that I'm not already pregnant?" Introducing a child into our relationship? That would qualify as beyond stupid.

He shakes his head and pulls me down, positioning himself, but I tense up, trying my hardest to prevent him from entering me. He looks up at me, and his eyes tell me everything I need to know. I push his hand away from under me and settle back down, minus one Jesse buried inside me. I keep my eyes on his, but they drop a little. He knows I've got him.

I turn and pick one of the foil packets from the box and then slide down until I'm kneeling on the floor between his thighs. He watches me rip the packet open and slide out the condom before I reach forward and gently grasp his cock, slip it over his head, and negotiate it down the full length of his shaft. We're both silent as I crawl back up his body and position myself back on his lap.

I raise myself, pushing forward so my breasts are within licking distance of his mouth. He takes full advantage, flashing a knowing smile and swirling his hot tongue around each nipple before clamping his teeth on the ends in turn. I've had two roaring orgasms, and with his teeth latched onto my nipple, there will be a third on the way soon. How does he do this to me?

I feel his hand under my backside, and he positions himself under me, the strange sensation of latex skimming my thigh. "Lower gently." His short, sharp instruction is delivered in a voice that, no mistaking, holds all of the power.

I do as I'm told, sinking slowly down onto him, and his steel rod of flesh finds my passage and slips past as he draws in a long, controlled breath. His head sinks back into the chair and mine drops onto his forehead, my eyes closed. I'm completely impaled by him. It doesn't feel the same, but it's still him inside me.

"Hold still." His minty breath heats my face as he wraps his big palms around my waist.

I wait. I can feel him pulsing inside me, and it takes every bit of strength I have not to contract around him. He needs a moment.

"You feel so perfect around me. How long do you think you could stand this without responding?" He pecks my lips and trails his tongue across my bottom lip. I wouldn't be able to hold back for long at all. I push my mouth to his, but he tuts and turns his face from me. "Not long then."

I pull back and he returns his face forward. "You're denying me," I say softly.

"It's a challenge."

"You're a challenge." I breathe and drop my face back down to try and claim him, but he turns his face again. I try to instigate some movement by rolling my hips, but he clamps his hands around my waist. It doesn't take much of his strength to hold me still.

"You need me." His voice is raspy, sexy as hell, and doing me no favors as I work hard to control my breathing, his cock still jerking wildly inside me.

"I need you." I know that these words mean more to him than I love you. His satisfied expression only confirms it. I lean forward to capture his lips, but he turns his face again. "How would you feel if anyone stopped you from kissing me?" I ask.

"Deadly," he states on a growl, returning his eyes to mine. He loosens his grip on my waist, and I take advantage of his lack of hold, bearing down on a moan. His eyes clench and reopen.

"Me too," I say firmly, following it up with a grind against his hips.

His cheeks puff out, and his hands shift to my hip bones, halting me in my tempting tactics. "Who has the power, Ava?"

"You."

His eyes twinkle. "Do you want me to fuck you?"

"Yes."

"Right answer." He lifts my hips and rams upward, yanking

me down on a guttural bark. I scream and grab the back of the chair. "Like that?" he asks as he withdraws and rams straight into me again.

"Oh God, yes!" My head rolls, my eyes close.

"Eyes!" he barks on another crash of our hips. "Feel it, Ava. Do you feel it?"

I drag my eyes open, my vision blurred. The pure, carnal, possessive expression on his handsome face makes me feel like the most desired creature alive. "I feel it."

He groans and smashes upward over and over, lifting and yanking me back down to meet every punishing advance of his hips. A sheen of sweat materializes on his brow, his jaw is clenched, and the vein in his neck is bulging. I grip tighter on the back of the chair, turning my knuckles white. I want to kiss him, but for one, he hasn't said I can, and two, our mouths will never stay joined. My core is twitching, the overused, overworked bud of nerves screaming for a break from such intensity, but I need one more—just one more.

"I'm close." My desperate words are disconnected and hardly decipherable. "Jesse, I'm close!"

"Wait!" He grates, and smashes upward again. The grip he has on my hips is nearly painful. "You'll wait."

"I can't," I cry, and he stops instantly, the lack of friction and rhythm chasing my orgasm away.

"You'll wait," he pants. He's twitching like mad within me, his breathing heavy and labored. "Control it, Ava."

"I can't control anything with you." I rest my head on his shoulder as the fire in my groin cools slightly.

"I know." He turns his face into my hair and kisses me. "I own you, so I'll control it." He circles his hips gently, stirring my abandoned orgasm. I can't argue with that claim. He totally owns me, and I'm under no illusion that he's talking only of my impending climax.

"I love you," I murmur against his damp shoulder.

He sighs. "I love you, too, baby. Shall we come together?"

"Please."

"Put those lips on me."

I slide my lips across his neck, to his jaw, straight onto his mouth, and he starts a lazy, languid rocking of my hips, back and forth, as I drown in his mouth's attention to mine.

Gentle Jesse—it's like I'm in a relationship with a dozen different men.

"Hmmm. You're delicious," he says. "I can feel you tightening around me. It feels so good." He guides my hips, grinding us together.

"You feel good." I clench my thighs and move my hands to his hair to pull him closer.

"Come for me." He delivers a few measured rotations, followed by a flick of his hips, and I roll gently over the edge on a long, satisfying groan into his mouth, my third release of the session not as body splitting, but no less earth moving or fulfilling. "Oh Jesus." His body goes rigid. I can't feel the sensations of his hot cum flooding me, but all the other signs of his climax are there. He holds me still in his arms. "You. Are. Amazing."

I grab onto his jerking cock greedily and draw him into me. It's pleasure embodied. *He* is pleasure embodied. "That was so good," I say, smothering his lips with mine. He lets me have my way, holding me as close as he can get me and circling teasing, feathery strokes on my hip bones. "It wasn't so bad, was it?"

"No, it wasn't, but it's still something between us."

"You want to trample the condom." I grin against his lips.

"I do." He pulls back and smiles. "You need to get ready or we'll be late."

I resume smothering his face. "Where are we going?" I could quite happily stay right where I am. "I'm comfy."

"For dinner. I made a reservation." He laughs lightly and cups my cheeks in his hands, pulling my face away. "Shower."

"Let me love you." I dip down and work my way to his ear, biting down gently.

"Ava," he warns, pulling me from my nuzzling. His eyes flicker with mischief as he reaches forward and traces the edges of his mark on my boob. "You'll always have this." He looks up at me. "Always."

I reach forward and draw my own little circle around my mark on his pec. "You should have your name tattooed on my forehead." I grin. "And then there will be no mistaking who I belong to."

He raises his eyebrows and pouts slightly. "Not a bad idea." He stands with me in his arms, and I resume my customary baby-chimp-style hold.

He takes us back upstairs, maintaining our connection until he reaches the bed, slips out of me, and lowers me gently to the sheets. He shakes his head on a disgusted snort and pulls the condom off, knotting it and chucking it into the bin.

"On your front. I need to cream you." He encourages me over and smoothes his palms over my bum cheeks.

"I need a shower." I sigh.

"I'll do it again after."

"You need cream."

"I'm fine. It's all about you." He settles himself on my bottom and squirts some cream on my back, making my shoulder blades fly up in shock.

"Where was the warning?" I gasp.

"Sorry." He laughs. "This might be cold."

I crane my neck around to look up at him and he dazzles me with his smile, which I know is reserved only for me. "You're so handsome," I mumble dreamily, settling my cheek back on the pillow. "I think I'll keep you forever."

"Okay," he agrees, laughing again.

"Where are you hiding my pills?" I throw the question into the mix casually, and the sudden stilling of his hands tells me I'm so right. He's hiding them, I know he is.

"What are you talking about?"

"I'm talking about the fact that my contraceptive pills have been growing legs and running away, and it's only been happening since I met you."

"Why would I do that?" His hands are moving in slow, cautious circles over my back.

"I'm not going anywhere, if that's what you're worried about."

"No, you're not."

"It's fine. I'll go to the doctor's to replace them," I say casually, and I'll be hiding them. I have no idea what I'm going to do if I am pregnant. Die on the spot, I think. "You'll just have to wear a condom until I can restart my course," I add.

"I don't like wearing condoms with you," he strains the words out.

"We won't be having any sex then," I conclude smugly.

"Watch your mouth!"

I laugh to myself. I don't know why. I should be raging, panicking, worrying. I can't even begin to imagine how he would be with me if I was carrying his child. Holy shit, it would be unbearable. I'd be wrapped in cotton wool, locked in a padded cell, and guarded for nine months. And how would he be with his children if he's like this with me? Waiting for this period is going to be the longest time of my life.

"You okay?" he asks.

"Fine," I answer quickly. "How long has Cathy worked for you?" I ask, diverting the conversation.

"Nearly ten years."

"She's fond of you."

"She is," he says quietly, and I know he feels the same way about Cathy. "Does she know about The Manor? Ouch!"

"Baby, I'm sorry!" His lips fall straight to my back, kissing me better. "I'm sorry, I'm sorry."

"I'm fine. Unravel your boxers." I feel him lift, and then the swift connection of his palm on my bum. "Ouch!"

"Sarcasm doesn't suit you, lady."

"Well?" I ask.

"Well what?"

"Cathy. Does she know?"

"Yes, she knows. It's not some secret society, Ava. There are no cloaks and daggers." He lifts from me. "You're done. Up you get."

"You kept it a secret from me," I mutter indignantly, sitting myself on the edge of the bed.

"That's because I was falling hard and fast in love with you, and it scared me to death to think you would run away from me if you found out." One brow arches accusingly, and I know what's coming next. "And you did."

"It was a bit of a shock." The events following my discovery still make me shudder, and I want to point out that I came back to him after the whole Manor bombshell. It was the drinking that really made me run. "I knew you were experienced, but I didn't anticipate it was because you owned a sex club."

"Hey!" He closes in on me and lowers me to the bed, dropping a kiss on my lips. "Let's not revisit old news. It's all about us, and now and tomorrow and the next day and then the rest of our lives."

"Okay. Kiss me." I grin.

"I'm sorry. Who has the power?" His lips are twitching as his eyes flick from mine to my lips.

"You do."

"Good girl." He drowns me in his mouth, giving me exactly

what I want, but all too soon he pulls away and I express my
annoyance with an over-the-top huff. "I'm ignoring you. Wear
your new cream dress." He gets up and leaves me to shower and
prepare for dinner.

*   *   *

I walk into the kitchen feeling very special in my new cream
dress, narrow gold belt, and new cream heels. My hair is swishing across my back, and my makeup is light. I skid to a halt
on my heels as I get my first eyeful of Jesse. He's on his phone,
listening intently, and he looks mouthwatering in his navy suit
and pale pink shirt. My roving eyes work their way from his tan
Grensons, up his long, lean legs, past his firm, perfectly toned
chest, and to his clean-shaven, devastating face. He's scowling.

I frown at him, and his eyes soften as he perches on a stool and
pats his thigh. I wander over and rest myself on his lap while I
search through my bag to find my gloss. His face goes straight
into my hair on an inhale, and his arm snakes around my waist
pulling me closer.

"So, what can you tell me other than that?" He's speaking
with little civility.

I turn and give him a questioning look as I sweep my gloss
wand across my lips. He ignores my obvious curiosity and kisses
me lightly on the cheek.

"It's fucking convenient that the other camera is broken," he
says shortly. "Have you checked the footage from outside the bar?"

Oh no!

He seems to take a relaxing breath. I squeeze his thigh and he
looks at me, then kisses my forehead. "Fine, let me know what
you find." He chucks his phone on the work top and it slides a
good few feet. "It's a fucking joke."

"You think it was Mikael in the footage, don't you?"

"Yes, I do."

"Do you think he drugged me?"

"I don't know, Ava." He sounds completely deflated.

"It's a bit farfetched, isn't it?"

"He hates me, Ava. He knows you're my Achilles' heel. He's been waiting for this."

I stand, turning to face him. "Should we go to the police?" I ask. Jesse's concern is really concerning me now.

"No." He shakes his head. "I'm dealing with it."

"Okay," I say quietly. I'm not arguing with him on this.

He smiles mildly, then narrows his eyes on me playfully. "I like your dress." His hand slides up the inside of my thigh and sweeps through the seam of my knickers.

"I like my dress, too." Damn, I'm panting again. My bag tumbles to the kitchen floor, and I grab the front of his suit jacket.

He slips his finger out and brings it up to my mouth, wiping the wetness straight across my freshly glossed lips. "I'm a very lucky man." He pulls me onto his lap and tilts me back, pushing his lips against mine on a long, lingering, sensual kiss. When he's taken what he wants, he pulls back and flashes me his smile, reserved only for me.

I return it, running my thumb across his full bottom lip. "That color doesn't suit you."

"No?' He pouts, and I laugh. He stands me up before grabbing the remote control for the sound system. "I want to dance with you."

"You do?"

"I do."

I smile when Foster the People's "Pumped up Kicks" fires from the speakers very loudly. Oh, he *really* wants to dance. I'm yanked into his chest, his palm rests on my lower back, and his spare hand grasps mine.

I place my other hand on his shoulder and look up at him on a smile. "You make me so happy."

His eyes twinkle, his luscious lips tipping at the corner. "I'm going to make you happy for the rest of my life, baby. Let's dance." He starts stepping backward out of the kitchen, and as soon as we're in the vast open space of the penthouse, I'm immediately twirled out and brought back in again before he starts guiding me around the room. I laugh and look up into his shining pools of green pleasure as I'm weaved between the furniture and twirled around while he smiles down at me. I'm guided from one end of the penthouse to the other, out onto the terrace, around the decking before being taken back inside.

"What are we doing?" I ask as we circle the sofa again.

"I don't know. Something between a waltz and a quickstep, I think." He grins at me as I continue to follow his lead. His eyes look like they could explode with happiness. "I think I enjoy this just as much as being buried inside you."

"Really?" I ask, completely shocked.

"No." He frowns. "That's probably the stupidest thing I've ever said."

My head falls back on a laugh, and he leans down, resting his lips on my throat as he directs me back into the kitchen. He lifts me up to his body, and my legs curl around his tight hips, my hands finding his hair. I hold his gaze and he stops his movements, studying me closely before placing me gently on the counter.

His palms cup my cheeks, his stare seeping into my eyes. He really doesn't need to say anything, but I know he will. It's like he wants to demonstrate how good he is at his newfound talent. He talks to me now.

His thumbs smooth over my skin. "Who has the power, Ava?"

I roll my eyes. "You do."

"You're wrong."

"I am?" I blurt. He holds the power. He's made that perfectly clear.

"You are." He smiles, and I frown. "You're the one with the power, baby."

"But you always insist it's you who holds the power."

He shrugs. "I like you stroking my ego."

I start laughing. "Are you joking?"

"No."

I stop laughing when he doesn't join me in my humor, even though it's pretty damn humorous. He burns holes through me with his stunning eyes.

"I hold the power over your body, Ava. When those beautiful eyes are full of lust for me, that's when I hold the power." He releases my cheeks and skates his palms up the insides of my thighs.

I tense, my mouth parting, my hands shooting up to clench his suit jacket in my fists.

He smiles, leaning in and placing his lips gently on mine. "See," he whispers, removing his hands from my thighs and then prying my grip from his chest. "The power's yours again."

I study him on a half-smile, completely getting it. "That's why you fuck me senseless, give me the countdown, and demand I kiss you when I'm mad."

He smiles. "Watch your mouth."

"You've completely exposed yourself. I'm never going to let you touch me again!"

He laughs, really hard. His chest expands and he throws his head back. I think I already knew that. That's why I run at the start of the countdown. I know what he's capable of when he gets his hands on me. His head comes back down, his eyes scanning my face.

"Well, Mr. Ward, given how much sex we have, I'd say you're the majority shareholder of power in this relationship."

I grin when he starts with the laughing again. It's a wonderful sight, the faint lines fanning his greens, making his eyes sparkle. "Baby, we will never have enough sex."

"That makes you a very powerful man then."

"Oh Jesus, Ava." He sweeps my hair away from my face and cups my cheeks. "I love you so fucking much. Kiss me."

"Feeling weak?"

He leans in. "I am." His lips brush gently over mine and I indulge him, handing him the control he craves, letting his tongue saturate my senses as he hums into my mouth and draws all of the power from me.

"Better?" I ask around his lips.

"Much. Come on, lady, we have a date." He places me on my feet before turning the music off and scooping my clutch from the floor. "Ready?"

"Oh, let me show you the message." I take my bag and retrieve my phone. I had almost forgotten about that.

"What message?" he asks on a frown. He clearly has, too.

"The one sent from John's phone." I scroll through my phone, my heart beating nervously. This is it. This is the moment I get this off my chest. I have it plain and clear, so he can't possibly argue with it. John wouldn't do this. "There." I hold my phone up to him and he takes it. His frown line creeps across his brow as he reads the message, a thoughtful look plaguing his expression. His eyes flick to mine and back to the screen. He's really thinking about this.

After what seems like forever, with me tense and him staring at the screen, he starts nodding mildly. "I'll be dealing with this." He tosses my phone on the counter. He doesn't look very happy at all.

I sag a little in relief. I think I almost expected him to defend her or say that it must have been someone else, but who else would do that? I don't need to say anything more. He knows, and I'm so relieved.

My phone starts singing and I scoop it up from the counter. Seeing Ruth Quinn's name flashing up on the screen, I let out a tired sigh and reject the call. She'll soon call the office and find out that I'm off work today.

"Who's that?"

"A new client. A pain in the arse new client."

He takes my phone and slides it back on the work top, then pulls me into his chest. "No work today. Are you ready for our date?"

I nod into his chest. "Yes."

His lips press into the top of my head and he releases me, holding his arm out in a very gentlemanly manner. I smile, thread my arm through his, and let him lead me out of the pent-house to the elevator.

We reflect in all of the mirrors around us. Everywhere I look, I can see him in all of his beauty, and me with my hand slipped under his suit jacket, unwilling to let him go. He glances down at me out the corner of his eye. "I should make you give me an apology fuck here and now," he says in a low, quiet voice.

"Do I owe you an apology?"

"You do." He returns his eyes forward, and I find them in the reflection of the doors.

"What for?" I quickly scan my mind for anything he might be referring to, and I come up with—in Jesse's world—way too much for him to hold against me. But this morning I've been compliant, and he has been quite reasonable.

"You owe me an apology for making me wait too damn long for you." His face is completely straight and his words full of meaning.

I smile and tuck myself into his side. I've not really had to wait very long for him at all, two crappy relationships aside. While he was battling numerous demons, I was blissfully unaware and going through the motions of any normal young woman. It's a strange thought.

The elevator door opens, and his arm drapes gently around my shoulder as we walk through the foyer of Lusso. "Clive." Jesse nods at the concierge, who nods brusquely in return before he continues with something that has his attention on his desk.

We emerge into the cool evening air and Jesse bleeps the DBS. "Oh, Kate rang. You should probably call her back."

"You answered my phone again?" I ask, but he just shrugs off my accusation.

I sigh and open my bag to retrieve my phone, but after a little rummage, I discover no phone. "Jesse, I've left my phone in the tower."

He makes a long, exaggerated point of demonstrating the inconvenience I'm causing. "Here." He passes the keys. "Hurry up or we'll be late for dinner."

"I'll be quick." I race off, back into the foyer of Lusso, throw a frown at Clive, who still ignores me, and press the code for the elevator. Why is it not on the ground floor still? I wait impatiently for it to return to base, then jump in.

I exit before the doors have completely opened and shove the key in the door, leaving it in the lock as I run into the kitchen. But I skid to a halt on a shocked gasp when I see two people sitting on barstools, both looking really very menacing.

CHAPTER THIRTY-FOUR

W hat...how...when..." I stammer and stutter all over the place. Where did they come from?

"Hello," Mum says, short and sharp. My dad just sits there shaking his head.

I can't work out if she's mad or not. I want to dive on them both and squeeze the life out of them; I've not seen them for weeks and here they are, but I can't gauge their moods.

"How did you get in here?" I manage to get a full sentence out.

"Oh, didn't you know? Your father is a retired cat burglar." Mum's perfectly threaded eyebrow raises at me, and Dad sits there looking all disapproving and moody.

"Mum?" I frown.

She sighs and stands. "Ava O'Shea, get your backside over here and give your mother a hug." She holds her arms out to me.

I burst into tears.

"I knew she would do that!" my dad grumbles. "Bloody women!"

"Shut up, Joseph." She gestures with her arms again, and I walk straight into them, sobbing like a child and wincing slightly as she rubs my back warmly. "Oh, Ava. What are you crying for? Stop it, you're setting me off."

"I'm so pleased to see you," I blubber into my mum's gray blazer and hear my father huffing his displeasure at the two women in his life bawling and sniveling. He's never been one for showing his emotions, finding any sort of affection highly uncomfortable.

"Ava, you couldn't avoid us forever, even if we are miles away. Let me look at you." She pulls me away from her body and wipes my tears away.

There is no denying I'm my mother's daughter. Her eyes mirror mine, all big and chocolaty, and her hair, which matches mine in color, is cut into a short, sweeping style. She looks good for forty-seven—really good.

"You have sent me and your dad wild with worry these last few weeks."

"I'm sorry. I've had a crazy few weeks." I try and sort myself out. My mascara is probably running down my cheeks, and I seriously need to blow my nose. "Hold up." I look at my mum and then my dad, who shrugs his big shoulders on a grunt. "How did you really get in?" I've been so blindsided with shock and emotion, I've forgotten that we're standing in Jesse's ten-million-pound penthouse.

"I invited them."

I swing around and find Jesse standing in the archway entrance with his hands resting loosely in his trouser pockets. "You never said," I splutter. I'm confused.

"I didn't want to row over it," he shrugs. "They're here now."

I look at my mother, who is smiling brightly, and I'm mortified to see that she's obviously affected by Jesse. I don't know why I'm mortified; he draws the same reaction from all women, and I need to remember that my mother is nearer to Jesse's age than I am.

"Urmm, Mum, Dad. This is Jesse." I gesture between them. "Jesse, this is my mum and dad. Elizabeth and Joseph." I hadn't planned for it to be like this. I hadn't planned it at all, actually.

"We've met," Jesse says.

My eyes fly to his. "What?"

"We've met," he repeats himself, which is not necessary, because I heard the first time.

His lips are twitching. Okay, I'm thoroughly confused. He sighs and walks toward us until he's standing in front of me, a bit close for comfort, considering my parents are just there and this is all a bit of a shock for them. And for me.

"I didn't go for a run this morning," he says.

"You didn't?" I frown. "You had your running kit on."

He laughs lightly. "I know. It's not what I would have chosen to wear to meet your parents, but desperate times." He shrugs.

"You're making up for it now, Jesse." My mum pats his suit-clad arm, and my mouth drops open.

What the fuck is going on here? I want to swear my head off, but my mum hates swearing just as much as Jesse. "I'm sorry." I reach up and rub my temples. "I'm confused."

"Sit." Jesse takes my arm and leads me over to a stool, taking a seat next to me. Mum resumes position next to Dad. "I spoke to your mum late last night. She was understandably worried about you and asked me lots of question." He raises his brow at my mum, who laughs lightly.

"Nosey, isn't she?" Dad tuts, and Mum slaps his shoulder.

"She's my little girl, Joseph."

"Anyway," Jesse continues, "I thought it was best for them to come and see for themselves that I'm not a raving loon, keeping you captive in our tower. So, here they are."

"Here we are," Mum sings. She clearly has no issues with the stunning man who is gently stroking my hand.

I try and recover from the shock. "So, you met them this morning? Why?"

"I felt I needed to explain myself," Jesse says. I look at him and could weep. I can't believe he's done this. "Ava, neither of us anticipated each other and for very different reasons. I know your parents' opinion means a lot to you, and as it means so much to you, it means a lot to me, too. My priority is you. You're all that matters to me. I love you."

I hear my mum hit the deck in her mental faint, and my dad, although emotionally detached, gives an approving nod. "All any father wants is for his daughter to be taken care of." Dad reaches over and puts his hand out to Jesse. "I believe you'll do good."

Jesse accepts my dad's offering. "It's my full-time job." Jesse smiles, Mum swoons, and I laugh.

Good God!

Jesse raises a sardonic eyebrow at me. He knows what I'm thinking. Are my mum and dad aware of how serious he is when he says that? I have to commend Jesse on his speech, though. He's won them over fair and square, and I do feel like I've had a huge burden lifted from my shoulders, but I'm conscious that they don't know Jesse's business nature and what he did when he drank. Or about the punishment he subjected himself to because he thought he had failed me, because he thought he deserves retribution—or the fact that I could be pregnant. I could go on forever. That's a whole other weight on my shoulders. Did he explain to them about the drinking? After Matt's call to them, they must be wondering.

Mum gets down from her stool and makes her way around the island, her eyes all glazed. "Come here, you silly sod!" She pulls me down from the stool and throws her arms around me. I hiss a few times, clenching my eyes shut. "You've got yourself in a right pickle. You've fallen in love, Ava. You should have told me."

Oh, I have got myself in a pickle, but for a whole lot more reasons than she knows.

"Right, are we eating or what? And I'm gagging for a pint." My dad drags me back to the here and now.

Mum releases me and straightens herself out. "Do you mind if I use your bathroom, Jesse?" she asks.

"Sure. Do a right and an immediate right again. By the gym. Knock yourself out."

"Pardon?" Mum blurts.

I laugh.

"I'm sorry." He smiles, flicking his eyes to me, then back to my mum. "Go for it. Like I said, right and right again. By the gym."

"Oh, thank you." Mum gives me an *oh-the-gym* look and grabs her purse from the work top, leaving me, Jesse, and my dad to make small talk.

"So, what do you drive?" Dad starts, and I groan. Dad's passion for big, expensive cars is going to be fed good and proper now.

Jesse pulls me back onto the stool. "A DBS."

"Aston Martin?"

"That's it."

"Nice." Dad nods and does a rubbish job of showing disinterest. "And the hotel is in the Surrey Hills?"

Jesse must feel me go rigid because he squeezes me slightly. "It is. I'll show you one day, perhaps on your next visit."

"Sure, Elizabeth loves anything luxury." Dad rolls his eyes. My mum is certainly high maintenance. "It's a nice place you have here." Dad looks around the kitchen and then back at Jesse.

"Thank you, but your daughter is responsible for that." He starts curling a lock of my hair around his finger. "I just bought the place."

"So, this is the big project that stole all of your time?" Dad muses. "You did a good job."

"Thanks, Dad." I'm more than relieved when I hear the front doorbell. Dad and small talk are not a match well made.

"Do you want to get that?" Jesse pats my bum and I stand.

"Who is it?"

"I don't know. Go and see." He pushes me away, and I leave Dad and Jesse to continue small talk as I make my way to the front door. No one can come up without knowing the code, so it has to be Clive.

I swing it open and find Dan, Kate, and Sam, all standing in the penthouse foyer, and my first thought is: Dan and Kate within a mile of each other? Bad news. But then Dan steps forward with a big smile on his face, and I all but throw myself on him, forgetting all back pain and awkward tension between him and my best friend.

"What are you doing here?" I squeeze him to me and he laughs.

"I'm doing as I'm told." He fights me off and holds me back. "You look good," he says on a bright smile. "Where's this new bloke I need to give the '*if you hurt her*' speech to?"

A wave of fear flies through me at the thought of Jesse accepting any such speech. "In the kitchen, but you don't need to do that."

He eyes me warily. "It's my job," he states firmly, and then looks past me into the penthouse. "Fucking hell!" he whispers as he cops a load of the space. He drops me and saunters off.

Kate steps forward with a clear look of trepidation on her pale face. She wraps her arms around me. "This has to be the most awkward situation I have ever put myself in," she whispers in my ear. "Fucking hideous."

I laugh. "Ease up on your grip." I shrug her slightly. "Does Sam know?" I whisper back.

"Sorry and no. He's fucking oblivious."

"Hey! Where's the love?" Sam removes Kate and throws his

arms around me gently. "You are one mad woman," he says quietly.

"I know."

"Don't do that again. Now, where's my man?"

"Kitchen."

He drops me and heads for the kitchen. I look at Kate, and she shakes her head. "If I could've got out of this, I would have." She lets out a stressed breath. "Come on." She takes my hand and we go back to the kitchen, finding Jesse making the introductions. Dan's cautious eyes flick between Jesse and Sam for a whole lot of different reasons.

Cathy appears from nowhere with Luigi and three waiters, and Jesse leaves the kitchen island chatter to have a word. I watch as he lets Cathy kiss his cheek, shakes Luigi's hand, and then points around the kitchen and through to the terrace. Cathy shoos him away and gives me a happy wave.

"What's happening?" I ask him when he joins me back by the island.

"We're having dinner."

"Here?"

"Yes, I arranged for Luigi to come in and do the honors. We'll eat on the terrace. It's a nice evening." He places me in front of himself and brushes my hair away from my face.

"I can't believe you did this."

He cocks his head to the side. "Whatever it takes, you know this."

My hands slide up his jacket sleeves to rest on his biceps. "You might get the loving brother speech." I smile apologetically. "Do you think you could humor him?"

His lips press into a straight line. "You mean another man telling me how to look after you? I don't think so."

My shoulders sag slightly. "Whatever it takes?" I whisper his words. I can't even begin to imagine how much it pained him to have to talk to my parents. It goes against all of his natural instincts.

He rests his finger under my chin and drops a light kiss on the corner of my mouth. "Whatever it takes," he confirms. "Come on."

He proceeds to direct everyone out of the kitchen and onto the terrace, where I find everything has been set for a meal. The outside dining table has been superbly laid, the patio heaters have been lit to take the edge off the cool evening air, and bottles of wine and beer are chilling in the drinks fridge by the huge built-in barbeque. I throw Jesse a questioning look. How did he manage all of this? He smiles and gives me a gesture of sleep. While I was snoozing most of the day, he was busy meeting my parents and preparing all of this? I'm still in shock.

I'm in a half trance as the people I love the most in the world converse, chat, laugh, and drink at the table, while Luigi and his staff prepare and serve a luscious Italian feast. Jesse keeps his hand firmly on my knee, choosing to eat one handed, squeezing every so often, particularly harder when Dan commences his older brother speech. I watch Jesse struggle to remain polite, and when my mother catches the line of conversation, I'm immensely grateful for her intervention. She admonishes Dan and smiles sweetly at Jesse before picking up her conversation with Kate, who has eased up slightly, although you can't ignore the tension that is bristling between her and Dan. Sam, however, is completely unaware and doing a good job of making my dad laugh hard with God only knows what stories.

"Kate's not her normal self," Jesse observes quietly, as he tops up my water glass.

"She and Dan have a bit of a history," I reply. "It's complicated."

Jesse's eyebrows rise in surprise. "I see. Did you enjoy your pasta?"

"It was lovely." I rest my hand over his on my knee. "Thank you."

"You are more than welcome." He winks. "Nothing stands in the way now, does it?"

"No, the path is clear." I smile and then melt when he gives me his smile, the one reserved only for me, his eyes twinkling in contentment.

"I'm glad you said that." He stands, halting all conversation at the table, all attention turning to him. He pulls my chair out. "Up you get." I stand on a frown. "Excuse us for a few minutes," he says to our silent guests before leading me away by my hand.

"Where are we going?" I ask his back.

He halts, turns, and drops to his knee in front of me, only a few feet away from the table. I hear my mum's sharp intake of breath and mine that follows shortly after. I look down at him with a gaping mouth and wide eyes as he takes my hand and looks up at me with crystal-clear greens.

"Shall we try this the traditional way?" he asks quietly.

I start to physically shake. "Oh God." I breathe through the melon-sized lump in my throat. I turn slowly and drink in the table and the occupants, all watching intently. My mum has her hand over her mouth, and my dad has a small smile on his lips. Dan is expressionless, and Kate and Sam are relaxed in their chairs with matching grins.

My heart commences to gallop in my chest as I return my body to face Jesse, my glazed eyes to his. He's only just met my parents. He can't land this on me—not in front of them.

"I've trampled them all," his eyes twinkle, "delicately...ish. I've even asked your father." The corner of his mouth lifts into a half-smile, and a small sob escapes my lips. "You must know how hard that was for me." He drops my hand and glides his palms around the backs of my legs to pull me closer, prompting my hands to rest on his shoulders. "Anything it takes, Ava," he whispers.

My hands drift up to find the back of his head, and my fingers thread through his dark blond hair as he looks up at me.

"Marry me, baby."

"You're crazy mad." I sob, bending to kiss him, my hands moving to the side of his face. "You crazy, crazy man."

"Will I be crazy mad and married?" he asks into my mouth. "Please tell me I'll be crazy mad and married to you." His hands pull me down to my knees, and he holds my shoulders firmly, his eyes swimming as he searches my face. "It's all about you and it always will be. For the rest of my life, it's only you. I love you, beyond crazy. Marry me, Ava."

I fall forward onto his chest in a sobbing mess and hear my mum burst into tears.

"Is that a yes?"

"Yes."

I hear his sharp intake of breath. "I can't breathe," he murmurs, falling back, taking me with him so we're sprawled on the terrace floor. He takes my mouth, kissing me adoringly. Once again, my challenging, neurotic ex-playboy will have me wherever and whenever he pleases. And he's completely unashamed of it. "I love you so much." He pulls my hand up and slips my ring back onto my finger before dropping a kiss next to it and engulfing me in his body again, squeezing me hard.

"I love you, too," I whisper in his ear.

"I'm so glad. You're the best birthday present I've ever had."

What?

I pull up and gaze down at him through my glazed eyes. He smiles, almost embarrassed. "It's your birthday?"

"It is." He starts nibbling his lip.

"Today?"

"Yes." He nods as he answers.

I narrow playful eyes on him. "How old are you?"

"I'm thirty-eight."

I break out in a full beam. "Happy birthday."

He blesses me with his smile reserved only for me and pulls me back down to his chest, sinking his nose straight into my neck.

I melt into him.

I love this man, in all of his perfection and in all of his challenging, unreasonable ways. He took me hard and fast. He made me fall in love with him. He made me need him.

He was so unexpected, so passionate, and so absolutely irresistible. And now he is wholly mine, and I am undeniably his.

I finally understand him.

I've finally got beneath this man.

The End

Bonus Scene

JESSE'S POV FOR *BENEATH THIS MAN*: THE WHIPPING

I can't feel the pain of the whip. There's no stinging or stabbing as the leather connects with my back. The only pain I feel is in my heart. It's the crippling agony of failure—failure to protect the only thing in my life of value.

Drink would've numbed this torture, but it also would have caused more pain...more failure. I can barely breathe through my guilt. I can't bring myself to face up to my wrongs—there have been so many—and all are potential triggers to drive my beautiful girl away.

I know Sarah is enjoying this. I saw the delighted sparkle in her sick eyes when she walked in on me with a bottle of vodka hovering at my lips. I could smell the ignorance and escape that bottle would provide, but I could also smell the remorse that would follow.

Punish myself. That's my only option. God knows I've put Ava through enough. And there's more for her to know. That is why I found it so easy to drop the bottle, remove my T-shirt, and fall to my knees. It gives me the opportunity to pray, too.

Even in my trancelike state I know this will never be enough, but I'm at a loss. I don't know what to do to make this better—to make myself miraculously worthy of her love. Maybe

I'm beyond hope. Maybe I'll always fuck up everything good that comes into my life. Maybe this is my penance—God giving me a brief perception of how my life could be, knowing I'll screw it up, leaving me more hollow and lost than before.

Or, maybe one day, I might get something in my life right.

I think I can hear voices. Or am I dreaming?

My back bows sharply, my head flying back as the leather meets my flesh again. I've lost the ability to speak, to make *any* noise, in fact. So what's that sound? It only takes me a split second to realize. It's loud. It's frightened.

It's my angel.

My head whips up, finding Ava in a physical struggle with John. She's screaming, yelling, thumping, and hitting him.

"Ava?" I just about form the single word that usually fills my heart with happiness. Just the sound of her name takes me away from all pain. But not now. She stills at the low husk of my voice, her face turning toward me. The distress and pain etched all over her beautiful features cripples me. She's here. How?

She cries out to me, kicking my dead muscles into action. My need to get to her is desperate. But nothing is working. My legs are like jelly, my mind still partly fogged. She looks me all over before her petite body folds in on itself and she falls to the floor at John's feet.

"Ava?" I finally convince my fucking legs to play ball and get me into a standing position. Fuck, I feel more pissed than any amount of vodka could achieve. I'm hoping this is all a bad dream, but when I shake my head and gain something near to full focus, my heart slows a little. She's sobbing, looking at me with nothing but pure agony gushing from those stunning eyes. "Jesus, no!" I start to rush over but something holds me back. It takes a few desperate moments to realize what. "Get the fuck off me!" I practically throw Sarah away and hurry to my girl. "Ava, baby. What are you doing here?" I join her on the floor, feeling her face out so I can see those eyes. When I find them, I hate what I'm confronted with—more pain. It's intensifying the closer I get, the more I look.

She's pushing me away, making me drop her from my hold. Panic sets in. "Ava, please!" John gets shoved from her path and she disappears through the door. My strength seems to return at the sight of her running away from me again. I push myself to my feet. "Fuck!"

John flicks a concerned face in my direction, weighing up my next move. He knows better than to ask. He takes his big body quickly down the corridor, and I follow.

I can't feel my legs, but they're moving fast. I watch her back disappear into the ladies' bathroom and I steam in after her, John in tow. The sound that greets me punches a hole through my gut. She's being sick.

"Ava!" I should be gently coaxing her from the cubicle, but my fear is growing by the second. I bang. "Ava! Open the door!" I hear shifting, but the door doesn't open. "Please." I let my head meet the door, my palms and chest pressed into the wood, as if this will make me a little bit closer to her. "Ava, please. Open the door."

Nothing.

"Who let her in?" I don't mean to punch the door in anger. "Fuck! Who the fucking hell let her in?"

"Jesse, I didn't let her in. I would never have let her in." John's big palm meets my shoulder, rubbing soothing circles into a piece of flesh that isn't welted. I don't need to look at his face to know he's being up-front.

We both look toward the door when Kate flies in, her pretty face looking back and forth between us. "What's going on? Fuck! Jesse, what the hell has happened to your back?"

"Nothing!" Fuck! I don't want the whole fucking world getting their fill of me and my fuckups.

"Don't fucking talk to me like that. Where's Ava? What the hell is going on? Ava?"

I flinch at her returned harshness, but I'm in no position to call her out on it. I deserve so much more than a tongue-lashing from Ava's best friend. I join her at the door. "She's in there. She won't come out. Ava? Please, Kate, get her out." I bang the door again for no purpose at all. She's not coming out while I'm here. I begrudgingly know that.

"Hey! Tell me why she's locked in there and why you're out here bleeding all over the place?" Ava's spunky friend hits me with a question I can't avoid.

"Ava walked in on something she shouldn't have seen." I'm vague, and Kate's raised brow confirms she's already aware of this. "She's freaked out. I need to see her." My panic is increasing with every second that I can't get to her.

"If you've fucked her over, Jesse!" she shouts. "Ava?"

"No! It's not like that!" My hand finds my hair and yanks. What the hell am I going to do?

"Well, what is it like then? She's in there throwing up. Ava?" Kate starts a gentler tapping of the door. "Ava, come on. Open the door."

"Ava!" I yell. I'll bash the fucking door down if I have to.

"Jesse, just go."

"No!'

"She's obviously not going to come out with you here. Hey, big guy. Get him out of here."

"Jesse?" John starts pulling at my arm, his rumble softer than usual, but there's an edge of *don't fuck with me* in his tone. I might be a nasty fucker when I want to be, but I've seen John in action, and even though I know I'd give him a run for his money, I don't have the physical strength required. He'd flatten me with his thumb. "Let's get you sorted out, you stupid motherfucker."

Reluctantly, I let John lead me from the ladies', hoping my

absence will encourage her out. I give Kate a pleading look, anything to make her see my turmoil. She'll never understand, but worst of all, I know Ava won't either.

John practically drags me back to my office. I can feel the stares of the members, the men probably feeling smug seeing me in such a fucking state over a woman, probably thinking I've got what's been coming for many years. They're all right. The women are probably itching to comfort me, to take my mind off things. It'll never work. If I lose this woman, there's only one thing that'll take away the pain. And I'm more than prepared to do it.

John lets loose once my office door is closed. I stand before his hulking frame and accept the rant I deserve.

"You stupid motherfucker!" His loud boom knocks me back a step. "Of all the fucked-up, sorry shit you do, this takes the fucking biscuit!" He actually prods me in my shoulder, only lightly, but it's enough to make me stagger. "I fucking told you! Stay away from the fucking drink. That didn't mean exchange it for the motherfucking whip!" I glance up and watch as he removes his glasses, something only done when he wants someone to appreciate how fucked off he is. He's *really* fucked off. The shades get pointed at me. "You are your own worst enemy, Jesse."

"I know," I agree quietly. I have no defense, nothing that'll make this acceptable. I'm going to try, though.

Sam's head pops around the door, disturbing us. He smiles a nervous smile, apologizes for the interruption, and then quietly leaves again.

John's attention is fired straight back at the sorry state of a man before him.

Me.

"I told you to put your shirt on. I told you to go back to your girl and make things right, not wallow in your own self-fucking-pity and join Sarah in her fucked-up sadistic shit! Be a fucking man, you stupid motherfucker!' His arms fly up in frustration. "And don't ever fucking question my security!"

"How the fuck did she get in, then?" I shout, John's words reminding me of that little mystery.

"I have no fucking idea, but I'm going to find out, you mark my word."

I'm about to yell some more, until Sam's random visit to my office quickly registers in my screwed-up brain.

"Fuck!" I curse, barging past John and thundering down the corridor. He was checking up on me, making sure I was out of the way, and he was doing it for a reason.

Barreling back through the Manor and in the door of the ladies', I halt when I find her standing and watching me, like she fully expected my arrival. There's a silent understanding that passes between our eyes as we study each other, Kate remaining silently to the side. Not prepared to be deterred, I walk forward and gather her in my arms, leaving the toilets fast. As I make my way to my office, Ava safely in my hold, I feel the most incredible amount of comfort. It's beyond what I could ever describe, and in this moment, I realize that every word that follows next has got to count. I'll *make* them count.

My foot kicks the door of my office shut, and I settle on the sofa, keeping her close, trying hard not to flinch at the contact of leather on my raw flesh. The numbness is fading, being replaced with a sting to accompany my slowing heartbeat. My face instinctively finds the soft skin of her neck, the smell of her hair easing me a little. Her tears, however, don't. "Please don't cry. It's killing me."

"Why?" Her soft question reaches my ears, stupidly catching me off guard. It's a question I should have expected, and it's one that now needs answering.

"I promised you I wouldn't have a drink." My reply is feeble. Perhaps I'm building up the courage to give her the answers she needs and wants—tell her exactly what a fuckup I really am. I mentally pray to God for forgiveness.

"You wanted a drink?"

"I wanted to block it out."

"Look at me," she says harshly, but I can't face her. I can't confront the hurt I've caused. "Damn it, Jesse, look at me!" She's moving, attempting to drag me from my cowardly hiding place. My hiss of discomfort stops her tactics. "Three." Her calm voice makes me go rigid. That and the one word that will lead to the answers much quicker than I'd like. I need to piece this together, make the most of the words I'm about to say. She's using my own manipulation against me. "Two."

"What happens on zero?" I already know the answer to this.

"I leave."

I raise my head fast, the confirmation hurting deeper than I thought it could. "Please don't."

Her face drops, all resentment seeming to fall away at my words. I didn't intend to make her feel guilty. She moves to sit astride me, her arms carefully encasing me. "Tell me what you were blocking out."

"Hurting you."

"I don't understand. I would rather you had a drink."

"You wouldn't." The small ironic laugh isn't stoppable. She really has no idea.

She sits back, determined to meet my eyes. I could never deny her. "I would rather face you with half a vodka distillery inside you than see what I just saw."

My head hangs. "Trust me, Ava, you wouldn't."

"Trust you? Jesse, I feel sick with betrayal." Suddenly, she's removing herself from my body, and the loss of her soft curves against my hard muscle is unbearable. I try to reclaim her but get shrugged off. It slices my soul. "I'm not leaving," she spits, making me retract my hands in shock.

She starts a dogged march around my office, the usual fond sight of her gently tapping her front tooth in thought doing nothing to relax me. My unease doesn't improve when she lowers herself on the opposite sofa, making a point of keeping out of my reach. I'm slowly forming words in my head, words to explain or make her feel better, but they're not in order yet. I'm not sure where to begin. I can do nothing more than watch as she sighs and starts rubbing comforting circles into her temples. I want to do that. I want to do anything I can to make her feel better.

"Is there anything else I need to know?" she asks, watching closely for my reaction to her unexpected question.

I try to hide my tensing body. "Like what?"

The look of disgust on her face is warranted. "I don't know, you tell me." Her arms catapult to the ceiling. "Why would I prefer this to drunken Jesse?"

Gritting my teeth, I move forward, trying to close the space between us. My elbows hit my knees and I mimic Ava's attempt to soothe the brain ache by rubbing circles in my temples, too. "Drink and sex go hand in hand for me." I say the words that'll commence the unraveling of my secrets.

"What does that mean?"

"Ava, I inherited The Manor when I was twenty-one. Can you imagine a young lad with this place and a whole lot of women ready and willing?" I've never felt so remorseful for my selfish ways.

"You mean the dabbling?" Her voice is quiet and cautious. She's already beginning to work this out.

"Yes, the dabbling, but it's all behind me." I move farther forward. "Now, it's all about you." I need her to understand this. It might make the rest easier for her to come to terms with.

"You drank and dabbled?"

"Yes, like I said, drink and sex go hand in hand. Please, come here."

I'm ignored. "So you didn't have a drink because you would have wanted to have sex?"

"I don't trust myself with alcohol, Ava."

"Because you think you will jump the nearest woman?"

Another ironic laugh falls unwittingly from my lips. "I don't think so. I couldn't do that to you." I should stab myself for my nerve and save her the trouble of dealing with this fucked-up arsehole any longer.

Her eyebrows shoot up. "You don't think so?"

"It's not a risk I'm willing to take, Ava." *Not anymore*, I add silently to myself. "I drink too much, lose reason, and women throw themselves at me willingly. You've seen it."

"You didn't look very capable of anything last Friday!" she shouts incredulously.

"Yeah, that's not my normal level of intemperance, Ava. I was on a mind-numbing mission." Shit, how the fuck am I going to do this?

"So, you usually maintain a steady level of drinking and then have lots of sex with lots of willing women? You've never had a drink when you've slept with me?"

I can't do this without contact, so I shove the table aside that's blocking my access and fall to my knees before her. "No, Ava. I have never been under the influence of alcohol when I've had you. I don't need it. Alcohol blocked things out for me, made me forget how hollow my life was. I didn't give a fuck about any of the women I slept with, not one. And then you fell into my life and things changed completely. You brought me back to life, Ava. I never want to touch the drink because if I start, I might not stop, and I never want to miss a moment with you." I'm a bastard. A desperate, hopeless bastard.

I can see the tears forming in her browns. I'm not sure how this can get any worse. "Have you had sleepy sex with anyone else?"

I do a shit job of hiding my exasperation at her silly question, sighing loudly. "No."

"What about a sense fuck?" She looks fierce.

"Ava, no! I've never cared about anyone else enough to need or want to fuck any sense into them." I find her legs and squeeze some reassurance into them. I don't expect it to work, but I'm willing to try anything. "Only you."

My hands are pushed aside and she's on her feet. "So on Thursday in your office, are you telling me that if you had drank the vodka, I would've found you nailing Sarah on your desk, not just looking cozy with her on your desk?"

What? Sarah? Is she insane? I jump up and stalk over to her, taking a firm hold of her small body. "No! Don't be so stupid."

"I don't think I'm being stupid. It's bad enough worrying about you drinking. I don't know if I can cope with the additional worry of you being drunk and wanting to fuck other women!" She's losing control, her scathing words making me jump back in shock, even though I have no right to.

I also have no right to reprimand her on her foul language . . . but I still do. "Will you watch your fucking mouth? It doesn't make me want to fuck other women. It just makes me want to fuck!"

"So I had better ensure that I'm with you when you have a drink then, hadn't I?'

Oh Jesus, yes, she had. But it's too late already. "I won't be having a drink! When will you listen to me, woman?" I'm losing control now, too, the plan to try and make these words count falling away fast. "I don't need drink." I fear I might tighten my grip too hard, so I release her, removing myself from her space and taking a march across my office to try and gather some calming thoughts. It's no good. Nothing will work. I jab my finger in her face. "I need you!" It's quickly brushed aside.

"You need me to replace drink and screwing."

Where the hell did she get that from? I need her to breathe; it doesn't get any simpler than that.

"You manipulate me."

"I don't manipulate you!" I defend, shocked, but I know I really do. Constant contact, making unreasonable demands, and blowing her mind with our joined bodies are all ways for me to keep her, but it's to keep her safe, too.

"Yes, you do! With sex! Sense fucking, reminder fucking. It's all manipulation. I need you, and you use it against me!"

"No!" I yell, thrashing out and sending the poison that has brought me to this hideous place in my life crashing to my office floor. The loud smashing of bottles and glasses recedes, and I find myself holding her arms firmly again.

"I need you to need me, Ava. It doesn't get any simpler than that. How many times have I got to tell you? As long as you need me, I look after myself...simple."

"How is having yourself whipped looking after yourself?" she screams.

My hair takes a severe punishing when I yank at it violently. "I don't fucking know!" I do. Desperation. Hopelessness. Desolation. Fear. There are four, and I'm not finished yet.

"I do need you, but not like this." Her defeatism worries me further, so I take her hands gently.

"Look at me." Her head falls and her eyes meet mine. "Tell me, how do I make you feel? I know how you make me feel. Yes, I've had a lot of women, but it was all just sex. Mindless sex. No feelings. Ava, I need you."

"How can you need me if I make you do this to yourself? You're more self-destructive now than you were before me. I've made you *need* alcohol, not want it. I've made you into an unreasonable, crazy man, and *I'm* certainly not stable anymore. Don't you see what we're doing to each other?"

Her words slice me, even though the first part of that statement is probably true. The last part, however, isn't. We're loving each other, that's what we're doing. Everything I do is because I love her. "Ava."

"And for the record, I hate the fact that you've slept around."

I take a deep breath, silently agreeing with her, but then she gasps and the horror-filled sound pumps fear directly into my veins.

"When you disappeared for four days..." Her words catch in her throat, trepidation splashed all over her beautiful face.

My eyes open farther, like I need her to see my remorse. My time is up. "They. Meant. Nothing. I love you. I need you."

"Oh God!" She collapses in front of me and starts a pain-filled cry. I've never felt more shitty, more unworthy, more desperate. "You were fucking other women."

I fall to my knees, taking a firm but gentle hold, shaking her a little, for what purpose I don't know. "Ava, listen to me. They meant nothing. I was falling in love with you. I knew I would hurt you. I didn't want to hurt you."

"You said you couldn't do it to me. You forgot to add *again*. You should have said you couldn't do it to me *again*."

"I didn't want to hurt you."

"So to remedy that, you fucked other women?" Her reasonable question leaves me without an answer. I ask myself the same thing every day, ten times a day. "How many?"

I wince. "Ava, please don't. I hate myself."

"I hate you too! How could you?"

"Ava, why are you not listening to me?"

"I am, and I don't like what I'm hearing!" She's moving, taking herself away. I make a panicked grab for her hips, placing my head on her stomach, my emotions completely taking over. My body starts to jerk.

"I'm sorry. I love you. Please, I beg you, don't leave me. Marry me."

"What?" Her tone is shocked, disgusted, everything I don't

want it to be. "I can't marry someone who I don't understand." And those words finish me off, making me crumble to the floor before her. "I thought I was working you out." Her voice is trembling. "You've destroyed me again, Jesse."

"Ava, please. I was a mess. I lost control. I thought I could fight you out of my head." I'm spitting words, frantic and flooded with panic.

"By getting pissed and fucking other women?'

"I didn't know what to do." I'm pathetic, but it's all I have. The overwhelming anxiety, fear, and dread at her being hurt hasn't improved. It never will. Neither will my dread of losing her. But my ability to run away from pure, raw, intense love has. My excuses for leaving her for those four days will never be good enough. Fear in a man like me is laughable, but that is what this woman reduces me to. A wreck. A tragic excuse of a man. I really don't deserve the love this woman throws at me. But I'm far too selfish to give it up easily.

"You could have talked to me," she says.

"Ava, you would have run away from me again."

"All of the apologies you've been giving me were because your conscience was eating away at you. It wasn't because you were drunk or because of The Manor. It's because you screwed around on me. You said you hadn't dabbled since way before me. You've lied to me. Every time I think we've made progress, more bombshells. I can't cope with this anymore. I don't know who you are, Jesse."

"Ava, you do know me. I've fucked up. I've really fucked up, but no one knows me better than you, no one."

"Sarah might do. She seems to know you very well." Her tone is flat, almost resentful. "Why?"

My body gives, my arse hitting my heels. "I've let you down. I wanted a drink, but I promised you I wouldn't, and I know what's likely to happen if I do."

"So you had yourself whipped?"

"Yes."

"I don't understand."

I don't show her the shame in my eyes. I don't need to. "Ava, you know I've led a colorful life. I've broken marriages, treated women like objects, and taken what's not mine. I've damaged people, and I feel like all of this is my penance. I've found my little piece of heaven, and I feel like everyone is going out of their way to take it away from me."

"*You* are the only one who's going to fuck this up. Just you. You drinking, you being a control freak, you fucking other women. *You!*"

"I could have stopped it all. I can't believe I've got you. I'm terrified you're going to be taken away from me."

"So you ask a woman I despise, a woman who wants to take *you* away from *me*, to whip you?"

"Sarah doesn't want to take me away from you." I frown, but obviously Ava disagrees, judging by the look of total shock on her face. And I know she's probably right. I could ignore it before Ava crashed into my life, but not now.

"Yes, Jesse, she does! You doing this to yourself is agony for me. You are punishing me, not you. I love you, despite all of the shit you keep landing on me, but I can't watch you do this to yourself."

"Don't leave me." My voice has taken on an unwarranted demanding tone, and I grab her hands. "I'll die before I'm without you, Ava."

"Don't say that! That's crazy talk."

Can't she see? I pull her to her knees. "It's not crazy. That nightmare I had when you were gone. Just like that—gone. It gave me a clue of what it would be like without you." The reminder brings all of the tormenting images back. Blackness. Emptiness. Indescribable pain. "Ava, it killed me."

"If I leave, it would be because I can't watch you hurt yourself—I can't watch you torture yourself anymore."

"You could never understand how much I love you." I clasp her face, but she fights me off again. "Let me touch you." The panic reignites, the visions of my nightmare now too near real.

"I do understand, Jesse, because I feel the same!" Her shout stops me from grappling to get her back in my arms. How can she feel like this? "Even though you've fucked me over completely, I still fucking love you, and I fucking hate myself for it. So don't you dare tell me I don't understand!"

"It's not possible." Damn it, she has no fucking idea! Anger surges through me at the very claim, and I reach forward, yanking her to me on a sharp intake of breath. "It's just not fucking possible!"

She doesn't fight me off this time. She's given in, letting me feel and hold her for a short while before she gently breaks away from me. "I'm going to get something to clean you up with." I'm not prepared to let her go, but she finds an incredible strength from somewhere, managing to shrug me off. "Jesse, I need to clean you up."

"Don't walk away from me."

"I said I would never leave you. I meant it." She walks out on me, leaving me on my knees and ready to pray some more. This is far from done, and despite her words, I'm not convinced she could possibly feel as strongly for me as I do for her. How could she? And there is nothing she can do to prove it.